BEYOND
ΩMEGA'S
SUNRISE

Eleni Papanou

COPYRIGHT

time, and in another space, reality, or dimension to use as he, she, or it chooses.

For updates, visit our website at:
http://philophrosyne-publishing.com

Book Cover design by Eleni Papanou

ISBN 10: 0988925230
ISBN 13: 978-0-9889252-3-6

Beyond Omega's Sunrise was grown and nurtured at:

Home Sweet Home in Makawao
Home in Tarpon Springs
IHOP
Home in Waianae
Home Depot
Kapolei Public Library
Starbucks - Waipahu
Tarpon Springs Public Library
Wailuku Public Library
AA Flight 6 en route to Maui from Dallas
Regency Hotel, Miami
AA Flight 7 en route to Dallas from Maui
Delta Flight 1196 - Maui to Los Angeles

For Barbra

Prologue

While I wasn't looking—and that doesn't happen too often considering I'm the Universe—My sun traveled to a place I'd forbidden him to go. Typical of the young generation. I was powerless to do anything. By the time I got to him, he had ventured too far for Me to alter his path. It's sort of like when you fall off a cliff. Once you take your second step off the precipice, there's nothing left for you to do but fall.

I know everything that goes on within My spherical body, but being all knowing doesn't give Me the power to undo what's already been done. Well...truthfully, I do have the power, but there's this unspoken rule among us upper-echelon lifeforms. Sheim, the one from whom I was begotten, kindly reminded Me that we permit mistakes. The results that evolve from them lead to new possibilities. Sheim also enjoys a good mystery. Remembering this truth helped diminish My fury towards Sun. Nevertheless, I was concerned. Because of his misdeed, Earth, who lived in an isolated pocket of space, would soon be affected in a manner that wouldn't be favorable to the lifeforms living upon her. All I could do was watch helplessly as Sun plowed towards a vast puddle of My energy that someone of his modest size couldn't digest. I warned him about consuming too much, but he was in a rush to grow up. Sheim told Me I had to let Sun fail if that was his fate. Eventually, I stopped worrying. Nothing lasts forever within Me. I have given birth to countless galaxies, many of which I've seen die. I developed a detachment to where I don't cry anymore. It's been over a billion years since I shed My last tear, but that doesn't make Me cold and unfeeling.

I was ready to shift My awareness elsewhere, limiting this arm of the Milky Way to passive observance. However, something caught My attention just outside Earth's atmosphere. I wouldn't have even noticed what was about to transpire had Sun not lured Me to this small, insignificant smudge of space. This was an extreme way for him to get My attention, but it worked.

A shuttle transporting winners of a lottery on Earth struck an alien vessel from a distant galaxy. The pilot of the shuttle was forced to make an emergency landing near the border of an English forest. More than half the passengers aboard were killed. Initially, the Custodians, who were the navigators of the alien vessel, regarded the lifeforms on Earth just as humans viewed ants. They rendered the surviving lottery winners unconscious and transported them to their ship for study. During the examination, the Custodians found something unexpected that made them take further interest in humans. This discovery made Me pay close attention to Earth over the next ten years.

Tracking and data collection implants were placed in the brains of the lottery winners. They were then returned a mile away from the crashed shuttle with their memories of the event erased. Rescue vehicles soon arrived at both locations, along with the usual barrage of military, reporters, and lawyers—all eager to know what caused the tragedy. None of the remaining lottery winners could explain what they had crashed into or how they ended up so far from the downed shuttle, which had exploded moments after the Custodians had intervened.

The whole incident made Me remember something I had long forgotten. Maybe I'll share My lesson learned later. I'm still undecided as I'm used to keeping secrets. And before you accuse Me of having anything to do with acquiring fast cars, dream careers, an ideal mate, or all of the above, understand that I'm innocent. If any of these wishes come true, it's either because you work hard, are blessed with attractive genes, or luck finds you— either by winning the lottery or by gaining a large inheritance. Still, I sometimes can't help but involve myself in sentient affairs, which is why I'm transmitting this story to my scribe. I like to remind sentients that I'm more than a passive observer.

And now on to Earth's final story: a story I intend to tell with a smile because I have no regrets. Without regrets there is no sadness, only being. That's what I am. Being.

1st Cycle

"Everything in life is
just for a while."
Philip K. Dick

Bad Review

Blaze Kenyon sat in a bathroom stall reading a scathing review of his book. He chose this isolated location to hide his anger over it. Yet if you happened to be standing in the men's room of Benny's Bar and Grill in New York City, province of the United Republic, at precisely 18:34 you would've heard him punch the stall door.

Blaze always knew he wanted to be a writer. After a mandatory two-year tour with the joined forces, he continued on to college and played guitar in a band to pay for the tuition. The band got turned down by every music company and eventually broke up. During that time, he had been dating a model. Her agent kept telling Blaze that his piercing blue eyes and muscular physique would lead to a successful modeling career. He eventually accepted the offer in order to pay off the remainder of his college tuition and quit soon after he'd earned a degree in English Literature.

Blaze soon became an overnight phenomenon with his first novel. In *Tales from the Mind of a Mad Guitarist,* the antagonist believed his Les Paul instructed him to kill guitar players until he was the last guitarist alive. On his trail was Drake Kent, detective by day and blues guitarist by night. The book was so successful, Blaze turned it into a series. Eleven books later, he was still going strong and received raving reviews for most of his work. There was only one critic, Trevor Forthright, who never had anything positive to say about Blaze's writing.

Blaze shook his aching hand that he had smashed against the stall door, then continued reading through Trevor's latest review on his translinker screen.

If Blaze Kenyon's music was as two-dimensional as his writing, it would explain why he failed as a musician. And it appears as if he's on his way to failing as an author with his latest in the Drake Kent series. Although Mr. Kenyon can dazzle a reader with his ability to create riveting and unique characters, he doesn't seem to understand the nature of suffering enough to realize that there needs to be a legitimate resolution in a character arc. Instead, he leaves the reader feeling emotionally manipulated by injecting tragic moments that seem to come out of nowhere. He further cheapens the experience by resolving them with a deus ex machina. A character's growth must be felt, not artificially enhanced at the last moment because the author couldn't figure his way out of the climax.

Blaze slammed his elbow against the side of the stall. He understood suffering more intensely than the average person. Three years earlier, he had lost his wife, Astrid, in the most horrific way imaginable. After they'd entered their apartment, they were ambushed by a madman who assaulted and murdered Astrid while Blaze was forced to watch. Blaze castigated himself over being too weak to save his wife's life. Nightly visits to the neighborhood bar ensued for the next six months, along with painful appointments at the local tattoo parlor.

A fighter pilot who turned up at one of Blaze's book signings inspired him to get his tattoos. The pilot was in the 3rd sector war and received two medals of honor. His well-developed forearms were covered with colorful tattoos. The one that caught Blaze's attention was of a hawk perched upon a triangle with an all-seeing eye.

When he returned home, he spent hours on the publink scanning through pictures of tattoos. After finding the one he'd wanted, he drank a pint of brandy and showed up at Tito's Tatts to get inked.

There was only supposed to be one tattoo, a necklace of stars. Because he was drunk and missing Astrid, Blaze instructed Tito to string the stars together with the inscription, *The illusion of security.* From that day onward, Blaze would recall what happened to Astrid each time he stared at himself in the mirror. He didn't care. He never wanted to forget her.

Blaze kept returning to Tito's until his whole neck was ornamented with an assortment of keyholes, keys, and locks. They symbolized that he was off limits to anyone who tried to harm him or anyone special in his life again. In the center of his chest was a large *Aum*. Branches extended from outside the Aum and were decorated with leave-shaped Yin-Yangs.

Blaze continued to add more branches until they met at the center of his back. He added lotuses and other auspicious symbols until his whole trunk was covered with ink. He then cut his hair into a mohawk and got more tattoos on his scalp of flowers and stars, several of which were further splattered against his upper cheekbone. Piercings came next: one snake bite and two silver studs on both sides of his bottom lip. Two more studs pierced the area between his brows. From that stretch of time to the moment where Blaze hid himself in a bathroom stall reading Trevor Forthright's latest review, over eighty-five percent of his body was covered with tattoos. I'll let you use your imagination over what portions betrayed his once pale skin tone. It's not that I'm embarrassed to mention it. I respect the privacy of My sentient children.

Whenever Blaze ventured outside, people either looked at him in disgust or were spellbound. Neither reaction mattered to him. The only responses that ever did came from Astrid, who told him his eyes spoke to the Universe. She was right. I heard him, but My attention was focused elsewhere at the time. I hear so many voices that it's nearly impossible to tune in to just one. As hard as this may be to believe, I'm not perfect. Sheim tells Me I'll be forever growing and evolving alongside My sentient children.

When Blaze had first gotten his tattoos, he believed he inherited the strength they symbolized. In reality, he was still the same introverted writer who preferred to be home alone, tapping into My creative stream. Everything he drew from Me appealed to him more than his material reality, particularly the present one in which he was throwing every known expletive at Trevor Forthright. Clenching one of his fists, he continued to read the blistering review...

Blaze Kenyon took the easy way out again with his latest book. It emerges as gimmicky as the previous books in the series. I don't know why Blaze—or I—bother with Drake Kent anymore. The character has become stale, and even a new shape-shifting lover from a neighboring star system fails to make him more intriguing. I hope Blaze Kenyon will rise to the occasion and give Drake the burial he deserves and then return to using his gift for words that we've all seen in his second book, The Sparrow's Whisper. It reveals his true artistry that he sadly traded for credit and fame.

Blaze slammed his foot against the stall door.

On the rooftop of Benny's Bar and Grill, Seth Marconi, owner of Marconi Aeronautics, had just landed his stretched flyer. For a man of his advanced years, he looked over a decade younger. He was fanatical about his appearance because of an acid burn that left the right side of his face scarred.

Seth reflected over a video file called, *"Final Message to Earth,"* visible on his translinker screen, then sent it off to the Universal Press Server.

His secretary, Anya Tanner, who sat in the front with him asked, "Why are we here, Mr. Marconi?"

Seth turned on the interior light, admiring Anya's light brown complexion. "You've been a loyal employee. Starting tonight, you can call me Seth. And to answer your question, I want to be with the commoners tonight."

Seth Marconi was a man of tremendous power and prestige. His self-proclaimed greatness was witnessed by all the *commoners* at ground level who'd seen his flyer land. Only those in law enforcement, the military, and people with a lot of credit had access to a flyer. Everyone else traversed along a poorly maintained primitive road system, either taking public transportation or hiring city-owned, air-powered cars. Off-world travel was also restricted to the Aristocrats, due to the high cost of space flight. Traveling in space became another bonus for the wealthy.

The survivors of the shuttle crash, who had been temporary captives of the Custodians, were winners of a lottery intended to promote Seth Marconi's newest fleet. Had the flight been completed, they would've landed on the spaceport and boarded a long-range cruiser to claim their grand prize: two weeks in the Mars colony at a luxurious spa where they would've indulged in the finest food and distractions outside of Earth's atmosphere.

Seth slid open the door to the flyer.

"You won't like it here," Anya said. "I know a place I think you'd like better."

"You recite your poetry here, right?"

"Yeah, but I don't think this'll be your type of hangout."

Benny's Bar and Grill was the local retreat for poets, musicians, and mystics. Anya was one of the poets who participated in the slams held every first Wednesday of the month.

"On any other evening, I would've agreed with you, but tonight is a very special night," Seth told her.

Anya craved a shot of whisky. The thought of hanging at Benny's with her boss and his guru, who was seated in the back of the flyer, wasn't her idea of a fun night out. The crowd that frequented the bar disliked the Aristocrats, which wasn't hard to understand considering the fact that they lived as royalty while the commoners were stuck working for minimal credit.

The commoners, which was how the Aristocrats viewed the lower financial class, voted to maintain the status quo. A flowery word, an offer of assistance, and a positive affirmation was all it took to keep the commoners from improving their lifestyle. Whenever a lofty promise was made, most of them quickly forgot that every previous promise made to them had been broken. The unfairness used to drive Anya crazy. She worked for Seth and saw through the lies. There were many times when she'd wanted to quit, but she appreciated her lifestyle. Her job got her out of the dungeon blocks, as they were called by the commoners who lived there. These living spaces were built so close together that there was hardly any privacy, and crime was rampant. It was similar to living in a prison. Guards surrounded the borders of the dungeon blocks to keep the violence from spreading to the rest of the island.

While Anya detested what was happening all around her, she was grateful for the many things she could do with her income. She gave her mother several credits every week for groceries and got her electricity back on after it had been switched off for almost six months. Although her mother never so much as thanked her for the assistance, Anya continued to support her without complaining. She released her sorrow over feeling unloved by slamming. Slamming saved her sanity and her life.

"Aren't you even curious about why I brought you with me?" Seth asked.

"Curiosity usually gets me into trouble. Why don't you tell me why we're here?"

"I want you to write an epic poem, spanning from the beginning of Earth's history up until tonight."

Anya nervously turned to look at the back seat where Seth's guru, Xavier Starfly, sat with his eyes half-closed. He wore a long seamless robe, and his luxurious black hair cascaded down too and rested upon the seat. His smile was continuous, only breaking when he ate and slept. It made Anya uncomfortable. She felt as though he could see right into her soul.

"Don't take what I ask of you lightly," Seth advised. "Your words will be immortalized for generations to come. How does that sound to you?"

"I don't think I can handle something that big," Anya said. "Not that I don't appreciate you asking me."

"I know you appreciate it, and don't underestimate yourself," Seth insisted. "Xavier chose you to be the deliverer of Earth's history."

Anya again turned to examine Xavier, who bowed his head.

"You should take this as an honor," Seth continued. "Xavier only selects those whom He identifies during His chanting."

"Mr. Marconi—"

"Seth."

"Seth," Anya repeated. "Why do you want me to do this?"

"Does there have to be a reason?"

"I can't write something unless I understand the motivation behind it."

Seth got out his translinker and handed it to Anya. On the screen was a daylight map.

"Do you see all the areas currently lit by the sun?" Seth asked.

Anya inspected the map.

"As we speak, all lifeforms currently under the sun's light are either dead, or in the process of dying."

Anya looked at Seth, who was smiling. His expression terrified her more than the news.

"Tomorrow morning, this city, and the rest of the world will meet a similar fate," he said.

"Is this for real?" Anya asked in a state somewhere between disbelief and panic, not knowing which one to commit to as she tried to take in the revelation.

"Tonight you won't hear anything more real than what I told you."

Anya went to get her translinker from out of her purse. "I have to call my mother and tell her what's going on!"

Seth clutched her forearm. "We have plenty of time," he said. "Right now we're going to engage in the conflict of your epic poem where I'll battle against the symbolic darkness of Earth."

"But if we're all dead, there won't be anyone around to read a poem."

"When Xavier first told me of Earth's impending destruction, I hired a team of astronomers to search for a habitable planet outside the Solar System."

"What about the Mars colony?" Anya asked.

"No one there will survive what's happening."

"Did you find a habitable planet?" Anya asked with desperate interest. Seth's proposal now seemed like a life preserver. She was willing to latch onto it as she had when he offered her a job after the shuttle crash, of which she was one of the survivors. Anya abhorred the idea of being stuck in space with Seth, but dying scared her more.

"We located the *perfect* world." Seth beamed. "While politicians fought over their petty issues, defunded the International Space Agency, and brought our scientific exploration to a halt, one of my astronomers found a planet with an atmosphere similar to that of Earth. We began construction on a colony nine years ago. It was a rush job in terms of building a whole civilization from scratch. Even so, a man with my resources can get the job done in a short period of time...unlike the government." Seth pointed to his head. "Greatness comes from here, not from a governmental body, which is nothing more than a compromised-over idea. An idea can't make an idea. Only mind can."

Anya fanned herself with her hand. The weather was unseasonably warm for an early April in New York. And even though the air conditioner had been on, her face was drenched in sweat. "Who are you taking with you?"

"Friends, colleagues, and artists whom Xavier believes will bring on a new Renaissance. As the writer of my epic, you'll be sitting beside me on the next shuttle out to the spaceport...along with your mother."

Anya exhaled after suspending most of her breaths for nearly the whole duration of their conversation.

"There will also be some members of the military to help keep the order," Seth noted. "But I'll be the one in charge...to ensure our new world will be free from corruption and crime. There will be no need for wars anymore. Xavier will teach everyone what it means to truly live free." He smiled and clutched the handle to the gun he'd hidden inside his blazer. "How does that sound to you?"

"Can I call my mother now?"

The Fallacy of Rules

In a hotel across town, Nestor Zaras had just stepped out of the bathroom, towel drying his shaggy brown hair. He tossed the towel onto the bed, picked up his camcorder, and played through footage he'd recorded of Seth Marconi and Xavier Starfly two hours earlier.

Seth gave the interview while seated behind a titanic crescent-shaped executive desk. Nestor was eager to question the man who owned the shuttle involved in the crash that almost killed him and his ex-wife. However, Seth wasn't eager to discuss past hiccups, as he called them. Whenever Nestor tried to change the focus of the interview to the business dealings of Marconi Aeronautics, Seth would maneuver the discussion back to his praising of Xavier Starfly, who chanted during most of the interview.

"Xavier Starfly is the real deal," Seth said. "I first met Him while I was working for my competitor. It's only because I listened to Xavier that I've been able to open my own company. He inspired me and helped me to see something that was beyond myself."

"Why doesn't he speak?" Nestor asked as Xavier spun around with his hands stretched out in the air like a bird in flight.

"He speaks the language of all living things," Seth responded. "It enables Him to foresee the future."

Seth wasn't lying. I speak an incalculable amount of languages, simultaneously. They all stem from Me, speaker of the protolanguage—also known as the parent language. The Hindus detected My song of creation and called it Aum, but truthfully I'm a lot more than a breeding machine. Aum is only the beginning of a myriad of labyrinthine frequencies that make up My language. Xavier's method of connecting to Me entailed writing down his predictions while he chanted. The notes of his chants resonated with various frequencies that allowed him to tap into what you humans perceive as the future.

Being a devout skeptic, Nestor was quick to point out all of Xavier's failed predictions. There was a valid reason for his less than accurate prophecies. If you're sensitive enough to connect to My main link, you're plugged in to all the information contained within Me. You'd have to sort through an astronomical amount of data to hone in on just one event. It's nearly impossible and not unlike playing telephone. With My frequencies bouncing around from sentient to sentient, by the time you connect to one particular event it's completely lost in the translation. Apart from Xavier Starfly's outlandish appearance, the resulting psychic tangle is why scientists failed to take personalities like him seriously. Extrasensory awareness isn't a science but part of My creative totality, which requires persistence, inspiration, and most importantly, an open mind. Still, the mind should not be so open as to believe I'd ever hand out the key to unlock the answer to *everything*. I never give that much away.

The outside traffic was getting noisy. Nestor turned up the volume of his transviewer to hear the remainder of Seth's interview.

"Earth's end will be arriving very soon," Seth stated with an entranced gaze.

"How soon?" Nestor asked.

"At sunrise...tomorrow."

Nestor laughed.

Ignoring the laugh, Seth continued. "There are some things about our Divine Universe that we don't understand, yet we analyze Her, give Her an age, and expect Her to play by our rules."

"Are you saying we shouldn't seek to understand the unknown?"

"To seek out knowledge is admirable," Seth said. "But what we do is make assumptions and mistake them for facts."

Nestor smirked. "What will happen to your fortune after we're all gone?"

"I know you're mocking me, but in the end I'll be proven correct. And as far as my fortune is concerned, I'd gladly give it away if it would help rid Earth of all the parasites."

"What parasites?"

Seth crossed his hands on his desk, twiddled his thumbs slowly, and said with a smile, "Humanity."

Nestor froze the frame and stared at Seth's eyes. During the interview, he never noticed anything amiss as he didn't believe what Seth told him. The still image spoke something altogether different.

Whatever lay beyond Seth's gaze made Nestor uneasy. He called his wife, Becky, to get himself out of his mood. When her face filtered onto his translinker screen, he smiled, revealing fine wrinkles around his mouth and cheeks. "Sorry I'm calling so late," he said. "I got lost in my work."

"That's okay." Becky grinned. "I'm used to that by now."

Nestor picked up a red silk scarf. "I'll be home by tomorrow night and make it up to you with gifts."

"I'll have your favorite dinner waiting for you."

"Eggplant Parmesan?"

"Pasta Carbonara."

"That's good too."

"Look Mom!" Nestor's son, Joey, yelled out.

"Your father's on the phone, Joey," Becky said. "Come talk to him."

"The sun is big!" Joey proclaimed.

Becky walked to the window and stared outside. "Wow!" She shielded her eyes with her free hand. "The sun looks twice its normal size—"

The conversation cut off. Nestor tried to reconnect and a recorded message played.

"We're sorry, but we are experiencing technical difficulties. Please try your call again later."

Nestor hung up, unconcerned. Disconnections were not that unusual after the last sector war. He was also eager to meet his friend, Randy, for drinks. He hadn't seen him in three years and was looking forward to the reunion. Nestor whistled a happy tune, unaware that part of the world had just been destroyed. Those who noticed Sun's peculiar behavior, like Becky, marveled over how majestic his light appeared that day.

Wager

Seth entered the men's room of Benny's Bar and Grill with Xavier Starfly and Anya, who stared at the urinals.

"I don't think I should be in here," she said.

"Tonight we stop playing by the rules," Seth told her. "Liberate yourself beyond the label of woman and relax."

Anya wasn't nervous about being in the men's room. She was nervous over being in the men's room with Seth Marconi on the eve of Earth's destruction.

"Did you find your mother?" Seth calmly asked.

"I called everywhere. I can't find her."

"We don't have much time," he warned. "The shuttle is leaving soon."

"Damn it, I know!" Anya tore off a paper towel from its dispenser to wipe the anxious sweat off her face. She didn't care if she sounded offensive. She was concerned for her missing mother.

"If I can't find her by the time we have to leave, someone else will have to write your..." Anya cut herself off when she heard the toilet flush.

Blaze stepped outside, and Seth stared at his tattoos in disgust.

Blaze smiled at Anya. "Welcome to the men's room, Anya. Taking in some of the male experience for your next slam?"

"Something like that."

With a quick look and gesture, Seth cued Anya to remain silent.

"Loved your last one," Blaze said. "*A Blight Called Emotion*. Felt as though you were speaking to me." He pointed at her. "But I'm winning the next one." He lifted a brow when Anya didn't come back with her usual competitive banter.

"Your friend is overconfident," Seth said to Anya.

Blaze recognized Seth but intentionally disregarded him. He blamed Seth for the shuttle crash. The chief engineer who studied the wreckage concluded there was a problem with the plasma thrusters. Had they been working properly, the accident could've been avoided. The surviving lottery winners sued Marconi Aeronautics. Seth threatened to fire Anya if she participated in the suit. Believing the Aristocrats would pay their way out of a guilty verdict, and not wanting to risk losing a steady paycheck, Anya abstained from joining in the suit. Her reasoning was accurate as the case was dismissed. The government purchased the contract to use Seth's fleet for future sector wars and dismissed the suit with a digital stamp that read: *insufficient data to process*. To make himself appear compassionate, the President of the United Republic gave the lottery winners twenty-five thousand credits and a handwritten conciliatory letter. Anya got a raise for her loyalty.

"Who are your friends?" Blaze asked Anya, hoping to bruise Seth's ego.

Seth offered his hand for a shake. "Seth Marconi, owner and CEO of Marconi Aeronautics."

"No one will be impressed about that here." Blaze turned to Xavier Starfly and pointed to his robe. "But you'll be a hit with that costume. You should seriously consider slamming."

Xavier bowed to him. Blaze shrugged his shoulders and walked over to the sink.

Seth smiled at Anya. "Call out your muse. We're about to start."

"Start what?" she asked.

Seth approached Blaze, who was washing his hands. "Might I have a word with you, Mr. Kenyon?"

Blaze glanced at Seth through the mirror.

"I got a proposition for you."

"Not interested," Blaze said as he shut off the faucet.

"I think you will be once I reveal the prize...but you'll have to accept my wager if you want to know what it is."

"I'll listen...if you can get it all out by the time I finish drying my hands." Blaze ripped a paper towel from the dispenser.

Seth faced Anya. "Get ready."

Blaze tossed the paper towel into the trash. "Too late."

"For some, it will be," Seth said.

Blaze glared at Seth, then smiled at Anya. "See you outside where the atmosphere is warm and the air, fresh." He headed in the direction of the door.

"What would you say," Seth asked, "if I told you that tomorrow morning all life, except for those of us who'll be leaving Earth...will be terminated?"

Blaze spun around, looked at Seth, then at Xavier who bowed his head again. Chuckling, he pointed his finger at Anya. "I get it now. Collin set this all up. This is by far the best gag he's ever pulled on me. I was almost ready to run to the nearest bomb shelter."

"This is no joke," Anya said. "Everything ends tomorrow."

Blaze felt a chill pass through him when he studied Seth's expression.

"Right as we speak, all life where the sun now shines is dying or already dead," Seth continued.

Blaze started to feel uneasy. "Why are you telling me this?"

"As a member of the *Killer Roboticrats*, I can't help myself from displaying my *caveman brain*," Seth sneered. "Isn't that how you phrased it?"

Anya eyed Blaze with worry as she now understood why Seth wanted to come here. He wanted revenge. Shortly after the lottery winners had received their government payoff, Blaze had done an improvised spoken word at Benny's to vent his feelings. Seth overheard one of his employees discussing the performance and later found a video of it on the publink. He played it back tonight on his translinker, observing Blaze's reaction.

The Killer Roboticrats;
They think they're powerful.
Look inside them;
They're weak.
Old game, new face,
The Killer Roboticrats are controlled,
By one remote control.
Killing, stealing, destroying,
It's all they know.
Lying, scheming, cheating,
Can't think outside their box.

Tightly wrapped, dark inside,
Nowhere to hide.
I opened one of you up,
Killer Roboticrat.

And I know what you're all about...

Shrimp cocktails, fine china,
Fancy flyers, shuttles,
Off-world excursions,
To partake in your diversions.
Cut off from reality,
Lost in your depravity.
Humankind suffering.
Immaterial.
Your caveman brain,
Drained.
Killer Roboticrat.
Destroy us, you destroy yourself.

You think in black and white.
Not seeing shades of gray.
No inspiration.
Just another plagiarized story.
Scurrying around town,
With your group of clowns,
Who all talk the same, act the same,
Drink the same, eat the same,
Are...the same.
Your freaky long-haired guru,
Makes more sense than you.
And he doesn't even speak.

You're the kid in the playground.
From where you never left.
You'll sacrifice your integrity,
For your compulsive need,
To be admired by all.
Nothing but a scared child.
Longing to fit in.
To join.
To belong.
To be liked.

Your face changed through the eons.
But your deeds follow a similar pattern.
Lands of ruins.
Deserted cities.
Destroyed lives.
Evidence of your osmosis psychosis.
If we don't stop you now,
We all lose.

The Killer Roboticrats,
Will destroy everything,
To get what they want.
Including themselves.
I know this firsthand.
I stared one of them in the eyes,
Behind them was emptiness.
No sadness.
No remorse.
Each time I see,
This killer roboticrat,
I'm reminded of the death,
The dread he left behind.

Of all the innocence lost.
This Killer Roboticrat,
Diseased in the brain,
Unable to refrain.
Credit and power; his drug.
Shot up, flooding,
His empty brain.
You know who I'm talking about?

"Seth Marconi!" All the patrons who knew Blaze's story could be heard yelling. A few also called out the President's name.

Blaze removed a letter from his pocket. "In my hand I hold a letter from the President, apologizing for the loss of life on Seth Marconi's shuttle. You know what I think of his apology?" Blaze rolled up the letter. "Anyone got a light?"

An audience member raised a lit lighter. Blaze walked over and waved the letter through the flame until it caught fire. After most of it had burned, a customer hurried over with a glass of water where Blaze dunked the charred remnants. Everyone in the room applauded. Blaze waved his hand in the air for them to quiet down. They complied, and he continued with his spoken word performance.

Without the Killer Roboticrats,
We'd all live in freedom.
No rulers to force us to serve them.
We'd be free to express,
Our creativity.
Each unique identity.
Free to live.
Free to love.
Free to just be.

But do we have the courage?
The desire?
The will to live free?
I honestly don't know any—

Seth shut off the video. "There's a little more. But judging by the defeated look on your face, I'd say you heard enough."

"I don't regret a word of it!" Blaze rammed Seth into the wall. "You killed them all!"

"Stop, Blaze!" Anya cried out. Then she softly added, "It's really happening. Everyone's gonna die."

"It's okay, Anya," Seth told her. "I can fill him in from here."

Blaze released Seth. "Whoever set you up to this, tell him or her I'm not buying a word of it."

"You have the right to ignore me," Seth said. "However, if you can convince everyone—and I do mean *every single individual* in this bar—that the world will end tomorrow, I'll save you a seat on the next shuttle out of here."

Anya waved her finger at Seth. "I agreed to write your epic, not to watch you torture my friend. I'll be by the bar." She stormed out of the men's room.

Seth smiled at Blaze. It was the kind of smile that outwardly displayed his contempt. "There's one positive aspect of this last night," he said. "And it's that I can do many things I wouldn't dare do on any other night." He quickly pulled out his gun and aimed it at Blaze, who lifted up his hands.

"I don't want any trouble here."

"You don't know a thing about *me*," Seth claimed. "And *you're* the disease. I abhor you and every other useless, pathetic body that thinks like you. I'm glad Earth decided to purge Herself from Her contaminators, although She should've done it a long time ago. This world was destroyed long before today with your vile and shallow idea of freedom. You, along with most of the people that waste the air they breathe, are too shortsighted to understand the true meaning of freedom. Because of your ignorance and unwillingness to take care of yourselves, we're always thrown into wars by the disorganizers that run this world."

"You can't shoot me in here," Blaze said. "There are witnesses." He glanced at Xavier Starfly, whose expression hadn't changed since he first saw him.

"I can do whatever I want." Seth laughed. "As of tomorrow, no one will be around to complain." He waved his gun, motioning for Blaze to leave. "Go now. Tell them what I told you, or I'll end your life earlier than the rest of the unproductive breathing machines out there."

"I'll convince them."

"If you do, I'll have to reconsider my near-perfect record at reading people. It's what kept me a very wealthy man. I would bet all my fortune on you agreeing with my assessment of Humanity before the sun rises. And when you do, it's going to break you more than you've ever been broken before."

"The only thing that will be broken is your record." Blaze rushed out of the men's room and gave his middle finger to the watchful eye camera that was recording him. He did this almost every time he encountered one.

Lieutenant Jeff Theobald was in his bedroom packing for a vacation to Australia. The trip was a present given to him by his girlfriend, Lynn, in honor of his forty-seventh birthday. She had just entered the room, surprising him.

"You're early," he said. "Didn't expect you for another hour."

"Hurry and finish packing."

"What's the hurry, babe?" Jeff wrapped his dark brown muscular arms around Lynn and kissed her. "We're not leaving for another few hours."

"There's been a change of plans. We have to be at the shuttleport in an hour."

"Why?"

"I'll fill you in on the way over."

Jeff's loving mood evaporated. "Fill me in now. You know how much I hate surprises."

"Trust me with this one. I had to pull a few strings to get you on my flight."

"I'm staying right here until you tell me where we're going." Jeff sat on the bed and crossed his arms. "Start talking."

Lynn clutched her forehead.

"Is the treaty with the Eastern Sector not being renewed?" Jeff asked.

"I wish."

"Now you got my full attention."

"Get your bags, and come with me. *Now.*"

"Are you pulling rank on me...Admiral?"

Lynn was six years younger than Jeff but had been commissioned five years longer. When both were in uniform, Jeff had to salute and address Lynn with her formal title. He'd sometimes playfully do the same at home.

"If I have to, I will."

Jeff extended his arms towards Lynn. "You're going to have to arrest me."

Lynn glared at Jeff.

"But I know you won't." He smiled.

"This isn't a joke."

"I'm starting to get that. Tell me what's going down. You know whatever you say will never leave this room."

Lynn tossed one of her hands in the air. "We've lost contact with all areas of the world exposed to sunlight. At first, we believed it was a massive solar flare, but what happened is much bigger. All life where the sun is now shining has been annihilated, and the same thing will happen here tomorrow morning."

Jeff thought about his father who lived on the West Coast. He felt nothing. "How long have they known?"

"Whatever happened to the sun has taken everyone by surprise, but we're going to survive this. We've been invited to the spaceport to catch Seth Marconi's cruiser out of the Solar System."

"To where? We've never explored that far out."

"Seth planned ahead like a good little squirrel. He's got a colony ready to be inhabited."

Jeff hurried towards the living room and picked up his translinker that was on the coffee table.

"Who are you calling?" Lynn asked.

"The hospital. I'm checking my mother out."

"You can't bring her."

"Pull some more strings."

"They won't approve. They're only taking people under fifty and without any medical problems."

"What a hypocrite! Seth Marconi is in his seventies."

"This is our only way out. And what's the difference anyway? Your mother doesn't even remember you. She won't even notice you're gone."

"I'll remember her!"

"I didn't mean for it to come out that way. I love you. I..."

"Leave now." He looked at Lynn as though he didn't recognize her.

"Not without you."

"If my mother stays, I stay."

"Don't do this to me. Don't make me leave alone."

"I'm not making you do anything you don't already want to do."

"Please," Lynn said while crying. "Come with me. I'm sure if your mother understood what was happening, she'd want you to save yourself."

"She would, but since she can't understand, I can't leave her."

"So this is it? You'd rather stay behind a stranger to someone than leave with me, who loves you...who needs you?"

Jeff looked away from Lynn, not wanting to be affected by her tears.

"I'm sorry I said that. I'm just so scared, and I don't want to lose you."

Never being the type to ignore a woman in distress—and to lessen his own, Jeff embraced Lynn. "I don't want to lose you either." He held her tight and squeezed his eyes shut even tighter. *This isn't happening. This can't be happening.*

Lynn pushed Jeff away when the thought of remaining with him entered her mind. "I wish I could stay with you, but I can't. I... I don't want to die."

"I don't want you to die either."

"If there's a chance to save myself, I have to take it."

"You don't have to explain yourself to me. You have to do what's right for you."

Jeff's supportive response made Lynn cry more intensely. "If you change your mind, I'll be at the shuttleport." She ran out.

Jeff gathered his gun and headed out after her.

Blaze spotted a young woman sitting next to Collin, his agent and brother-in-law. Collin had been trying to get him to start dating again. Blaze headed to the bar to avoid the encounter, get a beer, and also to re-run the conversation he just had with Seth, who was sitting at the opposite side of the bar with Anya and Xavier Starfly.

Anya unsuccessfully tried to quell her anxiety with a third shot of vodka. When the bartender and owner of the establishment looked her way, she called out, "Pour me another one Floyd, and keep them coming."

Blaze ignored the trio as he clung to the last thread of hope that Collin set the whole thing up with Anya's help. *The gun was nothing more than a prop.* He laughed to himself believing that was the likely explanation.

Collin and Blaze's friendship was marked by practical jokes, embarrassing moments, and when they were both still single, seeing who could get the girl first. Not a typical relationship for an agent and an author, and I marveled over how the two managed to get eleven books published.

Collin was the ideal agent for Blaze. He wasn't the usual stodgy-type who called you up only to discuss business. Blaze signed with him because he knew Collin was the kind of guy he could call up for a game of pool and a pint of beer. He also tolerated Blaze's crude sense of humor because he was equally as crude.

It was inspiring to watch Collin and Blaze during the early phase of their relationship. Together, they emitted frequencies that I easily and eagerly digested. Unfortunately, every table is eventually emptied of the feast presented upon it. After Astrid had died, the jokes stopped, and Blaze became a social recluse. Collin stood by his friend during this difficult period, and Blaze thought highly of his loyalty as he was starting to give up hope for the human race. He demonstrated his appreciation by introducing Collin to his sister, Tara. The endorsement was rare as Blaze never trusted any man with his sister. He was always overprotective and became even more so after Astrid's murder. Tara and Collin got married the following year, and Blaze then had to deal with two matchmakers.

Floyd came over with a beer and placed it in front of Blaze. "From the man at the end of the bar."

Blaze looked at Seth and raised the bottle in a thank-you gesture, then got up to join Collin and the mystery woman. Standing with his hands on his hips, he stared down at Collin.

"It's not what you think," Collin said.

"What am I thinking?"

"That I signed you up for that kundalini meditation class. It wasn't me; it was your sister's idea. I warned her—"

"Not even close." Blaze swiped Collin's beer bottle, took a long swig, and slammed it down on the table. "This is by far the worst prank you've ever played on me."

"One, I didn't play a prank on you; two, drink your own beer, and three, meet Talia." Collin showcased her with both his hands.

Blaze pulled out a chair and sat. "Hi Talia." He smile at her, then glanced at Seth.

Collin looked over to see what was monopolizing Blaze's attention. "I can't believe it." Collin laughed. "That's Seth Marconi! And he's with that crazy guru of his."

"Oh yeah," Talia said. "Xavier Starfly."

"That's him," Collin said. "He made a prediction about the sun destroying Earth."

Blaze grabbed Collin's arm. "If this is one of your pranks, let me in on it now because I'm not laughing."

"If there's a prank going on here, someone else set it up."

Blaze let go of Collin and guzzled down half his own beer.

"Talk to me, bro," Collin said. "What's going on?"

"Tell me everything Starfly said...everything that has to do with the sun."

"It's nothing substantial," Collin assured him. "As with all those phony psychic-types, Starfly wasn't specific, but Seth believed him and started looking for outer Solar System planets where he could build his own space colony." Collin turned and observed Seth who raised his drink towards Blaze. "Why the sudden fascination with the paranormal?"

"Marconi just told me that all life where the sun is now shining is dead. Think he's trying to get even with me."

"For what?" Talia asked.

"He played a video of an old spoken word performance I did about him a few years back. The man can hold on to a grudge."

"What a weirdo." Talia stirred her drink with a cocktail straw.

Collin glanced at Seth again. "Think he was just bored and wanted to watch one of the serfs make a fool of himself in a bar full of drunk people or..." He got out his translinker.

"You don't believe him?" Blaze asked. "Do you?"

"When Seth Marconi speaks, people listen. And verify."

With Collin busy on his translinker, Earth's possible destruction was placed in the nether-district of Blaze's mind. Still refusing to believe the end was approaching, he returned to seething over Trevor Forthright's review of his latest book.

Talia attempted to catch his attention with a few smiles and when that didn't work, she said, "You don't talk much."

"Don't have anything to say tonight."

"Why not?"

Blaze narrowed his eyes. "Do you know anything about suffering?"

"What do you mean?"

"I'm not sure." He checked Talia out. She tasted sweet to his eyes: red hair, petite, unusually large eyes. Collin knew him well.

Talia examined the tattoos around Blaze's neck. "The illusion of security. Sounds so negative."

"It's the reality of our age," he told her. "None of us are safe. Even with the joined forces patrolling our streets and all the watchful eye cameras filming us every time we use the toilet and take public transportation. Our city still has the highest murder rate in this country."

"You can either react to it or ignore it," Talia said.

"To what?"

"Suffering. Are you a reactor or ignorer?"

"A little of both, I..."

"Are you sure?" Collin responded into the phone with a raised voice.

Talia and Blaze both looked at Collin.

"Yeah. Yeah. Call me as soon as you can confirm any of it." He hung up.

"What did you find out?" Blaze asked.

"This may not be anything but"—Collin glanced at Seth Marconi—"according to one of my contacts, there's an unusual amount of shuttle activity tonight, particularly around all the world capitals."

Talia nervously asked, "Do you think it's true?"

"Don't panic yet. I'm waiting on one more—"

Collin's translinker rang. "This should be it." He answered.

Talia and Blaze listened closely.

"Are you certain?" Collin asked. "I will. Thanks." He hung up. "Communication has ceased in all areas currently exposed to the sun."

"Oh my God!" Talia put her hands over her mouth, and tears streamed from her eyes.

"It's a large solar flare," Collin said. "That's what the latest press release from the Universal Press Server is saying. Utility companies are debating whether they should power down until all this is over." He looked at Blaze. "Why did Seth tell you this?"

"He bet me I couldn't convince everyone in this room that the world will end at sunrise."

"What do you win if you succeed?" Talia asked.

"I get to go off world with him to his space colony."

"Can you get me a reservation?" she asked.

"I don't think I'm going to make the flight," Blaze said.

"What are you going to do?" Collin asked.

"Play along." Blaze tapped a fork against his bottle of beer and stood. "May I please have everyone's attention?"

The patrons spoke loudly and failed to hear him. Blaze chugged the remainder of his beer and hurled the bottle that shattered after smashing into the mirrored wall behind the bar. Everyone stopped talking.

Floyd gestured toward a crack in the mirror. "What the hell is wrong with you, Blaze? There's a more civil way of getting everyone's attention." He pointed to the stage.

"Sorry Floyd. I'll pay you back tomorrow for the repair—if we're all still around for me to pay you."

"I'm flagging you. No more booze."

Blaze gestured towards Seth Marconi. "See that old smug-looking man at the end of the bar?"

All eyes in the room were now on Seth. Anya downed another shot of vodka, and Xavier continued to smile his usual smile.

"Is that Seth Marconi?" one of Benny's regulars guessed.

Blaze clapped his hands. "Pour Rocco a beer, Floyd. He's correct."

"Thought he looked familiar," Floyd said as he grabbed a mug.

"I had an interesting conversation with Marconi in the men's room. He said all parts of the world exposed to sunlight have been destroyed. He then bet me I couldn't convince you all that we're going to die tomorrow morning."

Floyd laughed. "Come on Blaze. Don't tell me you fell for such a ridiculous story."

Everyone in the room laughed, except for Talia, Collin, and Seth's group.

"What do you think, Blaze?" Rocco asked. "Is Marconi telling the truth?"

"Collin just confirmed we lost contact with areas around the world currently lit by the sun."

Everyone in the room started talking at once, either to each other or into their translinkers.

Blaze nodded at Floyd who blew into a referee's whistle that hung from around his neck. Everyone quieted down.

"There's no reason to worry yet," Blaze told them. "This could be nothing more than a solar flare."

"How can we be sure?" a nervous female cried out.

"My friend is looking into this now. If you want more information, talk to Marconi. But you better ask him now. He and his pal Smily will be going off-world tonight."

Three customers left the bar after hearing the news. Those who remained, including a minor league baseball team, returned to drinking, playing darts, and shooting pool.

Satisfied he'd won the bet, Seth got up to leave. Xavier and Anya followed him towards the door.

Blaze cut them off near the exit. "Have a nice flight."

"I will," Seth said. "I was once again proven correct and will leave here with a clear conscience."

"You have no conscience," Blaze said.

Seth looked at all the people partying in the bar. "You can observe the indifference of Humanity here. This bar is a microcosm of the world. Even as the evidence continues to present itself, most of them won't care until it's too late. It's this shortsightedness that kept us destroying ourselves."

"What about those who *do* care?"

"History has always shown that they're eventually taken down. There are never enough of them to maintain peace. War always comes with a whip in hand, ready to strike you until you're bleeding so hard it never stops, even after you return home."

Blaze peered at Seth, finally detecting some emotion in his expression that quickly vanished before it could take root.

"Why did you do this?" Blaze asked.

"I wanted you to witness the indifference. And now that you have, you'll suffer for it."

"You're too late. Someone else beat you to it. I was already suffering."

"Really? According to Trevor Forthright, you don't understand the nature of it." Seth smiled. "Too bad you won't be joining us."

"I'd rather die tomorrow than get locked in a floating metal coffin with you." Blaze looked at Anya who turned away.

"Take care of yourself, Anya."

Blaze walked away with a defiant grin on his face, but it didn't last. There still existed the unresolved matter that the world would no longer support life the next morning.

As with most humans, Blaze believed the scientists' assertion that Sun was middle-aged and would be shining for at least another seven billion years. While Sun definitely has a few billion years left in him, what scientists failed to consider was the fact that accidents happen and that Sun has a mind of his own. He orbited through a high concentration of My energy, and Earth didn't react well to the radiation that began to flood her atmosphere, burning everything to a cinder.

Anya, Xavier, and Seth hurried out of the bar and into an awaiting flyer. After Seth's bet with Blaze, Anya wondered whether she'd be better off remaining on Earth. Spending months on a long-range space cruiser with a sanctimonious Aristocrat like Seth might be worse than death. Additionally, she hated how she left things with Blaze. Anya turned against everything she believed in to save herself and her mother. She wept silently on the way to the shuttleport.

Blaze returned to his table to tell Collin he was leaving.

"Where are you going?" Collin asked.

"If the world is going to end tomorrow, I have something to take care of before it happens."

"I didn't get confirmation for that yet."

"You will."

"What makes you so sure?" Talia asked.

Blaze thought back to his encounter with Seth in the men's room. "The way Marconi looked at me was more intense than Bradley Simpson's energy-sapping stare."

Collin's and Talia's faces turned white.

"I didn't sleep for a week after I read that book," Talia said.

Bradley Simpson was a character from one of Blaze's books. He was an alien serial murderer who traveled to different planets and killed people with a stare that pierced and siphoned their life force. The character was dubbed *Most Sinister Immortal Villain* by the *Horror Market Voice*.

"Keep your translinker on," Collin told Blaze. "I'll call you as soon as I hear back from my contact."

Blaze grabbed hold of Talia's hand and kissed it. "If this were any other night, I would've asked you to go to the science fiction convention with me next weekend."

Although Talia was his type, Blaze was lying. He normally didn't lie to a woman. Nevertheless, if the world were about to end, he preferred not to leave anyone with a bad impression of him. He also fancied Talia's smile.

How humans react to devastating news is the most accurate method for identifying the potency of their spirit. The higher the grade of spirit, the better they deal with tragedy. There's nothing better than the end of the world to engage in a character study, and each time I bear witness, I learn from My mistakes and improve on the new worlds and sentients I create with My call. It's never the same. I always rearrange My frequencies into patterns that even surprise Me at times. Sheim said that's the beauty of potential. It can lead anywhere.

Approaching the Rubicon

The Aristocrats believed they ruled over all humans because they had more credit, power, or both. Had they fathomed the countless lifeforms that evolved ahead of them, they would've presented themselves with a little more modesty and treated the commoners and each other with respect. I can't fault their arrogance as in My youth, I also had an elitist attitude towards some of My sister Universes. After My first galactic children had exploded into life, I developed a temper that was equally as volatile. Sheim disapproved of My behavior and threatened to uncreate Me.

The thought had terrified Me enough to fall into line. It also made Me realize that if I had it My way, I would've generated life that feared Me, as well. Hence, Sheim taught Me a valuable lesson in humility and compassion.

Aboard Seth Marconi's flyer on route to the shuttleport, Anya was polishing off another glass of champagne. She was trying to drown out the sound of her conscience.

Anya's mother, dressed in clothing geared more to her daughter's age, eyed Xavier Starfly who sat beside her in the back. She then peeked her head between Seth and Anya.

"Thank you for bringing us along, Mr. Marconi. Anya said many good things about you, and I can see why."

"Like what?" Seth smiled anticipating the answer. Anya was a loyal employee, but she never outwardly demonstrated her admiration.

Anya's mother had to think fast as her daughter mostly complained about Seth. "She said you were a compassionate man, always out to help people in need."

Seth quickly turned to Anya. "I never knew you viewed me in such high esteem."

Anya sipped some more champagne to prevent herself from telling Seth what she truly thought about him. She couldn't get her mind off the way he treated Blaze. *I should've said something.* That thought had been building inside her since she left Benny's.

Seth returned his focus to the slowly building traffic on the street below. Several videos of his encounter with Blaze at the bar had been recorded and uploaded to the publink. So far, the only people heeding the warning were end-of-the-world cultists and conspiracy theorists.

"I'm not feeling well." Anya rubbed her belly. She felt nauseous from the combination of stress and alcohol.

"Hold on a little longer. We're almost there." Seth smiled at Anya, who was young enough to be his daughter. He was attracted to her and never felt this strongly about a woman since the passing of his wife. That relationship didn't end well, and she died before their issues could be resolved. Seth wanted to ask Anya out on several occasions, but there was something about her that made him feel vulnerable. The last time he felt that way was when his wife threatened to leave him. He never wanted to love that intensely again. It made him feel as though he had no control over himself, and Seth always had to be the one in control. To submit to anything or anyone reminded him of the day he received his scar.

"You've been quiet since we left your hangout," Seth said. "Are you thinking about my epic?"

"I'm trying not to think."

"If you're worried about making it out in time, you can relax. We'll be out of the Solar System before dawn."

Anya's nausea intensified. She turned up the air conditioner to maximum level and took a few slow deep breaths.

"Are you upset about Blaze?" Seth asked.

Losing what composure she had, Anya flung the glass against the front window. "You went way too far tonight. Way too far!"

"He deserved it, Anya. He and all of his kind destroyed this world long before tonight."

"I can't do this!" Anya glared at Seth. "You were so mean to Blaze. I can't believe you said all those cruel things to him over a spoken word piece he did years ago."

"Calm yourself down," Anya's mother urged.

"How can I calm down? Everyone's gonna die tomorrow morning, and Seth is treating it as if it's a game."

"On the contrary, I don't think it's a game," Seth countered. "I only made the wager to demonstrate to Blaze and your friends how we brought the destruction on ourselves."

"And who are you to show anyone anything?" Anya questioned. "You're just as screwed up as the commoners! You don't know a damned thing more than us!"

Anya's mother leaned in between the two front seats. "Mr. Marconi, you have to excuse her. She's normally not like this. It's the alcohol. She can't handle it too well."

"That's not true," Anya said. "What Seth did tonight is heartless." She pointed her finger at him. "The only symbolic darkness of Earth is *you.*"

"Do you honestly believe that?" Seth asked.

"Of course she doesn't," Anya's mother said.

"Stop answering for me! *I do.* He tortured those people at Benny's and enjoyed doing it!"

"If that's how you honestly feel," Seth said, "I don't see how you can write my epic."

Anya didn't apologize, didn't plead to be forgiven, didn't even say another word. She was relieved she wouldn't be joining Seth, and her stomach no longer writhed in disapproval.

"I'll leave the both of you off at the entrance gate," Seth said. "You won't be joining us on our flight."

"Please, Mr. Marconi," Anya's mother sniveled, "don't leave us here to die."

"I'm sorry, Mrs. Tanner, but I only have room for people who share my vision."

Anya and Seth remained as silent as Xavier Starfly until they landed at the shuttleport.

"You can take the flyer," Seth said to Anya without looking at her. He wouldn't have let her go if he did. "I won't be needing it anymore."

Nestor sauntered along MacDougal Street. An avid people watcher, Greenwich Village was one of his favorite places to find inspiration. After he had crossed Bleecker Street, he passed by an outdoor cafe where a large crowd had gathered around a man seated at one of the street-side tables.

"You're all heartless!" He shouted with a drunken slur into his translinker. "You've lost your humanity!"

Because of his gray tousled hair and disheveled clothing, the locals hardly took notice of the angry man and continued with their dining. Tourists passing by on the sidewalk broke from their routine to aim their translinkers and camcorders at the shouting man, hoping to capture a legendary New York City diversion to show to their friends.

"People have a right to know!" the man decried into his translinker.

Nestor went over to see what all the excitement was about. He grabbed his camcorder, in case there was something worthy of shooting, and then worked his way to the front of the crowd on the sidewalk.

"I will not remain quiet! I don't care if I cause a panic! I, Warren H. Beasley, refuse to die with blood on my hands!" He rubbed his sweaty forehead. "This is all wrong. People have a right to know. I can't do what you're asking. No! I won't do what you're asking!" He flung his translinker against the wall of the restaurant, leaned his elbows on the table, and hid his face behind his hands.

Everyone was now staring at him. The manager came rushing out. Nestor stepped in his path and showed him his press pass. "Let me handle this."

The manager nodded and went back into the restaurant.

Nestor walked up to Warren. "Is everything all right?"

Warren unglued his face from his hands. "What?"

"Heard what you said about people having the right to know."

"Oh, that. Never mind." Warren got up to leave. "Won't make a difference anyway."

Diners went back to minding their own business, and the tourists grew bored and departed.

"It'll make no difference because no one cares," Warren said.

"I do." Nestor held up his camcorder. "It's my business to care."

"What kind of business?"

"I'm a documentarian. I can help get your word out."

"I don't think you'll want to hear what I have to say."

"You told whomever you were speaking with that we all have a right to know. Tell us."

"It's too late," Warren lamented.

"For what?"

"To produce a documentary." He sat back down and picked up a bottle of beer. "But I'll tell you anyway." He took a sip of his drink. "Normally, disclosing what I'm about to tell you would get me *disappeared*, but that's the least of my worries tonight."

Nestor sat and aimed the lens of his camcorder at Warren, panning down to his trembling hand that held the bottle, then back up at his face.

"State your name for the record before we begin."

"Warren H. Beasley. I'm a plasma physicist with the ISA."

"Just a while ago, you were talking with someone who made you upset. Can you tell me why?"

"The sun brightened without warning, without reason. We detected an increase in cosmic rays, but the sun shouldn't be reacting the way it is."

Newlyweds, Sylvia and Greg, who were at a nearby table overheard what Warren had said and listened intently.

Nestor zoomed in for a close-up of Warren's panicked face. "What do you think happened?"

"It's reacting to something, but what that something is, I...I can't explain. We lost contact with all areas that are now under sunlight. Most of the United Republic melted seconds after the corona had dilated." Warren showed Nestor a daylight map on his translinker screen. "We narrowly missed the cutoff."

Sylvia and Greg went over to look at the map, and a man who was sitting alone at another neighboring table began to record the discussion with his translinker.

"When did this happen?" Nestor queried mechanically. After all the years behind a camera, he was an expert at shutting off his emotions.

"A little over an hour ago."

Nestor now felt something. He stopped filming. "That was around the time the call to my wife was interrupted."

"If your wife is in an area where the sun is presently shining, she is more than likely dead."

Sylvia squeezed her husband's hand and asked Warren, "Are you sure?"

"God help us all. I'm sure." He sipped some more beer.

Nestor got out his translinker and called Becky. He got the same recorded message and thought back to his wife's final words: *The sun looks twice its normal size.*

"I'm sorry," Warren said after Nestor had hung up.

Nestor's body felt as if it were being crushed by the pressure of his dread, but he still had lingering doubts about what Warren had told him. *Everything can't end just like that, without any warning. There has to be signs.*

Sylvia asked, "What does that mean for the rest of us?"

"Enjoy your last night alive," Warren said. "Whatever is happening to our sun is not conducive to life on this planet."

Sylvia hugged Greg. "Did you hear that? We're all going to die!"

Warren sipped his beer, then burped. "Sleep late, and you won't feel a thing. That's what I plan on doing."

Now the patrons were all very interested with what was going on at Warren and Nestor's table.

"Don't listen to this nut," Greg said. "He's drunk."

"Only just a little," Warren said. "I'm going to have to get a lot more drunk to forget about what I know, so I can die in ignorant bliss."

"Can you verify your story?" Sylvia asked.

"Unfortunately, I can't. All of us with a lower security clearance were locked out of the live satellite feed. Only one is still in orbit. The rest are all fried."

The man who'd been recording the conversation on his translinker asked, "Is the government aware of what's happening?"

The question made Nestor go back to filming even though his whole body was shaking.

"I was told they're on their way to the spaceport and will be leaving the Solar System, supposedly to keep order in case there's something to come back to," Warren said. "But there won't be. There never will be."

"Are you telling us the truth?" Sylvia asked as she wiped tears from her eyes.

Greg pointed his finger at Warren. "You're a very sick man! Can't you see what you're doing to her?"

"I lied many times in my life, but not tonight," Warren said.

"What if he's right, Greg?" Sylvia asked. "We'll never see our families again." She got out her translinker and tried to call her mother.

"He's crazy." Greg held his wife's arm. "Come on. Let's get out of here."

Sylvia hung up after getting the recorded message. "I can't get through."

"It's only a solar flare," a patron called out as she read a headline on the publink. "No big deal. The sky isn't falling."

Greg held his wife's hand. "See that? Everything's going to be okay."

Sylvia looked at Warren, who softened when he detected her fear. "Go to the concert and have fun."

Sylvia left it at that. Denial was her way of tackling her conflicting thoughts as it was for most humans on this night. Greg paid the tab, and the newlyweds left.

Most of the diners discounted Warren, believing the headlines. As for the rest of the East Coast, it was business as usual. Nevertheless, Warren's disclosure had been recorded, and Nestor knew this was going to be a crazy night once the story hit the publink.

"Were there any eyewitnesses?" he asked Warren.

"A fishing vessel in the Indian Ocean had the best view. The crew witnessed the destruction and called in the event as it was happening. They saw the sky turn red over the horizon, and they could feel a blast of heat coming towards them." Warren clasped his hands together. "I envied them. To see something like that and live long enough to digest the magnitude of the experience...it's priceless." Warren managed to sound both whimsical and solemn.

"Did they send back any pictures?"

"If they did, we would have seen them. Ten minutes after they had called in to report what happened, the Universal Port Authority lost contact with them."

Nestor put down his camcorder and studied Warren's expression, attempting to ascertain whether he was of sound mind. Most of the diners also doubted Warren's sanity. After three sector wars, doomsday messages became a normal part of city life across the United Republic.

Despising how he was being visually scrutinized, Warren picked up a fork and pointed it at Nestor then at two college-aged boys who were laughing at him. "Order your favorite dish because this will be your last meal. As of tomorrow morning, you'll all be dead." Warren stood and overturned the table.

Nestor continued filming him.

"I know what you're all thinking. You all think I'm crazy. But you'll all soon know I'm right moments before you're all fried to a crisp." He ran off, and Nestor hurried after him.

Warren sprinted across the street and narrowly missed getting hit by a car. He ran down the stairwell of a subway station yelling, "The end is tomorrow! The end is tomorrow! Repent your sins! Repent your sins! The end is tomorrow!"

Believing Warren was a religious zealot, Nestor ended his pursuit. Solar flares had caused blackouts before, and he surmised that was probably what happened. He tried to contact Becky again. The dreaded recorded message played.

The sun looks twice its normal size. Nestor could hear his wife's voice vividly, as if she were standing beside him. He didn't like the troubling thought that followed. *What if Warren wasn't crazy?*

2nd Cycle

"All that we see or seem is but a
dream within a dream."
Edgar Allan Poe

Down the Slide

Videos of Warren H. Beasley's outburst and Blaze's announcement at Benny's were uploaded to the publink. Because there was no official word out, only a small majority believed Warren and Blaze. The rest bought the solar flare cover story. Trusting the compassion of a governmental body was an effective mental defense to hide behind and easier to deal with than the reality of what was to come. Those who were skeptical of authority were either reconnecting with their relatives or hiring cars to leave the major cities of the East Coast. Grounded travelers, like Gary and Sylvia, were in their hotel rooms coming to terms with the prospect of never seeing their families again. Although not fully convinced by Warren's story, they took his advice and cancelled their wake-up call.

People of the clergy were also among the first to react to the news. At St. Augustine's Church in Lower Manhattan, Father Stephen had just finished watching Nestor's interview. After forty-one years of serving God and his congregation, he was good at reading people, and he could see that Warren was terrified. Father Stephen tried to call his first cousin who lived in Arizona and got the recorded message. He placed several more calls to people he knew out of state. Everyone he called from the Central Time Zone to the Pacific Time Zone yielded similar results. He contacted the Bishop, who sounded equally worried.

"Keep your doors open," the Bishop said. "Tonight, St. Augustine's and every church, mosque and temple will be a full house whether the story is true or not. Panic can make people react in unpredictable ways."

Father Stephen agreed. He needed help and knew where to get it.

In the auditorium of the attached parochial school of St. Augustine's, a group of young unwed mothers were in the middle of a meeting. Leading the group was Pearl, a paunchy social counselor who came out of retirement to help Father Stephen.

He walked into the meeting room as Deirdre, one of the attendees, was talking about how her boyfriend left her when he found out she was pregnant. She was deliberating over a possible abortion.

Pearl spotted Father Stephen, excused herself, and went to him.

"We need to talk privately," he said.

Pearl followed Father Stephen out to the hall where he played her Warren H. Beasley's video.

"This has to be a hoax," she said.

"Let's pray it is and that God hasn't given up on us."

"Do you...believe that man?"

"The interviewer is attempting to confirm or deny the story. I'll reserve my judgement until then."

Pearl gasped. "Christina! She lives in Oregon."

"You know where she lives?" Father Stephen asked surprised.

"I hired a private detective to find her but never had the nerve to contact her." Pearl did the sign of the cross. "What if it's true? What if I never see her again?"

"You can go home if you want. I can handle things on my own here."

"No," Pearl said. "I want to help. I have to help. It's the only way I'll get through tonight without thinking the worst happened."

Father Stephen nodded, concerned about his cousin and all the other people that he couldn't get in touch with.

"I have to leave for about an hour," Pearl said. "There's something I need to take care of."

"If that something is Opal, I insist you leave right now."

"Can you continue with the meeting, Stephen? I'd rather not frighten the girls until we're absolutely certain."

"I will...but I won't be as effective as you."

"They only need someone to talk to."

"Let's hope that's the only thing they'll need tonight."

Nestor's ex-wife, Rajni, was at the craft fair selling her custom-design gameboards. Her smooth olive skin and blue eyes made her look like an exotic china doll. She brushed some brown curly strands of hair away from her face that failed to be contained by a hair clip. She smiled at a boy who was begging his father to buy him a backgammon board with a Chinese horoscope theme. He was fixated by the large Yin-Yang painted in the center.

Rajni loved mythology, particularly from Ancient India. She grew up playing Pachisi and Leela with her maternal grandmother. The symbolism behind the games had captivated her. Pachisi was about life, which encompassed skill, free will and luck, whereas Leela was about destiny. When Rajni first started playing Leela, she would get frustrated each time she slid down a snake. Her grandmother would patiently explain how fortune could turn in her favor and not to give up. Rajni failed to understand the meaning until she landed on the tallest ladder and shot up to the lead, winning her first game.

"Just because you're at the bottom doesn't mean you can never rise again," her grandmother said.

Rajni's love for games developed into a lucrative hobby. The boards for sale on the display table were backgammon, chess, Leela and her preferred game of them all, Pachisi. All were intricately hand-painted, and two of the Pachisi boards were inspired by Hindu mythology. When Rajni first saw a picture of a Vimana—a mythological flying palace in Hinduism, she pondered over the possibility of life on other worlds and imagined piloting her own. Her grandmother told her anything was possible and never to stop dreaming.

Rajni's favorite Pachisi board had Vimanas suspended within lotus flowers for the nests, and the home space was represented by a large Aum contained within a white lotus. The board beside it had a Sri Yantra Mandala in the home space. The nests were Mandalas of Ganesh, Lakshmi, Dhumavati and Kal. This was Rajni's best-selling board in the Pachisi mythological line.

The boy continued to badger his father about the backgammon board, and an elderly female artist who operated the concession stand next to Rajni's came over, shaken. "You have to hear this, Raj." She played the video recorded at Benny's on her translinker.

On screen was Blaze, who was in the middle of his announcement. "Collin just confirmed that we lost contact with areas around the world currently lit by the sun," he said.

"If that's supposed to be a joke, it's not funny." Rajni said as she started to put her boards away. It was nearly quitting time.

"I thought so too," the neighboring artist said, "but he appears to be right. We lost contact with the whole West Coast, and every other part of the world exposed to sunlight." She showed Rajni the daylight map.

"What does that mean, Daddy?" the boy asked.

"It's only a solar flare," the father assured his son. "They happen all the time."

The scared look on the boy's face moved Rajni, and she gave him the board he admired.

"That's very kind of you," the father said, "but you don't have to do this."

Rajni smiled at the boy. "Enjoy the game."

"Thank you, Miss." He traced the Yin-Yang with his index finger. "I can't wait to learn how to play it."

"This world needs more people like you," the father said to Rajni, then walked off with the boy.

"He's right. It's probably just a solar flare," the artist speculated. "We're in the middle of an active sun cycle."

"Not as active as that tattooed man's imagination," Rajni said.

"You might have a point. I think I heard it mentioned that he's a novelist."

"He can't be that good if he comes up with such an unbelievable premise." Rajni packed her remaining boards, got her cane and pushed her way through a swarm of bodies, which wasn't easy for someone of her petite size and frame, let alone her current physical condition. When she got to the street side, traffic was at a standstill. The subway station was over a mile away. She could've hired a car or taken the bus, but to Rajni that would've meant giving in to her illness. A diagnosis of multiple sclerosis had already destroyed her successful career as a ballerina. She refused to give up what was left of her mobility, even though she knew the excruciating effort it would take for her to get to the subway station.

On days like this, Rajni felt more eighty-five than thirty-five. What was once a task she never had to think about now had to be methodically planned and executed. Her favorite coffee shop was two blocks away. She would stop there to rest and have an espresso. The historic book shop, a block and a half farther, had a couch inside. Rajni knew the owner, and he let her rest there even though she never bought a book.

With her itinerary all figured out, she slowly walked forward, conserving her energy so that she'd make it to her first scheduled stop. The phantom smell of a freshly brewed espresso put a little extra determination in her stride. She laughed over how the little things motivated her more than they did before she was first diagnosed with multiple sclerosis. Rajni then became teary eyed as she considered how much she had lost.

Jeff spotted the shuttleport ahead. He flew his flyer towards the entrance gate, and he called in to land. He was warned not to proceed any farther.

"I'm Lieutenant Jeffrey Theobald. I have clearance to land here."

"Not tonight; you don't," answered the flight coordinator. "We're in the middle of running some military exercises."

"I know what's going on in there. I was invited by Seth Marconi."

"One moment please."

Silence followed, and Jeff nervously tapped on the wheel. He was a task man and regularly honed his attention on pressing matters as they arose. He pushed the pending end of the world to the sidelines for the moment. Right now, his priority was seeing his sixteen month old daughter, Darla, for one last time.

"I'm sorry, but I can't let you inside," the flight coordinator said. "If you'd like to land in the visitor lot and contact your party from there, it's on the north side."

"I know where it is." Jeff flew towards the visitor lot and called his ex-wife after he had landed.

"I need to see you, Gwen," he said the instant her face appeared on screen. She was in one of the hangars, holding their daughter. Standing beside her was her husband, who was an admiral.

"Where are you?" she asked.

"In the visitor lot. They won't let me in."

"They're running exercises tonight."

"Spare me the scripted answer. Lynn got me a ticket out on Marconi's shuttle, but I chose to stay."

"Seth Marconi? Invited you?"

"Why do you look so shocked?"

"I just saw the line going into his shuttle. The darkest skin I saw was of the suntan variety."

"He also has something against the elderly."

"Your mother?"

"He wouldn't let me take her."

"She doesn't even remember you, Jeff. If you had a way out, you should've taken it."

Jeff shook his head, only now noticing the similarities between Gwen and Lynn. "After what you told me about him, I'm even more glad I didn't."

"Call him. Tell him you changed your mind. Once you get to Mars, you can go your own way."

"He's not going to Mars."

"Where is he going?" Gwen asked surprised. "There are no other colonies."

"He built one outside the Solar System." Jeff paused, then added, "I wish I could get you and Darla onto that flight."

"We'll be okay. The colony is like a fortress, and they say that since Mars is farther out than the Earth, we'll be safe."

Jeff didn't feel as certain, but he kept his concerns to himself. "I want to see her before you take off. Can you come to the gate?"

Gwen muted the audio from her end. She leaned towards her husband and asked if she could go to the gate.

Jeff closed his eyes and sighed after the Admiral had looked into the lens of Gwen's translinker and nodded.

"We'll be there," Gwen said. "But only for a couple of minutes. We're taking off soon."

Jeff watched Gwen get out of a jeep on the other side of the fence with his one-year-old daughter in her arms. She approached the gate, waved her arm in front of the scanner, and the gate opened. Jeff entered, and Gwen let him hold their daughter.

"So good to see you, Darla." He hugged her tightly, never wanting to let her go again.

"Come with us, Jeff," Gwen said. "With a little coaxing, I'm sure I can have Paul get you on our flight."

Jeff gazed at his daughter, whom he still held in his arms. "I can't." He ran his hand through her red curls.

"You're never going to see your daughter again."

"You didn't seem to care about that when you planned on leaving without telling me." Jeff stopped himself from continuing. He didn't want to end the night arguing. "Have a good life, Gwen, and give our daughter one."

Gwen began to cry.

"I'm not mad at you," Jeff said. "I'm not mad at anyone anymore." He smiled at Darla. "I can't be. Not with a face like this staring back at me." He handed Darla back to Gwen.

Gwen smiled. "You're an honorable man, Jeff." She kissed Darla's cheek. "I'm going to make sure our daughter knows it."

The jeep's headlights flashed, and Jeff walked out of the restricted area. Gwen shut the gate and headed back to the jeep with Darla.

Jeff got into his flyer and watched the jeep drive away until he could no longer see its taillights. He then took off to complete his next task, trying not to think about whether Mars was out far enough.

Confrontations and Obstructions

Blaze eyed Trevor Forthright's door and then checked the time on his translinker. It was nearing 9:00 PM. A combination of beer, anger, and hurt—along with the fear that everything really would be over—made Blaze knock. He refused to die before telling Trevor what he thought of his latest review.

Trevor, who was one year away from retiring, opened the door to his apartment and squinted his eyes. "Blaze Kenyon?"

"Live and in person, but I'm not here to autograph your book."

"You know I delete your books after I read them." Trevor leaned his hand against the door frame. "Why are you here?"

"To tell you you're way off this time."

"Put it all down in your next attack piece about me. I'm in the middle of watching a movie with my wife." Trevor went to close the door, and Blaze pushed it back open.

"I've suffered enough to know it's you that has no understanding of suffering."

"Are you drunk?" Trevor looked out into the hallway, worried his neighbors might be disturbed by the exchange.

Blaze thrust his finger forward. "And you're an uninspired, pompous, literary evangelist who needs to be knocked off his pedestal."

Trevor's wife, who was in the living room, grew impatient waiting for him. This was one of the few nights the couple had to spend together. Trevor was either working on his reviews or writing his magnum opus that had taken him ten years, so far, to write.

Ivy was a lonely woman existing on the glory of her past. She'd won numerous beauty pageants, including the title of Miss New York. A string of plastic surgeries and hair weaves kept her sparkling on the outside, but she felt dull inside. She escaped her tedious life through either a book or interactive program on the transviewer.

"Who's at the door, Trevor?" she called out.

"Blaze Kenyon," Trevor yelled back.

"Blaze Kenyon?" Ivy picked up her translinker and looked at the bookmarked page of the latest Drake Kent novel she was in the middle of reading.

"Yes, Ivy. Blaze Kenyon."

Ivy sprang from her chair, ran to the door, pushed Trevor aside, and extended her hand to Blaze. "It's an honor to meet you, Mr. Kenyon."

Blaze couldn't resist the charming older woman. He took her hand and kissed it. "Delighted to meet you."

Trevor winced.

"My husband never told me you were coming. I would've prepared something."

Trevor glared at Blaze. "He was just leaving."

"So soon?" Ivy asked. "Why don't you come in for some coffee, Mr. Kenyon?"

"I don't want him in our home, Ivy," Trevor said. "He's drunk and belligerent."

"Thank you for the invitation, Mrs. Forthright," Blaze replied. "I'd love some coffee."

"Come on in," she said ignoring her husband. "And you can call me Ivy."

"As long as you call me Blaze." He smirked at Trevor and followed Ivy inside.

"Have a seat," Ivy told Blaze as she rushed past the kitchen table to prepare the coffee. "Do you believe in synchronicity?"

"As a novelist, I see it more as a reality than belief." Blaze pulled out a chair and sat.

"I was just reading your book when the doorbell rang, and here you are, sitting in our kitchen." Ivy smiled as she placed a filter into the coffee machine. "It's serendipitous."

Trevor rolled his eyes, and Blaze slapped his hands on the table. "Have a seat, Trev."

"Leave now," Trevor told him. "Or I'll call the police and have them forcibly remove you."

"What's wrong with you, Trevor?" Ivy scooped some coffee grounds out of the container and poured them into the filter. "He's a famous author. Stop treating him like a convict."

Blaze waved at Trevor and smiled.

"I didn't invite him," Trevor said.

"If he needs a formal invitation, I'll grant him one." Ivy started the coffeemaker and got out a large jar of biscotti.

"Which book are you reading?" Blaze asked.

"The latest in the Drake Kent series."

Trevor tossed up his hands in defeat and sat down.

"What did you think of it?" Blaze asked.

"I loved it! I didn't agree with Trevor's review. He can be a little too over-critical. I thought Drake Kent's decision to let Bradley Simpson leave Earth and travel with a group of monks was believable."

"The man killed over one hundred and thirty-seven women during his murder spree," Trevor countered.

"But he never wanted to kill anyone. He even told Drake he felt like a robot. Whenever he killed, it was as though someone else's hands were strangling his victims. And that's how Drake eventually discovered the microscopic alien burrowed inside Simpson's brain."

Trevor shook his head. "That sounds even more preposterous hearing it aloud."

"Why?" Ivy placed some biscotti on a plate, then set it on the table.

"By the turn of a page, Simpson is miraculously healed after a band of space monks arrive with the antidote to rid him of the infestation. They then go on to explain how he used to be one of them before a nefarious alien abducted him and fed off the energy produced by his compassion. Kenyon let Simpson completely off the hook." He picked up a biscotti and took a bite

"He's not off the hook!" Blaze said. "Simpson endured years of suffering under the influence of the alien. But his true sentence began once he became aware of his condition. He knew that no matter how hard he tried to make up for what he did, it would never be enough. His inability to stop the alien from making him kill people would be forever on his mind. But all you saw was a madman who killed without remorse because you think I don't understand the nature of suffering."

"By your own definition, you don't," Trevor said.

"Wasn't aware I had one."

"You wear suffering like a badge, which is why your characters all end up sounding whiny and apologetic. After a time, they have to face the consequences of their actions. That's how real life operates. There are no magical beings that can undo what we've done in this life."

Ivy poured some coffee into the cups and served the feuding men. "You're taking this far too seriously, Trevor. Everything doesn't have to read like a Greek tragedy. Most people buy books because they need an escape. After all the wars we've been through, everything seems so dark and gloomy in this sector. Reading an uplifting book makes me feel as though I exist in a happier world."

Trevor poured some sugar into his coffee and stirred. "My wife has a valid point. Most reviewers praise your work for that same reason. Why do you care so much about what I think?"

"Have you ever lost someone you love?" Blaze asked.

"I've been in two sector wars, so I've seen a lot of great men and women fall."

"Were any of them murdered in front of you...while you were forced to watch?"

Trevor remained silent. He had heard about what happened to Astrid.

"Be glad you never witnessed the murder of your wife. Be glad you never had to see the terror in her eyes that would haunt you every waking moment of your life because you couldn't do a damned thing to save her. If you can show me how to remove my badge, I'll gladly do so...right now."

Ivy warned Trevor with her eyes to keep his mouth shut. She wanted to say something comforting, but no words that seemed adequate came to her. She topped off Blaze's cup with more coffee and hoped her smile and hospitality was enough.

"Thank you, Ivy," Blaze said as his translinker rang. He looked at the screen. It was Collin. "I need to take this." He connected to the call.

Collin's voice sounded rushed and panicked. "Link to the UPS with my ID: seven, alpha, delta, six, three, four."

"What's going on?"

"The meaning of now is now!"

Collin's frantic demeanor sobered Blaze up. "Give me the codes again."

"Seven, alpha, delta, six, three, four. Go to the live feeds and scroll down to Nestor Zaras."

Blaze opened the file, played the video and when it got to the part where Warren H. Beasley paraphrased what Seth Marconi had told him, he pounded his fist on the table.

"What's wrong?" Ivy asked.

"He's drunk," Trevor said. "That's what's wrong."

Blaze switched on the external speaker so Ivy and Trevor could listen in. Ivy started crying after Warren said, "Enjoy your last night alive. Whatever is happening to our sun is not conducive to life on this planet."

"Is any of this confirmed?" Blaze asked Collin.

"Nestor Zaras—the guy who interviewed Beasley, is trying to verify that now."

Blaze's thoughts were racing. "How long ago did the interview take place?"

"About a half-hour ago," Collin said. "It's raw footage. Nothing is confirmed yet, but this is moving beyond coincidence."

Ivy reached for her husband's hand. "Trevor, I'm scared."

Trevor glared at Blaze. "Your problem is with me. Don't take this out on my wife."

Ivy carefully scrutinized Blaze's face and then turned to Trevor. "He's serious."

"Your sister is freaking out," Collin informed Blaze. "Get here as soon as you can."

"On my way now." Blaze disconnected the call.

"What kind of depraved game are you playing?" Trevor asked.

"Not as depraved as the game Seth Marconi played with me tonight." Blaze recounted the bet Seth made with him earlier at Benny's.

"You believe that man was telling the truth?" Ivy asked.

Blaze had taken a liking to Ivy, and he struggled to find the right words to announce her death sentence.

Ivy yelled, "Is it true? Are we all going to die tomorrow?" She clenched Trevor's hand so hard that he winced.

"We're a resilient species." Blaze forced a smile and hoped it appeared genuine. "I don't believe the Universe is ready to give up on us just yet."

Trevor could tell Blaze was attempting to assuage Ivy, and he saw him in a way he hadn't expected. Although he was honest in his reviews, he read Blaze's books with a prejudice he wasn't aware existed until now. Trevor had always prided himself as a man who never judged anyone by appearance and found it troubling that he was surprised to find compassion in Blaze. He knew Blaze volunteered his time at the local VFW and visited veterans who were institutionalized due to PTSD, yet Trevor refused to acknowledge it because of the novelist's tattoos. He viewed Blaze as a thug with a gift for words, a thug who more than likely got his wife killed. *Sometimes a man sees what he sees because of his own prejudices.* Trevor admitted to his own, as many other humans did, on this last night.

Ivy smiled at Blaze, seeing who she wanted to see in this dark hour: Drake Kent, her ideal man. He came alive for her in the pages of Blaze's books. Wherever trouble ensued, Drake Kent showed up to save the day. Ivy was going to die in her happy little fantasy world, and Blaze was contented to maintain it for her. He answered all of Ivy's questions when she asked about his future installment of the series. Blaze never actually planned the next book, and some of the ideas he came up with on the spot made him wish he had time to write it.

Pearl's estranged twin sister, Opal, sat on the couch with her feet on the coffee table, drinking a beer and watching the transviewer. When the sisters were children they were identical. Now, Opal and Pearl didn't even look related. As a retired commander from the joined forces, Opal maintained her self-discipline by eating healthy and working out five days a week. She was lean and muscular and could do twenty pull-ups and a hundred push-ups. Impressive for a seventy-three-year-old human form. Opal kept her gray hair long and loosely braided on her right side. Apart from the generic ponytail, it was the only other way she could style it herself. Whenever she desired a fancier up-do, she used to go to Pearl for assistance. Since the twins hadn't spoken in years, Opal had gone to sticking with her trusted side-braid. She typically left her apartment wearing clothes meant for women half her age, and men still stared at her from behind. The shock on the men's faces when they first caught sight of her wrinkles amused Opal. "My muscles haven't sagged, but I can't do a damned thing about the face," she'd respond with a chortle.

Opal clicked on a news-site where it was now being reported that a large X-class flare had struck the Earth and that blackouts were occurring all over the world.

The doorbell rang, and Opal's parrot, Rufus, mimicked the sound. Opal got up and glimpsed through the peephole. When she saw Pearl's face, she returned to the couch. The doorbell rang again.

"I know you're in there!" Pearl yelled. "I can hear your transviewer!"

Rufus carried on with his imitation of a doorbell.

"Open the door now, Opal! This is an emergency!"

Rolling her eyes, Opal got up and opened the door. "What do you want?"

"Did you hear the video?"

"All I hear is your mouth."

"We have to end this now." Pearl invited herself in.

"I didn't say you could come in."

"I don't care," Pearl said. "You're going to listen to me tonight, and I won't take no for an answer."

Opal went to the closet and grabbed her jacket. "I'll leave then."

Pearl got out her translinker, found Warren H. Beasley's file, and played it.

Opal held back her laughter until the end. "Is that why you came here tonight?"

"Stephen made a few phone calls. He couldn't reach anyone in the Central and Western time zones."

"It's a solar flare. The whole world is experiencing blackouts, so you can go now. The end is not near."

Pearl remained where she was, and Opal headed for the door. "Enjoy the apocalypse without me. I'm going for a walk."

Pearl grabbed her sister's arm. Opal swung around with her fist clenched, ready to strike. It was an instinctual reaction born during her tour in the 1st sector war.

"Violence was always your way of dealing with things," Pearl said.

"Did you come here expecting a hug and forgiveness?"

"All I want is a truce. If that scientist spoke the truth, we'll never have the chance again to make peace."

"So what? We won't know the difference because we'll be dead."

Pearl put her translinker in her purse. "If you want to stay angry, that's your choice. But I'm going to say what I came here to say. You can either listen or ignore it."

Opal covered her ears with her fingers.

"Stop acting childish! I'm sorry for what I did to you, but I have no regrets. You can either accept my apology or continue to ignore me as you have for the past ten years. Whatever your decision, I made my peace."

Opal crossed her arms. "You made a lot more than that."

"If the story is true, we won't see each other again." Years of pent up emotions spilled out, and Pearl wanted to tell her twin she loved her, but the words refused to come out. Her tears had no such restraint. "I'll be at St. Augustine's if you want to talk." She hurried to the door.

"It was always so easy for you," Opal told her.

Pearl turned to face her. "I thought the same about you."

"You hurt me, but you say you don't regret it. I don't understand how you can say that."

"Christina."

Opal looked away.

"I haven't seen her in years," Pearl said. "She won't even talk to me."

"You only have yourself to blame for that."

"I tried reaching out to you."

"You didn't try hard enough."

"What do you want me to do?" Pearl asked. "Throw myself off the George Washington Bridge? Would that make you feel better?"

"It would be a great start."

"To hell with you! I'm trying, but you won't even budge an inch." Pearl opened the front door.

"Come back," Opal said. "I'll make a few calls to put your mind at ease."

Pearl shut the door. "Thanks."

"I should be thanking you. I could use a good laugh tonight."

"What if it's true?"

"I'll make peace with you."

Opal was still in touch with those she served with. She began her round of calls, believing she'd end up making Pearl look foolish. But after she'd finished talking with a recently retired admiral, she was convinced Warren spoke the truth.

"Looks as if we'll be making peace tonight," Opal said calmly. "All communications cut out. Shuttles filled with Aristocrats and select members of the military are taking off from all around the world. They're headed to the Mars Colony. The ISA issued a phony press release stating that we're in the middle of a solar storm. They're hoping it will calm people down." Opal shook her head. "We fought and died for them, and this is how they thank us. By leaving us down here to fry like bacon. Spineless bastards."

"I'll never see my daughter again," Pearl said to herself and started to sob.

Opal tossed her hand up. "If it's any consolation, we'll be joining her soon."

"How can you be so cold?"

"Sorry. My heart was ripped out long ago. I haven't felt anything in ten years."

"Come to St. Augustine's with me," Pearl urged. "Helping others will make you feel something again."

"You know I don't like churches."

"There will be a lot of scared people. We could use someone like you."

"Ah, so now you need a soldier to protect you? Peace isn't as easy as you believed it to be. Maintaining it requires the threat of violence."

"I don't want to get into a personal or philosophical debate tonight. What's done is done. I want us to start over, Opal. Make the effort with me. Please. We more than likely won't get another chance if what your friend says is true."

Opal thought about the chaos that was about to be unleashed on the city. To her, reacting to the call for order was as instinctual as waking up in the morning. "I have to get dressed and grab a few things."

"Don't even think about bringing your gun," Pearl said.

"We'll need it. The city is going to be a madhouse tonight."

"We'll be inside. Leave it here. A gun will scare everyone."

"Including the criminals."

Rufus squawked. "Rufus happy birdy."

Pearl glanced at Rufus. "Is that the same Rufus?"

"Yes, and he goes with us," Opal answered.

"Oh, good. He'll help calm the children."

"Rufus gets skittish around kids."

"Wonder where he learned that from," Pearl said.

Opal went into her bedroom, got dressed, and snuck her gun into her tote bag.

Nestor arrived at the cafe where he was to meet Randy. He took a seat at an outside table. The street scene that night was typical for Greenwich Village. Most of the population continued to believe a solar flare was responsible for the blackouts. Nestor also clung to that last fragment of hope and tried calling Becky again, hanging up when he got the recorded message. He searched online for news updates and stopped when the email icon flashed. In the dropbox was a video from MatrixMaster, a fourteen-year-old, pimple-faced, conspiracy-loving genius. He regularly gave Nestor tips and story ideas, which were more-often-than-not verifiable. Also included in the delivery was a video of Blaze's revelation at Benny's. Nestor played it and then watched MatrixMaster's video.

MatrixMaster sat at his desk with a large banner behind him that read, *Disconnect from the Lies and plug in to the Truth*. With a shaky voice, he said, "Hi Nestor. If you're opening this video message, you're still in the East Coast. Something weird is going on with the space weather, and even I'm having trouble verifying things over here. Communication is cut off in all areas under the sun's exposure. The media is reporting that it's only a solar flare, but I'm not buying what those empty-heads are saying. Whatever's happening is being closely guarded. I checked the shuttle departures within the last three hours. Many of the who's who of the world are aboard those shuttles and headed to the spaceport for some *convention* on Mars. I'm not buying that either. Rumor has it that Seth Marconi is heading to a space colony he built outside of the Solar System. Can't confirm that one for you, unfortunately. If this turns out to be what my dog leaves on the grass during his morning walk, I'll be finishing up something else I have for you. You're going to love this one. Want a hint?" MatrixMaster smiled. "Hah hah hah, I'm not telling. You're going to have to wait."

His expression turned grave. Peering directly into the camera, he said, "If this turns out to be true, which I'm leaning toward believing it is, I'm sorry for your family...for all of our families. As for me, I'm off to play virtual house with my virtual girlfriend. I'll die virtually happy because my brain won't know the difference. It's better than freaking out like the rest of the sheeple will be doing pretty soon. MatrixMaster out."

Nestor tried Becky again, and when he heard the recorded message, his chest tightened. Blaze's video, his interview with Warren H. Beasley, and the message from MatrixMaster couldn't all be a coincidence. Nevertheless, admitting the world will end tomorrow morning is not the type of truth you immediately accept. You confirm, and then confirm again until you have nothing left to do but accept your fate.

Nestor made a few more desperate calls to people he knew on the West Coast, hoping to hear a live voice. His friend Randy arrived while he was connecting to the seventh name on his auto-call list.

"Sorry I'm late." Randy pulled out a chair and sat. "You okay? You look whiter than my cat." He waved to a passing waitress. "Two dark ales for me and my friend." Fanning himself with his hand, he said, "Woo whee, it's hot tonight. Seems more like summer than early spring." He picked up a napkin and blotted the sweat from the bald spot on the top of his head. "Why aren't you saying anything? I usually can't get a word in."

"What did you find out?"

"Hello to you too, old friend. How long has it been since we've last met? Oh...three years. Has it been that long?"

"Did you get my message?"

"Along with that video you sent me? Yeah, I got it. I didn't need to check anything out. Beasley's insane—but entertaining. Much more so than that tattooed author who's spreading the same piffle. Just goes to show you, people will believe anything."

"How do you explain that we lost contact with everyone exposed to sunlight?" Nestor asked.

"We're in the middle of an active sun cycle. The flare affected the satellites. Nothing unusual."

Nestor shook his head.

"You don't believe any of that crap, do you?" Randy asked.

"MatrixMaster just shot me a message. All the government officials took off for some convention on the Mars colony."

"If it'll make you feel better, I'll check the UPS again and see if there are any updates."

The waitress brought over their beers. Randy picked up his bottle and took a sip.

"When are you calling?" Nestor asked.

"Relax, the night is young. We have at least another eight hours until sunrise." Randy smiled.

"Call now!" Nestor insisted.

Randy raised a brow. "Have another beer, man. You're way too tense." He got out his translinker and connected to the Universal Press Server. He soon confirmed everything that MatrixMaster, Warren H. Beasley, and Blaze had said.

"Still doesn't mean that physicist—who sounded like he guzzled down the liquor inventory of that cafe you were at—told you the truth. An X-class flare is common." Randy laughed as he continued to look at the screen. "What a head-case!" He then widened his eyes. "Now *this* is interesting."

"What?" Nestor leaned toward Randy to get a look at his translinker screen.

"There are several videos here of Warren H. Beasley running around and yelling that the day of tribulation has arrived and that God is seeking his revenge by turning the sun against us." He pointed his finger in the air. "Woh-hoh-hoh, this gets even better. Some of Xavier Starfly's followers joined Beasley in chanting, 'The end is here, there's nothing to fear. After we're dead, we'll be joined by a cosmic thread.'" Randy shook his head while laughing. "You can relax, Nestor. This is too hysterical to be real."

"When has an X-class flare ever caused half of Earth's communications to be cut off?"

Randy made another connection on his translinker. "If you're still not convinced, I know someone at the observatory in Hilo. I'm forwarding your footage to him."

"Then what?"

"We wait."

On the way back to the city, Anya had to listen to her mother chastise her as she always had.

"Why did you have to be so selfish?" Mrs. Tanner complained. "For once, couldn't you keep your opinion to yourself? What difference does it make about honor when you're dead? You're just like your father, all self-righteous, thinking you're above everybody else. What makes you so special?"

She continued on with a series of more questions until Anya landed on the roof of her mother's apartment building.

"Don't bother staying!" Mrs. Tanner opened the door.

"This is our last night, Mom. Can't we have some peace tonight?"

"The only way I'll find peace is with you not around," Mrs. Tanner grumbled as she got out of the flyer. She leaned down and glared at Anya. "When I look at you, I feel nothing. Nothing at all. I don't know who you are because you're certainly not my daughter."

It was too much. Anya felt tears begin to roll down her face.

"Go ahead and cry. You deserve to suffer because you didn't only kill yourself tonight. You killed me. Goodnight, you miserable little bitch!" She slammed the door and marched off.

Anya collapsed onto the steering wheel and sobbed because she realized her relationships had been a series of abusive ones. There was her ex-husband, whom she left after he had almost beat her to death; Seth, whom always made her work extremely long hours without even saying thanks; and her mother, whose treatment tonight was only moderately worse than what she had dished out since Anya was a child.

I saw that the dark frequencies Anya emitted were attempting to extinguish the light from within her. Then words started to emerge in her mind and strung together into poetry, untangling most of the darkness. I bathed her with some extra Light to keep her going a while longer. Nevertheless, it would be up to Anya to receive and transmit My gift of Light.

Saints and Sinners

It took Rajni over an hour to make it to the subway, and her legs were throbbing. A line of frantic people who started to doubt the International Space Agency's story stretched all the way up to street level. As Rajni neared the stairwell, people plowed and pushed to get ahead of her, not even considering that her cane might be the only thing that kept her from falling. Rajni moved off to the side, concerned that she'd get thrown down the stairs or trampled on if she tried to enter the station. Her father's store, and their apartment that was in the same building, were another thirteen blocks away. Traffic was at a dead stop, and all the cars in the vicinity were either hired or stolen.

Rajni limped to a nearby building with a small flight of stairs and sat. She tried calling her father. When he didn't answer, she wept.

People walked by unfazed. Rajni hated feeling helpless. Hated that she couldn't just spring onto her feet and run home.

Watching Rajni sitting all alone, one might think I'd have a change of heart about Sun's misdeed. Admittedly, the idea of a cleansing once had its appeal, especially when I witnessed such selfishness on display. Sheim attempted to temper My thirst for vengeance by explaining how darkness is eventually overcome by Light. When I was calm enough to lie back and observe My first offspring produce their star children, I knew Sheim was correct, which is why I gave up judging long ago.

On this last night, the light that would shine over Rajni's pain stood a few yards away. A police officer and his partner had been unsuccessfully fighting off the frenzied horde by the subway station. One of them yelled, "Get back to the flyer. They're gonna need the joined forces to contain this!"

As the two headed back to their patrol flyer, Brenner, the younger officer, noticed Rajni's tears and her cane. He went up to her.

"Need a lift?"

"Oh, yes. Thank you. Thank you so much." She struggled to get up.

Brenner assisted Rajni to the flyer where his partner, Hank, was waiting with the engine running. Once they got inside, Hank took off and flew over the traffic.

Rajni shuddered as she stared down at people beating, pushing, and kicking each other to get into the subway station.

"Crazy night tonight," Brenner said to Rajni.

"That's an understatement."

"Never saw anything like this before," Hank added. "Even the last sector war wasn't this bad." He shook his head as he looked down below. "Animals. They're all animals."

"Don't insult the animals," Brenner said as he got out his translinker to see if any new information was posted on the publink.

"Is all this because of what that man with all the tattoos said?" Rajni asked.

"Along with Warren H. Beasley."

Rajni's baffled expression made Brenner continue. "He's a plasma physicist with the ISA. He caused a disturbance at a cafe in the Village. Some documentarian shot an interview with him. He claimed the sun was behaving weirdly, and they couldn't figure out why."

"I didn't see that one."

"It was uploaded to the publink about an hour ago, but his story hasn't been verified yet."

Brenner showed Rajni a daylight map displayed on his translinker screen. "People lost touch with their families in exactly the areas that Beasley said were destroyed."

"It's really happening then?" Rajni asked.

"Don't jump to any conclusions yet. This could all be nothing worse than a large solar storm like the Carrington Event of 1859."

"This happened before?" Rajni asked with a trace of relief.

"The storm was so powerful the aurora lights could be seen all the way to Hawaii," Hank said. "What a sight that must've been."

"You think that's what's happening?" Rajni asked.

"Probably," Brenner told her as he scanned the publink for more news. "But we'll have a bigger mess to clean up because we're more dependent on electric power. Back then, the worst that happened was that a few telegraph operators got a little shock."

Rajni leaned back against her chair.

"Jesus," Hank said, "they'll probably place us back on twelve hour shifts as they did during the last sector war."

"I'd rather have that future than the one Beasley mentioned," Brenner said, then smiled at Rajni. "But I'm sure it's just a solar storm."

Pearl and Opal entered St. Augustine's. It was nearing full capacity. Opal set Rufus's cage on a large donation bin.

"Not there," Pearl said.

"Only for a minute." Opal opened the cage door.

Rufus hopped onto her hand, climbed up her arm and rested on her shoulder. He gently pecked the side of her cheek—his version of a kiss.

A crowd came over to admire Rufus. Used to being only around Opal, he shrieked.

"There, there, Rufus," Opal petted his head. "We'll go find a quiet corner for you." She picked up the cage and asked her sister, "What can I do to help?"

Pearl glanced over at Father Stephen who was comforting an older woman. "Help Stephen calm people down."

Opal did as requested, but she was surprised Pearl asked her to comfort people. She had a tendency to blurt out whatever came to her mind. Opal preferred the truth, no matter how hard it was to hear. And she gave it out just as honestly. As a survivor of the 1st sector war that left half the population of the West Sector dead, Opal didn't want to waste time on pretense. She figured the transviewer was filled with enough fantasies to keep people locked in ignorance if that's how they chose to live.

When Father Stephen finished consoling the older woman, Opal approached him.

"It's so good to see you, Opal." He hugged her and smiled at Rufus. "And who's this?"

"Rufus," Opal said.

"The same Rufus from over twenty years ago?"

"That's me," Rufus said.

Father Stephen laughed. "How old is he now?"

"Almost thirty-six," Opal said.

Father Stephen petted Rufus. "I bet you're glad to see the twins together again. It's been too long."

"It's been even longer since I've been in this church." Opal glanced at Pearl who sat on one of the rear pews comforting Deirdre.

"The Lord doesn't wear a watch," Father Stephen said. "He'll always make the time for you."

Opal wasn't religious, but she admired Father Stephen. They grew up together and spent a lot of their childhood in the neighborhood playground.

"Pearl says you need help in the comforting department," Opal said. "Don't know if you remember, but I'm not the nurturer in the family. That's my sister's specialty."

"I think you underestimate yourself, Opal. When I married you and Harry, all I had to do was look at the expression of love and devotion in his face to recognize the kind and compassionate spirit in you."

Although she knew Steve meant well, hearing about Harry awakened old wounds. Opal felt lonely since her divorce. She found it hard to trust another man and spent most of her time alone. Having Rufus around kept her from giving up.

Opal's reunion with Father Stephen was interrupted when a frantic woman entered the church, pulling her daughter by the hand.

"Help! Somebody help me!" she screamed as a few people hurried over to her.

Father Stephen nodded his head at Opal, signaling her to assist. Opal handed her cage to Father Stephen and went to the woman whose shirt was torn.

"Things are getting crazy out there!" the woman said while her daughter clung to her jacket, sobbing. "I couldn't find a car to hire. I headed home on foot, and a man came to us from out of nowhere and stole my purse. He didn't hurt us, but he frightened the hell out of my daughter." The woman looked around at the church. "Can I stay here until my husband comes for me?"

"That's why we're here." Opal had an uneasy feeling and wanted to get her gun. Pearl had inspected her tote before they entered St. Augustine's and found it. She forced Opal to leave the gun in the trunk of their hired car.

The girl stepped away from her mother and stared up at Rufus. "What's your bird's name?"

Opal shifted her head down towards the girl. "Rufus."

"Can I play with him?"

Opal looked at Pearl who was still soothing Deirdre, then back at the girl. "What's your name?"

"Molly."

"Rufus is a very special bird. Whoever I let hold him has to promise to take good care of him. Do you understand?"

Opal looked at the mother for approval, and she nodded.

"Stretch out your arm in front of you, Molly," Opal said.

"Does it bite?" Molly's mother asked.

Opal cringed at the disrespectful tone of her voice. "He doesn't bite."

Molly cautiously held out her arm.

"Go play, Rufus," Opal prompted.

Rufus hopped onto Molly's forearm and walked to her shoulder. Molly giggled.

"Show Molly some love, and give her a kissy kiss," Opal said.

Rufus gently pecked Molly's cheek, and she laughed again.

"Kissy kiss," Rufus said, and Molly's mother joined in the laughter.

"I'd like you to do me a favor, Molly." Opal looked over at Pearl who waved and then returned to the conversation with Deirdre.

Opal leaned down in front of Molly. "Can you keep an eye on Rufus for me? I have something I need to take care of."

Molly glimpsed at her mother. "Can I, Mommy?"

Her mother nodded.

"Remember," Opal said to Molly, "Rufus is a very special bird. You're the only one allowed to hold him." Opal gently stroked the side of Rufus's face. "I'll be right back."

"Right back, right back," Rufus said.

"I'll take good care of him," Molly said. "I promise."

Opal never left Rufus with a stranger before, but she had to get to her gun. She sneaked to the door and slipped out with no one noticing.

I sighed, thinking about the dichotomy of hope displayed in St. Augustine's and everywhere else on Earth. Hope can make some people feel helpless to do anything while empowering others to take action. In Opal's case, it strengthened her resolve. Not knowing the full extent of Sun's wrath kept her fighting spirit strong. Pearl hoped as well, but hers came in a prayer, hoping her god would show up in the final hour to save them all. Such a polarity I've known, but it would take on a whole new twist by the time the night was over. If there's one thing you can take from this comment is that I don't do reruns.

Jeff checked out the clock on the dash after he had touched down in Outer DC. It was nearing 10:00 PM. He connected to the publink and heard the end of Warren H. Beasley's rant. It was now the most clicked on story in the part of the world lit by Moon, who shined brighter than he ever had before.

Jeff headed towards the hospital where his mother had lived for the past fifteen years. Whenever he came here, the surrounding dilapidated buildings made him recall the final days of the 2nd sector war, shortly after his tour had ended. He was in DC when the Pentagon was bombed. His mother was working inside when it happened. She spent three months in a coma, and when she awoke she couldn't remember her own family. Six months later, the senior Mr. Theobald ended up having an affair with a nurse he met in the hospital cafeteria. His visits to his wife dropped down to one hour every Sunday, then to once a month. He eventually stopped visiting her altogether. Mrs. Theobald never noticed the difference. Jeff noticed and confronted his father about the affair, punching him after he had compared his mother to a vegetable. The altercation happened fourteen years before. It was the last time father and son had spoken. Even with the end of the world in the offing, Jeff had no desire to make amends.

He passed the nurses' station and entered his mother's room. She was watching some old comedy program on the transviewer that was blaring loudly. Jeff lowered the volume.

"Hey! Why did you do that?"

"We're going for a ride."

"Not until after my show." Mrs. Theobald grabbed the remote control from Jeff and turned the volume back up.

"Come on, Mom. I don't have time for this tonight."

"Why did you call me that? I don't have any children."

Jeff rummaged through the closet and got out a red floral dress and jacket, dreading the typical disjointed conversation he'd have to participate in tonight. A part of him regretted not leaving. *Lynn was right. My mother would never have even noticed me missing. What difference would it have made if I never showed up?* Jeff hadn't cried since the bombing that injured his mother, but he came close to it now. He handed the dress to his mother, who stared at the transviewer in a glazed expression.

"Put this on," he said.

"Shh!"

Jeff threw the dress and jacket on the bed, tore the transviewer off the wall and slammed it on the floor.

Mrs. Theobald started to sob.

"I'm sorry, Mom." He hugged her. "I didn't mean to scare you."

She pushed him away as a nurse ran into the room. Mrs. Theobald walked in a circle, clapping her hands together, and crying.

"I'm going to have to ask you to leave, Lieutenant Theobald," the nurse said. "You're making the patient upset."

"She's my mother! And I signed her release papers."

The nurse looked at the shattered transviewer.

"Bill me." Jeff picked up the jacket and dress from the bed, grabbed his mother's hand, and dragged her out of the room.

The nurse left after them, relieved to have one less patient to deal with tonight. Two of the nurses failed to show up, believing the end was nigh.

"Where are you taking me?" Mrs. Theobald asked terrified.

"Out to a restaurant."

Her demeanor instantly shifted at the mention. "You didn't have to break my transviewer to get me to leave this prison. Sounds like fun!" She laughed. "But I'm not leaving without my hat."

"We don't have time."

"Not without my hat!"

Jeff hurried back to his mother's room with her following him. "Where is it?"

Mrs. Theobald pointed to a brown cloche hat with a red carnation. It was sitting on top of the wardrobe. Jeff got it and went to place it on his mother's head.

Mrs. Theobald seized the hat and put it on. "I'm not an invalid." She admired herself in the mirror and smiled. "Now I'm ready."

Jeff clutched her hand and rushed out.

"Can you get me some potato chips and cherry cola? Alone they're yum, but I like eating them together. I take a bite of a chip and then a sip of cherry cola and swirl it all together. It's deli-eli-licious."

"I'll get you a lifetime supply if you move faster."

Mrs. Theobald beamed as Jeff flashed his ID at the guard who opened the front door.

"They never let me have that here. They say it's not good for me, but I don't care. This nice boy sneaks potato chips and cherry cola to me every Sunday."

"That was me."

"It was?" Mrs. Theobald squinted her eyes and tried to recognize Jeff, but her brain was too damaged to make the connection. "Can't remember, but thanks. That was very kind of you."

Trevor walked Blaze to the door. "You should've gone with Marconi," Trevor said.

"Sometimes death is preferable to bad company." Blaze smiled.

Trevor opened the door and stepped outside with Blaze.

"Did you come here to tell me off before the world ended?"

"I couldn't let you get away with your critique unanswered," Blaze replied.

"A wise decision. There wouldn't have been enough time to write your rebuttal on your pubpage. I was looking forward to reading it."

"Was it more entertaining hearing it delivered in person?"

"That all depends. Do you believe Seth Marconi?"

"He had Bradley Simpson's energy-sapping stare."

"I'm glad you didn't mention that to Ivy." He shook his head.

"Maybe I should've kept the call private."

"I think you calmed her sufficiently."

"How about you?"

"At my age, you're lucky to get out of bed each morning. Putting an exact time on death is oddly easier to deal with. And you?"

"I've almost been there...twice. It's a lot easier the third time around."

"You understand suffering," Trevor said. "I saw that tonight in you. What I don't understand is why your characters never did."

"Some things are just too private to reveal to the world."

"Even on this alleged last night?"

"Maybe I'll write a poem."

"Pity no one will have time to read it."

"I will." Blaze turned to leave.

"Send me over a copy."

"As long as you promise to trash it as you did with all my other work."

"If we have enough time, you know I will."

"If we run out of it, I win." Blaze smiled and walked away.

Trevor was ready to return with a comeback, but he kept it to himself. There was an ulterior motive behind his restraint. Ivy would award him for respecting Blaze when they retired to the bedroom. Trevor figured that if he had to die, he'd go out with a big bang, and preferably, more than one.

Games, Guns, and Gore

Jeff and his mother were in the flyer. He turned on the navigation display and called in Langley Base.

"Where is Langley Base?" Mrs. Theobald asked.

"In Virginia."

"How far is that?"

"It'll take us a little over an hour to get there."

"That long? Can you get me my potato chips and cherry cola first?"

"When we get back."

"That's too long. Go now."

"We don't have time."

Mrs. Theobald opened the door. "I'm leaving then."

"Okay! We'll hit a quick stop on the way over."

She smiled and shut the door.

Jeff lifted off and when he looked down at the highway, the traffic was stopped.

"Oh boy, oh boy. Lots of cars down there," Mrs. Theobald said. "Almost as many as the pre-sector days."

"I wouldn't know. I wasn't alive then."

"I was. You didn't miss much. It was like a zoo back then. There was no order."

Jeff had a feeling he was going to get a taste of what his mother was talking about. He'd encountered enough violence during his tour in the sector war and preferred to die in peace. "Do you like boats?" he asked.

"Boats? Oh yes, I like them very much. My father used to take us out on his fishing boat every Sunday. It was nice and quiet. Almost felt as if all the problems of the world disappeared while we were out at sea."

Jeff enjoyed hearing his mother talk about the past. It was when she sounded most lucid. "Got a boat moored at Langley Marina. Would you like to go out?"

"I would!" she clapped. "But after you get me my..."

"Potato chips and cherry cola."

Mrs. Theobald's smile reminded Jeff why he stayed on Earth. It no longer mattered that she didn't remember him.

Opal made it to her hired car and waved the palm of her hand in front of the ID scanner. The trunk popped open, and she retrieved her gear. A female screamed while she was buckling her combat belt around her waist. Opal grabbed her gun, sprinted across two blocks, and stopped at an alley where a man had a woman pinned to the ground. The woman fought back with all her might but was nearing exhaustion.

Opal aimed her gun at the assailant and fired a warning shot. "Stay where you are! I won't miss again!"

The assailant sprang to his feet and tried to run.

Opal shot his leg. "Last warning! Stay down, or you won't be getting up after the next one!" She hurried over to the woman. "Are you all right?"

"Thank you so much." The woman cried as she tried to cover herself with her torn shirt. "If you didn't show up, he probably would've killed me."

Opal took off her jacket and placed it over the woman's shoulders. "What's your name?"

"Heather."

"You're safe now, Heather." Opal called the police. With the confirmation that they'd all be dead at sunrise, she wanted the woman to make it home safe to die with her loved ones rather than out on the street.

A pre-recorded message came on: "All our cars are out now. If you need assistance, activate your tracker. A squad flyer will be sent over when one becomes available."

"He's getting away!" Heather pointed at the assailant who hobbled towards the street corner.

"Stay down!" Opal yelled as she clipped her translinker onto her utility belt.

The assailant limped faster, and Opal shot him in the back. He staggered forward and fell.

Heather clutched Opal's arm. "What's happening? Why is everyone acting so crazy tonight?"

"Did you hear about the solar flare?"

Heather nodded.

"The streets are going to get even more dangerous. Do you live nearby?"

"My apartment is five blocks away, bu—but I'm afraid to walk alone."

Opal glanced at the assailant dying on the street and then back at Heather. "I'll take you home."

"Thanks...again. Seems kindness is in short supply tonight."

One look at the circus on the main street made Opal reach a similar conclusion. She wanted to take the car, but it was running low on air. Every air pump station was as busy as the traffic, and she needed to get back to St. Augustine's. She called Father Stephen to tell him what had happened and walked Heather home. Her husband hurried out as soon as he'd seen them. After he had heard about Opal's heroics, he wanted to give her a financial award.

"If you want to thank me, donate some credits to the injured veteran survivors of the..." Opal froze, remembering there wasn't going to be a tomorrow.

"Were you with the joined forces?" Heather's husband asked.

"I was career."

"Do you know if there's any truth to what that physicist said?"

"Whatever loose ends you have, tie as many of them up as you can tonight."

"Are we all going to die?" Heather asked.

Opal looked directly into Heather's eyes. "It's looking that way."

Heather teared up and hugged her husband while Opal wished Pearl were here to handle this.

"I saw the way you fought your attacker," Opal said. "You're a strong woman."

"No. I'm not."

"You are. That's why you're here, with your husband."

"I'm here because you saved me."

"What I learned during my military career is that the side that works best as a team emerges the victor. We proved that during all three of the sector wars. Whenever one of us was down, we knew if we hung on long enough, one of our comrades would be around to save us. You hung on tonight, and I was your comrade. Because of that you're going to die on your own terms."

Heather looked up at her husband and wept.

"Don't let that monster destroy your last memories," Opal said. "Don't give him power over you. You were the victor tonight."

Heather held both her husband's hands. "I thought I was going to die without seeing you again." She turned to face Opal. "Thank you for bringing me home to him."

Opal waited until the couple went back into their apartment. She then bulldozed through the ever increasing crowds to get back to St. Augustine's where, unbeknownst to Opal, two gang members had just entered, firing their guns into the air.

Nestor tapped his hand on the table. The suspense was driving him crazy. If everything was normal, he'd be on a shuttle now returning to his wife and son. He got out his translinker and opened an image of Becky and Joey, wondering if he'd ever see them again. He then cycled through the usual questions regarding life after death. Becky believed in heaven. Nestor thought when he died, that would be it for him. He would be no more. Thinking about the end put things in a new perspective for him. He worked hard to find success as a documentarian and even won some awards. None of that mattered to him now. *Is this it? Is this how we say good-bye?* He gazed at the image of his family and then at Randy who was enjoying his plate of linguini with clam sauce.

"Are you gonna eat yours?" Randy asked.

Nestor pushed his plate towards Randy who eagerly took it. "You'll regret this when you find out tomorrow morning will be just like any other day."

"Hope you're right." Nestor reflected on the image again and was startled when he heard gunshots.

"The lunatics will be out in droves tonight." Randy eyed people hurrying by the sidewalk. "They're probably gonna take advantage of the panic."

Nestor's translinker rang, and he quickly answered. An older man's face flashed on screen.

"You look disappointed to see me," he said with a light Italian accent.

"I could never hide anything from you, Vinny."

"I'm sorry it took me so long to call back. Your message surprised me. What brought you here today of all days?"

"Had an interview with Seth Marconi. But he spent most of the time talking about his guru's end of the world nonsense."

"Let us hope it is nonsense."

"Did you watch the videos?" Nestor asked.

"Yes. Is it true?"

"We're checking on it right now."

"Everyone's starting to act *pazzo* around here," Vinny told him. "If it gets worse, I will close early tonight."

"That might be a good idea. There's a lot of looting going on."

"Is Rajni home?"

"No. I'm worried about her being out there all alone. She should be back soon. If not, I'm going to hire a car and pick her up...if I can find one."

"I'll call you later to see how you're both doing."

"That is very kind of you to still think of us."

Vinny looked off camera when he heard gunfire. "There's a gang outside fighting."

"Don't get involved, Vinny. Call the police."

Randy raised his fork that had linguini wrapped around it. "All the flyers are restricted to city emergencies until this is over."

Vinny shook his head "You won Nestor. All these years I thought it would be me, but after tonight, I concede. I will add one-thousand credits to your account tomorrow...if we're still around."

"Hold on to your credits," Randy said. "This will all blow over by the morning."

"Whatever the outcome, Nestor was right...the United Republic will never return to her former glory. We have turned into savages."

"Not all of us," Nestor said.

"There isn't enough of us to make a difference. Only a miracle can turn things around." Vinny looked away from the camera lens. "And you were also right about miracles. I no longer believe in them. We're all damned."

"From the ashes something new is always built," Nestor blurted out.

Randy gaped at Nestor while he was chewing on his linguini. "Come again?"

"You?" Vinny added. "Optimistic? That scares me more than the gunfire outside."

"I'm with you on that one, Vinny," Randy said as he placed his hand on Nestor's forehead. "You feeling okay?"

Nestor was even more shocked over his comment than Randy and Vinny. He believed what he said, when he said it. Now, he had no idea why or how it had come to him.

Randy swiped Nestor's half-empty beer bottle. "No more for you. It's melting your brain."

Vinny glanced off to the side, and a loud gunshot followed. "I have to go. They just executed a kid."

"Stay inside, Vinny," Nestor said.

He nodded. "I'm going to lock up now."

After hanging up with Vinny, Nestor examined the street scene using his documentarian perspective. Everything seemed surreal. Customers enjoyed their dinners, unfazed by the traffic that continued to build on the streets.

Nestor got out his camcorder to capture the mood. "It's either heaven or hell tonight, depending on what you believe is going on." He panned the camera from the diners to the street.

"I wouldn't know. I'm agnostic until I hear back from my contact." Randy took a sip of Nestor's beer and smiled.

Rajni thanked Brenner and Hank and got out of the flyer. She walked to her father's convenience shop. No customers were inside. The door was locked, and she waved her wrist in front of the entrance scanner. A buzzer sounded, and she opened the door. "Papà?" Rajni heard groans and ran behind the counter where her father lay bleeding from a bullet wound on his chest. "Papà!" She put her gameboards and cane on the counter and knelt down beside him.

Vinny grabbed her jacket sleeve. "Quiet," he whispered loudly.

"What was that?" a male voice called out.

"Your lazy ass not helping me," said another, deeper male voice. "Get back in here and carry the rest of this crap out."

Vinny pointed to the drawer. "Get my *pistola*."

Rajni stared at the drawer nervously.

"Ora ottengalo," he said in a low voice.

Rajni heard the men shout to each other and reached for the drawer.

"If you see one of them, don't hesitate to shoot," he whispered. "Do you understand?"

"I can't, Papà," Rajni protested as she struggled to hold the gun in her left hand that was almost completely numb from the multiple sclerosis.

"Use your other hand."

Rajni gripped the gun in her right hand, and it felt awkward. She stared up at the monitor as the men entered the main part of the store. Rajni's arm shook as she held the gun, and she tried to conceal her frantic breathing.

"Come on Carlo, hurry your ass!" The deeper male voice yelled. "We gotta get to the other stores before someone else hits 'em."

Rajni aimed the gun upward as the two looters exited the store. She breathed a sigh of relief as the door opened. But Carlo and his observant partner never left. He spotted Rajni's cane and gameboards that weren't there before.

Carlo's accomplice picked up the Pachisi board with the Vimanas, admired the artistry and then glanced over the counter at Rajni. "Hey, check this out. There's a girl here, and she's—" A bullet landed between his eyes, and he fell backwards.

Rajni waited for Carlo to stick his head over the counter next, but he chose to live for a while longer and ran off.

Rajni scrutinized her father's condition. He was bleeding badly. She got out her translinker and called for a med-flyer. "You have to come quick. My father's been shot." She stopped to listen to a recorded message delivered by a cheerful voice.

"Due to the current crisis, all our med-flyers are out on rescue. Please set your translinkers to tracking, and we'll send one over as soon as it becomes available. We're sorry for the inconvenience, and we will work diligently to return the city's operations back to optimum performance. Thank you and have a great evening."

"They are not coming," Vinny said.

Rajni hurried to the door and locked it. "I turned on my tracker. They'll be here." She got some towels and an unopened medical kit from behind the counter. She then tore open her father's shirt and quivered at all the outpouring of blood. Rajni pressed one of the towels against his wound. "With everything that's going on tonight, you'd think there wasn't anyone decent left in this world."

"The same opinion has crossed my mind this evening."

"I thought the same way earlier. Until a friendly policeman saw me near the subway station and gave me a lift back on his flyer. I should've had him come in with me."

"You couldn't have known."

Rajni opened up a bottle of peroxide, and Vinny grabbed her forearm. "It's too late for me. You must leave *now*. It isn't safe here. That video of the scientist scared a lot of people and many of them are not right in the head." He coughed. "It is very cold in here."

Rajni took off her coat and went to put it over her father. He pushed his hand forward.

"Blood is hard to get off clothes."

"Stop being stubborn, Papà. I will not leave you."

"Go to Uncle Frank's. He will watch over you."

"Who will watch over you?" Rajni asked, tears flowing.

Vinny placed his hand over her hand. "I love you very much, Bambino. I want you to always remember that."

"No, Papà!" Rajni caressed his cheek and continued to cry. "Don't leave me. Hang on a little while longer. A med-flyer will be here soon."

"I don't want your crying face to be the last thing I see. Please... smile for me one last time."

"When we get to the hospital." Rajni peered at her father's face and could see death creeping into his eyes. She took some slow breaths to stop her crying and stretched her lips into as real a smile as she could deliver.

Vinny lifted his hand and placed it on the side of her face. "Beautiful. You are beautiful, just like your mother."

Rajni wanted to weep again after hearing those words, but she successfully held it back.

"Don't be sad. I will be with your mother in heaven looking down on you." He squeezed Rajni's hand, then relaxed his grip completely.

Rajni lay beside her father, hugged him, and yearned for her world to end next.

One Last Slam

Anya sat by the bar at Benny's finishing up her fourth shot of vodka. Floyd handed her another one with his usual apprehension, but he didn't think it was his business to tell Anya she was an alcoholic. If he did that, he'd have to do the same to half his customers. He wasn't in business to be a counselor, although he sometimes felt that way.

Anya downed her shot as the minor league baseball team discussed the video of Warren H. Beasley that Floyd had played on the transviewer.

"He probably had an axe to grind with the ISA," Shortstop said.

"What about the man with the tattoos that was in here before?" Second Baseman asked sincerely. "He said the same thing."

"Could've been the scientist's son," Umpire said.

"Or part of the same alien species from the planet Nutzoid." Shortstop laughed.

The rest of the team joined in, and Anya slammed her shot glass on the bar.

"Easy Anya," Floyd said. "They're drunk."

Anya's anger and hurt smothered her. The only way she knew how to get out of that mood was through the spoken word. She stumbled toward the stage, almost tripping over a snag in a mystery-colored rug. So many dirty shoes trod upon it, Floyd had forgotten its original shade.

Anya stepped in front of the microphone and tapped on it.

Floyd yelled out from behind the bar, "Did you lose your calendar, Anya? Slam night isn't until next Wednesday."

"I know. But I need to get this one out tonight."

Floyd nodded and switched on the microphone and light over the performance platform.

"Everyone quiet down," Anya said. "Got something important to tell you all tonight."

The baseball team kept talking loudly, unable to hear over their own voices.

Floyd blew his whistle. "Everyone tune your ears to Anya Tanner. She won the most slams here since we started Slam Wednesdays twelve years ago."

"Need you to play for me, Floyd," Anya said.

Floyd grabbed a bongo drum from behind the bar and joined Anya on the stage. He sat, placed the drum on his lap and began to play a medium-tempo beat in quarter time.

Anya stared up at a light bulb hanging from the ceiling. She closed her eyes, and a lucid stream of verse flowed into her. Words soon drifted into her consciousness, ready to be spoken. Cupping her hands around the microphone that smelled like a mixture of various alcoholic beverages, she spoke softly, keeping her gaze fixed on the light overhead.

Under the lightbulb moon,
I'm illuminating, ruminating,
Contemplating...

Anya slowly lowered her head and looked ahead at the audience.

I stand beneath this beam alone,
Terrified, angry, sad, confused.
I stand exposed before you.

Anya pointed her index finger forward and slowly panned it around the room. She stopped when she got to the baseball team.

You, over there!
You're all about to be exposed!
You're all exposed!
We're all exposed!
No more secrets.
No more places to hide.
We're all deposed and then reposed,
Like toy soldiers, and little dolls in little doll houses.

It's too late to reposition ourselves.
Our fate signed, sealed, delivered,
Before we drew our first breath,

Concealed during our living.
Revealed right before our dying.

There's no more time to regroup.
No more time to philosophize,
Proselytize, synchronize.
No more time to organize, industrialize, prioritize.
No more time to fantasize.

Anya quieted her voice as she listened to the words racing ahead in her mind.

Because I now realize...
There's no more time.
We've run out of it.

A combination of screams and heckles came from the audience. But there were a select few who connected to Anya's words. She fixed her gaze on them and lifted the microphone off the cradle.

The last laugh will be on all of us.
Once we realize the truth,
We'll all finally be in agreement.
That's right.
We're all gonna agree real soon.
Tonight we'll all be drawn,
On the same page,
Standing upon the same stage.
All for one; one for all.

Anya paced from side to side. The tempo of her voice quickened.

We'll soon all agree.
There'll be no more time to dream.
No more songs left to sing.
No more bonfires at the beach.
No more vacations.
No more favorite food,
Or shopping for trendy clothes,

Shuttles falling from the sky.
Cars disintegrating.
Buildings collapsing.
All life evaporating...
Right before our eyes.

No one to paint a landscape,
To direct a movie,
Write a book.
All that records our culture,
Will forever be destroyed.

Think about that one over your next beer or shot!

Anya stopped and looked at Floyd who was lost in his playing. Her words hooked him right into the beat. Anya slowly turned and faced the audience.

When it's gone, what remains?

Before you answer,
Let me continue.
I left out a few things.

Cities and streets, hammered.
Towns and villages, battered.
Sectors and states, splattered.
Provinces and towns, shattered.

Shall I go on?

No fish, birds, reptiles, amphibians.
And all the creepy crawlies,
That make you scream in the night.

Oh. And one more thing.

Anya pointed her finger upward.

There'll be no more people.
Our identities displaced,
Defaced, then erased.
What will stay behind,
Once everything is taken away?
Who'll be around to remember us?
Will anyone remember us?
Who'll remember all that we did?
All that we've become,
Once we're all gone?
Why did we wait so long?
To ask these questions?
If we had the courage to ask,
We would've stopped fighting,
Each other and in battle,
Over little things that don't matter.

Anya felt tears coming and stared back up at the lightbulb. She closed her eyes and quieted her voice to almost a whisper.

All our languages, arts, and sciences.
All our dreams and inspirations,
Materialized into our reality.
What were they all for?
Who will remember them?
Who will appreciate them?
Who will remember us?
Does anyone know?

Everyone in the room became silent. Even the baseball team no longer found Anya's delivery funny. What came out of her mouth reached out and embraced everyone in the room that night.

I don't have an answer.
But what I do know,
Is that our ideas will continue,
Because ideas never die.
Maybe they'll recycle.
Get reinterpreted,
By some unknown alien race,
In some distant place,
In some other time and space,
The heartbeat of our existence, they'll embrace.
Our ideas that made us who we are,
 Will continue to exist.
And from out of them we'll persist.
Even if our species is forgotten,
We'll exist forever, eternal.
Immortalized by our endeavors.
Loved for our passions.

Contained...
In a cosmic creative stream.
Downloaded by another slam poet.
In another time,
Another place,
Another space.
I wish I could be around.
I'd applaud him, her, or it.
But I'll be there in spirit.

Anya put the microphone back in the cradle. She bowed her head, and almost all the patrons clapped their hands.

Floyd stopped playing his drums. "Seth Marconi wasn't kidding?"

Anya nodded. "You played the best you ever had, Floyd." She hugged him fast, then ran towards the door. There, she was surprised by Blaze, who stepped in front of her.

"That was beautiful, Anya. How you come up with all those rhymes so fast never fails to astound me."

"I screwed up. I screwed up bad," she said.

Blaze hugged her. "Why? Because you're not on Seth Marconi's space cruiser?"

Anya stepped back. "No. That was the only smart thing I did. It's everything before that."

Blaze always admired Anya, and he wanted to ask her out on several occasions, but he had stopped himself. He could see things moving forward with her, and he never wanted to move forward with someone else again.

"Who are you spending the night before everything goes kaboom with?" Blaze asked.

"Myself. You?"

"I'm heading over to my sister and brother-in-law's. You can come along if you like."

"Thanks, but I'd rather be alone."

"I understand." Blaze crossed his arms. "So this is it. This is the last time we'll see each other."

Anya cried over the finality of how that sounded.

"I'm glad I got to see your last slam."

She hugged him once more. "Take care, Blaze."

Anya left, and Blaze walked up to the stage, where Floyd was still playing his bongo.

Several customers got up and followed Anya out.

"Looks like Anya convinced quite a few more," Blaze said as he gazed out at the almost empty room.

The few who remained—including the baseball team—had gotten over Anya's performance and returned to their barroom antics.

"She convinced me." Floyd stopped playing. "Almost."

"I'm already convinced."

"Why did you come back then?"

"Your turn, Blaze!" Rocco called out.

Floyd started to play a slow rhythmic beat. "I'll play for you."

"Don't think I can top Anya's performance tonight."

"Why don't you tell us about the end of the world again," Shortstop called out. "That was the funniest thing I heard all night."

Blaze swung around. "You think it's funny?"

"Hysterical!"

"Did you win your game tonight?" Blaze asked.

"We did."

The whole team cheered.

"What do you get from winning?"

"Victory."

"Define victory."

"Winning," Shortstop said. "Being the best."

"What does that mean?" Blaze started to feel some words emerging. Grabbing Floyd's bongo, he said, "Fill everyone's glass, Floyd, and put it on my tab."

"We'll take two more pitchers here!" Umpire shouted.

"You sure about this?" Floyd asked.

Blaze nodded.

"Shit, now I'm convinced." He took back his bongo and returned to the bar. When everyone crowded him, he blew his whistle. "Calm yourselves, and face the speaker on stage! I'll bring over your drinks only if you give him your undivided attention."

Everyone turned to face Blaze.

"We're all yours, Blaze!" Rocco called out.

Blaze set his translinker to record. "Greetings to all my friends at Benny's Bar and Grill. When I first came here, I asked Floyd, 'Who the hell is Benny?' You know what he said?"

"My pet meerkat that I had when I was a kid," Floyd yelled out.

"Did he really say that?" Shortstop asked.

"He did, and I believed him, just as I believe Seth Marconi."

"I have a bridge to sell you then!" Third baseman yelled out.

Blaze closed his eyes and began his slam.

Laugh, joke, jeer,
But don't you dare deny.
It's another crazy, hazy night at
Benny's Bar and Grill tonight.
But hear me now, hear me loud.
I'm a good judge of character.
I sense what makes people tick.
That's why I'm an author.
A very successful author.
I had best-sellers turned into movies,
Sci-fi musicals and interactive games.

I write stories that entertain you.
But you don't see the hours I work.
The mental pain I endure.
Placing words in precise order,
Just so you can understand.
Hours, days, weeks, months; I write.
I go to sleep at night with a story.
Wake up with the perfect scene,
Before I roll out of bed.
Every moment, ever day of each year,
I live each character in my head.
Why? For what?
I drove myself to exhaustion.
But in this end, I realize,
I'm nothing more than a liar.
I earn credits,
 From making up stories.
My subconscious believes, perceives,
Invents my lies.
I bring them to life,
To make you disappear.
To make you forget your misery.
But you don't know my misery,
My pain, my anguish.
What is the meaning?
The purpose of success?

I used to think my words,
Would exist beyond my death.
I'd be immortal, existing forever.
Admired,
As all the literary masters before me.
Even though my stories are shallow,

Gimmicky, without meaning.
Just as the extremely shrewd
Trevor Forthright expressed.

I hid away,
My deepest darkest secrets.
Always held myself back,
From expressing my truth.
So here I stand before you...
I admit that I'm a liar.
A very successful liar of the written word.
And on this last night...
My words will forever be forgotten.
But, at last, I speak my truth.

All the minutes, hours, days, and weeks mean nothing.
After you read the end,
There is nothing left to be said.
My books will be forgotten.
I'll be forgotten.
We'll all be forgotten.
What was it all for?
This thing we call existence?
Why do we do what we do?
Work hour upon hour,
Rather than stopping,
To appreciate life.
To smell a flower...

On this last night,
I see only one face before me.
Her delicate face and large eyes
That saw straight through me.

I wish I could believe,
That we'd be together again.
Wish I could touch her soft skin,
Hold her hand, walk in the rain,
For one more time.
Laugh at people walking by.
Then everything would've all been worth it.

Blaze hopped off the stage and walked over to the table where the baseball team was seated. He lifted the pitcher of beer and poured the brew into the glass of Second Baseman, who he noticed was paying close attention to him.

Go home.
Go home to those you love.
There's nothing here,
Worthy of your time.
Go home and live.
Live your life fully awake.
At least, for this last night.
That's what I'm trying to do.
Because I have nothing left,
Other than to say, "The end."

Blaze stopped recording, emailed his performance to Trevor Forthright, then went to the bar. Shaking Floyd's hand, he said, "Keep filling them."

Several patrons followed Blaze out of the bar, including Second Baseman. Blaze paused to look up at the sign hanging over the door. Memories of all the good times he'd had here fused with the flashing of blue neon that displayed the name of the bar he'd been visiting since his college days. Refusing to succumb to sentimentality, he left.

Those who remained kept filling their glasses, numbing themselves to the reality that was getting harder to ignore.

After the baseball team had left Benny's, Floyd and Rocco played their last game of rummy 500.

Anya sat at home crying. Her mother had just hung up on her after having berated her again for getting them kicked off Seth Marconi's flight. She understood nothing would fix their relationship, including the end of the world. Some wounds cut too deep, bled too hard to coagulate.

Anya took an almost-full bottle of sleeping pills and turned in for the night. Lying on her bed, she closed her eyes and felt relief as her consciousness dispersed into the place where awareness hides away in sleep and in death. Moments before her death, she witnessed a golden star that shone on her. It erupted into a fountain of colorful rays, and she felt herself detach from her body.

"I see, I understand, and I'm ready to let go."

And she did.

Unexpected Encounters

At St. Augustine's, Vince and his fellow gang banger, Tom, were having fun with their guns. They were members of the Hell Dragons and were distinguishable by their fire red mohawks and dragon tattoos on the right side of their heads.

"Everyone get down on your knees *now!*" Vince yelled. "The first head I see that comes up will be blown off!"

Everyone else sat on the pews, except for Rufus who perched on Molly's shoulder. "Stay here with me, Rufus," she whispered. "Those men will hurt you."

Despite the warning, Rufus was restless and decided to go for a fly.

"Rufus, no," Molly whispered as she watched him soar up towards the rafters.

"Who said that?" Tom asked.

Molly cried, and her mother drew her closer.

Vince pointed toward Rufus. "Look! Up there! It's a bird!"

"Want me to shoot it?" Tom said.

"Don't you dare harm one feather on him. I like birds. It's people I can't stand," Vince told him, two hours after he had consumed a bucket of fried chicken with a double order of gravy.

Vince walked down the aisle. "All right everyone, listen up. Take off all your jewelry and whatever other valuables you got and pass 'em towards the center aisle. My friend's gonna come 'round and collect 'em."

Pearl, who was seated in the front pew, unhooked her watch and tossed it into the designated aisle.

Deirdre whispered to her, "I can't give away my cross. My mother gave it to me."

"I'm sure she wouldn't want you to lose your life over a piece of jewelry. Take it off."

"Maybe they won't see it."

"A cross can be replaced. You can't."

Deirdre's eyes filled with tears. "I can't. It's the only thing I have left of her."

An insensitive person might've judged Deirdre as being materialistic, but Pearl understood that Deirdre had never gotten over the loss of her mother.

Pearl held her hand. "Let it go. Your mother will always be alive in your memories. They can never be stolen."

Deirdre held on to the cross. Her tears multiplied and began to fall down her face as Vince headed towards her.

Two flights up from her family's shop, Rajni knocked on her Uncle Frank's door, but he wasn't answering. She called and left a message on his translinker. She then went upstairs to her apartment. When she unlocked the door, someone grabbed her from behind.

"Guess who this is?"

Rajni recognized the voice and even the name that went with it. *Carlo.* He had followed her upstairs.

Rajni fought fiercely to break free.

Carlo pushed her inside and pinned her against the wall. "Where's your gun?" he asked.

The rage emitting from his dark brown eyes terrified Rajni. "In my purse."

Carlo grabbed the purse and threw her to the floor. She scooted away from him until her back hit the couch.

Carlo got out the gun and inspected it. "How did you get your hands on this illegal beauty?"

"My father was in the joined forces."

"Everyone serves in the joined forces, but they usually don't let you leave armed." He pointed the gun towards Rajni. "I came here to give you the same thing you gave to my brother."

Rajni closed her eyes and prepared herself to die. With her father gone, she no longer cared what happened to her.

Carlo was enraged by the calmness of Rajni's expression. He wanted her to suffer before he killed her. He pulled her up by her shirt and threw her onto the couch.

"You were a naughty, naughty girl tonight."

"Not as naughty as your brother."

Carlo slapped her face. "Bite your tongue off bitch, or I'll cut it out of your mouth."

Rajni glared at him. "Your brother murdered my father. I'd shoot him again if he were here."

Carlo slapped her harder. "You gotta lot of nerve considering your current circumstance."

The doorbell rang, and Carlo placed his index finger in front of his lips to hush Rajni.

At the door was Rajni's Uncle Frank. Banging on the door, he shouted, "Rajni, are you in there?"

Carlo shoved the barrel of the gun against the side of Rajni's head and whispered, "Say one word, and I'll shoot whoever's on the other side of the door. Understand?"

Rajni nodded her head and squeezed a pillow that was beside her.

Frank banged harder and yelled out her name. He waited for a few moments and then wrote a note, slid it under the door and left.

Carlo went over to the door, picked up the note, and read it aloud. "I found your father. I'll be downstairs waiting for you. Love, Uncle Frank." He crumpled the sheet and threw it at Rajni's face. "Does *Uncle Frank* have anything worth stealing?"

"He's got nothing! Leave him alone!"

"Maybe I will." Carlo sat next to Rajni and placed his hand on her thigh. "If you do something nice for me."

"How nice?" Rajni asked.

Carlo leaned toward her and whispered in her ear, "Very, very, very nice."

Mrs. Theobald was fixated on the street scene below. "It was never safe to leave the house before the formation of the Western Sector," she said. "My father always had a gun in his holster with his finger on the trigger."

Jeff wasn't a fan of the Western Sector. He romanticized the days of old, when nation states existed and had their own rulers.

Nevertheless, he allowed his mother to discuss her love for the first sector president, a man she eventually grew to despise. It was Mrs. Theobald who influenced Jeff's rebellious politics. The only reason he volunteered to stay in the joined forces longer than the mandatory two years was because he got his own flyer and had the freedom to travel off world.

He located an out of the way neighborhood to avoid the intensifying maelstrom and landed in front of a quick stop. Mrs. Theobald went in with him, still dressed in a hospital gown. Jeff gave his mother her dress and escorted her to the bathroom.

"I'll be waiting for you by the register," he said.

"With my potato chips and cherry cola?"

"They'll be waiting for you too."

"You're a good man." She smiled and entered the bathroom.

Jeff went down the snack aisle and got what his mother requested. On his way to the register, the lights went out.

"Do you have a flashlight?" Jeff asked the young female clerk.

"There's probably one here, but I'm not sure where it is."

Jeff placed the merchandise on the counter. "Got one in my flyer. Be right back." He left and returned quickly with a flashlight.

"Who shut off the lights?" Mrs. Theobald yelled out. "I can't find the door to the shelter."

"This isn't a raid," Jeff explained. "It's just a blackout."

"I can't see you," Mrs. Theobald said.

Jeff aimed his flashlight to the ceiling. "Look up. Do you see the light?"

"I see it!" she exclaimed.

"Follow it to where it's shining from, and you'll find me." His eyes adjusting to the semi-darkness, Jeff searched behind the counter for the fuse box. "It's not here." He shone the light on the young female clerk and then on himself. "I'm Jeff, by the way."

"Sirene."

"Don't worry, Sirene. I'll have the lights back on for you."

Mrs. Theobald approached, and he gave her the chips.

"I'll pay for these when the electricity comes back on," Jeff said to Sirene.

"They're on me." She smiled. "Thanks for helping."

"I didn't do anything yet." Jeff walked into the back room and found the fuse box. He flipped the switches off and then on. Nothing happened, and he then surmised that the lights would never be going on again. The certitude of his assertion made him think of Darla's fate. Playing the hero had always kept him detached from his emotions, and tonight was no exception. He returned to Sirene and his mother who were both going to need his strength.

"The lights won't be turning on for the rest of the night," he said to Sirene.

"Did they explain why this is happening?" she asked.

Jeff gazed at her young face, not wanting to answer either way. "They say it's a large solar flare."

"Is it dangerous?"

Jeff looked out into the empty lot and back at Sirene. "It's not going to be safe in here. You should lock up and leave now."

"I can't. My boss will fire me, and I can't afford to lose the credits."

"Looters have taken over the streets tonight. Stay here any longer and you may lose more than a few credits. Where do you live?"

"The curfew zone in Old DC," she replied nervously.

"Come on. I'll take you home."

Jeff sighed as he thought about the zoo he was going to have to land in. There were no active patrols in the curfew zone, and violence had become a normal part of life for its residents. The inhabitants there had little to look forward to, but some were motivated by the desire to escape from the bleak environment.

Sirene, in particular, had high ambitions. She was studying to be a psychologist and had managed to examine Jeff and his mother before the lights went out. Jeff's devotion to his unwell mother made Sirene view him as loyal and honorable. She felt safe leaving with what her father had referred to as "a dying breed of man." That wasn't an exaggeration during this last period of Earth's history.

Blaze stopped over at his apartment to get a framed picture of Astrid. He had plenty of images of her stored on his translinker memory drive, but none were large enough to catch the depth of her eyes. If the world was going to end tomorrow, he wanted them to be the last image he gazed upon. Blaze took a final look around, switched off the light, and left without the slightest hesitation. As he headed down the corridor, he passed a young boy who sat cross-legged against the wall, crying. Blaze had seen him around before but never paid him any attention. He never had the patience for kids, especially sniveling ones.

When Blaze stepped outside, he was almost run down by a stampede of frightened people. Blaze thought about the boy all alone upstairs and went back to check on him.

"Where's your mother?" he asked.

The boy shrugged his shoulders.

"Are you locked out?"

The boy shook his head.

"You should go inside." Blaze looked around the hallway and then back at the boy. "When will your mother be returning?"

The boy shrugged his shoulders again.

"Do you know how to talk? It's easier to communicate that way."

"Of course, I can talk. I'm not a baby. I'm seven."

"Great." Blaze clapped his hands together. "I'm Blaze. And you are?"

"David."

"Where's your mother?"

"At work."

Blaze glanced at his watch. It was almost 11:00 PM. "Where does she work?"

"Marconi Aeronautics."

As Blaze was doubting the story that David's mother was at work this late at night, all the lights in the building turned off.

"What happened?" David asked. He sat up and clutched Blaze's jacket. "I'm afraid of the dark."

Blaze rummaged through his pocket, got out his keys, and fumbled around for the flashlight. He found it and turned it on. "I'll take you to your mother."

"What do you think happened to the lights?" David asked.

"I don't know." Blaze waved for him to follow. "Let's go."

David hesitated. "Why do you have those tattoos?"

"I like them."

"My mother told me not to talk to you because you're a gang member."

Blaze shone the flashlight beam on his face. "I'm too old to be in a gang."

David nodded his head and followed Blaze to the fire exit as the elevator was no longer working.

Blaze opened the door to the stairwell. Screams and pounding footsteps echoed from all around. His legs trembled as the reality of what was happening finally awoke in him.

"I don't want to go in there," David said, looking into the darkness.

"It's our only way out of here."

"I'm staying here."

"Do you want to find your mother?"

David nodded and followed Blaze into the dark stairwell.

Peace Warriors

Nestor and Randy were almost finished with their dinner when the electric power had gone out. Under candlelight, the patrons discussed how Moon appeared unusually bright.

Randy's translinker rang. He answered, and a few seconds later he said, "The blackout is on the whole East Coast? Are you sure?"

One of the diners nearby asked, "Are they saying what's causing it?"

Randy gave the diner a worried glance, hung up, and then turned to Nestor. "Beasley spoke the truth. My contact said no one over there was allowed to talk to the press out of fear of causing a panic. This event just happened. No warning." Randy paused to take a sip of his beer, then continued. "He had to call me back from inside a bathroom stall. Not sure why he bothered. They listen to all outgoing conversations."

The scientist who gave Randy the information knew the risk he had taken but didn't care. When he left the bathroom, he expected two joined forces officers to be waiting for him. What he didn't expect was that they were instructed to execute anyone who dared to defy the chain of command. When the scientist stared into the barrel of a gun, he was comforted to know Humanity wouldn't survive this latest threat.

Several of the patrons who'd heard Randy's conversation with the scientist, fled. The few who remained behind searched for more information on the publink. The solar flare story was still the official word.

With the death of his wife and child now confirmed, Nestor was too devastated to form any cogent thoughts. "I got to get out of here." He stood.

"We have to tell everyone," Randy said.

"Tell us what?" asked a waitress who handed him the bill.

"My friend will explain." Nestor walked away.

Randy got up. "Give me the scanner now."

The waitress handed it to him, and Randy waved his hand across the scanner. "Take as big a tip as you want." He handed her back the device.

He was already halfway across the street before the waitress thought to yell, "Are you serious?"

Not hearing her, Randy caught up with Nestor and panted. "I'll forgive you for sticking me with the tab if this is about your family."

Nestor stopped and turned to face Randy. "Of course it's about my family! The world ended for them a little under three hours ago! Should I go out and celebrate?"

"All right! You don't have to shout. We're soon gonna be part of the casualties as well."

Nestor started to pace back and forth. He didn't know where to go, what to do, what to say.

"Beasley's right. People have a right to know," Randy said.

Nestor got out his translinker.

"Who are you calling?"

Nestor waited through ten rings and then disconnected. "She's not there."

"Who?"

"Rajni." Nestor rubbed his forehead. "Go home to your wife."

"I'm not leaving you here all alone. You can stay with us tonight. We'll celebrate the end together." Randy laughed to himself. "I always wondered how I'd handle news like this."

"You seem to be handling it well."

"What else can I do? It's gonna happen whether I want it to or not. I can either go home and cry for the rest of the night with Jeanie or try to make these last few hours worth it." Randy let slip a few tears. "So...are you coming?"

"I'd rather be alone."

The alarm on Randy's translinker rang. On screen was a video file, *Seth Marconi's Final Message to Earth*.

"What is it?" Nestor asked.

Randy clicked open the file and played it.

Seth Marconi was sitting in his backyard garden. Behind him loomed a stone-wall with water trickling down. On either side of him were exotic plants and flowers. Beside Seth sat the taciturn Xavier Starfly with his usual smile.

"Greetings Earthians," Seth said. "I uploaded this message to the Universal Press Server before my departure. To ensure you didn't hear me before the right time, I encrypted this message to keep it from being accessed until this moment. As you all figured out by now, part of the world has been destroyed by the sun. At first consideration, it would seem like a helpless situation, but I promise you this is all the Divine's way of maintaining balance and order in the Universe."

Seth stretched his hand towards Xavier. "This was explained to me many years ago by Xavier Starfly, the great sage that you see sitting beside me. I wanted Him to speak directly to you, but He declined with a nod of His head. Don't be offended by His refusal. Xavier doesn't say much...even to those of us who are His most loyal disciples. He only spoke to me four times. Our first discussion occurred when I encountered Him on a street corner; the second, when He suggested I build my business; the third, when He told me the sun would destroy Earth, and the fourth time was last week, when He announced that today would be our day of reckoning.

Xavier saved my life. Without Him, Marconi Aeronautics would never have even entered my mind. Without Him, I would've remained a broken man.

"I served my two years in the 1st sector war. The cargo craft I was in got shot down, and I was taken prisoner." Seth ran his hand across the scar on his face. "Although many people have asked me about my scar, I kept the story to myself at the request of Xavier. He thought my story would be more effective if I waited until this moment."

He covered his face with his hands. "I'm sorry. I still find this hard to talk about." He took a deep breath, looked at Xavier for comfort and then continued. "During my interrogation, one of the guards spilled acid on my face. That night, when I lay in my bed, the acid still burned. The heat built within me, and it got so intense I thought I was going to go up in flames. I was convinced my body melted away and that nothing remained. I sought after the Light that would carry me to the heaven promised to me by my religion, but all I experienced was coldness and blackness. The most intense fear seized me when I realized everything that defined who I was would die with me. The only thing I could count on was what existed here, in this moment. I didn't want to end. I was terrified of death, terrified of slipping into a cold, dark abyss. So, I continued to fight each day. I hung on, and I survived. I lived the next five years growing rice and was whipped whenever I didn't move fast enough. All I ate every day was rice." Seth laughed. "To this day, if you serve me rice, I'll throw the dish off the table."

Seth held out a whip in front of him. "One day, in my fifth year at the prison camp, a guard came to my door and let me out. There was a shuttle outside, ready to take me home. The 1st sector war was over, and they were doing a prisoner exchange with our side."

Seth looked down at the whip in his hands. "I saw this on the guard's desk and asked if I could take it, and she nodded at me. I wasn't sure why I asked for it until now." Seth cried honest tears. "This whip isn't a torture device. It's the hand that holds it that's the torture device—that commits the violence. We were ruled by the whip for too long, and now we're finally free of it."

Seth closed his eyes, and Xavier Starfly placed his hand on his shoulder.

"I'm okay. Just give me a moment."

Xavier nodded and leaned back into his chair.

Seth took a deep breath and looked straight into the lens. "After the war, I moved to London and started college. I was eager to live my dream of becoming a cruiser pilot, but I couldn't forget my experience in the prison camp. Each time I stared into the mirror, the scar on my face served as a constant reminder that I was empty. I went out searching for something to help fill me with life again and thought I found that when I met the woman who became my wife. She saw me beyond my scar. Things were great between us and got even better when I was commissioned to pilot a cruiser in New York. I was living my dream until my wife grew distant. The more I tried to fix things between us, the further she pulled away from me. I felt lonely and unloved until I found Xavier Starfly chanting on a street corner. He was holding up a placard that read, 'Reconnect with the Light inside you. You are all lost.'"

Seth glanced at Xavier. "I went to Xavier and asked Him to help me find my Light—not that I believed He could. I was desperate. He began to turn around in a circle, flapping His arms and chanting. He then stopped, got out His notebook, and started writing while continuing with His chant. All the while, I felt this energy swirling and building at the base of my spine. It shot upward and was followed by a thunderous explosion that immersed me in rapturous unbound happiness. Xavier then said to me, 'You are free. You are love.' He was right. I was never unloved. Love always exists here." Seth touched his chest.

"I became Xavier's first disciple. His lessons were taught by example. He demonstrated peace and happiness, and I learned from Him how to find those qualities within me. During one of our sessions, I had a flash of inspiration. I could develop fighters that were superior to those of the Eastern Sector. I studied engineering and worked day and night until I could find the right idea, the right design to make the West Sector gain the advantage in space."

"The leap drive came to me in a vision while I was meditating. Xavier wisely told me to refrain from giving my idea to my boss. 'It is you who must present this to the world. You are the warrior for peace,' He told me. I eventually got some backers to invest in my cruiser, and soon after that, Marconi Aeronautics was born. It took many years for us to build our prototype. Fifteen years ago, our fleet destroyed the Eastern Sector's defense shield. The 2nd sector war ended the next day. Unfortunately, we didn't stop them fast enough to save what was once our nation's capital. But I don't blame warships, bombs and machines for what happened to us."

Seth held up the whip again. "We have brought our own destruction upon us. All our hands hold the whip that we've collectively turned against ourselves.

As Xavier's disciples, we've been forgiven for our transgressions and have been promised that we would survive the cleansing. Be consoled in knowing that the knowledge of our species will continue. We will plant our seeds for a New Earth. Good-bye, good luck, and die in peace."

"What a lunatic!" Randy clipped his translinker onto his belt.

"And a good salesman," Nestor said. "For a moment I almost blamed myself for what's happening to the sun."

"People are gonna be panicking after they see this." Randy pointed his thumb toward himself. "I'm panicking." His translinker rang, and he answered. "Yeah, Deb. I know. I'll be home soon. I'm bringing Nestor with me."

"I'm heading back to the hotel."

Randy covered the mouthpiece. "You're what?"

"I'm tired. I'm going to take Beasley's advice and turn in early."

Randy put the phone back to his ear. "I'll be home in a while. Yeah, yeah, I will." Randy hung up. "You can't be serious."

"Very." Nestor said. "My preferred way of dying is in my sleep. That way I won't feel a thing."

"How can you walk away from this?"

"What would you like me to do?"

"What you do best. Speak. Go out with a big crash bang boom, and finish your last documentary. Then come spend the night with us."

Nestor shook his head. "This is one documentary I don't want to finish."

"You've got no choice." Randy looked starkly at Nestor. "You won awards because of your ability to sway people to your cause. And I could use some swaying myself."

"The only place left to sway people towards tonight is their graves."

"Do you really want Seth Marconi to have the last word?" Randy looked at the street that was carpeted with cars and people. "The UPS still isn't admitting to any of this either."

"Everyone knows now. Seth got the news out."

"You know most people look to the government and media for confirmation. Until they say 'the end is near,' everyone will continue thinking it's nothing but a solar flare, even though they're scared out of their minds because they can sense something is off. They're gonna need some comforting words. It's not right to leave them hanging."

"I'm sure MatrixMaster has a few videos out by now."

"No offense, but MatrixMaster isn't the soothing type. He's probably telling everyone that some advanced alien species is behind all of this."

"Who's to say they're not?"

"Seriously man, you were one of the first to break this story. That gives you credibility." Randy smiled. "If anyone can make the eve before Armageddon easier to deal with, it's you. What do you say?"

Nestor crossed his arms. "I prefer the term apocalypse. It's nondenominational."

Randy shook his head. "Why do you always have to be such a wise ass?"

"Me?" Nestor pointed to himself. "It was you who spent the whole night joking about what's happening. I'm trying to see if doing the same will make Becky's and Joey's deaths easier to deal with." Nestor wiped tears from his eyes. "As you can see, it doesn't. I don't want to be awake any longer knowing they're gone."

"I know it sucks. What happened to Becky and Joey isn't fair. None of this is fair. There's nothing I can say, nothing I can do that'll make you feel better right now, so I'm not even gonna try. All I can say is I love you and that you've been a great friend to me." Randy softened his voice. "And as your friend, I know that working behind a camera always helped you deal with this crappy world, and it can help you deal with it tonight until we're all put out of our collective misery."

Nestor handed Randy the camcorder.

He aimed the camcorder at Nestor and began recording. "Don't you wanna die knowing we made a difference? That's what we always talked about when we were in college."

Nestor gazed at Randy. "That was a long time ago. We didn't know any better."

"And we still don't." Randy chuckled. "What's your point?"

Nestor lifted his brows and then peered at the now empty cafe they were at previously. "I'll need a few shots first."

Randy handed Nestor the camcorder. "Okay I'll join you for a bit, but I have to call Debra back. She's scared out of her mind."

"How are you taking this?"

"Debra's handling this better than me. I hope you're right. I hope that from the ashes something new will be built...along with us in it."

Light Journey

Blaze and David stared up at the dark building that belonged to Marconi Aeronautics. The street seemed eerily silent in contrast to the mob running amok on the main avenue a block away. Looters that had banded together in droves, smashed windows and stole anything they could carry.

Blaze rapped on the main door with his keys until he saw a flashlight beam.

"What do you want?" the guard from inside yelled. Seeing all of Blaze's tattoos, he decided not to open the door.

Blaze pointed to David. "I'm looking for the boy's mother. Her name is—"

"There's no one else in here. The last of them just headed to the shuttleport."

David stared up at the tattooed man his mother told him he wasn't supposed to talk to. "What now?"

"You come with me."

"Where?"

"My sister's."

"But I want my mother."

"We'll try to call her again later." Blaze scanned the surrounding street that was now flooded with a rabble of people, cars, tanks, and buses. "We have to get out of here." He snatched David's hand.

David pulled himself free. "I'm not going anywhere until I find my mother!"

Blaze's patience had been exhausted. "Your mother's never coming back," he blurted out before he could stop himself.

David backed away, then ran off.

Dashing after him, Blaze called Collin on his translinker. "Tell my sister I'm going to be a little late."

Seth Marconi stood behind a pulpit in a large conference hall aboard his space cruiser. He was wearing a robe, similar to the one worn by Xavier Starfly, who stood by his side. Three hundred people sat in attendance, including David's mother. She was invited by one of the board members with whom she was having an affair. Even after her eighth glass of champagne, her guilt over leaving her son behind remained strong.

"Ladies and Gentlemen, welcome aboard the Dreamflyer, my newest imperial-class, long-rage cruiser," Seth said. "You're about to witness one of mankind's greatest innovations embark on a flight outside our Solar System and on to our new home. We'll live in a world built for a thinking human, a human of dreams, and a human who lives to be inspired by the sanctity of life.

"As I look at some of your faces, I sense the trepidation and worry of what you're leaving behind. Once you see that you're missing an illusion, you'll wake up and look forward to starting your new lives."

Seth projected a live montage of Earth on a holographic screen. Various areas around the world were shown where the inhabitants had surrendered to chaos. People ran in the streets, fighting, hitting and screaming. Car horns honked, buildings were ablaze, and soldiers blindly fired their weapons into panicked crowds.

"Do you miss this?" Seth asked.

Everyone in the room yelled, "No!"

"Do you want to return to this?"

"No!"

"Are you glad you left this all behind?"

"Yes!" everyone yelled out.

"On our new world, laws will be written for the honorable man. No longer will we be reacting to the scourge that created wars and illness. We'll honor loyalty, integrity, faith, and honesty."

The passengers, mostly made up of Aristocrats, clapped and cheered as Seth stepped aside to make room for Xavier Starfly. They fell silent when he spun around with his arms spread high like an eagle. He began to chant, and his voice became louder and more disturbed. He then stopped, stretched open his eyes, and his lips quivered when he internalized what he'd most feared.

"Why?" Xavier cried. "Why couldn't I see?"

Seth approached Xavier who pushed his hand toward him, closed his eyes, and stood motionless for a few moments until he connected to My music. He then opened his eyes and smiled, knowing I'd never abandon him.

"Greetings, faithful followers," Xavier said. "I have been dreaming of this day for the past twenty-four years. In my fifteenth year of life, I fell off a ladder. The doctors told my parents I was going to die. I almost did, but then the most beautiful music, that was more than just a combination of notes, played for me. It was a language. I tried to match the pitches with my inner-voice and failed on many attempts. Just as I was about to give up, I connected to one of the pitches by feeling it as opposed to listening to it. I did the same with every pitch until I matched them all. A healing took place within me, and when I opened my eyes I knew I had many years left ahead of me.

"When my parents spoke to me, their words were inadequate. My own words were inadequate. They failed to express the true reality of life eloquently expressed by the Divine Voice, who healed me with Her beautiful language. Most of the words I spoke were meaningless by comparison. I stopped speaking and sang to the Divine Voice in Her language. She rewarded me with the gift of foresight. To this day, thirty-four years later, I only speak through Her in the Mystic Chant. But tonight is a momentous occasion because we are about to go home."

Everyone clapped, and Seth said, "We are honored that it's you who's leading us."

Xavier nodded and continued. "At times, I doubted the validity of my visions. As the years passed, I questioned myself. Did I truly experience the sweet, mystic music or did I trick myself? It wasn't until this very day that I knew our time had come. And I was relieved to know I wasn't a fraud. Even with all these gifts bestowed upon me by the Divine Voice, I doubted my connection.

"My message from the Divine Voice to you is to prepare to go home. We'll all start anew, but we must always remember to nourish the ground we walk on and demonstrate respect by not forcing our wills upon each other. If we can't live by respecting each other's right to freedom of self-expression, we'll die in bondage. So

I ask you to make your peace now. Free your will from the conditionings bestowed upon you by mortal confusion, and liberate the Light within you for the journey it will soon be embarking on."

Everyone in the room clapped again.

"All of us will be free in our new colony," Seth said.

More applause followed.

"Please, I must explain what's happening," Xavier said. "The final message of the Divine Voice has just been given to me."

Everyone looked at Xavier in anticipation.

"Seth thinks that his space colony is inspired by the Divine Voice. He believes where we're going is to a beautiful place on a beautiful world. In essence, we are going home, but not to the home Seth Marconi believes." Xavier began to cry. "When the Divine Voice revealed Her final plans for us, I was frightened, at first. I thought I had failed her, but She reassured me that I was living up to Her expectations." Xavier smiled at Seth and bowed his head.

The ship started to vibrate, and everyone in the room talked at once.

Seth looked at Xavier, startled. "I thought we were going to be saved!"

The engine shook, rattled and jerked, throwing everyone to the floor. Xavier clung to the podium until the engine silenced and all the electric power shut off. The Dreamflyer was dead in space with less than three hours of oxygen left.

"You must prepare yourselves for the journey you're all about to take," Xavier said. "Make peace now. No one is going to get a free ride. Not here, not on Earth, not anywhere." Xavier placed the palms of his hands together and bowed.

Xavier's ability to so eloquently convey My message illuminated My mood. I set off a few supernovas, all in unchartered areas of space. When that happens, sensitive individuals experience a moment of unexplained euphoria. And now you know one more of My little mysteries.

Opal arrived at St. Augustine's where two male gang members had been standing guard at the entrance. She snuck around to the side of the building and peaked through a window. The lit candles inside the church gave her a clear view of Tom waving his gun in the air. She called the police and was surprised to get a live operator on the phone. "I got a hostage situation here at St. Augustine's. Need a rescue team here as soon as possible."

"Sorry. You're gonna have to call back later. We've been swamped over here since the electric went out."

"I'm a retired commander with the joined forces, and I want a rescue team here now! We have hostages!"

"And I'm a frustrated operator who has to tell you the same thing I told the last five-hundred people; there's worse than that happening tonight. You're gonna have to handle this on your own."

Opal hung up, got her gun, and crept toward the front of the building. She easily spotted the gang members under Moon's glow and shot one of them in the leg. He limped away, and his partner took off ahead of him.

Inside St. Augustine's, Tom picked up Pearl's watch and then looked over at Deirdre. "What's that shiny thing around your neck?" He pulled back Deirdre's hair and saw a chain. He yanked her shirt and pulled her to her feet. "You didn't listen. I don't like to be ignored."

"Please don't hurt me. I'm pregnant!"

Tom checked her out. "You don't look pregnant to me." He whistled to Vince who came over. "What do you think of this one?"

Vince inspected her. "I like."

"Me too. Think I'll take her."

"Hope this crisis lasts all night. We're gonna acquire tons of merchandise."

Pearl got up and stood in front of Deirdre.

"Check out the fat old troll," Tom said. "Either she's brave or retarded."

Vince leered at Pearl. "If you don't want a shot in your head, move!"

"I can't let you take this woman."

"Really? And who's gonna stop me?" Vince looked around the room and then pointed at Pearl. "You?" He burst out laughing and then glared at her. "Who should I take in her place?"

I could feel Pearl accept her fate in this moment. She recited the *Hail Mary* to herself and a calmness swept through her. She was no longer afraid.

"Take me instead, I—"

"What kind of sicko do you think I am?" Vince clubbed Pearl on the head with the butt of his gun.

Pearl fell to the floor and struggled to get back onto her knees.

"I don't do old hags," Vince told her.

When Pearl looked up, Vince's gun was aimed at her face. She turned to Deirdre who was crying. "It's all right. Don't be afraid. God is with you."

"Please!" Father Stephen pleaded. "Have some compassion tonight! It's your last night to redeem yourself in the eyes of the Lord." He gazed at Pearl, unable to mask his worry.

"If I believed in your god, I'd join the other team," Vince said. "Hell seems like a lot more fun." He laughed at Pearl and then shot her in the head.

As Pearl's energy form escaped from her body, an agonizing scream blared from the balcony of the church.

Vince glanced up, and a bullet landed between his eyes. Another one struck the back of Tom's head. Their energy forms shot out and traveled blindly as they had very little Light within them.

Light is necessary for a life-form to reanimate. The dimmer the Light, the longer it takes to find a new host. Despite that, during this solitary Light journey the form has time to reflect upon its previous life and plan for a brighter future. Vince and Tom would require several Light journeys before they could get a glimpse of it.

On the Edge of the End

From inside the flyer Sirene looked down at all the backed-up traffic, then over at Jeff. "Are you a police officer?"

"I'm with the joined forces."

"For how long?"

"Twenty years this spring."

"Does the reason I can't get through to my parents have anything to do with what that scientist said about the sun?"

"What about the sun?" Mrs. Theobald asked. "It looked very beautiful today. More shiny than usual, in fact."

"He said the corona enlarged, and no one could explain why," Sirene said.

"Scientists think they know everything, but they're as ignorant as the rest of us," Mrs. Theobald said.

"Is it true?" Sirene asked Jeff.

"Yes."

"Are we all going to die?"

"Die? Why would we die?" Mrs. Theobald questioned.

Jeff peered at his mother through the rearview mirror. "I don't know all the details."

"You're with the joined forces," Sirene said. "How could you *not* know?"

"Being in the military doesn't give me access to everything."

"Don't worry dear," Mrs. Theobald assured. "Predictions hardly ever turn out to be true. Just last night, the meteorologist said it was going to rain today. It didn't. So if they tell you the sun is going to shine tomorrow, you can bet all your potato chips that it's going to snow instead."

While Sirene struggled to accept the truth, Mrs. Theobald slurped some of her cherry cola, unconcerned about Earth's last night of human civilization. Jeff envied her.

While Mrs. Theobald was oblivious to the destruction, on this night, the screams of Humanity were louder than in any other world within Me. Those who resisted were quieter, but I heard them the loudest. They hid in their homes, in churches, synagogues, mosques, and temples; up mountains and in caves. Some even hid in the sewers and garbage receptacles. Anywhere to get away from the madness of Humankind's final hours.

In tears, Opal leaned her back against the rails of the balcony. She didn't want to move, didn't want to look down at the aisle below where her sister lay dead. As though sensing her sorrow, Rufus flew down from the rafters and landed on her shoulder. Opal caressed the side of his face as Father Stephen approached.

"She's dead because of me, Stephen."

"I don't know how you can say that. If you didn't show up, more of us would've died."

"Those bastards wouldn't have made it in past the entrance if I brought the woman I rescued back here with me. But I wanted to be the type of person you believe I am."

"My impression of you has been confirmed again tonight."

"You wouldn't say that if you saw me trying to comfort her. All I managed to do was scare her." Opal laughed. "I actually talked to her as if she was one of the soldiers in my unit. Compassionate and kind? I'm neither. You're confusing me with Pearl. She was the good twin, while I was the one who got into trouble and made my parents sick with worry."

"You weren't so bad." Stephen sat beside Opal. "Your most nefarious deed was painting Old Lady Tredwell's bedroom window black." He smiled reflectively. "I can still picture her face when she told my father she thought the sun burned out." Stephen stopped himself. "Tonight is the first time I feel awful for laughing over that memory."

"I've done far worse than that. Compared to Pearl, I could've passed for Satan herself."

Father Stephen laughed. "You still like to exaggerate."

"I don't think I am. There's this darkness inside me I couldn't let out. I wanted to keep hating Pearl for what she and Harry did to me. But when I found out there would be no tomorrow, I missed all the days we wasted not being together."

Father Stephen put his hand on Opal's forearm. "I know Christina is Harry's daughter."

"She told you?" Opal asked surprised.

"Pearl was in a lot of pain over what she did to you, but what hurt her most was losing your trust."

"Every time I looked at Christina, all I could think about was the betrayal." Opal shook her head. "Poor Pearl. She never got the chance to say good-bye to her. And on top of that, I had to go and be my usual insensitive self. You know what I told Pearl?"

"It's not important."

"That we'd be joining Christina soon." Opal wept.

Father Steven hugged her. "We should hold a service. For both of them."

"Yes. Pearl would want that."

Pearl lay on a bed with her arms crossed in front of her. The candlelight reflecting on her face made it appear as if she were sleeping. Father Stephen knelt on the floor beside her, gazing at a silver charm bracelet around her wrist. He ran his index finger under the chain, positioning it beneath an angel. "She was my angel."

Opal handed Father Stephen a blanket. "She is an angel."

"Are you a believer now?"

Opal looked at her sister. "I want to believe I'll see her again."

Father Stephen draped the blanket over Pearl. "I loved her."

"Out of appreciation, or is this a confession?"

"Both."

"Nothing like the end of the world to make a man honest."

"I loved her since we were kids."

"It never took much effort for my sister to attract attention. Growing up, I always felt like the ugly duckling, swimming yards behind her and getting pushed out of the way by her admirers."

"You looked exactly the same."

"I know. Sounds crazy even to me now."

"But you were always the one with the strength."

"A lot of good that did me." Opal looked at Pearl's covered form and then back at Father Stephen. "Why didn't you tell her?"

"I knew she belonged to Bertrand."

"Is that why you became a priest?"

"No." He smiled. "I heard the call and responded."

Opal shook her head. "I never even heard so much as a whisper."

"You will. Someday..." Stephen shook his head. "And yet another word to strike from my irrelevant words list."

"Are there many?"

"So many that this is going to take some time to get used to."

"Don't put in any extra effort," Opal said. "By tomorrow, it won't make a difference."

"Changes can be made as long as we're alive to make them."

"I've changed enough for one night. Now it's time for me to go home and rest." Opal hugged Father Stephen. "I'm honored to have known you."

"You shouldn't be alone tonight."

"It's only been me and Rufus during these last ten years. Seems right that I meet my end with the two of us sitting on the balcony."

Father Stephen picked up Pearl's purse from the nightstand and handed it to Opal. "You should take this. Maybe something in here will help connect you to Pearl."

Opal left the church and plodded home as people rushed past her. She tried hard not to imagine what Pearl's last moments were like. Pearl on her knees, Father Stephen pleading for her life, and her not there to assist. *If only I were there five-seconds earlier. That's all I would've needed*, she kept repeating to herself. On top of her torment, all the screaming and honking, all the yelling and threats, all of Humanity displaying its ugliness on this last night broke her spirit. She cried, begging to see a spark of hope somewhere, anywhere. She wanted to know she didn't waste her years in the joined forces protecting a false ideal and losing her husband as a result of all her time spent away from home. Her intention was to serve and protect, but every step she took, each block she passed, all roads she crossed, demonstrated a crushed ideal, the falsity behind her conviction. *Lies. All lies.* She fought so that the greedy could remain in power. She almost died for them, and what did she get in return for her heroics? A medal and a title. They seemed so important when she received them, but now their insignificance couldn't have been more obvious.

Last Documentary

Rajni lit a few candles on the coffee table and eyed her father's bottle of whisky. She wasn't much of a drinker, but she now craved a shot.

Carlo pulled her back onto the couch. "We can have a lotta fun in the dark," he said. "Under the candlelight you look pretty." He rubbed the barrel of the gun against Rajni's cheek. "Too pretty to mess your face up with a gunshot. But don't think for a minute you're gonna live past tonight. After we're finished, I'll shoot you in the heart and break it like you broke mine when you killed my brother."

"Your brother killed my father. Consider us even."

Carlo pushed her onto her back and lay on top of her. "I'm gonna take what I want from you and then I'm gonna go to your uncle. What's his name again?"

The hatred inside Rajni boiled over. All her restraint evaporated. "What I had to endure over the last twelve years is far worse than anything your pathetic little brain can come up with!"

Carlo grabbed a tuft of Rajni's hair and pulled hard. "Who are you calling pathetic?"

"Go into the bathroom. There's a mirror in there that will answer your question."

"I think you got me confused for yourself." Carlo twisted Rajni's hair and pulled harder. "You're the pathetic one. You got a nice apartment with lots of pretty stuff, and you come home alone."

"What makes you so sure I'm alone? My husband could be coming home any minute now."

"You got no husband. I can tell by looking at this place. There are no electronics in here. Just a bunch of useless frilly girly crap."

"There's more to life than having stuff."

Carlo laughed. "What's life all about Dr. Self-Righteous?"

"Living, experiencing, enjoying."

"Yeah, true. But you stole my brother's life. He won't be able to do none of those things."

"Either kill me, or shut up," Rajni said.

Carlo got off her and studied her expression under the glow of the candlelight. He then grabbed the whisky from the coffee table. "I'm trying to figure out if you're playing me." He opened the bottle and gulped down the equivalent of two shots.

Rajni sat up. "I'm not playing you. Either kill me, or get the hell out of my apartment."

"Think I figured you out." He pointed his gun at Rajni. "You wanna know how I know you're not playing me?"

"I could care less."

"I'm a good people reader." He swigged down some more whisky.

"Then you know what I think of you."

"The same as what I think of you." He slammed the bottle on the coffee table. "How come you wanna die so bad anyway?"

"I'm sick."

"You don't look sick."

"That's what makes it worse. No one can see how I feel, and they treat me as though I'm normal. But I don't feel normal."

"Maybe you're sick in the head." Carlo laughed, and his translinker rang. When he recognized the caller as one of his friends, he answered. "I'm avenging Georgie's death. What do you want?" Carlo connected to the publink. "Yeah, I'm searching now. I'll be at our usual spot in about an hour. Get everyone together."

Carlo's gun shook when he arrived at the headline his friend had told him about.

"What's wrong?" Rajni asked.

"Thought my friend was joking." Carlo nervously opened a video file and tilted the screen for Rajni to see.

Rajni gasped when she saw Nestor and Randy sitting at the cafe. A few tealight candles were flickering on the table, and a small crowd was gathered around them. The flames illuminated Nestor's face as he spoke.

"My name is Nestor Zaras, and I have some news I regret to bring to you tonight. A few hours ago, I released a video of Warren H. Beasley who claimed the sun's corona expanded. An astronomer from an observatory in Hilo confirmed his claim. Most of the government is on their way to the Mars colony, but they more than likely won't survive what's coming. I'm sure most of you think they'll get what they deserve, and I agree with you. But some of our leaders of industry also knew of this disaster ahead of time. They left Earth for an outer Solar System space colony constructed by Seth Marconi. I'm sure the news is making many of you mad. Why should they be the ones to survive? It's not fair. I know. The lack of fairness is something I've been struggling to understand through each documentary I've produced. I never did find any answers other than the fact that unfairness sometimes wins. It won many times throughout our history. And like it or not, it's going to win again tomorrow morning. Where can you find comfort in that truth?"

Nestor picked up a glass of water, took a sip and then continued. "My friend wanted me to make this statement because he believes I'm a good speaker, and that I can comfort all of you. The truth is there's no pleasant way to state that by sunrise tomorrow, we'll all be dead. My advice to all of you is to go home and be with your families, even if you can't stand them. Don't let your hatred win out, even against Seth Marconi and his friends. Don't waste tonight on hatred. You'll gain nothing from it. In the end, family matters most, and that's where I'd be right now if mine were here with me."

Nestor wiped away a few tears he couldn't hold back. "Die in peace. Die loving someone. The Aristocrats have stolen a lot from us since they came into power, but love is beyond their reach. That's the strength we have over them. Hold on to it as tightly as you can on this last night. Love to all. That's all I have to say." He got up and walked off camera.

The screen turned black, and Carlo shut off the video. He nervously paced around the room. "We're all gonna die in the morning? Is that what he meant?"

"Yes," Rajni wiped her eyes with her shirt sleeve.

"This has gotta be a joke. Right?"

"My ex-husband isn't a comedian."

"He's your ex-husband?"

All Rajni could manage was a nod.

Carlo placed his gun in his pocket. "No sense in me killing you now. You'll get your wish at sunrise."

"I never wished for everyone to die."

"I wanna keep hating you for what you did, but I don't anymore." He peered at Rajni with a seriousness he hadn't expressed in years. Carlo, the criminal, transformed into Carlo, the wizened street philosopher. "We're all equally screwed up." He peered at Rajni. "Some of us are just better at hiding it."

"Not some. We all are."

"Does that mean we're all damned?"

"I hope not."

"I'll let you enjoy your last night alone." He picked up the whisky bottle, chugged some down, and set it on the coffee table. "Still wanna die?"

"Not like this," Rajni said.

"I think we're getting exactly what we deserve." Carlo left the apartment.

Rajni ran to her translinker and called Nestor, who happened to be on his way to her apartment. He was worried about her and Vinny.

"Rajni!" he shouted with tears in his eyes. "Thank Shiva, God, and Allah you called! Did you hear me? Did you hear about the sun?"

"I heard. Why are you in New York?"

"I'll explain everything later. Can I come over for a game of Pachisi?"

"I'm blue."

"I'm red. Fire up the dice, and I'll be there in ten minutes."

Coming Together

Jeff landed the flyer in front of the patrol station. He drummed his hands on the steering wheel and waited for the guard to come outside to check his credentials. When no one came out, Jeff went to the border booth to investigate. The door was left ajar and inside, two guards lay dead on the ground. There were typically more than two, but the joined forces were called out to help with the chaos going on outside the curfew zone. But after Nestor's broadcast, many soldiers quit on the spot. There was nothing to defend anymore.

Jeff grabbed his gun and went out to assess the perimeter. Old DC had become a ghost town. Every side road Jeff looked down was practically empty. Only a few street people meandered about, salvaging through trash cans, unaware that their end was nearing.

Jeff ran back to the flyer and got inside. "We're going to have to go all the way in."

"Your flyer won't last two minutes in there," Sirene said.

"These aren't easy to break into." He started the engine and took off.

"Oh my God!" Sirene said as she looked down at the curfew zone, most of which was on fire. "They're destroying themselves."

"It's like a large bonfire down there," Mrs. Theobald observed.

"There's probably an even bigger one farther in, and we're going to fly right into it," Jeff said.

"We should've brought along some marshmallows." Mrs. Theobald pressed her hand on the glass, remembering she said the same thing to her father after the Eastern Sector had bombed a neighborhood near her house.

Not comprehending the meaning of the comment, Sirene smiled. Mrs. Theobald reminded her of her late grandmother. Even their skin tone was almost the same shade of brown. "Your hat is beautiful."

Mrs. Theobald smiled at Sirene. "My father got it for me for my sixteenth birthday." She looked back out the window, mesmerized by the crackling flames. "It's as if the fire is dancing and swaying to music." She sipped some of her soda.

"Your mother is a lovely woman," Sirene told Jeff.

"I'm not his mother," Mrs. Theobald said.

Jeff switched on an infrared camera as the flyer touched ground behind a large apartment complex.

Sirene looked out into the barren street. "So this is what peace looks like here."

Jeff unfastened his seatbelt. "That can only mean the gangs are in New DC making trouble." Turning to his mother, he said, "Be back in a few minutes." He opened the door and stepped out of the flyer.

"Alone?" Mrs. Theobald asked as Sirene climbed out of the flyer. "You're going to leave me in here all alone?"

"For a while. But when I get back, I'm going to take you on the most thrilling boat ride you've ever been on in your entire life."

"Really?" Mrs. Theobald beamed.

"Maybe we should take her with us," Sirene said.

"She'll be safer in here." Jeff popped the trunk, got another bag of potato chips, and handed it to his mother. "Stay in here like I ask, and I'll get you another can of cherry cola."

"I knew this was going to be the best night of my life." Mrs. Theobald tore open the bag of chips.

Jeff and Sirene walked away from the flyer, and Sirene kept looking back. "Are you sure she'll be all right?"

"My mother doesn't like playing follow the leader, and I want to get you home safely. I can't do that while chasing her around."

Mrs. Theobald turned on the audio system and selected a classical music playlist. She chose her favorite composer, Ludwig van Beethoven and selected "Moonlight Sonata." Her father used to play it for her to comfort her whenever the bombing raid sirens rang. The somber melody never failed to calm her. Mrs. Theobald closed her eyes and swayed her body to the beat of the music as she ate her chips. Loud laughing and yelling pulled her out of her musical reverie.

Across the street, some teenagers stood around a bonfire they'd started in a trash bin. Mrs. Theobald, finally free after years of being confined to a few small rooms in a hospital, decided to join the party. She slid open the door, climbed outside, and ambled towards the adolescent gathering, leaving her bag of chips behind.

Blaze caught up with David, who stood in front of an alley where a man was assaulting a woman. Recalling his vow to never watch another woman die in front of him, Blaze gave David the picture of Astrid and ran towards the assailant.

The assailant pointed a knife at Blaze and charged him. Blaze stepped off to the side and seized the assailant's arm. As the two struggled for control of the knife, the woman ran out of the alley.

While Blaze fought to get the knife out of the assailant's hand, David spied Opal who was fending off two delinquent teenagers. They stood in the middle of the street as the surrounding buildings were in flames.

The younger of the two examined Rufus's covered cage. "Hey old lady, what do you got under there?"

"None of your business."

"Come on. Show me."

"Go home to your parents. It's not safe out here."

The older boy, who towered over Opal, flashed a knife in front of her. "Feel safe with this."

Neither of the youth had noticed that Opal was armed, and the younger boy went to snatch the cage.

Opal seized her gun and shot him in the chest. The older youth ran off, and she shot him in the back. She readied to fire another round when he continued to run. "Die, you punk bastard!" Her body trembled at the sound of her own voice, and she dropped her arm to her side.

Off the battlefield, Opal had never shot anyone without a warning. She looked down at the boy she'd shot first. He was dead. Opal was about to cry when David approached her from behind. She quickly swung around with her gun ready to fire and froze when she saw him. "You shouldn't sneak up like that! I could've shot you!"

"My friend is in trouble!" David yelled. "A man is trying to kill him! You gotta come quick!"

Opal followed the boy to the alley where Blaze was twisting the assailant's arm. His knife was lying on the ground.

"Freeze!" Opal called out.

The assailant pushed himself free, and when he squatted down to pick up the knife, Blaze kicked, pounded, and punched him until he collapsed. Believing Blaze was the assailant, Opal shot him.

"You shot the wrong person!" David yelled.

Blaze dropped to his knees, and the assailant headed for the fire escape after he had seen Opal's gun. She shot him before he reached the first step.

"Call a doctor!" David yelled to Opal and then ran over to Blaze.

Opal glimpsed at Blaze and then at her gun. She distinctly heard Pearl's voice telling her how she only understood violence. "I'm sorry," she said and ran off.

Blaze clutched the right side of his abdomen that bled profusely. "Go find shelter. The streets won't be safe from now on."

"I don't wanna be alone."

"I know you're scared, but you have to listen to me and go now."

"I have nowhere to go." David cried.

Blaze slowly pulled himself onto his feet, and David gave him his picture of Astrid. As he gazed at her image, the woman whom he'd saved returned.

Her eyes went right to his wound. "We should go now. I found two policemen. They were shot by looters right in front of me."

"I can't go too far," Blaze told her. "Take the kid and find shelter."

"I have transportation. One of the policemen gave me the override code to his patrol car before he died."

"A flyer would've been better."

"And a car is better than nothing." She put her arm around Blaze and helped him walk. "I'm Kay."

"Blaze. And thanks for coming back."

"I couldn't leave you after what you did for me. You're either brave or suicidal."

"A little of both."

"I can take you to the hospital."

"Not enough time. I need to get to Bensonhurst."

"You've been shot. You need a doctor."

"It's only a flesh wound."

Kay could see Blaze's injury was serious, but she owed him her life. "Don't know where Bensonhurst is, but if that's where you want to go I'll take you."

Sirene unlocked the door to her parents' apartment and called out for them. No one responded. Jeff kept his gun aimed and ready to fire as Sirene went inside and searched every room. No one was home. She ran out of the apartment and pounded on the door across the hall.

"Mrs. Bellamy! Are you home?" Sirene sobbed. "Mrs. Bellamy!"

Mrs. Bellamy opened the door. "Sirene?"

Sirene hugged her neighbor.

"What are you doing here?" she asked.

"I'm looking for my parents. Have you seen them?"

"They told me they were going into the city to find you after they heard that man's message confirming what the scientist said."

"What man's message?" Jeff asked.

"About how tomorrow we're all going to die."

"Why didn't you go with my parents?" Sirene asked

"The walk would've been too much for me," Mrs. Bellamy said. "I would've just slowed them down. My legs haven't been very reliable lately. I was going to head off to the church around the block, but I heard gunshots and got scared. I came back here."

Sirene gave Jeff a pleading stare.

"Mrs. Bellamy, would you like to join us?" Jeff asked while thinking that Mrs. Bellamy and his mother would probably get along.

Sirene smiled at Jeff, pleased that her assessment of him had been accurate.

"I have a flyer," Jeff said. "You'd only have to get yourself downstairs."

"Only downstairs, ey?" She rubbed her chin. "Can I bring Spunky?"

Jeff raised his brows.

"Her cat," Sirene said.

"I won't leave without my Spunky."

Jeff was allergic to cats, but he said yes anyway as he wouldn't have to deal with it for too long.

While Mrs. Bellamy put Spunky in his cage, Jeff played Nestor's message on his translinker.

"I was hoping it wouldn't be as frightening hearing it for the second time," Mrs. Bellamy said as she picked up her cane, "but it was."

"I'd rather my mother not hear this." Jeff placed his translinker in his pocket.

Sirene nodded. "I wish I never heard it."

"Ignorance is certainly bliss this evening." Mrs. Bellamy peered into the cage at Spunky. "Isn't that right, Spunky? You're as happy now as you are on any other day because you don't know what's coming at sunrise."

Mrs. Bellamy slowly followed Jeff and Sirene to ground level. When they arrived at his flyer, some kids were attempting to steal it. Jeff gestured for Mrs. Bellamy and Sirene to stand behind him.

Jeff got out his gun and shot into the air. "You have five-seconds to get out of there!"

The kids ran off, and Jeff sprinted to his flyer. Mrs. Theobald was nowhere to be found. He had Sirene and Mrs. Bellamy wait in the flyer and went to look for his mother.

Jeff cautiously walked past burning buildings and displaced people, showing them his mother's picture. No one recognized her, and he was about to head back when he spotted a woman pushing a shopping cart on Pennsylvania Avenue. She was wearing his mother's hat.

Jeff approached the woman, and she shined her flashlight on him.

"Hmm. This street is filled with you outer city folk tonight."

"Did you see one come by?" Jeff asked.

"Yep."

Jeff showed her the picture of his mother, wearing the same cloche hat. "Was this her?"

"Yep." She held onto the hat with both her hands, thinking Jeff was going to take it from her.

"Do you know where she went?"

"Yep."

"Where?"

"Don't work for free."

Jeff looked at the watch Lynn had given him for his last birthday. He unclasped it from his wrist and handed it to the woman.

"A gang took her to the White House," she said. "Better get over there quick. Heard they do weird satanic rituals in there."

One Last Game of Pachisi

The traffic stood still en route to the Brooklyn Bridge. Kay put the car in park and looked in the rear-view mirror that was filled with a swarm of headlights for as far back as she could see. David stood on his knees staring out the back window.

"Put on your seat belt," Kay said.

David turned to face her. "Why? We're not moving."

"Maybe we should rethink our plans." Blaze inspected his wound that had been wrapped with an old tee-shirt of Kay's.

The car horns and screams gave him more pain than the bullet that pierced his skin. He checked his translinker for new information about the blackout, and the Universal Press Server was still reporting that Earth was in the middle of a solar storm.

Kay tapped her fingers on the steering wheel. "Any news about the traffic?"

"Border security closed all the bridges and tunnels a few minutes ago. We're stuck here."

"Can you try my mother again?" David asked.

Blaze pretended to make the call and waited several seconds. "She's not answering."

"Where am I going to stay?"

"You can stay with me." Blaze's translinker rang. He answered, and Collin's face displayed on the screen.

"Where are you?" Collin asked before Blaze could utter a greeting.

"They closed all the bridges and tunnels out of here. I'm not going to make it. Where's my sister?"

"She's at Mrs. Maretti's calming her down. She's been moaning non-stop since I got home, talking about God's wrath being upon us. Think she drank more than her usual one bottle of wine per day."

"Does my sister have her translinker with her?"

"No. But she should be back soon."

Blaze checked the battery supply on his translinker. "I'm running low on power, and I'm not sure how long the satellites are going to be working. Tell Tara to expect my call within the next couple of hours."

"Affirmative. Hey, did you hear the live broadcast from Nestor Zaras?"

"What broadcast?"

"Jesus Christ, Blaze! What are you doing out there?"

"Helping an abandoned child, saving a woman from a rapist, and getting shot. What have you been doing?"

"You got shot?"

"Never mind me! The message!"

"Okay, okay. Go to the main news link. Marconi's story has been confirmed."

"I'll call you later." Blaze hung up and clicked onto the news site link and shuddered when he read the headline: *Seth Marconi's Final Message to Earth.* Below that was a link to Nestor's broadcast.

"What is it?" Kay asked. "Your leg is shaking."

Blaze contemplated over whether he should wait until David was away before he told Kay the news, but that wasn't likely to happen. "A few hours ago I had a run-in with Seth Marconi."

"I was supposed to go on a business trip with my husband on his next shuttle out."

"Why are you still here?"

"I missed the call. There was a message from one of Seth Marconi's associates telling me to pick up a ticket at the shuttleport kiosk, but I was late. A common occurrence for a world security agent."

"And you're not allowed to have your translinker with you for security reasons."

"How did you know?" Kay asked.

"One of my characters is a WSA agent."

"You're a writer?"

"Tried to be." Blaze stared at the two files on his translinker screen. "Did your husband tell you about what's going on with the sun?"

"No. But I heard a massive solar flare struck Earth."

Blaze kept silent and let Nestor be the courier of bad news for a change. He played the video and after it had ended, Kay stared ahead emptily.

"Are you okay?"

"I should feel bad, but I don't feel anything," Kay replied.

"You're in shock. Once it wears off, you're either going to scream or laugh on the inside as I'm doing now."

David sniffled. "On the inside of what?"

Blaze looked back at him. "This car." He peered at the traffic. "Be right back." He stepped outside and climbed onto the hood. Headlights shone from every conceivable direction. "We're not going to be able to turn back," Blaze called out. He slowly maneuvered himself back onto the ground.

David stuck his head out the window. "What are we gonna do?"

"Walk." Blaze opened the back door. "They've been doing it in New York for centuries."

David got out of the car and wiped his eyes. He'd been quietly crying since hearing Seth's message.

Kay reached into her purse and pulled out a gun.

"Why didn't you have that with you when you were attacked?" Blaze asked.

"Got it from one of the downed officers. When I ran over to assist him, he gave it to me."

Blaze held out his hand.

"You know how to use this?" Kay asked.

"I spent two years in the joined forces."

"Everyone spends two years in the joined forces."

"I was in active combat."

Kay gave the gun to Blaze, and the three of them crept back towards the violently pounding heart of Manhattan.

Rajni opened the door and hugged Nestor. "I'm so glad you're here. I didn't want to be alone." She wept. "Papà is dead."

"When? I talked to him only a couple of hours ago."

"Two men robbed his shop and murdered him." She wiped her eyes. "I killed one of them."

"Where's Frank?"

"He'll be up shortly. He's in the shop paying his last respects to Papà."

They walked into the living room that was now lit up by every candle Rajni owned.

"It's an asylum outside," Nestor said.

"You should've been here a while ago."

Nestor sat on the couch, and Rajni filled him in about her encounter with Carlo.

"This night has confirmed my worst fears," Nestor said.

"What is that?"

"That Seth Marconi is right about us. We're all parasites, him included."

Rajni shook her head. "You're still as gloomy as ever."

"It's hard not to be after you take off your communal lens and see the truth for what it is."

"What is the truth?"

"That we're all screwed. And I'm dead inside. What's speaking to you now is nothing more than a machine."

Rajni understood what Nestor meant. She felt the same for too many years to remember what it felt like to be alive. "What brought you to the East Coast?"

"I shot a documentary. It was supposed to be about Seth Marconi, but he made Xavier Starfly the focal point of our discussion."

"The chanting prophet?"

"The one and only. And Marconi knew what was happening with the sun while he was talking to me." Nestor punched the inside of his hand. "I can't take this waiting! I can't take being alive while my family is dead! I can't take that those Aristocrat bastards are going to survive this and that we're going to die because we didn't have the right connections."

Rajni spied Nestor's camcorder sitting unused on the couch, picked it up and started to film him. "Nestor Zaras, since this is your last night alive, do you have anything you want to be remembered for before your demise?"

Nestor looked into the lens. "I became nothing tonight." He picked up the half-consumed, uncapped, bottle of whisky from the coffee table.

"Rebuild yourself into something for one last time," Rajni said.

"No thanks." Nestor took a long sip. "I like being nothing. Makes things easier."

"This will be your last will and testament. Maybe in a thousand years someone will find this and base a history course out of your life."

Nestor laughed and pointed his finger towards the lens. "I hope you're not as brainless as us."

"Do you have any words of wisdom or advice you'd like to pass down?"

"Barter for services, don't create villages with more than one hundred people, and above all else, don't start any new religions, philosophies, political parties, and nationalities because they'll eventually kill you all as they almost killed us a few times over."

Rajni put down the camcorder. "Were you going to call me if none of this happened?"

Nestor thought reflectively for a moment. "No."

"Why not?"

Nestor held Rajni's hand. "This still feels so natural."

"I know," Rajni said as all her suppressed feelings for Nestor came to the surface while she looked at him.

"That's why," Nestor said.

"Is it wrong, considering the circumstances?"

"I don't know what's wrong or right anymore," Nestor said. "The only thing I know for sure is I don't want to die alone." He drank some more whisky. "Or sober."

"Wonder if there's some deep cosmic lesson we have to learn from all of this," Rajni said.

Nestor grabbed the camcorder and aimed the lens toward Rajni. "Your turn."

Rajni leaned towards the coffee table, picked up the bottle of whisky, and took a swig.

"What have you been up to these last four years?" Nestor asked.

"Fully immersing myself in all the 'ings that irritated you. Sitting, drinking and brooding."

"They never bothered me."

Rajni took another sip of whisky. "Don't lie to me tonight."

"I'm not lying." He continued filming Rajni. "Except for the drinking part. I hated that part of you."

"We all can't be as perfect as you," Rajni said as she brushed her fingertips across the front of her neck.

"I'm not perfect."

"Could've fooled me. The way you kept picking apart everything I did made me think I was in the presence of Lord Shiva."

Nestor deleted the last recording. "There. All gone. I don't want the people from the future to mistake me for a deity or hear about our marital problems."

"Maybe it would be safer if we don't talk for the rest of the night."

"Great idea. I'll turn myself off now." Nestor leaned back into the couch and put his feet on the coffee table.

Rajni took the camcorder from Nestor and peered at him through the viewfinder. "Why did you leave?"

"I didn't leave."

"You packed your bags and left to be with another woman because you got her pregnant. That sounds like leaving to me."

"You were already gone before then. You kept yourself locked up in your room reading books, drinking, brooding and doing the rest of your 'ings."

"I was right. They did bother you."

"And whenever I asked you what was wrong, you wouldn't give me anything."

"So, I'm to blame for your affair?"

"It's not about blame. I was lonely. I came home from work each night, and we barely said a word to one another. That was never us. We always had a lot to say and then something went wrong. I analyzed it from every angle, and I couldn't figure it out. Can you tell me now?"

Rajni handed Nestor the camcorder, and he started to film her.

Nestor exaggerated clearing his throat. "Rajni Zaras will now reveal her truth to all of you lovely and beautiful mutants of Earth's future generation. Watch with extreme caution as the words you hear may cause you to learn a thing or two."

Rajni smiled. This was her first real one since her father's birthday one year earlier.

"When we first started talking during our shuttle flight, I thought it was going to be nothing more than the typical polite conversation you have with people while traveling. But I had such a great time. It was so easy being with you...before the crash, of course." She smiled again.

"Of course," Nestor smiled back. "I never found anyone else who loved playing board games as much as I did."

"You made me feel better than I had in a long time."

"Can't take all the credit. One round of Super Pachisi made you forget you were air sick."

"I lied. It was vertigo." Rajni peered directly into the camcorder lens. "About two years before that flight I was diagnosed with multiple sclerosis. My career as a ballerina was officially over."

"You told me it was a knee injury."

"My right leg went numb, and I had trouble walking. I went to the doctor, and he told me I had a muscle spasm. He gave me some muscle relaxants, and the numbness went away. I thought everything was okay. Then six months later, I started to experience vertigo."

Rajni gazed at the candle. Concentrating on the flickering flame disconnected her from everything, making it easier for her to speak. "One morning, I got out of bed and fell. I couldn't stand up and had to call for an ambulance. An MRI was done on my brain, and that was when I got the diagnosis that destroyed a career I worked hard for since I was a little girl. My symptoms soon got worse, and the pain was so bad I didn't want to wake up anymore. After spending six months doing nothing but sleeping and taking tranquilizers, I made an appointment with the Compassionate Endings Clinic. After I hung up, I couldn't wait to take the small pill that would put an end to my suffering forever." Rajni wept and looked at Nestor. "I was due to check in after we returned from our trip."

Nestor put down his camcorder and took Rajni in his arms. She continued to cry.

"Why didn't you tell me this?" Nestor asked.

"Remember what I told you about the shuttle crash? The experience I had?"

"You saw a mirror image of yourself looking down at you and say something. Can't remember what."

"'We fix, so you continue.' After I heard those words, all the pain from my illness went away. When I awoke, you were looking down at me. I believed I was cured. But a year later my symptoms returned. I didn't say anything because I refused to accept my disease had come back."

"Did your parents know that you were on your way to the clinic?"

"They didn't even know I had multiple sclerosis. The truth would've been too much for my mother to handle. She had her cancer to deal with, and I didn't want her to waste her energy worrying about me. After she died, I kept the lie going until I needed a cane to get around." Rajni picked up the bottle of whisky. "You accused me of being an alcoholic, but my unsteady gait was caused by my disease." She handed the bottle to Nestor. "I drank, but not that much."

"You should've told me."

"Wish I did, but back then it was easier to be viewed as an alcoholic than as an invalid." She laughed to herself. "Sounds so stupid now, hearing myself admit this out loud. I'm glad I got it all out."

Nestor examined the bottle. "Whose is this?"

"Papà's."

Nestor slugged down some of the whisky and handed it to Rajni. "Now what?"

Rajni took a sip. "How about one last game of Pachisi?"

"Since there are only two of us, I insist on Super Pachisi."

"As long as I'm blue and yellow."

Rajni left the room and came back with her Pachisi boards. "I started making these to earn some extra credits." She handed them to Nestor who inspected them.

"They're all beautiful, but this one stands out for me." Nestor placed the board with the mandalas on the table. "You didn't make any of them with a Roman Mythological theme?"

"Not yet."

"Your nana would've been insulted."

Rajni set up the game, and they played while discussing what had happened in their lives in the past four years. When Rajni moved her third yellow piece into the home nest, several gunshots were fired. The two scrambled to the window and spied two gang members walking away from a man they'd left to die in the middle of the road.

"Got a flashlight?" Nestor asked.

Rajni ran to the kitchenette. She opened a drawer, pulled out a flashlight, and handed it to Nestor.

"Stay here." Nestor raced toward the door.

Rajni followed him. "I want to help."

"You had enough excitement for tonight." Nestor opened the door and left.

Rajni waited for a few moments, then went after him.

A Party in the Truman Balcony

Jeff entered the White House from the North Lawn ruminating over Nestor's message. Although he knew what was coming, Nestor's words extracted Jeff's own distrust of authority and anger that a narcissist like Seth Marconi would survive and a good woman like his mother would soon be reduced to ash. Jeff once believed in the idea of justice. After tonight, he understood it was a human concept rather than fact and that justice was only possible if everyone played by the same rules.

The state of the White House shocked Jeff. He'd read about the condition of the premises but wasn't prepared for what he saw up close. He was stunned by the destruction of the Entrance Hall. He'd been in the White House only once, but once was enough to remember its former beauty. He recalled the President and First Lady walking down the Grand Stairwell to greet everyone. The once bright red carpet was faded and torn, and the marble columns in the Cross Hall had been spray-painted over. Smashed bottles, fast food containers, and shattered crystal from the chandeliers littered the floor.

Jeff heard music and laughter emanating from upstairs and unholstered his gun. He cautiously climbed the stairs towards the sounds.

Reaching the entryway of the Yellow Oval Room, Jeff hid at the side of the door and took a quick peek inside. The room was in a similar state as the Entrance Hall. He could see a group of teenagers in the Truman Balcony, five boys and one visibly pregnant girl.

The recalcitrant teens were part of the hidden youth. On any other normal day in Old DC they socialized, mostly in their apartments because the streets were filled with gangs. There was hardly any adult supervision for the hidden youth. Parents who remained together both had to work. Tonight, Old DC was the safest area in the whole city because there was nothing worthy of stealing there. The hidden youth saw this as their opportunity to rule the streets, even if it were only for one night.

Jeff edged up a staircase towards the balcony, keeping to the side so as not to be seen. Nearing the top, he spied his mother dancing and spinning around with her arms stretched towards the sky.

"I never felt so alive in my life!" she yelled out.

The hidden youth, of which seven were present, clapped.

Jeff jumped out into view and flashed his gun. "Everyone stay cool, and you'll be okay."

Mrs. Theobald looked at her son. "You're just in time for the party. I hope you don't mind that I didn't wait for you."

"We have to go now." Jeff aimed his gun at Jericho, believing he was the leader of the group because of his large build, shaved head, and body piercings on his lips and outer brows.

"I'm not going anywhere with you," Mrs. Theobald responded. "I want to stay here and party."

"Grandma loves us more than you," Jericho said.

His friends all laughed.

Jeff shot the radio, and everyone fell silent.

"Why'd you do that, Tin Man?" Jericho asked.

"We're leaving now." Jeff took his mother's hand, and she pulled it away.

"Don't you dare come here and disrespect my friends!" she yelled.

"These are not your friends." Jeff stared at Jericho. "They're a gang."

"I'd rather be part of a gang in Old DC than from the phony world you come from," Jericho said. "I wouldn't wanna fight in all your phony wars that kill innocent people. And you think that makes you superior to us?" Jericho spit. "You're nothing to us."

Everyone applauded. Jeff normally would've been offended by Jericho's proclamation, but he agreed with him tonight. He had allowed himself to be used to advance the lives of those higher up than him. All the spilled blood of his brothers and sisters had been paid back by betrayal when the cowards they fought for fled into space.

"I don't care if they're in a gang," Mrs. Theobald said. "They treat me kindly, unlike all those nurses back at the hospital who talk to me as though I'm a baby." She mimicked their voices,

"'Would you like some pudding, Mrs. Theobald? Or would you prefer Jell-O today?' They never bother asking if I want something else, like maybe pumpkin pie or chocolate layer cake or even a cheese strudel." She sighed. "It's always the same thing, day in and day out."

"Know what you mean," Jericho commented, more to himself than Mrs. Theobald. He then looked at his girlfriend. "Except for you, Blossom. You're the only thing around here I can stand to look at every day."

Blossom held his hand. "Along with all our friends...old and new."

"Them too." Jericho kissed her gently on the lips. "But they're not as beautiful."

"That's for sure," Mrs. Theobald said. "I barely looked into the mirror since the day I turned fifty."

Jeff walked over to his mother. "If you come with me, I'll get your hat back. I know how much it means to you."

"And I know that you and all those bores at the hospital think I'm a senile old woman. But let me tell you something...just because I have trouble getting my thoughts together doesn't mean I'm ignorant." Mrs. Theobald began to cry. "I understand a lot, but I can't connect things in a way that make sense to me."

"I don't think you're senile...or ignorant," Jeff told her.

"The way you look at me tells me you're lying."

Jeff glanced at Jericho and then at Blossom. "How far along are you?"

Jericho put his arm around Blossom. "Seven months."

"Are you the father?" Jeff asked.

"None of your business," he replied angrily.

Jeff saw right through Jericho's act of bravado. He looked at Blossom and thought about the life growing in her that would never be born, and it changed his whole demeanor toward the group. They were still children—inexperienced, uneducated, and most of them never set foot outside Old DC.

Jeff walked over to the railing of the balcony. Under Moon's glow, he could see the Washington Monument looming ahead. The relic of a grand ideal that once made everyone within the United Republic very proud now depressed him.

Mrs. Theobald giggled, and Jeff turned around to face her.

"Let's go, Mom." He holstered his gun.

"Stop calling me that!" Mrs. Theobald yelled.

"Leave with me now, and I'll take you on that boat ride."

She pointed at Jeff. "I know what you're up to. You're trying to trick me so that you can take me back to that prison. I'm never going back again. Never!" Mrs. Theobald crossed her arms. "You're going to have to shoot me first. I'm sick and tired of sitting in one small room, eating bland food, and watching the transviewer all day. It's as if my life is passing me by without me in it." She cried again.

Blossom walked over to Mrs. Theobald, and put her arm around her. "I'm not going to let you make her upset."

"What do you want from her?" Jeff asked.

"Nothing. She wanted to join our party, and we let her."

Blossom's tender gesture softened Jeff. "We have to go, Mom," he said quietly. "We don't have a lot of time."

"I already told you, I'm not going anywhere."

"What's the rush, Tin Man?" Jericho asked. "Join the party. It's safe here tonight. All the gangs left to go looting because of that solar flare. We got this whole place to ourselves until things get back to normal."

"Have any of you checked the news updates in the past hour?" Jeff asked.

"News?" Jericho repeated. "Why should we bother with the news? It's all about war, poverty, and death. We don't need to hear about any of that shit. We're living in it."

The hidden youth cheered him on.

Jeff took a moment to contemplate the options of telling them the truth or letting them die in blissful ignorance. "Do you want to know why the electric is really out?"

"Electric's always out in Old DC," one of the boys called out.

Jericho shrugged his shoulders and flipped his palms up. "Not newsworthy material here."

"It's worldwide," Jeff said.

Blossom rubbed her belly. "What's causing it?"

"Something has happened to the sun, and it's not a solar flare."

"What is it?" she asked.

Jeff peered at all the kids and then at Blossom. "As of tomorrow morning, all life here will be no more."

Jericho appeared stunned for a moment and then laughed. Everyone else laughed along with him.

Jeff got out his translinker and hesitated for a moment. He still didn't want his mother to hear about their impending deaths. Nevertheless, after studying the faces of the hidden youth, he thought back to when he was their age. He would've wanted to hear the truth, and he didn't want to deprive them of that. He clicked on Nestor's message and turned the screen toward the hidden youth. "I hate to ruin your party, but I think you need to listen to this."

Jeff played the message, and everyone listened attentively. After it had ended, Blossom started sobbing.

Jericho hugged her. "Don't you worry, baby. That was nothing but a truckload of shit."

Mrs. Theobald walked up to Jeff and slapped him across the face. "Why did you come here and terrify them?"

"It's the truth. They have a right to hear it."

"You gave it to them with a smile. I saw you. You wanted them to suffer."

"I'm not smiling." Jeff shook his head.

To the casual observer it did appear as if Jeff were smiling. The edges of his lips curved upward, ever so slightly. When he was a boy, Mrs. Theobald would tell all her friends that her son was the happiest child in the world.

"You have to come with me," Jeff said to his mother.

"And go where?"

"My boat. Remember? I told you about it in the flyer."

Mrs. Theobald wouldn't move. Blossom held her hand. "Go with your son."

"He's not my son."

"If you come with me, you'll be out at sea," Jeff pressed. "It'll be much prettier out there with all the water shining under the moonlight."

Mrs. Theobald smiled at Jeff. "That does sound like fun." She walked over to Jeff. "Let's go."

Jeff nodded his head at Blossom. "Thanks for your help, and I'm sorry."

Blossom sniffled and caressed her belly.

Jeff and his mother entered the Yellow Oval Room.

Jericho hurried after them holding Blossom's hand. "Hey, Tin Man!"

Jeff turned around.

"Take us with you."

"I have no room."

"If you have no room for them, then you don't have room for me," Mrs. Theobald insisted.

"Please," Jericho pleaded. "Give our baby his last night in a beautiful place."

"He's a boy?" Mrs. Theobald clapped her hands and beamed. "How sweet. Did you think up a name for him yet?"

"Not yet," Blossom responded, only now realizing the severity of Mrs. Theobald's condition.

"What d'ya say, Tin Man?" Jericho persisted. "Will you give our son a memorable last night?"

Jeff sighed and then nodded his head. "Follow me."

When they reached the State Floor, Jeff looked towards the East Room. He told the others to wait and went inside. Jeff recalled a classical concert he attended there with his first wife.

In the center of the room, the lid of the grand piano was torn off, and the body of the piano including the mahogany eagle legs were spray-painted over. He glanced up at the portrait of George Washington that was also spray-painted over.

Blossom entered the room. "Your mother is getting restless."

Jeff remained fixed where he stood, lost in the reverie of the past. "You should've seen this room before all of this."

"Must've been beautiful."

"I used to think so. But I now see it as nothing but a symbol. I fought to defend a symbol when I should've fought to defend you, Jericho, my mother, and the rest of your friends." Jeff looked back up at the portrait of George Washington. "Unlike a symbol, you're all real." He laughed. "Guess it's better to learn later than never."

"Tin Man! Blossom! You coming or what?" Jericho yelled from outside the East Room.

Jeff found it hard to move his legs. This was it, the last time he'd ever see the White House, the last time he'd see anything in Old DC or anywhere else. The finality hit him, and it almost knocked him to the floor.

Chorus of all Living Things

Blaze gazed at Astrid's picture as he limped alongside Kay. His legs started to go numb, and he could barely feel his feet against the pavement. David had been clutching his hand, terrified of all the people running in every direction on the street.

Kay scanned the area and noticed a five-story building with an already looted food market. "We need to clean your wound."

Blaze nodded, and David took a step back. The crowd frightened him.

"You can have all the chocolate you want when we get there," Blaze said.

"There probably won't be any left."

"Then any other treat you find in there."

"I don't want a treat. I just want my mother."

"I'll try to call her once we get inside."

Crossing the street turned out to be like charting a course through an asteroid field. Legions of humans pushed, shoved, rammed, and hit everything that got in their way of reaching a sanctuary they'd never find.

David clung to Blaze who kept his other hand on the grip of the gun, ready to shoot. When they made it inside the store, some people were grabbing supplies off the shelves but they kept to themselves. And for the few people who gave Blaze the odd look, all he had to do was show them the gun, and they'd move in the opposite direction.

"Is he gonna be okay?" David asked Kay.

"He'll be fine." Kay found some isopropyl alcohol, gauze, and a bottle of whisky. She handed Blaze the whisky. He uncapped the bottle and took a generous sip.

"Take off your shirt," Kay said.

Blaze did as commanded. He was eager to get out of his bloodstained clothing.

Kay admired the intricacy of Blaze's tattoos and his well-developed chest. She then thought about her husband and felt guilty for admiring another man. Tending to Blaze's wound kept her from breaking down. "This is going to hurt." She poured some of the rubbing alcohol onto the cotton pad. "A lot."

Blaze raised the bottle. "Makes all pain go away." He took a long swig.

When he put his arm down, Kay pressed a piece of gauze against his wound.

Blaze gasped. "You weren't kidding!" He gulped down some more whisky.

After Kay had dressed his wound, they went to leave. Blaze extended his arm to block David's path when he witnessed a frenzied group of teenagers beating a police officer. "It's too dangerous to go all the way back to my place."

"Where can we go?" Kay asked.

Blaze pointed to the ceiling.

"How about my mother?" David asked.

"We'll call her upstairs."

"You don't have to pretend around me anymore. I know she left me."

"Don't give up."

"She's done this before. One time she left me alone for three days. No one even noticed."

Blaze recalled a time when he saw David sitting outside his door by himself. He walked right past him, just as he had almost done again tonight. "I won't leave you alone." He put his hand on the boy's shoulder.

The trio quietly headed upstairs, wishing. Blaze wished for an afterlife where he'd see Astrid again, David wished his mother loved him more, and Kay wished she was on Seth Marconi's shuttle with her husband.

They weren't alone. Everyone was wishing tonight. And hoping.

Nestor approached the man lying in the middle of the street. He cautiously scoped out his surroundings. The building was on a side street, and there wasn't a lot of activity going on there. Nevertheless, being alone made Nestor stand out. He wanted to get back to the safety of Rajni's apartment, but Nestor was too much of a good Samaritan to leave someone to die alone.

The man groaned when Nestor leaned down to check his pulse.

"Sit still. You're losing a lot of blood."

The man wouldn't have been able to move, even if he wanted to do so; he was nearing death. Nestor knew this, but he didn't want the victim to die thinking the worst of Humanity, even though he believed it himself. He opened a bag with some medical supplies he had grabbed from Vinny's store. As he tore open a bottle of peroxide, one of the gang members who had attacked the man returned. He snuck over from behind Nestor and whacked the side of his head with a bat just as Rajni and Frank exited their apartment building.

Nestor collapsed onto his back. Frank shot the assailant, and the bullet pierced the side of his head. A dim energy form catapulted from out of his body before his remains slumped onto the pavement.

Frank and Rajni rushed to Nestor's side.

Rajni kneeled beside him, weeping. "Don't die on me. Not until we finish our game."

"You were winning anyway." Nestor looked at Frank. "Watch out for her."

"I will."

Nestor held Rajni's hand and told her, "Die happy. Make your last moments count."

He closed his eyes, thought about Becky and Joey and smiled as he pictured them. Before he took his last breath, he witnessed the golden star. His energy form then shot out from his body and into the depths of My space.

Back on Earth, Frank spotted the gang, which was heading back to search for their friend.

"We gotta go, Raj," he said. "They're not gonna be happy when they find out I shot one of them."

"We can't leave Nestor here!"

"We'll be joining him if we don't leave now."

Rajni reluctantly left with her uncle, and they ended up back at her apartment. They could hear the gang shouting and breaking things downstairs.

Frank snuck a look out the window. "We got trouble."

"What's going on?" Rajni asked.

"One of them just lit up a firebomb and tossed it into the store."

Rajni came over and looked outside as one of the truculent youth hurled another fire bomb into her father's shop.

"We have to get out of here," Frank said.

Rajni grabbed her tote-bag and cane. The two hurried towards the stairwell yelling, "Fire!" but hardly anyone was left in the apartment building to hear the warning. When they got to the lobby, Frank readied his gun, and he and Rajni cautiously headed outside. Three of the gang members approached them.

"We don't want any trouble," Frank said.

The three hooligans stepped aside when they noticed Frank was armed. Rajni and Frank walked backwards slowly, keeping an eye on the gang. When they got to the main street, people were still stampeding over each other.

"My church is nearby," Rajni said. "Maybe we can find shelter inside."

"I'm an atheist, but there's no time to be picky tonight."

"Papà never told me you were an atheist."

"I told him, but your father insisted I was mistaken."

Rajni laughed. "Sounds like him."

The Dreamflyer was within minutes of running out of oxygen. Seth hid himself in his office with Xavier, who sat with his back against the wall chanting and writing in his notebook.

Seth sat at his desk and drank from out of an almost empty bottle of champagne. "I can't believe I spent all these years following a delusional man." Chuckling, he pointed the bottle at Xavier. "But all was not lost. I did build a successful company thanks to you." Seth got up, walked to the window, and stared out of his space coffin. "I still can't figure out how you predicted what happened to the sun. What was it? A lucky guess?" He leaned his forehead against the glass and sighed. "So much effort...so much time spent to make our new home. It was all for nothing."

He turned around, and Xavier now stood in front of him.

"Why?" Seth asked. "Why did you mislead me? I trusted you."

Xavier handed him his notebook.

"All these years, I wanted to understand what you wrote in here." Seth tossed the notebook across the room. "Now, I couldn't care less. I don't buy into your crap anymore."

Xavier held on to his smile.

"What do you have to be so happy about? We're about to die."

Xavier returned to where he was seated before and closed his eyes. Seth picked up Xavier's notebook and spent his remaining energy looking through it. As disillusioned as he felt, Seth still wanted to know his life meant something. He opened it up, and there was only one page that he could understand. It was addressed to Seth.

Let's chant before the rising of the sun.
We're conflicting matter, but our hearts beat as one.
Together in peace within Your most sacred space.
We're all flowers in Your immeasurable vase.
Our petals soft, our stems neatly aligned.
We sing in reverence to Your astral mind.
From within this Universe everyone sings,
They sing in the chorus of all living things!

I pour out my soul to Your infinite sea!
I cast my eyes upon Your shimmering beauty.

Until they close, I'll live only to face,
This moment, a present, I can't ever replace.
The night is fleeting; tomorrow is nearing,
I'll embrace the sun's rising
With neither crying nor fearing.
I'm drifting along and accept all that it brings.
I sing in Your chorus of all living things!

I bow to Your greatness; I know You can hear me.
Emitting my voice without guilt or self-pity.
Now I will listen and hear Your sweet song.
Nothing can stop me from singing along.
Uprooted from here, I'll grow in Your vase.
I'm ready to bloom in Your warm embrace.
From inside I'll flourish as one of Your seedlings.
I'll sing in Your chorus of all living things!

Tonight, Humanity says its good-bye.
Some weep and some laugh,
Others scream and ask why?
We ignored Your whole vision for fame and for power.
Is it any wonder our world has gone sour?
We accept Your verdict. You've proven your case.
One day You'll make us a more suitable place.
Forgive us and carry us on top of Your wings.
We'll continue Your chorus of all living things!

Seth ripped all the pages in the notebook. "I was a fool to listen to you!" He tossed the notebook at Xavier, hitting him in the face. "Do you have anything to say about that? Anything at all?" Seth yelled.

Xavier pointed at him and said, "Our end is but a stopover at the starting point to somewhere else."

Seth fell onto his back and wept until he took his last breath and witnessed the golden star.

Waiting on Tomorrow

Opal returned to her apartment and let Rufus out of his cage. He scuttled up to her shoulder.

"I don't deserve your kindness, Rufus. Tonight I became a murderer." She cried, remembering the teens she'd killed and the terror in David's eyes after she had shot Blaze.

Opal walked over to the sliding door and opened it. A cool breeze entered. "It's still a little too chilly for you." She shut the door. "If you weren't here, I would've shot myself by now." She petted his head. "But I would never leave my pretty birdy."

"Pretty birdy. Rufus pretty baby."

"You are."

She sat on the couch, leaned back, and threw her legs on the coffee table as she always had done. However, Opal didn't have the transviewer to occupy her mind. "There's nothing left to do now but wait."

Opal picked up Pearl's purse from the coffee table. She unzipped it and went through the contents. Inside the wallet was a picture of her and Pearl when they were kids. She also found several prescription bottles. Opal couldn't recognize any of the medication names, but she quickly perceived that her sister had been seriously ill. She got out Pearl's translinker and searched for any files that would reveal the mysterious disease. It took her under a minute to find the answer. A postoperative medical transcript revealed that she had stomach cancer. It was terminal as it had spread to her liver. Pearl opted out of treatment preferring to live out her remaining days without prolonging her pain. Opal cried again because, until tonight, she believed Pearl deserved to suffer for her betrayal.

Opal thought back to the time before the shuttle crash when things weren't so complicated. Each year, they left their husbands behind to vacation together. When Pearl heard about Seth Marconi's lottery to celebrate the maiden voyage of his new fleet, she bought two tickets. Pearl knew if they won, Opal would be thrilled. After their names were announced on the transviewer, Opal jumped off the sofa with such force that she pulled a muscle in her back. The week she spent confined to her bed with muscle relaxants would've been unbearable had she not spent her time studying the technology used to build the shuttles. By their departure date, Opal had memorized all the schematics and couldn't stop talking about them with Pearl, who would've rather discussed an article in the recent issue of *Counselor's Circle*.

For the first twenty minutes into their shuttle excursion, Opal enjoyed the thrill of being among the first to fly on Seth Marconi's new shuttle. She kept sending text messages to her joined forces buddies, boasting about the flight. It was all in fun, but the fun soon ended when one of the engines began to make a menacing sound. Being a pilot herself, Opal instinctively knew the flight was in peril. The shuttle pilot soon confirmed they were going down, and Opal doubted they'd survive. So did Pearl.

Squeezing Opal's hand, Pearl said, "I have to tell you something about Christina."

"What about her?"

"She's Harry's daughter. Please forgive me."

Opal pulled back her hand. "Damn you for saying this to me now!"

"Forgive me," Pearl cried, "please."

"Never! I hate you, and I want you to die knowing that!"

Both sisters looked forward to their deaths, and both dreaded having to deal with Pearl's disclosed secret when they found themselves alive with the other surviving lottery winners. After the rescue team had arrived, Opal wanted nothing to do with Pearl or Harry. She returned the betrayal by telling Pearl's husband, Bertrand, about what happened, but she got no payoff out of her vengeance. Pearl had already confessed to Bertrand, and he'd forgiven her. That made Opal all the more angry. *Why did he forgive Pearl?* Opal couldn't even look Harry in the eyes because she encountered betrayal in them. While she trekked through the Eastern Sector trying to avoid the enemy, her sister and husband were enjoying a life of ease and pleasure upon her bed.

After the crash, Opal cut off all ties to Christina, whom she had been close with. She missed her niece, but it was too painful to look at her.

Opal tossed Pearl's pills across the room and wept. *No victory exists within vengeance*, admitted the surviving twin. She lamented over the lost years, both with her sister and with the ideal she lived by when she served in the joined forces. All she came out with was that her whole life had been a waste. What she stood for, what she believed in were all based on lies. Lies she told herself and lies that had come unmasked. She lay on her side and sobbed.

Rajni found comfort looking at the large cross that hung over the altar, even though she hadn't been to church in years. She lost her faith long ago.

The pews were filled with people praying. Frank and Rajni sat on the floor. Frank leaned his back against the wall. He closed his eyes and sighed thinking about Vinny, but the only words he could manage to get out were "What a night."

Rajni knew better than to press her uncle. He was guarded with his emotions as was her father. She looked at a line of people waiting at the confession booth. "I'll be back." She got up, wanting to unload her own confession that was too heavy for her to carry alone. As she waited for her turn, Rajni thought of her discussion with Nestor. Everything she couldn't tell him surged out in ten years' worth of repressed tears.

An older woman, standing in front of Rajni, handed her a tissue.

"Thanks." Rajni blew her nose.

"You look familiar," the old woman said.

"I've been coming to this church since I was a child. I also went to school here."

"I sing in the choir."

"So did my mother, Shanti Consenza."

"I remember her. She had such a lovely soprano voice."

Rajni cried again. Thinking of her mother always produced tears. They were very close.

"How insensitive of me." The old woman took Rajni's hand. "She didn't leave us so long ago."

The door of the confessional booth opened, and a young woman exited.

"We'll talk later." The old woman entered the booth.

Rajni was relieved when she left. Discussing the loss of her mother on the same day her father was murdered, on the eve before the end of the world was too much sadness to endure for one night.

After the old woman had come out, Rajni entered the confessional and sat.

The priest opened the slot.

Rajni did the sign of the cross. "Bless me Father for I have sinned. It's been over twelve years since my last confession. I was diagnosed with multiple sclerosis. After that, I didn't value my life anymore. All I wanted to do was die until I saw my father and ex-husband die in front of me. Now I want to live," she said while weeping. "I don't want to die anymore, Father Thomas. I want to live. I never wanted to live so much before in my life, and now I can't. That's so cruel. Not to care and then care when it doesn't make a difference. I would've preferred not to care. Not to feel anything. It made things easier."

"You have to step outside yourself to realize you've been blessed with a gift. God thought you worthy of saving tonight. Understand this, and you'll die knowing your spirit has awakened after a long slumber."

"What gift, Father? Tell me because I don't feel saved. I fought against my spirit for the last ten years, and I'm so mad at myself for allowing it to happen. I can't help but think I'm being punished for it." Rajni closed her eyes, cupped her hand around the front of her neck, and said quietly, "Sometimes I feel as if I'm possessed by Kali."

"Rajni...sorry...I know I shouldn't identify you by name, but considering the circumstances—"

"That's okay, Father Thomas. I feel better knowing you're speaking directly to me."

"It doesn't matter what you've done before tonight as long as you die in peace. You can only do that if you see the gift that you've been given is who you've become. Perhaps that's why you've been relating to Kali. I've studied Hindu mythology in college, and I remember her as the destroyer of the ego. That's what's happening to you, and it can be frightening to feel liberation for the first time."

"I can't see how that will do me any good now. We'll all soon be dead."

"It's better to live for a moment and die than to be alive for an eternity without living."

Rajni cried harder.

"Don't waste these last few hours. Do something that makes you happy. Make these final hours count."

Rajni recalled Nestor's last words to her. *Die happy. Make your last moments count.* "Thank you, Father." Rajni left the confessional and returned to Frank.

"Did it help?" he asked.

Rajni sat beside her uncle and hugged him. "I'm so glad you're with me."

"Me too."

"I'm ready now."

"For what?"

Rajni reached into her tote-bag and pulled out a Leela gameboard. She hadn't played the game since she was a child, but felt like it tonight. "How about one last game?"

"You're on." Frank picked up the board and examined the elaborate drawing of snakes and ladders. "We're all going to slide down the big snake tonight."

Rajni got out the pawns and the dice. "Maybe there's a chance we'll land on a ladder and climb again."

Frank placed the board on the ground. "Maybe."

Mrs. Bellamy and Mrs. Theobald stood by the rail on the lower deck as Jeff sailed his boat out to sea. The glow of all the fires traced the shoreline until the orange flames turned to specks and then eventually disappeared in the distance. Jeff glanced at a picture of Darla on the translinker. He then advanced to a picture of his first wife, who'd died in the shuttle crash. They hadn't been getting along the last two years of their marriage, and Jeff had considered a divorce. In spite of that, he recalled the good times as many humans typically do upon reflection.

Jericho entered the bridge and stared out the window. "Looks like we're floating in space."

"This is one of my favorite places to be, besides space." Jeff said as he clipped his translinker to his belt.

"It sure is spacious out there. In old DC, you're always bumping into people. It's sometimes hard to hear yourself think."

"I'm not a people person either."

"Explains why you got this boat." Jericho approached the helm and admired the wheel. "I always wondered what it was like to steer one of these."

Jeff lifted both his brows. "Are you asking?"

"Yeah. I'm asking."

Jeff stepped back. "Be my guest."

Jericho positioned himself in front of the wheel. "What do I do?"

"Keep her steady and hold her gently."

"You mean I should treat her like Blossom." He snickered. "I get it." He turned the wheel slightly left, then right. "What's her name?"

"Whose name?" Jeff asked.

"Your boat's."

"Kara."

"Kara." Jericho gazed at Jeff. "She must've been very special."

"She was. I'll never forget her."

"Know what you mean. I feel like that about my woman." Jericho shifted the wheel and smiled as he looked out into the dark sea. "I get why you like this."

Jeff crossed his arms. "Why?"

"Feels nice."

"As nice as Blossom?"

"Not that nice. But close." Jericho stared ahead solemnly. "My kid'll never see any of this. Guess it's not so bad. I lived this long, and I'm only seeing it now cuz you feel sorry for Blossom and the baby."

"It's not like that."

"Come on. Would you have invited me, Blossom, Mrs. Bellamy, and *Spunky* if the sun wasn't going all crazy up there?" Jericho pointed to the ceiling.

"I wouldn't have met any of you if it wasn't."

"A convenient answer."

"And also the truth."

Blossom entered the room. "What are you two talking about?"

Jericho pointed to himself. "Check me out, babe! I'm steering!"

Blossom hurried over to Jericho. "Can I try?"

"Go right ahead," Jeff said.

Jericho stepped out of the way, and Blossom took the helm. The two men stood at the sidelines and watched the sea.

After the novelty had worn off, Jeff dropped anchor and left the bridge to give Blossom and Jericho a little privacy.

Jeff joined Mrs. Theobald and Mrs. Bellamy, who stood on the lower deck staring up at the moon.

"Do we have a bottle of champagne?" Mrs. Theobald asked him.

"Ooh, that's a lovely idea; I can go for a glass of bubbly," Mrs. Bellamy said. "Alcohol would definitely make these last hours easier to deal with."

"Last hours?" Mrs. Theobald repeated. "Why is everyone acting so gloomy this evening? It's a beautiful night to celebrate. We couldn't have asked for better weather. It's warmer than it usually is for this time of year."

"I wish I could be as happy about the end as you are," Mrs. Bellamy said.

"Life doesn't end until you do, dear. You're not ended yet. You're still here, talking to me. And as long as we can talk, we can party."

Mrs. Bellamy turned to Jeff and nodded her head. "She's right. It's a wonderful night for a celebration. I don't see why we should all be depressed. Better to go out with some good cheer."

"And one last buzz," Jeff joked.

"I appreciate how you think, Lieutenant." Mrs. Bellamy chuckled.

"It's about time you loosened your collar," Mrs. Theobald added.

Jeff tilted his head up towards the fly deck. "Don't start the party without me ladies. I'll be right back."

From the top of the grocery store building, Blaze, Kay and David looked up at the sky that glistened clear as crystal. The Moon was producing enough light for the trio to spot four lounge chairs and a picnic table on the roof of the fourteen-story building. Kay and David headed for the table, while Blaze continued standing, mesmerized by the open sky. Being a romantic, he mused over how the end of the world was a once in a lifetime event and one he wanted to experience. He felt disappointment that he wouldn't be around to write about it.

The event was to be very small by comparison to other similar events within Me, but I could understand Blaze's conflicting sense of terror and awe. I can be an enigma to those who don't understand My nature. I don't have to make sense. Sense comes from predictability, which was never My style. I live for the unexpected, the unfathomable potential, the surprising dream that comes true. I can be such a romantic.

Blaze sat on the roof's ledge and stared down into a dying city that appeared as if it had been swallowed by a dark pit. A cacophony of screams, shots, sirens, and car horns emitted from out of the depths making Manhattan sound more like Hades than a thriving city. Blaze stared at the picture of Astrid to calm himself.

David sat beside Blaze. "I never saw the moon so bright. Is it because of the sun?"

"Probably," Kay said as she joined them.

"Will it hurt?"

"I don't know," she answered honestly.

"From what I heard, we're going to die instantly and won't feel a thing." Blaze intended David to view a quick painless demise as something preferable over a prolonged and agonizing one. His assumption was proven wrong when David started wailing. Blaze began to feel as though he were the Angel of Death.

Kay hugged David. She wanted a child of her own, and this was the closest she was going to get to having one in her present human form.

Blaze stared up at the moon. "It's getting hotter."

Kay nervously checked the time on her watch. "And nearing dawn."

"What made you join the WSA?" Blaze asked, hoping to get Kay's mind off their pending death.

"I wanted to be a field agent," Kay told him. "But I froze during my battle simulation test, and they said I would be best suited for office work."

"Did you like your job?"

"Hate it. I'm relieved that I don't have to show up tomorrow." She laughed.

"What did you do there?"

"I worked as a translator. I speak five languages: German, Chinese, Arabic, Spanish, and French."

"Au revoir monde," Blaze said.

"Parlez-vous Français?"

"No, but my late wife did."

"She was French?"

"German, but she didn't know how to speak it." Blaze laughed.

David got onto the ledge and sat next to Blaze. "Why did she speak French then?"

"She was born in France, but her parents were Germans." Blaze glanced at his translinker screen for the time. "It's now 8:00 AM in Paris. You know what that means?"

"Most of France has been turned into a pot of fondue," Kay said.

"Oui Madame," Blaze said.

Blaze and Kay laughed, and David failed to perceive their underlying stress.

"What's wrong with the both of you? We're gonna die, and you're laughing? I don't find people dying funny! I don't want to die!"

Blaze turned to David and hugged him. David tried to push himself away, but Blaze held on to him tightly.

"I'm scared," David said, giving up the struggle.

"That's why we're laughing. We're trying to be less scared."

"Is it working?"

"Not really." Blaze got off the ledge and kneeled in front of David. "Could you maybe give us some tips to make this night better for us? I don't have any children. This is all new to me."

"I don't have children either," Kay said.

David widened his eyes. "Since you don't have kids, and my mother is missing, maybe we can be a family. Just for tonight."

Kay's eyes filled with tears.

"I wanna die with a family, even if it's a pretend one."

Blaze placed his hand on David's shoulder. "Okay son, your pretend father is now telling you to find something to laugh about because laughter is the best medicine for sadness." Blaze chuckled over the comment. He was surprised over how easily he fit into a paternal role.

"I don't find anything funny," David replied.

Kay walked over to the table and grabbed some potato chips from out of the grocery bag. "Eat your vegetables." She handed the chips to David. "You'll feel better with a full tummy."

"These aren't vegetables."

"Potatoes are vegetables."

"But they're junk food!"

"Don't argue with your mother," Blaze quipped. "Eat your veggies."

David giggled, opened the bag and removed a chip. "Did my mother really leave me?"

"I'm sure your mom would be here if she could," Blaze said.

"Why did you tell me she wasn't coming back?"

"Because I'm an impatient jerk."

"You're not a jerk."

Blaze never wanted children. Neither did Astrid. Tonight Blaze thought he would've made a decent father.

"My mom was wrong about you, and so was that shooter." He sighed. "I miss my mom."

Blaze's translinker rang, and he answered.

"Blaze!" Collin yelled as soon as his face presented on screen. "Why didn't you call us back? We've been worried about you. Are you okay?"

"Is that my brother?" Tara peeked her head into the camera's viewing area. "Blaze, oh Blaze," she said while sobbing. "I'm never going to see you again."

Blaze studied his sister's face in the glowing candlelight. She was younger than him by three years, but her petite size and blonde pixie haircut made her look even younger.

"My translinker's almost out of juice, Tara."

"I heard you got shot. Are you all right?"

"It was just a flesh wound. Let's say what we have to say before it's too late."

"We've already passed too late," Tara said.

"I love you both," Blaze said.

"We love you too."

Collin put his arm around his wife. "We'll stay on until the end," he said.

Blaze introduced Kay and David to his family. He wanted to make a wisecrack about getting together for drinks when they arrived in hell but stopped himself. It wasn't only for Michael's benefit. Blaze didn't get his own humor anymore. He didn't get a lot of things tonight and that depressed him.

"Can you sing for us?" he asked Tara.

She sniffled. "What do you want me to sing?"

"The song you sang to calm me down when we were kids." He hoped her voice would have a similar effect on David.

"'Winter Wind'?"

"That's the one."

Tara crooned slowly and softly in a lovely alto voice. She effectively calmed her audience along with herself.

Her sad concert drifted through My space and into the ears of David, Blaze, and Kay on the opposite side of the Brooklyn Bridge.

Winter Wind, where are you, when I'm calling?
I'm alone, when you're not with me.
I close my eyes, and I count the days.
When you take me far away.

I'm afraid when it's dark, and it's raining
When you're near, I can hear you breathing.
Please stay with me, so my eyes can see.
All the love I left behind.

Yesterday is far away.
When I feel your breath on me.
Carry me, far away.
Show me what I can't see.

Take me home, Winter Wind.
Won't you hold me?
Take me far where no one can find me.
Please guide the way to another day.
Where I know I'll want to stay.

One bar remained on the battery display of Blaze's translinker. "Bye Sis...Collin," he said. "I love the both of you always."

The screen went black. Everything went black. A sorrowful black. The shouts from the pit of hell hushed, and the fantasized family gazed at the sky and patiently awaited sunrise. Blaze clutched his wife's picture across his chest and had his other arm around David who had indeed calmed. And although Kay was

216

curious about the identity of the woman in Blaze's picture, and why he carried her with him everywhere, she never made an inquiry.

To the Beauty of Life

Sirene stood alone on the fly bridge and stared up at the moon as everyone had done at least once on this night. Mesmerized by the brightness she almost forgot she stood on a boat.

Jeff walked over and stood beside her. "I'm sorry you couldn't find your parents."

"I don't want to talk about them."

"We can talk about whatever you like."

"Let's talk about you." Sirene turned to face him.

"Except that."

"If neither of us want to talk about ourselves, what is there left to talk about?"

"Hell if I know. They want to have a party downstairs. Want to join them?"

"Maybe later." Sirene tossed her translinker into the water. "Battery's spent."

"Do you want to try your folks again?" He handed his translinker to Sirene. "There should be enough power for another call, providing the satellites are still operational."

Sirene tried to connect to her parents but couldn't even get a signal. She handed Jeff his translinker and stared out emptily into the sea. "I wouldn't have minded so much—not seeing my parents, if I knew they were all right."

Sirene would've been comforted to know her parents were at a small church, just outside of Old DC. No one was able to make or receive calls from their location because of a weak satellite signal.

I had no problem receiving Humanity's signal. Each individual thought pattern transmitted simultaneously, contemplating life, death, and whether it would see its family again in some other plane of existence. I wanted to offer a reassuring word, but Sheim blocked my frequencies from reaching Earth.

"You'll never learn," Sheim said and left me to contemplate further.

Sirene always had a difficult time with spiritual questions. She was a rationalist and preferred to see evidence before committing to a particular viewpoint. Not having any immediate answers made her nervous.

"So you're not going to tell me your story tonight?" she asked Jeff.

"I don't like to talk about myself."

"Who will I tell? We'll all be gone by morning."

"That's true."

Sirene turned and gazed directly into Jeff's eyes. "Talk to me because right now our conversation is the only thing keeping me from going overboard."

Jeff looked off to the side. "I have too much to say to squeeze into one night." He laughed nervously. "I wouldn't even know where to begin."

"What happened in your childhood to make you so guarded?"

"You sound more like a shrink than a store clerk."

"Interesting you should say that. It's my—was my major. Cognitive psychology. Since I won't be practicing, I'd like to have at least one patient to prove these last five years weren't a waste of time and that I should've been traveling the world instead."

"If a boy came to your office and told you he killed a shopkeeper, what would you tell him?"

"I'd ask him why."

"What if he told you he didn't want the shopkeeper to die? He had no idea the kids he associated with would harm anyone."

"I'd tell him he'd hurt for a while, but he'd eventually recover over time."

"What if he never did?" Jeff stared out to sea. "What if each time he went to sleep at night, he recalled the shopkeeper's terrified expression before he was shot."

"Did the boy pull the trigger?"

"No. But he was there. He yelled for the kid holding the gun to stop. The kid shot the shopkeeper at point blank range and laughed about it afterwards."

"Did the boy tell anyone?"

"He did. After he found out the shopkeeper died."

"Why does the boy think it's his fault? He tried to stop the shooter."

"The boy couldn't stand the shopkeeper. He was their landlord. He threatened to throw them out of their home for not having enough credits to pay the rent. The boy wanted to get even with him, and he persuaded a gang to hit the landlord's store. But when he saw the landlord's face, the boy realized he made a mistake. By then it was too late." Jeff faced Sirene. "What would you tell him?"

"I'd tell him to let go. He did wrong, but he turned his life around and did good things with it."

"Good intentions sometimes bring about even worse consequences. And that's all I have to say about that subject."

"Think we could both use a party right now," Sirene said.

Jeff extended his hand towards her. "Shall we?"

Sirene took his hand, and they went downstairs where Mrs. Bellamy and Mrs. Theobald were drinking champagne.

"How did you find my stash?" Jeff asked his mother.

"I went into the galley to try to find where you hid the chips. I never found them, but I found your champagne. There are a few more bottles remaining to keep us partying till dawn."

Blossom and Jericho came out while Jeff and the others were indulging in their bubbly drinks.

"They got booze!" Jericho said.

Mrs. Theobald handed both Blossom and Jericho their own glass of champagne. "I had these ready to go for you."

"You make all other grandmothers look bad." Jericho turned and pointed at Jeff. "What time you got, Tin Man? Wait—no way. Can't call you that anymore. You grew a heart."

"And I only have a few more hours to use it." Jeff glanced at his watch. "It's now 0300."

Blossom got nervous and gently caressed her belly. Jericho held her free hand. Jeff, Mrs. Bellamy, and Sirene stood silent, and Spunky entertained himself with a mouse he just saw scurrying across the floor. Apart from Mrs. Theobald, he was the happiest of the group.

Mrs. Theobald placed her hands on her hips. "What is it with you people tonight? Feels like I'm at a funeral."

No one spoke, and she shook her head, disappointed that her first night of freedom brought her to a group who seemed as dreary as those back at the hospital.

"It's almost impossible to get a party going with you." She raised her arms towards the heavens. "Enjoy this night. Enjoy the gentle wind blowing against your skin. This night is special."

Where Mrs. Theobald stood made it seem as though Moon had intently beamed a spotlight down on her. Pointing towards the sky, she said, "The moon never looked so vibrant in all my life."

Everyone craned their necks towards the sky. Jeff's eyes begged to be filled with the tears he had held back for so many years, but none came.

"She's right," Mrs. Bellamy agreed. "The moon looks lovely."

"Lovely," Mrs. Theobald repeated. "And we were brought together under this lovely moon for a reason. When you admire its beauty, how can you not celebrate the beauty of life? The beauty that we're all a part of." Mrs. Theobald pointed at Jeff. "If that man didn't bring me here tonight, I would've been locked up inside a tiny room. I would've missed this special night. And I'm glad I didn't because I'm the only one around here who can cheer up you sad sacks of rotting onions. And trust me when I tell you, you don't want to be in the same room as rotting onions. They smell awful."

Mrs. Theobald raised her glass. "Let's share a toast to the beauty of life and everything in it."

All the others raised their glasses and repeated the toast to humor Mrs. Theobald. They then sipped their champagne.

"That's it? That's the best you can give me?" Mrs. Theobald rapidly snapped her tongue while shaking her head.

Jericho rolled his eyes. "This is pointless. We're all gonna die."

Blossom slapped the side of his arm.

"Say the words as though you mean them," Mrs. Theobald prompted. "To the beauty of life and everything in it!"

"To the beauty of life and everything in it," the others said.

"I don't believe any of you. Again!"

They repeated it louder.

"Again!"

"To the beauty of life and everything in it!" everyone yelled, and they all believed it. In that instant, at least.

"That's acceptable." Mrs. Theobald stared at her glass of white sparkling beverage. "Champagne is the only other drink I prefer over cherry cola." She took a sip.

Jeff walked up to his mother and handed her the last bag of potato chips. He stared at her in awe. This was the most lucid he'd seen her since before the bombing. He wanted so much for his mother to recognize him, but he accepted that he'd die a stranger to her. "I love you, Mom," he said, not caring if she disapproved.

Mrs. Theobald smiled. "If it makes you happy to call me Mom, go right ahead, but only for tonight."

"Only for tonight." Jeff hugged his mother and finally allowed himself to cry.

Sunrise

Sun made his entrance on time. From their lounge chairs,
David, Blaze and Kay watched as his first rays touched upon Earth's
atmosphere, igniting a brilliant carpet of red haze that spread out in
an instant. Blaze had enough time to squeeze Kay and David and
say, "Wow," after which a blast of heat hit their bodies, incinerating
them. They never felt a thing.

Jeff and his crew stood on the fly deck when Sun's rays first
touched the Earth.

"How lovely," Mrs. Theobald said.

"I agree," Mrs. Bellamy responded as she petted Spunky.

Jeff also agreed, but he paid his reverence in silence and held his mother's hand.

Blossom rubbed her belly. "Bye bye, Jay Jay. I love you."

"Jay Jay?" Jericho said.

"Couldn't decide between Jericho and Jeff." She smiled and placed her hand on Jericho's cheek. "I love you."

"I love you too, babe," Jericho said. He placed both his hands on Blossom's belly. "Bye littlest sweetheart. Wish we had time to meet—" He quickly kissed Blossom and wept while doing so.

Sirene rested her head on Jeff's shoulder. "I'm not scared."

Jeff kissed her forehead and then saw a golden star flash before him.

Rajni and Frank were in the middle of a game of Leela when Sun's rays first entered the church. Rajni had just maneuvered her piece down the longest slide. Neither she nor Frank had a thought. Neither said a word. They held one another's hands and smiled. The golden star exploded in front of Rajni, taking her energy pattern with it.

Literary critic, Trevor Forthright rolled to his side and kissed his wife after a very eventful evening that had broken all records in their thirty-seven years of marriage.

Opal sat on the balcony with Rufus on her shoulder. The last couple of hours were warm enough for him to be outside. Together they sat and gazed out at the sun. When the first glow of light appeared, Opal said, "Look at the pretty sun, Rufus." She stroked the top of his head.

"Pretty birdy, pretty birdy, pretty birdy," Rufus said.

Seconds later the golden star appeared to Opal and Rufus, and they were no more.

The lottery winners were no more.

The last of the Earth dwellers watched in awe as Sun outstretched his rays towards them—close enough to bring about their extinction, but far enough to allow some microscopic particles to escape and seed life elsewhere. There were also a few anomalous energy forms that were at risk of being destroyed. I took a deep breath and blew them safely past Mars, which was also destroyed. They flew out of the Solar System and caught up with the energy forms that had left before them.

Back on Earth, all that mattered to humans ended. Culture ended. Everything Anya had spoken of in her final slam came to pass. She would've appreciated her accuracy had she decided to stick around a while longer.

3rd Cycle

"Life is not a problem to be solved,
but a reality to be experienced."
Soren Kierkegaard

Gathering

Six of the lottery winners aboard Seth Marconi's doomed flight opened their eyes and were blinded by a radiant white light.

Blaze wasn't aware that he was standing until he took a step forward. He felt his abdomen. His wound was fully healed. He sensed the others around him and took a few more steps, bumping into Jeff.

"Watch where you're going," Jeff said.

"Who are you?" Blaze asked.

Opal walked with her arms extended in front of her, trying to get her bearings straight. "I'm Opal Halifax, retired commander of the joined forces, and I demand to know where I am!"

"Lieutenant Jeff Theobald here, Ma'am! Active member of the joined forces. It's an honor to meet you."

"Oh my God! Opal? Is that you?"

"Pearl?" Opal said in shock. "You're alive? How can that be?"

"Of course I'm alive! How else would I be talking to you?" Pearl froze when she recalled Vince's gun aimed at her head. "Where are we?"

"I don't know," Opal replied. "Can't see a damned thing in here."

"I'm Nestor Zaras. Does anyone know where we are?"

"Nestor!" Rajni yelled.

"Rajni! Where are you? Becky? Joey? Are you here too?"

Nestor walked with his hands in front of him and bumped into Blaze. "Sorry."

"I'm here, Nestor!" Rajni kept talking until Nestor grabbed her hand.

"Rajni?"

"Yes, it's me," she said. "Where are we?"

"I don't know."

Nestor called out for Becky and Joey, and the rest of the lottery winners shouted out the names of their loved ones.

"Everyone quiet down!" Blaze yelled out, clutching his head. All the shouting along with a low humming sound was giving him a headache. "Does anyone have an aspirin?"

"Why don't we all introduce ourselves and see if we can figure out how many of us are in here," Opal said.

"Blaze Kenyon here."

"Author of the Drake Kent series?" Opal asked as she petted Rufus who was on her shoulder.

"That's me," Blaze said.

"I'm Pearl Levenworth, Opal's sister."

"I'm Rufus."

"Rufus is here?" Pearl asked surprised.

"You know he goes wherever I go," Opal replied.

"Does anyone know where we are?" Nestor asked.

"I'll let you know once I figure it out," Opal said after she had grasped Pearl's arm.

"Does everyone remember the catastrophe?" Nestor asked.

"I can still feel the heat on my face," Jeff told him.

Pearl cried. "We're dead."

"I don't think so." Jeff walked around the area slowly, trying not to bump into anyone. He stopped when he hit a wall. Running his hand across the surface, he felt a vibration.

"Do you hear the humming?" Blaze asked. "Sounds as if we're in some kind of machine."

Opal rubbed her forehead. "Think that's what's giving me a headache."

"Me too," Nestor massaged his temples.

The rest of the lottery winners also complained of headaches.

"We should search for a way out of here," Blaze suggested as he walked around with both arms outstretched, searching for a door. "What's the last thing everyone here remembers?"

"I was out on my boat," Jeff recalled. "The sky lit up in a flash. I saw this gold light, and that's the last I remember."

"Did it look like a star?" Pearl asked.

Before Jeff could respond, Nestor said, "I saw that, right before I...did I die?"

"I thought you did," Rajni said, "but now I'm not so sure. Uncle Frank and I had to leave you because the gang came back."

"I don't understand. How can I be here then?"

"I don't know," Rajni said.

The remaining lottery winners acknowledged seeing the same golden star, which made Pearl panic.

"That must mean we're dead." Pearl held the cross that hung from her neck and whispered the *Our Father*.

"We can't be dead," Rajni said. "I still have my multiple sclerosis symptoms."

"And my lower back aches," Opal said.

"How does that explain me then?" Nestor asked.

"And me?" Pearl wondered. "I was shot."

The humming grew louder, and the lottery winners groaned and became nauseous.

"This is making my vertigo worse than it normally is," Rajni said as she felt around for something to grab on to.

"I got you." Nestor held on to her.

"Who has you?" Rajni said.

"We have to find a way out of here!" Pearl yelled. "I can't take this sound anymore. The pain is too much!"

"Take deep breaths. You'll be okay," Opal assured her.

Pearl cried. "I have to tell you something."

"It better not be another revelation," Opal warned. "We may live through this disaster as well."

"I don't have any more secrets to reveal," Pearl said. "All I want is your forgiveness."

"I know...but you do have one more secret. Why didn't you tell me?"

"Tell you what?"

"I found the pills in your purse."

"I didn't want you to come back out of pity."

Opal didn't say anything. She'd successfully cut off her emotional attachment to Pearl and believed she wouldn't have contacted her even if she had known she was sick. That was one confession Opal preferred not to share.

The whiteness cleared, and the lottery winners found themselves wearing gray jumpsuits and standing in a room shaped like a hexagon. The door was now open, and they all slowly stepped outside. An arched building loomed across a vast circular meadow. Directly in the center was a large, round marble table. Tall trees bordered the perimeter continuing behind the colossal, metallic hexagon they had just stepped out of. The structure was quite an engineering accomplishment, stretching high in the sky.

There were only two pathways out of the circle, one on the east side of the meadow and the other on the west. The area was surrounded by a maze of mountains with rows of forest and clearings in between.

Kelly, the male shuttle pilot of the doomed flight, arrived to greet the lottery winners. He was fifty-three at the time of the crash and appeared exactly the same as he had back then—right down to his salt and pepper beard and mustache. With him was Astrid and Hiroko, who also hadn't aged since their arrival here. Luna, barely into her tenth year, held Hiroko's hand. She had lived on the outskirts of London and witnessed the golden star several hours before the others. She ran towards the lottery winners, calling out for her parents.

"Welcome to your refuge," Kelly said. His voice and appearance both conveyed his years of experience flying in two sector wars.

Hiroko smiled warmly. Her long black braided hair cascaded down to her elbows. Standing beside her was Astrid, petite and cherub in appearance with fine freckles on her cheeks.

Blaze stared at her with his mouth agape. "Astrid?"

Astrid took a few moments to recognize him underneath all his tattoos. Her eyes sprang wide when recognition hit. She ran to him, and the two embraced.

"I missed you so much, *votre mon seul et unique amour!*" Blaze said.

"*Moi aussi!* They told me the rest of you would not make it here because of what happened to Earth," she said with a French accent. "They told me you were all a miracle!"

Rajni peered at Blaze, "I saw his video," she said quietly to Nestor. "I thought he was nuts."

"That's Blaze Kenyon," Nestor said. "He was on the shuttle with us."

"I don't remember him having tattoos."

"He got them a few years after the crash, shortly after his wife was murdered."

Opal trembled as she examined Blaze's tattoos. She knew he was on the shuttle, read his books, and saw pictures of him with his tattoos. Nevertheless, she only now recognized him as the man she'd unwittingly shot. The fires from the surrounding buildings gave off sufficient light to see him, but not enough to recognize him as the famous author whose books she'd read.

"That man probably spent a year in prison for each of those tattoos on his body," Pearl stated.

"That man is Blaze Kenyon, and he's no criminal," Opal said.

Pearl examined Blaze again, then spotted Hiroko and Luna, who was crying. She headed over to them.

Jeff also edged closer to them, but he was more interested in Hiroko.

"Why are you crying?" Pearl asked Luna.

"I can't find my parents."

"You're a counselor," Hiroko said to Pearl in a light Japanese accent. "Perhaps you can help."

"How did you know?"

"They know everything," Luna told Pearl. "It's creeping me out."

"Who are *they*?" Jeff asked.

Hiroko turned to face him.

"I remember you," Jeff said to her, "from the shuttle crash. How is it that you're here?"

"This will all make sense to all of you soon," she said.

"Did anyone else come with you?" Pearl asked Luna. She then glanced at Hiroko who shook her head.

Luna didn't miss the cue. "That can't be. I was with my parents when the sun went crazy."

"What's your name?" Pearl asked.

"Luna."

Opal came over to talk to Jeff and plan a countermeasure for what she believed was a possible hostage situation. Jeff was surmising the same thing. Military minds think alike.

Luna's eyes immediately went to Rufus.

"That's Rufus," Pearl said, "and the shoulder he's perched on belongs to my twin sister, Opal."

"You don't look like twins," Luna noted.

"Not anymore, but we used to when we were your age," Opal explained.

Astrid and Blaze approached them, and the lottery winners engaged in the typical introductions, during which Luna began to cry again.

"Why don't you let Luna hold Rufus?" Pearl said to her sister.

"He needs some time to adjust." Opal petted Rufus. "He's been through quite an ordeal."

"So has she."

Opal looked down at Luna. "Would you like to hold Rufus?"

"A parrot's not going to make me feel any better. Finding my parents will."

Opal glared at Pearl.

"But I'll hold him," Luna said. "I like African Grays."

Opal smiled at Luna's knowledge of parrots and guided Rufus onto her shoulder.

"Does he speak?" Astrid asked.

"From what I remember, he doesn't stop." Pearl made a chitchat gesture with her hand.

"Rufus speaks over fifteen-hundred words, and he can even sing," Opal said.

Luna's face expressed her disbelief.

"Why don't you ask him his name," Opal said.

"What's your name?" Luna asked.

"I'm Rufus. What's your name?" he replied.

The lottery winners laughed, including Luna. After she had caught herself giggling, she returned to her solemn expression.

Kelly approached, clapping his hands. "What an amazing bird!"

Blaze took advantage of the distraction to reconnect with Astrid. He held her hand and gazed into her large deep blue eyes. "Please tell me we're not dead and that I'm really here with you."

"We are not dead."

"If we were dead, I don't think we'd be wearing jumpsuits," Jeff said.

All the lottery winners examined their clothing.

"How can any of this be possible?" Blaze asked Astrid. "You died three years ago."

"As you can see, I am very much alive," Astrid said.

"She's right," Hiroko added. "We're not dead."

"What are we then?" Jeff asked, probing Hiroko.

"The shuttle crash ten years ago...were any of you on the flight?" Kelly asked.

"I was," Jeff said.

"Me too." Pearl pointed to Opal. "As well as my sister and her bird."

"His name is Rufus," Opal said.

"My name is Rufus," he restated and then went through a few more sound effects he had picked up through the years, including the sound of an egg cracking, the rattling of keys and a zipper unzipping.

Rufus continued his vocal acrobatics as everyone revealed being aboard the doomed flight, except for Luna who simply replied, "This is weird."

"Tell me about it." Opal snickered.

"I don't know how much you were told about the flight, so this may come as a bit of a shock to all of you," Kelly said. "We got caught in an electrical storm. This alien craft showed up and hovered in front of us. I didn't recognize it as being one of ours."

"What was it? A UFO?" Jeff laughed.

"Yeah, and it was real. Seth Marconi spotted the thing first. Thought he was drunk."

"What does that have to do with us now?" Jeff asked. "The crash happened ten years ago."

"Both Kelly and I thought we died on the day of the crash," Hiroko said. "It was difficult for us to comprehend that we were still alive."

"Astrid arrived here after we did," Kelly said.

"Where do the aliens fit in?" Rajni asked, now more fascinated than concerned over the mysterious environment.

"I can communicate with them," Astrid said. "The Custodians speak in vibrational tones when they need to tell me something, and I am somehow able to understand them. They told me some of you would not be joining us because of a tragedy that befell Earth. It made them lose their connection to you." She looked at Nestor. "Your signal was lost before everyone else's. They were very surprised when you arrived. The Custodians later told me they were able to reclaim all of you and that you were all a miracle."

"Marconi's here?" Blaze asked.

"He and Anya went up one of the mountains. They haven't returned yet."

Nestor leaned in towards Jeff and whispered, "Could we be part of some military psychological operation?"

"This is no experiment," Kelly stated. "You're all here."

"How about the Mars colony?" Jeff asked. "Did it survive?"

"They never mentioned anything about the colony, but they did say that the whole Solar System was singed," Astrid said. "So, as you can see, this place is your refuge."

Jeff closed his eyes and privately mourned the loss of his beloved daughter.

"So where are we then if this isn't Earth?" Pearl asked.

"Like Astrid just said, this is your refuge," Kelly said.

Blaze gazed at Astrid. How he wanted to believe his wife was here, but he found Kelly's explanation too outlandish to believe, as did Nestor who just didn't believe anything ever.

"What are we supposed to do now?" Pearl inquired.

"Move into your unit. The dormitory is over there." Kelly pointed to the curved building.

"Can we leave if we want to?" Jeff asked.

"We cannot," Astrid said.

Jeff scanned the perimeter. The surrounding mountains seemed more like bars. "Are we prisoners?"

"We're not really sure what we are. But the Custodians have been taking good care of us," Kelly replied.

"Custodians," Opal repeated. "The...aliens, right?" She asked, still not willing to believe the explanation.

"Yes." Astrid smiled at Opal, then held Blaze's hand to reassure him. "And they give us everything we want." She pointed at the hexagon. "Inside is the pillar. It reads your deepest desires and lets you live them."

Kelly shot Astrid a look to not say anything more.

"Why don't we let everyone settle in before we resume?" Kelly advised. "This can be overwhelming."

"I agree," Hiroko said. "We will continue the orientation after everyone is all settled."

"What about my parents?" Luna asked.

"Follow me," Kelly said and walked ahead.

Pearl took Luna's hand. "You can stay with me until we find them."

The curved building appeared smooth and had no doors or windows. In front of the structure were eight round glass panels on the ground.

"To get inside your units, you stand on your assigned panel," Kelly explained.

Astrid pointed to each panel, from left to right. "Kelly, Seth, Hiroko, Jeff, Pearl and Opal, me and Blaze, and Anya...if she comes back, and the last one belongs to Rajni, Nestor, and Luna."

Rajni and Nestor stared at each other and then at Luna.

"Why do I have to go with them?" Luna protested. "They're not my parents."

"I know."

"Then how come I have to go with them?"

"Your parents aren't here, and a girl your age cannot be left alone," Astrid said.

"When are they coming?"

"They're not."

Luna cried, and Pearl held her hand.

"Why aren't they coming?" Luna asked.

"Where we are now, it's not an easy place to find," Astrid said.

"Can't we call them?"

Astrid looked up at Rajni, who still couldn't figure out why she and Nestor were selected to watch out for a child. She had no experience in the art of child-rearing.

"I think we're too far from the satellites to make a call," Opal said. "It would be impossible to contact them."

"When can I go home?"

"You cannot," Astrid said. "None of us can."

"Why not?"

"This is the assignment given to us," Kelly answered coldly. "You're to stay with Rajni and Nestor."

Luna petted Rufus's head. "I'd rather stay with Opal and Pearl."

"The rooms are already assigned," Kelly told her.

"I don't care!" Luna glared at Kelly. "I want to stay with Opal and Pearl."

"Perhaps she should stay with them," Hiroko suggested. "She seems to have bonded with them."

"It makes no difference!" Kelly said loudly.

All the lottery winners stared at him.

Astrid gently placed her hand on Luna's shoulder and spoke softly. "You must go to your assigned unit. That is what they want."

"Who are the Custodians?" Jeff asked. "You still haven't told us about them. And what do we get for following along?"

"You eat," Kelly replied

Jeff shook his head. He didn't appreciate feeling like an animal being trained, especially since he wasn't aware of who was doing the training.

Opal stepped in front of Kelly. "I'm not doing anything until I meet them, and they tell us exactly where we are and why we were brought here."

Jeff stepped beside her and crossed his arms. "Same here."

Kelly shook his head. "At ease, soldiers. Your ranks don't mean anything to the Custodians. The sooner you start to cooperate, the easier it will be for you. For all of you."

What Rufus Wants

Nestor explored one of the bedrooms where there was only one double bed and a bureau. The adjoining bedroom looked exactly the same. He went out to the living room where Rajni sat on the couch massaging her thighs.

"Did it pass your inspection?" she asked.

"Both rooms only have one bed each."

"I want my own room," Luna demanded. She'd been standing by the front door since they entered the unit.

Rajni stared up at Nestor. "I'll share with you."

"Are you sure?" Nestor felt uncomfortable sleeping on the same bed with a woman other than his wife. He still considered himself a married man.

"I'll take the one on the left." Luna barreled across the living room, entered the bedroom and slammed the door shut.

Nestor went after her.

"Leave her alone," Rajni said.

"She's probably missing her parents. I know I'm missing my wife and son."

"Give her some space to calm down."

Nestor nodded and went to sit down beside Rajni. "What do you think is going on here?"

"The only thing I can tell you is we're not dead. My legs are hurting from the walk back from the hexagon."

"But I died, Rajni."

"We left you. Maybe you survived."

Nestor felt his head. "I was hit pretty hard. I don't feel a bump or any pain."

"I'll gladly trade places with you." Rajni lay back against the couch.

"How can you just sit there?"

"Because I'm too dizzy to execute a pirouette."

Nestor felt his head again.

"And I find all of this intriguing," Rajni said.

"Intriguing? In what way?"

"If aliens really brought us here, a question I've been asking since I was a child will finally be answered."

"I forgot about how much you loved the paranormal."

"It's not so paranormal anymore. We're here, and this is all real."

"But none of this makes any sense. I'm completely healed."

"Nothing ever made sense to you before this happened. You told me that's why you became a documentarian, to answer the questions you had about life and get paid to travel while doing it."

"I still have questions, but I'm not getting paid anymore."

"But you're still traveling." Rajni smiled, hoping to cheer Nester up.

"To travel, you have to have freedom of movement. What if we're some kind of exhibit, placed here to be studied and harvested like cattle?"

"You could've made the same argument before all of this happened."

"I did...for my philosophy term paper in my junior year at college. And now I'm making a similar reactionary comment to this present inexplicable reality. And even if this...new reality is explained to all our satisfaction during the orientation, you can bet your life that some other inexplicable phenomena will present itself rendering everything once again inexplicable."

"You're giving me a bigger headache than the one I got from the humming in the hexagon. Can't you just take in what's happening, without making it into a grand mystery that needs to be solved?"

"I lost my wife and son, and I was shot. That's hard to overlook."

"I understand. But torturing yourself over what may or may not be happening isn't going to make you understand this situation better. And it's not going to bring back your family...or mine." Rajni cried thinking about her parents and Uncle Frank.

"All of our memories seem to be connected to a gold star," Nestor noted. "What do you think it means?"

"I thought it meant I was dying."

"Me too," Luna said as she opened the door. "My mom said everyone sees the Light of God before dying and that it means we're evolving."

"An interesting theory," Nestor said, even though he didn't believe it. He didn't want to hurt Luna's feelings.

"No, it isn't!" she said. "My mother wanted to calm my brother down. He was scared about what that weird scientist said about the sun, so she told him it had to do with evolution to calm him down."

"Did it work?" Rajni asked.

"It worked so well that the whole neighborhood got involved." Luna crossed her arms. "My mom got all the kids to paint a picture of the things they'd miss about Earth so they could remember what it looked like before everything changed."

"What did you paint?" Nestor asked.

"Nothing. The whole thing was a stupid idea."

"Your mother sounded like a very smart woman," Rajni said.

"What do you mean by *sounded*?"

"I didn't mean anything."

"You think she's dead! Why can't you tell me the truth rather than treat me like a baby!" Luna ran into her room and slammed the door.

Opal ran her hands against the wall, fascinated by the smooth texture.

"Which room do you want?" Pearl called out from inside one of the bedrooms.

"I don't care." Opal continued to feel the wall, wondering about the material from which it was made. She turned to Rufus, who was perched on her shoulder. "This place is extraordinary." She petted his head.

"I want Luna," he said.

"She made that big an impression on you?" Opal asked surprised. "The whiny ones usually annoy you."

"I want Luna," he said again.

"We'll go for a visit soon."

"Luna, Luna! I want Luna!"

"Yes, yes. She's not going anywhere. None of us are going anywhere."

Opal pressed her hand against the wall and gasped when she felt a warm vibration. "But I don't think I'll mind staying here for a while."

"You don't mind?" Pearl asked. "Before you were ready to start a mutiny with Lieutenant Theobald."

Opal turned to face her sister, who was now in the room with her. "Did you notice the material this building is made of? Whoever can create such technology is someone I'm interested in meeting."

"I see you still love your gadgets."

"This isn't a gadget, Pearl." Opal glided her hand against the window's surface that felt the same as the wall. "It's alive. It's breathing."

Pearl shook her head. "Haven't you figured this out yet? We're dead."

"We're not. Didn't you hear what Kelly said?"

"I don't care what he said. I know we're dead," Pearl insisted. "We have to be dead."

"Why do we *have* to be?"

"That's the natural order of things. We live, we die, and we go to heaven."

"I want Luna," Rufus said and then started screaming the girl's name.

"Hah!" Opal said to Pearl. "You just reminded me why I stopped going to church. All those rules and regulations made me realize religion is nothing but a load of—"

Rufus nipped Opal on the side of the cheek.

"Ow! What's gotten into you, Rufus?"

"Luna, Luna, Luna, Luna," Rufus said.

"What's that bird going on about?" Pearl asked.

"He wants to see Luna."

"He cheered her up. You should take him."

Opal rubbed the side of her face. Rufus never bit her before.

"Luna," Rufus continued.

Opal stroked his cheek and sighed. "All right. You win."

Opal and Pearl stared at all the panels, not recalling which one led to Luna's unit.

"I can't remember," Pearl said. "Can you?"

Opal shook her head, and Rufus flew off her shoulder. He landed on the last panel on the right side of the building.

"You trained him well," Pearl said.

"Not that well."

Pearl and Opal walked over to Rufus who flew back onto Opal's shoulder.

"See. We have to be dead."

"Will you stop with that already? We're not dead." Opal stood on the panel, and nothing happened.

Pearl knocked on the building, then quickly retracted her hand. "It's moving!"

"I know."

Opal pressed her hand on the wall. "And it matches the pulse of your heartbeat."

"Does it really?" Pearl's curiosity overshadowed her fear. She placed her left hand on the building and her right hand over her heart. When she felt the pulsing of the wall sync up with her heartbeat, she laughed. "It does! How about that!"

"Luna," Rufus said.

"We didn't forget you, Rufus." Opal stroked his belly.

A hum reverberated from all around them. The twins turned towards the hexagon. A large light pillar erupted from the roof, shot up into the sky, and pierced through the clouds.

"Whoever's in there now might be able to show us how to make a house call," Opal reasoned.

They made their way to the hexagon. Pearl was exhausted. She panted heavily trying to keep up with Opal. When they arrived at their destination, Pearl slowly maneuvered her plump body to the ground for a rest. Opal went to help her.

"I can do this myself," Pearl objected.

"Why must you be so stubborn?" Opal asked.

"Can we please sit here in silence without arguing?"

"I don't even know why you came with me."

"I want to make sure the child is okay."

"Looks like the Custodians are in need of counselors. Perhaps I should change careers."

Pearl leaned her head back against the wall and closed her eyes. Tears came pouring from them.

Opal sat beside her sister and held her hand. "I'm sorry, Pearl."

"So am I."

The two remained silent until Astrid stepped out of the hexagon.

"What are you two doing here?" she asked. "Our orientation will not begin until this evening."

"How are we supposed to get in touch with each other? I didn't see a doorbell or translinker in our unit," Opal said as she helped her sister to her feet.

"Why should we see a doorbell when we can't even see the door?" Pearl asked.

"I want Luna," Rufus said.

"You'll see her soon." Opal petted him.

"Everything will be explained during the orientation," Astrid said.

"I want Luna." Rufus flapped his wings.

"He is very determined," Pearl said.

"In that case, we better give him what he wants." Astrid smiled and caressed Rufus's side wing with her index finger.

Opal sat beside Blaze and avoided looking at him because every time she did, she recalled shooting him. Pearl tried hard not to stare at his tattoos.

Blaze sensed he was making the twins uncomfortable, and he got up to leave.

"You're a very good storyteller," Opal said. "Your Drake Kent Series is my favorite."

"Seems to be everyone's favorite." Blaze sat back down and pointed at Opal. "You look familiar."

Opal's heart beat fast, and she squeezed the front of the sofa cushion. "Get that all the time. I have a familiar face."

Blaze nodded. "Well, I'm glad to hear you appreciate the series." He leaned forward and spoke quietly. "Believe it or not, I'd sometimes forget I had other books published. I considered devoting the rest of my story ideas to Drake Kent. Astrid talked me out of it."

Astrid came out of the bedroom. "I am glad you listened. You would have severely limited yourself to the testosterone, beer, and football crowd."

"You're insulting one of our guests who happens to like Drake Kent," Blaze said.

"My apologies." Astrid smiled as she held three chain necklaces with crystal spheres. She handed one each to Blaze, Opal, and Pearl.

"Don't care much for jewelry," Opal said.

"Don't be so rude, Opal." Pearl smiled at Astrid. "They're lovely." Pearl put hers around her neck.

Blaze inspected the sphere. "I'm with Opal. This isn't my style."

"They are used for communication," Astrid said. "If you want to visit someone, you need to have the crystal with you when you stand on the panel. This will let the person inside know you're calling on them. You will also need it to enter the hexagon."

"I want Luna," Rufus proclaimed and fluffed his feathers.

"In that case, I better take it." Opal slipped the chain around her neck.

"I can see who's the boss in your relationship." Blaze laughed.

"You got that right," Pearl agreed. "Rufus is the only one I know that can get Opal to do what he wants. No human ever had that kind of power over my sister."

Astrid petted Rufus. "He certainly is an amazing bird."

Recouplings

Astrid lay naked on Blaze's bare chest, tracing his Aum tattoo with her index finger. Although he appeared vastly different since their last meeting, she was ecstatic to be with him again. Nevertheless, Blaze still didn't trust the current circumstance he found himself in, even after a highly charged reunion.

"Talk to me," Blaze said as he examined the very sterile looking bedroom. It was the ideal writing room for him.

"What would you like me to say?" Astrid asked.

"Anything. You don't know how much I missed your accent." Blaze kissed her.

"And I missed you. As troubled as I was when the Custodians told me they lost your signal, I could not believe I would never see you again."

"Tell me about them."

"They are a very advanced intelligence. Compared to them, we are like mice."

"Are you trying to make me wish I wasn't here with you?"

Astrid leaned onto her elbow and examined his tattoos. "You have changed a lot since I last saw you."

"I didn't have an easy time after you...after I thought you died."

"How did you think I died?"

"You...don't remember?"

"Last thing I remember is going to sleep after my performance." Astrid rolled onto her back and stared at the ceiling. "I miss my cello. The only time I get to play it is in the pillar, but it's not the same."

Blaze could see she was in pain and couldn't bear making her hurt any more. "You left my world after a brain aneurysm stole you away from me."

"Did I feel anything?"

"I don't think so. You had a smile on your face." He looked away from Astrid, not feeling comfortable about lying.

"I am happy to hear that." She kissed him. "Are you hungry?"

"Starving."

Astrid left the bedroom and returned with four small black cubes on a plate. Blaze didn't notice them because he was admiring her naked body.

Astrid handed the plate to him. "I saved these for you."

"What are they?"

"Food." She got back into bed.

Blaze picked up one of the cubes and examined it. "You're kidding?"

Astrid shook her head and smiled.

Blaze tossed the cube into his mouth and chewed. "Tastes like nothing."

"For now."

Blaze was about to question Astrid about what she meant, but her smile pushed his concerns to the back of his mind. "I missed you so much." He hugged her. "I never thought I'd see you again."

"How long did you think I was dead? We have no calendar here."

"Three years. You have no way of keeping time here?"

"Kelly made a sundial. He also tracked the days before my arrival but soon stopped when he realized there was no reason for doing so." Astrid turned away from Blaze.

"What's wrong?" he asked.

"I have something I must tell you, and it may upset you."

"I can never get upset with you, Astrid"

"I am glad to hear you say that because I never lied to you, and I don't want to start now."

"You can tell me anything. You always could. Things aren't any different now"—Blaze looked around the room—"except for this strange environment."

"And it can get lonely here. I had a hard time adjusting. I do not think I would have lasted here without Kelly."

"What are you trying to say, Astrid?"

"I was in a relationship with him."

The words seared Blaze's heart. "Do you love him?"

"Yes. However, not in the same way I love you. I told him if you ended up here with us, I would return to you."

"I don't know what to say, other than I don't like Kelly all that much and that next time I see him I'll want to knock him on his ass. But I can't blame you. You've been alone here...and I've been lonely without you."

"Have you had many relationships?" Astrid asked.

"Why don't we forget the last three years happened and continue from right now? It'll be as if we were never apart."

"I can go along with that."

"And the less I know about you and Kelly, the easier it'll be for me to talk to the guy."

"He is a very nice man. I am sure you will get along with him once you get to know him."

"I'm not so sure. Apart from you, everything else about this place is alien to me."

"Like what?"

"Everything. The hexagon, this building, the food, the mountains that surround this place. It's just so..."

"Alien." Astrid giggled.

Blaze adored Astrid's laugh. He rolled her onto her back and kissed her.

Rajni returned to her unit after a short walk. She kept active daily to prevent her leg muscles from atrophying but also because she didn't want to forget how to use them. Each step she took was planned, and the slightest miscalculation led to a fall.

Nestor noticed her left leg dragging as she walked to the couch. He remembered seeing her walk similarly when they were married and had blamed her gait back then on her drinking. He got up to assist her, and she pushed him away.

"I'm not an invalid." Rajni slowly lowered herself onto the couch.

"I know. I only wanted to help."

"Don't."

Nestor gave her a sympathetic glance, and Rajni rolled her eyes. "I liked it better when you thought I was a drunk."

"I'm still trying to figure that one out. Why you'd rather have me believe you were an alcoholic."

"I hate when people feel sorry for me. I was treated differently, and it depressed me. It was as though I had a label stitched onto my shirt that read, '*Sick person here; treat her as if she lost her life and has nothing left in life to do but die.*'"

Nestor thought about Becky and how effortless communication was with her. With Rajni, each conversation was a Russian roulette of words.

Rajni perceived Nestor's displeasure, given away by his finger tapping on his thighs. "My apologies that you have to room with someone who isn't as perfect as you."

"I'm not perfect." Nestor was tiring of this particular label, which to him felt as repulsive as the word, "sick" did to Rajni.

"If Anya doesn't return, I'm going to ask for my own room." Rajni stared at the bedroom door. "Good idea. I don't want to share a bed with you."

"I planned on sleeping on the couch."

"I insist that you do." Rajni sounded cold, but she cried inside when she recalled Nestor's life slipping away in front of her.

"I love it when we agree," he said.

Luna's bedroom door opened, and she slowly stepped outside her sanctuary.

Nestor smiled. "Welcome back." He patted the cushion. "Would you like to have a seat?"

"Does anyone know what day it is here?"

"If this were the same place from where we came from, today would be Saturday."

"Are any of you Jewish?"

"I'm Catholic," Rajni said.

Luna peered at Nestor who shifted around on his seat. "I was raised Eastern Orthodox."

"What are you now?" Luna asked.

Rajni glanced at Nestor, wondering how he'd respond.

He cleared his throat. "Nothing...I'm nothing."

Luna squinted her eyes. "What does that mean?"

"I don't like to discuss religion with people of faith."

Luna crossed her arms. "I can take it."

"It can sound upsetting."

"I don't get upset by stuff like that. My parents were—I mean are—always debating about religion. My father never came to the synagogue with us, and it made my mother upset."

"Did he practice a different religion?" Rajni asked.

"They're both Jewish, but my father is an atheist. My mother doesn't think that's a good excuse for him not coming with us. What do you think?"

Nestor smiled. "Sounds like my kind of guy."

"So what's your reason?" Luna asked.

"My reason for what?"

"For not believing in God."

"Rajni doesn't appreciate this type of discussion."

"Why do you care now?" Rajni said as she grazed her fingers across the front of her neck. "You already told me all about how the Western Civilization's idea of God is childish and immature, and you compare those of us who worship Him to kids who believe in Santa Claus."

Luna snickered, and Nestor was relieved she wasn't upset. But he was.

"Why did you blurt that out?" he asked Rajni. "What did you want to accomplish?"

"To prove that you're a condescending elitist! You would've made a great Aristocrat!" Rajni got up, stormed to the bedroom, and slammed the door.

"There's a lot of that going on today." Nestor smiled at Luna. "Anything else you'd like to talk about?"

Luna returned to her room and shut the door. Nestor sighed and wondered how he ended up with two of the most temperamental women of the group.

Right after the Dreamflyer had crashed, Seth Marconi encountered the same golden star experienced by the lottery winners. He then awoke in the hexagon with Anya. After the whiteness had dispersed, they met Astrid outside of the hexagon.

"Welcome home," she said.

Anya and Seth looked at each other and then at Astrid.

"Where are we?" Anya asked.

"I cannot answer that."

"Why not?" Seth asked as he scanned the surrounding mountains. "Are we dead?"

"You are not dead," Astrid told them.

"Do you hear that?" Anya said. "I hear music."

Astrid and Seth gawked at Anya because they heard nothing.

"There's no music," Seth noted. "There's no sound at all. Not even a bird."

Anya's face lit up. "The music! It's coming from over that mountain!" Anya pointed towards the peak beyond the dormitory.

"I don't hear anything," Astrid said.

"I gotta go!" Anya ran towards the mountain.

Seth and Astrid chased after her as she headed for the western path.

"You must stay here!" Astrid yelled. "It's not safe away from the refuge if you do not know where you are going, and it will be getting dark soon!"

"I know what's up there!" Anya yelled back.

Astrid gave up the chase and allowed Seth to carry on with the pursuit.

Seth soon caught up to Anya, who was now walking.

"What do you think you'll find?" Seth asked.

"I'll know it when I see it."

The two followed the path northward until they found another trail that led up the mountain. It took a half-day of climbing for Seth and Anya to arrive at the apex. At this height, they could see that the mountains were carved into concentric rings, and they seemed to stretch out infinitely.

Seth slowly turned around and observed more of the same on the southern side. "We're in a giant annular maze."

In the near distance was a tall spiraling peak that from Seth's perspective appeared to be the central point of the maze. Motioning to it, he said, "We can get a better view from up there."

Seth was an adventurer as much as he was ruthless. His travels usually included some physicality such as mountain climbing, bike riding, sailing, skiing, skydiving. He had climbed Kilimanjaro and the Himalayas. He even rode his bike across the European continent and conducted his business while on the road. During the trip, Seth was barraged by reporters whenever he stopped for a break. He ended each interview with the phrase, "It's good to be rich. You can do whatever the hell you want." He'd then hop onto his bike and ride off. Seth had a talent for manipulating the media. Nevertheless, at this moment, he wasn't working anyone. He'd become a follower, trailing behind his secretary.

Anya stopped and pointed towards the horizon. "Over there! It's the golden star! The same one I saw before I died!"

"You saw it too?"

Anya turned to Seth. "What did you see?"

"A bright gold star materialized in front of me while I was on the Dreamflyer. I thought it meant I was dying, but now I'm not so sure we're dead."

"Do you see it now?" Anya asked. "It's in front of that peak you just pointed at."

Seth glanced up at the heavens. "All I see now is a moonlit sky. None of this is connecting. I left Earth. I know I did."

"We gotta find a way to cross these rings."

"Unless you have wings to fly, there's no way we can make it over—"

"I'm going to check it out." Anya rushed ahead on the trail, and Seth followed after her.

The two paused when they came to a natural stone bridge that stretched across to the next peak. Anya smiled. "Beautiful. This whole place is beautiful." She gazed out into the horizon.

Seth gawked at Anya, who to him appeared as though she were intoxicated.

"It looks too narrow to walk on," he cautioned. "We should return to that complex and find out where we are."

"I can sense a presence calling to us."

"I'm going back," Seth said, desperately trying to reclaim his leadership role.

Anya stepped onto the bridge and began to slowly walk along the hazardous crossing.

"Come back here, Anya!"

She advanced without hesitating. Seth hopped onto the bridge and followed behind her.

"I guess you never arrived at your promised land with Xavier," Anya said as he caught up to her.

"How did you figure that out?" He laughed under his breath. "Do you really think I'm the symbolic darkness of Earth?"

"I did..." Anya lost her balance and spread out her arms.

Seth put his hand around her side to assist.

"I'm okay. I just gotta keep talking. Makes it easier for me to keep going."

"You've been with me for ten years. How long have you felt that way about me?"

"Ten years." Anya stared into the horizon and recited a poem as she carefully continued stepping along the crossing.

He has no eyes to see the light.
He has no lips to speak the right.
No nose to smell the flowers,
Beneath the plane of heaven's towers.
He has no ears to hear.
The beauty of a soundless cheer.

A shroud he wears upon his face.
To seek and find the human race.
But what he fails to comprehend,
Reality has never been his friend.
And what he thinks he already knows.
Recreates his destined flaws.

He is the man without a face.
Now he must run a quicker pace.
For what he doesn't want to see.
Is the only thing that can set him free.
Face unmasked; future past
Coming fast; he cannot last.

His shelter isolates his zone.
He melts into a blank unknown.
Here he fits within the scheme,
Of an ordinary person's dream.
He screams to wake himself up.

As his true will pleads to erupt.

The answer is quite obvious.
He must find his inner-conscience.
Lingering on in quiet sleep.
He can faintly hear his silent weep.
Dripping down along his cheek.
He knows he is the master freak.

Anya reached the end of the bridge and jumped onto the ground. Seth trailed behind her.

"I wrote that poem the second year after I started working for you," Anya told him.

"Why didn't you quit?"

"The pay was too good, and I had to take care of my mother." Anya's eyes became watery as she thought about their last discussion. "She never thanked me. Didn't expect her to, but it would've been nice to hear."

"I wish you wrote my epic. You know me well," Seth said glumly as he looked up at the tall spiraling peak they were now directly in front of.

"You wouldn't have liked what I would've written. I don't lie in my poetry. I try not to lie about anything. Lies make everything heavy. All I want to feel is..." Anya pointed towards the horizon. "Light!"

"I see it too!"

They walked towards the precipice, and Anya's eyes lit up. "It's showing me the way!" Anya laughed like a school girl and went to take a step forward.

Seth pulled her back. "That's a long drop."

"Don't you see the lights? They're showing us the way." Anya pushed herself away from Seth and jumped off the mountain. She remained suspended in mid-air and continued walking forward.

After Seth's shock had worn off, he picked up a rock and tossed it over the edge. It fell. He sat and hung his feet off the ledge. Nothing kept them from following the law of gravity. He watched as Anya continued onward, without looking back. When she disappeared from Seth's line of sight, the light exploded, brightened and then disappeared.

Seth jumped onto his feet terrified. "Anya!" He called her name out repeatedly until his voice gave out. Everything around him was dark, and he couldn't locate the path back to the refuge. He sat and ruminated over Anya and her poem.

Everything was quiet, not even a bird in the sky or the sound of crickets. The silence was unbearable. Seth rolled onto his side and told himself if he could survive being tortured he could easily survive a night without noise. He thought about everything from the 1st sector war to his wife, and finally to losing his fortune, and his religion. He was now a man without a face, in the dark. All alone.

House Calls

Opal stood on Nestor and Rajni's panel, and her crystal sphere lit up. "Oh look at this!" She held out the crystal. "This place is like an amusement park for adults!"

"Or an insane asylum."

Rajni opened the door, and before she could utter a word, Opal asked, "How did you know we were here? Is there a doorbell?"

"Ask one question at a time," Pearl said. "You're overwhelming the poor woman."

"Can I help you?" Rajni inquired as Rufus flew over her shoulder and into the unit.

"There's a bird in here, Raj!" Nestor called out from inside.

Rufus's eagerness to leave hurt Opal, and she began to cry.

"Are you crying?" Pearl asked in disbelief. "All because Rufus flew away? We've got bigger problems than that."

"Why don't you come in." Rajni put her arm around Opal and led her inside just as Luna opened her bedroom door to see what all the ruckus was about.

Rufus flew to her and perched upon her shoulder.

"See that," Pearl beamed. "Everything's okay."

Opal sat on the couch. She was happy that Rufus comforted Luna and tried to conceive why she'd reacted so emotionally. That wasn't how she usually handled conflict. As a joined forces officer, Opal dealt with far worse situations. Even a three day hike through the jungle dodging enemy fire failed to break her.

Nestor sat beside Opal. "You came at just the right time. She locked herself in her room and refused to come out."

"Don't thank me. Rufus insisted on coming here."

"What an amazing bird!" Nestor said.

"I'm a pretty bird," Rufus responded. "Kissy kiss." He delicately pecked Luna's cheek, and she laughed.

Pearl leaned in and whispered to Nestor. "I'm a retired counselor. Come get me if Luna needs to talk. Or even you and Rajni."

"I don't need a shrink," Luna said. "I'm going out for a walk."

"We don't know if it's safe here," Rajni warned.

"You can't take Rufus with you," Opal said to Luna. "You can only hold him in here."

A chime sounded. Opal and Nestor scanned the room.

"I can't find a speaker anywhere." Nestor glanced at Opal. "Can you see where it's coming from?"

Opal shook her head. "I found nothing. It's as if the sound is coming from all around us"—she gestured toward her head—"and inside us."

"That's impossible," Nestor said.

"But not as impossible as whatever material the Custodians used to construct this building."

Nestor nodded as he continued to survey the room.

Pearl whispered to Rajni. "I see you have to deal with the same thing. My sister hasn't stopped going on about how extraordinary everything is around here."

The door chime sounded again.

"Guess I'll answer." Rajni went to the door and pressed a small button on a panel. The door slid open.

Astrid smiled from the other side of the doorway. "My apologies if I have come at the wrong time." She held out three crystal spheres. "These are for you."

Luna stepped outside with Rufus on her shoulder. "Those are so cool!"

"Glad you like them." Astrid handed one to Luna and gave the other two to Rajni. After she'd explained their purpose, Luna asked if it was safe to walk outside.

"Very safe," Astrid said, "as long as you don't climb any of the surrounding mountains."

"Can I go out now?" Luna asked Rajni, not understanding why a stranger had control over her actions.

Rajni nodded. "Have fun."

"I will." Luna went back inside to deliver Rufus to Opal.

"I want Luna," Rufus said when Opal extended her arm to him.

"We have to go now, Rufus. You can see Luna tomorrow." She directed her hand closer to Rufus who bit her thumb.

Opal looked at Rufus and cried. Hurt and embarrassed by her emotional display, she ran out of the unit.

Pearl caught up with Opal, who was heading toward the western side of the refuge. "Let's talk," Pearl said out of breath.

"You got five minutes. After that, my warm-up will be over, and you'll be miles behind me."

"Keeping your pain to yourself won't help you."

"I don't like leaving my bird in the hands of strangers."

"Did you say *bird*? Is this truly Opal Halifax speaking about Rufus, discounting his name and treating him more like a possession?"

"It's me."

"Then I never knew you."

Opal stopped and thrust her finger in Pearl's face. A fresh outpouring of tears rained down her cheeks. "You never knew me because you never took the time to know me. I'm not a machine! I can be hurt!"

Pearl didn't need her training as a counselor to figure out this went beyond Rufus. "You're right. I didn't."

"Is that why you betrayed me so easily?"

When Pearl didn't answer, Opal ran off. Pearl watched her until she disappeared into the western path, then slowly made her way back to her unit.

Rajni, who'd been outside watching Luna enter the eastern path, noticed Pearl struggling to walk. Forgetting about her own limitations, she ran over to assist.

"Thank you, dear."

"How is your sister?"

"Don't worry about her. She'll be all right."

Rajni assisted Pearl to her unit and helped her onto the couch. She was glad to be able to help someone else for a change, but her own legs had become fatigued by the walk.

"You can stay for a while if you'd like," Pearl said. "I could use the company."

"So could I." Rajni eased herself onto the couch.

"What's your disease?" Pearl asked.

"I'm surprised you noticed. People usually think I'm drunk."

"Takes one to know one. I have cancer. It's inoperable."

"Multiple sclerosis. It's a lifetime prison sentence."

Pearl closed her eyes. "We can't be dead."

"Because we're still sick," Rajni said.

"Where do you think we are?"

"I'm too disoriented to even guess."

"What if this is hell? It would explain why we're suffering."

"Luna wouldn't be here if we were in hell," Rajni said.

"I died after being shot, and none of you could've survived what happened."

"But we did." Rajni thought about the vision she had after the shuttle crash. "We fix, so you continue."

"What?"

Rajni recounted her vision to Pearl. The two then mused over various places they could possibly be, from another dimension to a distant planet. None of these scenarios comforted Pearl. The uncertainty of where she was or whether she died from a bullet that pierced her skull eroded the foundation of her faith.

After Rajni had left, Pearl slowly got onto her knees and prayed. She went through one *Our Father* and ended with ten *Hail Marys*. Pearl kept praying until she perceived the same connection she felt each time at mass. Pearl promised herself to do this once a day. Her faith was the only thing that kept her from giving up.

Secret Places

Luna continued along the eastern path with Rufus on her shoulder. She stopped to admire Kelly's sundial. Rocks of varying shapes and sizes encircled a thick branch positioned in the center.

"11 AM. Plenty of time until lunch."

"Lunch time. Cracker time," Rufus said.

"I'm not even hungry."

"Hungry, I'm hungry."

Luna giggled and headed eastward while Rufus continued his vocalizations. Luna speculated over where they could be. Were they in Gan Eden? Was Gan Eden even real? She wanted to believe it could be now more than ever because her family was gone. Luna started to accept that she'd never see them again, but she stopped short of sorting through the implications. She was disappointed that she was the only Jew amongst the lottery winners and puzzled over why it mattered to her. She had friends of all faiths, including her best friend Jodi who was Protestant. Thinking about her made Luna cry. She caressed Rufus, and the action comforted her, reminding her she wasn't alone.

The farther from the refuge Luna walked, the more spacious her mind became. She forgot everything that was bothering her and continued her stroll until she arrived by a cliffside. The path veered to the north and south. "Which way should I go, Rufus?" Luna looked left, and then right.

Rufus flew off her shoulder and headed northward.

"Rufus come back!" Luna chased after him. He flew in a circle until Luna caught up, then continued ahead.

Luna chased him until she came to a narrow opening between two ridges. "A hidden path!" Luna gazed up at Rufus who circled overhead. She entered the crevice, and when she emerged from out of the other side, she found herself in a clearing with another mountain directly in front of her.

Rufus flew towards the south. Luna continued the pursuit until he landed on a rocky ledge protruding from the cliff face. When she neared him, Rufus took off again and led her to a path due west. Luna ran until she reached a dead-end.

Rufus flew down and landed on her shoulder. "Almost there. Follow me."

"I'm tired, Rufus."

"Almost there. Follow me."

Rufus took flight again, and Luna followed him around one last bend. When she turned the corner, Luna's mouth flew open as she gazed upon a garden of sunflowers, spanning all the way to the next row of mountains. Rufus descended and perched on her shoulder.

"You really are an amazing bird, Rufus! This place is so cool!"

Luna ran to the sunflowers and got lost between the tall stems. When she got tired, Luna stopped and plucked a flower off its stem. Rubbing her fingers against the petals, she thought about how her family and Jodi would appreciate the beauty here. She cried, and the loneliness inside her swelled and begged to be released. Luna slowly raised the sunflower up to the sky and began to sing "Sh'ma Yisrael." Luna had sung the sacred hymn many times before, but she now connected to each word. Her voice was clear, each note perfect in pitch, and she sang with committed intention. Her crying intensified, but she continued. She felt joined to her family through her singing. After Luna had finished the song, she lowered her arms and petted Rufus. "This is our secret place. We won't tell anyone about this garden. Okay?"

"Lovely Luna. Lovely flowers," Rufus responded.

"We should go back. Rajni and Nestor are probably worried."

Rufus flew off her shoulder and guided her back to the path. She turned to have another look at the sunflowers, and Rufus landed on her shoulder.

"I feel better Rufus. Every seven days, we'll return here and sing together."

Opal ran for two miles and stopped when she spotted a cranny. The sun shone high in the sky, and she knew she had enough daylight to do some exploring. She crammed herself through and ended up in the next ring. The path directly in front of her split to the north and south. So she wouldn't get lost, Opal noted Sun's position in the sky, then headed south until she came across a smaller mountain. To the east was a lush, tropical environment of ferns, lower lying trees, orchids, air plants and palm trees. She pushed through branches and leaves, enjoying the cool breeze that brushed across her skin. All her worries were obscured by the beautiful scenery, and she wanted to distance herself more. She continued on for another quarter mile until she spotted a waterfall that emptied into a large wading pond. She washed her face then sampled some of the water. Deciding it was safe, she drank some more.

Opal got up and decided to head back, but she took a different path that ended on the eastern side of the oasis where there was a cave. She realized the error, but her curiosity made her continue. She entered into a large cavern with an indigo glow reflecting off the walls. A crackling sound lured her farther inside to investigate. She entered a narrow passageway that widened into another cavern. An indigo fire burned in the center, floating several inches off the ground. Opal lay on her side to examine the enigma. She couldn't identify anything that would explain how the fire was produced. Something about the flames drew her to them. She sat up, placed her palms in front of the blaze and felt at peace. A tingling sensation between her inner brow made her want to shut her eyes.

"Commander?"

Opal bolted up and breathed out in relief when she saw Jeff. "What are you doing here?"

"Exploring." He had initially gone outside his unit to clear his head. When Jeff saw Opal wandering off, he went after her. He thought that being in the company of another soldier would help get his mind off Darla, and he also wanted to discuss their current predicament. However, it was the flames that caught his attention now.

"What's your take on it, Lieutenant?"

"I can't even venture a guess." Jeff walked around the fire. "I never saw green fire before."

"It's indigo."

"Looks green to me." He moved toward the flames and placed his hand over his chest. Each beat of his heart produced a euphoric sensation that pumped into every cell of his body. "And I'm having the...oddest reaction to it."

"The tingling between your eyes?" Opal asked.

"In my chest. It's similar to the feeling you get when you're intensely happy."

Puzzled, Opal stared at the fire. "I'm not color blind, and I know you can't be because you're on active duty." Opal rubbed her chin.

"Yet we're seeing a different color," he said.

"Fascinating."

"You took the words right out of my mouth, Commander." Jeff walked around the fire. "The flames seem to be reacting to nothing."

"Before you arrived, I was trying to figure the same thing out."

Jeff halted and looked at Opal. "I read about you during basic training. You made quite an impression."

"No time for hero worship now," Opal replied. "We need to figure out where we are."

"Think I agree with the kid. This is one weird place."

"And impossible." Opal pointed to the fire. "This shouldn't exist." She stared into the flames. "But here it is existing."

Jeff smiled at Opal's curiosity because she wasn't the only one enthralled by the environment. "If this were a base, I'd request to be assigned here...temporarily."

"And I'd come out of retirement to explore it, but there's something about this place I don't trust. What's your take?"

"I never trusted any situation I was in."

"We should keep watch over everything going on here."

Jeff nodded. "How about getting Blaze to help?"

Opal shook her head. "Did you pick up on how he looked at Astrid when he first saw her? He can't be trusted. How about Nestor?"

"Maybe. We should keep an eye on him for a while first. He asked if I thought this was a PSYOP."

"He could be testing your reaction," Opal surmised.

"My thoughts exactly."

"We'll keep a close eye on him then."

"Agreed," Jeff said while trying to figure out a logical explanation for the differing colors of the fire.

"We'll meet here again and report our findings," Opal said.

"What about Kelly, Hiroko, and Astrid?"

"We'll have to monitor where they go each day."

"When do you want to meet?"

"Every two days. Same time." Opal went to unclip her translinker from her belt and then remembered she didn't have it any longer. She chuckled when Jeff did the same automatic action. "We really are creatures of habit."

"There's a large sundial near the start of the eastern path," Jeff said. "I caught the time before I left. It was roughly 1400 hours. Took me about two hours to walk here."

"We'll rendezvous two days from now at the east ridge, at the end of the entrance path, at 1300 hours."

"I'll be there, Commander."

"We should get going now. The orientation meeting will be starting at 1700. You leave first, and I'll follow behind you."

Jeff saluted her. "Pleasure to serve with you, Commander."

"At ease, Lieutenant. You don't need to stand at attention." She smiled. "Although a little hero worship might be fun after we figure things out." She winked an eye and left feeling more alive. She needed a sense of purpose to get her mind off Rufus.

Opal approached the western path, and Seth Marconi ran towards her. Without her gun in hand, she hurried toward the security of the refuge.

Seth looked crazed with his arms flapping about wildly as he ran. This was not how he typically presented himself, but he believed Anya was in peril.

"I'm so glad I found someone," Seth told her, gasping.

Opal quickened her stride and prepared herself for a fight. "I'm not alone."

"My friend is in trouble. We have to organize a rescue team to find her."

Opal took another look at Seth. Upon recognizing who he was, she slowed her pace. "Where is she?"

"We climbed that mountain." Seth pointed towards the peak. "When we got to the top, we crossed a stone bridge and saw a gold light."

"Did it look like a star?"

"You saw it too?"

"Me...along with everyone else here."

"Do you know what it means?" Seth asked. "Are we dead?"

"We're not dead."

"Are you sure?"

"As sure as I can be."

"Then it's more imperative that we keep away from that star. When my friend went towards it, she disappeared. I think she might've gotten electrocuted."

"There's a meeting starting shortly. We'll get a team up there to find your friend." She extended her hand towards Seth. "I'm Opal."

"Seth."

"I know. Heard you were here. They're expecting you back at the refuge."

"Do you know who *they* are?" Seth asked. "The ones who are running this place?"

"I know as much as you do. Maybe we'll get some answers at the meeting."

The Hexagon

The lottery winners were gathered in front of the hexagon when Opal and Seth arrived. Opal observed Rufus on Luna's shoulder and went over to say hello to her beloved bird. She leaned down and petted Rufus. "Hi pretty birdy."

"Pretty birdy. I'm a pretty birdy," Rufus said.

Opal extended her arm for Rufus to climb on to, but he turned his head away. Pearl came over and rubbed her back to demonstrate her support.

Blaze pointed his hand towards Seth once he spotted him. He delighted in Seth's disheveled appearance and became agitated when Astrid gazed at Seth sympathetically. "That bastard doesn't deserve your pity."

"I agree," Nestor said. "If I weren't an atheist, I'd believe Seth Marconi is the devil."

Seth's eyes widened when he recognized Blaze. "Blaze Kenyon?" Seth asked.

Blaze crossed his arms. "I'm surprised you remember my name."

Seth was even more taken aback when he noticed Hiroko, who was with Jeff. "Hiro? How did you get here?"

"The same way you did," Hiroko explained. "Do you recognize these people?"

Seth observed everyone and when he exchanged glances with Jeff, he put it all together.

"I remember you." Jeff glared at Seth.

"They're the lottery winners from your shuttle that crashed ten years ago," Hiroko clarified.

Seth looked down at Luna.

"There were no babies on the flight."

"We haven't been able to figure that one out yet," Kelly said.

Nestor eyed Seth suspiciously. "Did you have anything to do with all of this?"

Opal and Jeff glanced at each other and then at Seth anticipating his answer.

"I admit I had a lot of power. But not over the sun." Seth rubbed the scar on his face. "We should all be dead, but for some reason we're not."

"You are correct. We are alive," Astrid confirmed.

"Anya disappeared. We have to find her," Seth said.

"What did you do to her?" Blaze yelled.

Astrid was curious about his passionate response. "Do you know her?"

"She's been a slam artist over at Benny's. We've been friends for years."

"How many years?" Astrid asked.

"We don't have time for this," Kelly interrupted. "We have to be ready to start tomorrow morning."

"Ready to start what?" Jeff asked. "You still haven't even told us what this place is."

"It's our refuge," Kelly said.

"But where is it?" Jeff pointed to Moon. "Are we on Earth?"

"Aren't any of you hearing me?" Seth said loudly. "Anya is missing! We have to go find her."

Blaze walked directly in front of Seth and thrust his finger in front of his face. "No one is buying your phony concern! You probably killed her!"

"That is enough!" Astrid said. "Please find a more civil way to deal with your disagreements."

"This isn't a disagreement!" Seth yelled. "Anya is missing! We have to find her now!" He peered at Blaze. "Will you go with me to find her?"

Blaze refused to recognize Seth's obvious concern even though his Bradley Simpson energy zapping stare was replaced by fear and confusion.

Jeff approached Opal. "We can head a search party, Commander."

Opal nodded. "Think it should be just you and me since we don't know what's up there."

"Thanks," Seth said, relieved. "I'm glad some people here are showing a little compassion—"

"Now's not the time for heroics!" Kelly yelled out. "We must continue with the orientation."

"You'll have to postpone it," Seth said. "We have to go look for Anya."

"It's almost dark," Hiroko noted. "We can't search for her now."

"Do you have access to flashlights?" Opal asked.

"We don't," Kelly said. "We'll have to wait till the morning."

"We can't leave her alone all night," Seth argued.

"She chose to leave," Astrid added. "I warned both of you not to go."

"And you're punishing her for a bad decision? This place has robbed you of your Humanity."

"Who robbed you of yours?" Blaze asked.

"Get over your petty need to look like the bigger man! This isn't about you or me! Anya is missing!"

Luna petted Rufus to keep herself from crying. Rajni placed her hand on Luna's shoulder to comfort her, but Luna didn't want to be comforted. She pushed Rajni's hand away.

"Climbing the mountains is dangerous," Kelly said.

"Who told you that?" Jeff asked.

Astrid cupped the crystal sphere hanging from her neck. "The Custodians. They tell me we must stay within the first two rings."

"Rings?" Jeff repeated.

"This place is a maze, and we're the rats," Seth said.

"I don't like any of this." Jeff shook his head.

"What you like or don't like is irrelevant," Kelly said. "We're here, and we're not leaving anytime soon. We'll have an easier time if we work as a team."

"How can we call ourselves a team if we don't search for one of us who is missing?" Nestor asked.

"Leaving was her decision." Kelly turned towards Seth. "If you want to go look for Anya, I won't stop you. But Astrid, Hiroko, and I won't be going up to find you if you disappear. We've been here longer than you and have a better understanding of how things around here work." Kelly inspected everyone to ensure they had on their crystal spheres. "We should all go inside now." He stood on the panel in front of the door to the hexagon. It slid open, and he entered.

Astrid and Hiroko followed behind him.

Seth hesitated and gazed up towards the mountain he'd descended from. The words from Anya's poem lingered. He was the man without a face, and had never felt that way more than he did in this moment. Seth wanted to go after her, but he was too frightened to climb the mountain alone. Gone was his adventurous streak, and he followed everyone into the hexagon.

Luna hesitated. "I don't want to go in there."

"You'll be okay," Rajni assured her.

"How do you know?"

"Astrid and Kelly are all right, and they've been in there before."

"I don't care."

Kelly stepped outside. "Is there a problem?"

"Luna doesn't want to go in," Rajni said.

"I can answer myself!" Luna leered at Kelly. "I'm not going in there."

"Then you won't eat."

"I don't care."

"Where are you going to get food for your bird?"

Luna thought about the sunflower field. There was enough food there for Rufus. She petted him again.

"Luna go, Luna go," Rufus said.

Rajni and Kelly shot a surprised glance at Rufus.

"Even the bird agrees with me," Kelly pointed out.

"His name is Rufus, and he wants me to go *away* from this place."

"I'm closing the door now," Kelly said.

Luna looked up at Rajni. "You can go."

"I'm staying with you."

"Then I'm going in." Luna pushed her way past Kelly and entered the hexagon.

Luna went to step on a circular glass panel in the center of the hexagon, and Astrid grabbed her arm. "Never stand on the panel when others are in the room."

"Why not?" Luna asked.

"Only one person at a time can be in here when the pillar is activated," Hiroko said.

"Why didn't it matter when we first arrived here?" Opal asked. "With all the scrambling around we did, I'm sure more than one of us stepped on it."

"It was set to retrieve your patterns," Astrid said. "I was told it could do either that or what we are about to show you now."

Rufus began to sing the first lines of "Dream a Little Dream of Me."

Hiroko pointed at him. "That is truly one amazing bird."

The lottery winners stared at Rufus, fascinated.

"And he is exactly in the pitch's center," Astrid added. She knew this because she had perfect pitch.

"He also seems to be a psychic," Hiroko said, amused. "That's exactly what you're all going to learn here today, how to dream a dream."

"What happens if there's more than one of us in here when the pillar is activated?" Seth asked, unimpressed.

"We don't know," Astrid admitted. "The three of us never attempted it before."

"So you just follow along with what they tell you? Without asking why you're here?" Seth looked around the room for support, but the only responses he received were angry stares from Jeff and Kelly. Out of everyone, they made him feel the most uncomfortable.

"I tried asking many times," Astrid said. "They will not tell me anything other than we must enter the pillar every day if we want to be fed. It bothered me for a while. However, when I started to listen to them, I had an easier time."

Seth shook his head, and Luna pointed to one of six circular panels on each wall. "What happens if I touch that?"

Astrid walked over to the panel. "This is the first station. It activates the pillar." She continued with the remaining panels in counterclockwise order. "In this next station, you will receive your daily nourishment, including water. In station three, you dispose of your rubbish. In the fourth, you deposit laundry or anything else in need of washing, and the fifth station has a shower. There's no water, but you'll be clean once you exit. The last one dispenses clean linens and clothing." Astrid returned to the first station and opened the panel. She pointed to a lens. "You must stare into the lens to be properly identified, and you must be wearing the crystal sphere while doing so. Stations two through six will only be accessible after you've completed your session in the pillar."

"Hold on, hold on one minute," Seth urged with a terror that stemmed from the time he spent as a prisoner of war. "What if we don't want to go along with this?"

"I hate to agree with him," Blaze added, "but I'd like to hear the answer to that one."

"You don't get access to the other panels if you don't enter the pillar," Astrid said.

"We're no better than caged animals in a zoo," Seth said, "brought here to entertain aliens who view us as inferior lifeforms."

"Sure you're not talking about yourself, Marconi?" Blaze asked. "From the way you sounded at Benny's, you believed you were above the rest of us *unproductive breathing machines*."

"He really said that to you?" Jeff asked.

Seth pointed his finger at Blaze. "I gave you a chance to get something out of our deal."

"Oh, you mean like a people treat?" Blaze pointed to the nutrition panel, and everyone laughed. He smiled at Seth. "How does it feel to know that being an Aristocrat means nothing here?"

"To hell with you, and everyone else here! I'll admit I've got flaws, but the rest of you are no better. You're abandoning a woman in need. Anya is a truly compassionate woman, much more so than all of you. You could've learned something from her." Seth touched the side of his face and spoke softly. "I know I did." He walked to the door and stepped on the panel. The door slid open, and he left.

"He's got a point," Jeff said. "If one of us is in trouble, we have to help—"

"We don't have to do anything, Lieutenant." Kelly glared at Jeff.

Astrid widened her eyes. "Anya is all right!"

"How can you know that?" Opal asked her.

"The Custodians just told me."

Opal shook her head. "This place seems to be getting crazier by the minute."

"You have to trust me."

"I trust you." Blaze held Astrid's hand.

Jeff peered at Blaze and then at Opal, who acknowledged his concern by slightly lifting her brows.

Nestor, who stood beside Jeff, leaned in and whispered to him, "What do you think?"

Jeff crossed his arms and took a moment to examine the environment. "Haven't made up my mind yet about anything." He smiled when he noticed Hiroko had been looking at him.

"I was also suspicious when I first arrived," she said. "If you would like to talk about..."

Hiroko gasped and rushed over to Luna who was about to look into the lens. She pushed her out of the way. "The pillar must never be activated when others are in here."

Rajni attempted to comfort Luna by holding her hand, and she pulled away.

"Get away from me!" Luna shouted.

Hiroko kneeled down in front of her. "I'm sorry if I scared you."

"You didn't."

Nestor came over and put his hand on Luna's shoulder. "What would've been the harm? She was only looking."

Hiroko stood. "Staring into the lens activates the pillar. An alarm sounds afterwards, and the door locks. You can't exit until after the session is over." She walked to the center panel. "You must stand here." She pointed to the ceiling. "The roof will slide open and from beneath you, a pillar of light will flow up and out of this structure. From outside, we'll all be able to see it. That's how we'll know the hexagon is occupied."

The lottery winners spent the next several minutes exploring the stations. Opal studied the panels, fascinated by the technology.

Pearl followed behind her. "You're enjoying this, aren't you?"

"How could I not?" Opal ran her hand across one of the panels. "It could take a lifetime to understand how this place works," Opal said, ignoring her sister.

Rajni placed her hand on the wall. "It's almost as if it's breathing!"

Luna touched the wall and gasped. "What if this whole place is the inside of a monster that ate us?"

Nestor felt the wall. "Monsters aren't real," he said unconvincingly.

"In my favorite movie, *Space Ex: The Ranger,* Space landed on what he thought was a planet. But he was really inside a giant spaceship eating machine. It converted everything it ate into electricity to feed its electric empire of killer robots."

Rajni laughed.

"It's not a comedy."

"Sorry." Rajni faked a serious expression. "Is this better?"

Luna rolled her eyes and walked away.

Nestor playfully whispered in Rajni's ear. "You never were the maternal type."

Rajni nodded. "It obviously skipped a generation. My mother always knew the right thing to say."

"Stop trying so hard, and you'll be all right." Nestor scanned the area around him thinking about what a fascinating documentary he could produce about this environment. He imagined all the different camera angles he could use to present the unusual structure.

"Why do I even care?" Rajni asked. "It's not like she's my daugh —"

She lost her balance, and Nestor put his arm around her. "I got you." He smiled.

"For now. But I need my cane...and meds."

Astrid overheard and replied, "There will not be any need for medicine here."

"Easy for her to say," Rajni said quietly to Nestor.

Astrid opened the door. "Does anyone have any more questions before we leave?"

"Do we have to come in here every day?" Opal asked.

"You do," Kelly answered. "We compiled a list in alphabetical order: Astrid, Blaze, Hiroko, Jeff, Luna, Nestor, Opal, Pearl, Rajni, Seth."

"You missed Anya," Blaze said.

"If she returns, she'll go before Astrid," Kelly said.

"How about you?" Jeff asked. "I didn't hear your name mentioned in your list of guinea pigs."

"The Custodians told me my participation is no longer necessary."

"Why not?"

"They didn't tell me why."

"How convenient for them." Jeff surveyed each wall. "How do we keep time here? I didn't see any time keeping devices besides that sundial outside."

"That's all we have." Astrid informed him. "And Kelly is always up by 6 AM. You can think of him as our personal alarm clock. He'll keep us all on schedule."

"Can we get some food now?" Luna asked. "I'm hungry."

Astrid opened up the food dispenser and removed a tray of nutrition cubes. "For tonight, these will be enough for all of you." She passed them around. "Tomorrow, you will be receiving your own supply."

Hiroko removed some bottles of water from the nutrition panel and distributed them to the lottery winners.

"What happened to not gaining access to the stations until after the pillar session is over?" Jeff asked.

"This is a special occasion," Hiroko said with a smile.

When Opal received her nutrition cube, she took a bite and creased her forehead. "There's no texture to these."

"Or flavor," Pearl added.

Jeff went to Opal and said quietly, "We need to talk."

"Come to my place after the meeting."

Pearl overheard. "What are you two up to?" she asked softly.

"We have some things to discuss."

"Including the missing woman," Jeff said. "We should go look for her."

"Agreed," Opal said.

"Didn't you both hear what Kelly said?" Pearl asked.

"Should we let her remain missing and possibly die?" Opal finished off her cube.

Pearl shook her head. "You always know how to get to me. If I had my strength, I'd go with you."

Luna approached Opal with Rufus on her shoulder. He was cycling through his impressive lexicon, cheering up the lottery winners who needed to be cheered.

"Thanks for letting me play with Rufus," Luna said. "Can I play with him again? He's a smart bird."

"Rufus is a smart bird and a pretty bird," Rufus informed everyone. He then did a realistic impression of a zipper closing and followed it up with a verse to "You Are My Sunny Day."

You are my sunny day.
When you're near clouds go away.
Shining down, don't ever leave me.
Beaming down, you make me happy.

Rufus held out the last note with a smooth and impressive vibrato. When he finished, everyone clapped.

"Thank you." Rufus bowed. "I'm a superstar."

Jeff laughed out loud. "What an amazing bird!" He was surprised by his enthusiasm. Since his mother's accident, he had been keeping his emotions to himself.

"Rufus is an amazing bird," Rufus repeated.

Opal smiled. "And another new phrase for you!"

Luna giggled, and Opal extended her arm towards Rufus who turned his head away.

"Why don't you keep him for another day?" Opal said trying to maintain the cool demeanor of a commander in front of her subordinate.

"Thank you, Opal," Luna said. "I'll take good care of him."

Opal watched Luna walk off with her beloved Rufus and hoped he hadn't abandoned her.

Pearl peered at Opal, wanting to comfort her but understanding her pain went beyond Rufus. Her betrayal separated her from the two most important people in her life. She already lost Christina and had no intention of losing Opal again.

Conflicting Signals

Jeff stood outside the hexagon, examining the structure. As suspicious as he was about the Custodians, he couldn't deny their mastery over technology.

"I never thanked you for helping."

Jeff turned and grinned when he saw that it was Hiroko, but it was short-lived. Her remark made him recall the day of the shuttle crash. "You don't have to thank me. It didn't make a difference."

"It did. I got a chance to say good-bye to my brother. He came to the hospital before my operation." Hiroko cried and wiped her eyes. "I'm sorry. Whenever I recall the worried look on his face, it makes me so sad. I promised him I'd be okay."

"I thought you were going to make it too."

"I also believed I'd pull through. Right up until my last memory." She smiled. "At least it was a pleasant one."

"Tell me about it."

"I laughed at a riddle the anesthesiologist told me before he put me under. I can still remember it."

"Don't keep me in suspense." Jeff's smile returned.

"What do you call an anesthesiologist who shows up for work wearing a rabbit suit?"

"What?"

"An ether bunny."

Jeff wanted to laugh, but the events of the crash were too vivid. After the shuttle had crashed, He spotted Seth gazing down at Hiroko. Seth ran off, leaving her behind. Jeff looked over at his wife and checked for her pulse. She was dead. As he was about to lift her, he heard Hiroko yelling for help. Jeff rushed over to her, picked her up, and raced towards the exit. Hiroko opened her eyes and looked at him. Jeff sensed a strong connection to her. He'd never reacted that way with anyone, including his own wife.

Outside the shuttle he ran into Seth, who was racing toward him. "You forgot your wife," he said as he handed Hiroko to Seth.

As Jeff ran back to reclaim his own wife's body, a warm blast struck him down, and that's the last he recalled. He awoke with the rest of the lottery winners a mile away from the shuttle crash.

Jeff peered into Hiroko's eyes as he had done when he was carrying her out of the shuttle. "I remember you telling the paramedics to help the other survivors because you were feeling okay."

"Apart from a headache, I thought I was," Hiroko said. "On the ride over to the hospital, I was talking and laughing with the medics. I even told Seth to contact you and thank you for saving me." She shook her head when she noticed Jeff's surprised expression. "He didn't tell you."

"The only time I heard from Seth was through a letter from an attorney that represented all the survivors of the crash. 'Due to the lack of evidence, we regret to inform you that your case against Marconi Aeronautics has been dismissed.'"

"That should surprise me, but it doesn't."

"The dismissal of the case or Seth not giving me your message?"

"Both."

Jeff peered into Hiroko's eyes, searching for any traces of deception. "Do you know why we were brought here?"

"All I know is that the Custodians saved us."

"For what?"

Hiroko shook her head. "Anything I say would be a guess, but we're safe here."

"I don't trust anyone who hides their identity. Until the Custodians show their faces, I'm not going to make it easy for them."

"When Astrid arrived they told her they'd never harm us because they care about us. They've remained true to their word."

"Sounds like they think of us as their pets."

"That's possible. We're not as highly evolved as them."

"So we just accept the collar around our necks without protest?"

"Did our dogs protest?"

"It's not the same. They were always our pets while we are intelligent beings that have accomplished a lot, socially and technologically."

"So have the Custodians. Their achievements are far more advanced than we could even imagine. What you view as major accomplishments wouldn't impress them."

Jeff shook his head.

"I know this is hard for you. But if you allow yourself to experience this place, you'll be humbled and appreciate what we have here. For me, it happened when I admitted that all my previous assertions about what it meant to be human were wrong. It isn't about ruling over my environment; it's about ruling over myself." Hiroko laughed. "I felt so foolish when I first realized this."

"I'll never enjoy living my life as someone's pet."

"When I first arrived I was upset, even more so than you. I took long walks around the first ring, and it gave me time to think about things. As contained as we are, it's very beautiful here. There are no sector wars, no checkpoints, and no watchful eye cameras monitoring everything we do. If anything, we're freer here."

Hiroko's last sentence resonated with Jeff. Yet when he stared at the mountains, they still seemed like prison bars. And the only way he'd have all he needed here was if Darla were with him. He glanced back at Hiroko. "I wish I could see what you see, but I can't."

"Give it time, and you will. And if I can help you in any way, please let me know. I owe you one."

"You don't owe me anything," Jeff said, "but I do need your help."

Seth hid behind the corner of the west side of the dormitory, observing the conversation between Jeff and Hiroko. He worried over what Jeff was telling his wife. Would he reveal his abandonment of the woman he promised to love forever?

After Seth had recovered from his injuries incurred during the 1st sector war, he moved to London and got a job as a shuttle pilot. He didn't go out much because of the scar on his face. He finally got the courage to attend a friend's birthday celebration, and life slowly began for him again.

Two years before his return to the United Republic, Hiroko was assigned as his co-pilot. The two soon learned they had a lot in common. Both had a love of museums and concerts. She was the first woman who didn't stare at his scar. The two started dating, and six months later they married. Seth wanted Hiroko to quit flying so they could start a family, but she loved her job and refused.

At first, Hiroko's independence didn't bother Seth. He was promoted when they returned to the United Republic, and his dream of piloting a space cruiser was realized. Soon, however, there was jealousy over Hiroko's working relationships with her new flight crew, particularly her co-pilot. This began to overshadow Seth's personal success. Whenever Hiroko talked about the camaraderie with her flight crew and how much they trusted her piloting skills, Seth would change the subject. He no longer felt like the center of her life, and the scar on his face became more glaring to him. Seth's obsession became a burden and made it hard for him to think and concentrate on his job.

Seth felt the same weakness resurrect in him at the refuge. What was Jeff saying to Hiroko? Why was she laughing after he spoke? Seth waited until Jeff went into Opal and Pearl's unit and then he approached Hiroko.

As she turned and saw him, Hiroko felt a trace of fear. "Seth, where did you come from?"

"I wanted to see how you were doing."

"I'm fine. I'm going inside to rest."

"I'm glad to see you."

"Me too."

"Why didn't they give us the same room?"

"I requested my own."

"Why?" Seth asked.

"I would prefer to discuss this at another time."

"You're still my wife, Hiro."

The words shocked Hiroko. She hadn't regarded Seth as her husband since her arrival here. "Three weeks before the crash, I had divorce papers drawn up."

"I kept asking you why you were pulling away from me. Why didn't you tell me?"

"You scared me. Every time I left the house, you asked me where I was going and who I was meeting. It felt like an inquisition."

"I loved you."

"That's not love. That's ownership."

"I've changed since then. I want you to know that."

"I'm glad to hear that, Seth. If you'd like to talk more, we can...at a later time. I need to get used to you being here."

"I feel the same way. All these years, I thought you died."

Hiroko stood on the panel, and the door slid open. "I'll see you later." She entered and shut the door.

Seth remained where he stood for a few minutes, confused by all his awakening emotions. Hiroko still had a hold on him.

Opal opened the door, and Jeff saluted, "Commander."

"At ease Lieutenant, and come inside."

He entered and thought how much of a privilege this would've been before the catastrophe, to be in the same room as one of the most highly decorated war heroes of the 1st sector war.

Pearl stood in the living room with her hands on her hips. "I hope you're not planning on going up there now. It'll be getting dark soon."

Opal pointed her thumb towards Pearl. "My twin sometimes confuses herself as my mother."

"I also want to find Anya, but you won't be of help to us if you go missing as well," Pearl said.

"I was reported missing once, and that was enough. I'm no fool." Opal looked at Jeff. "We'll leave at 0600. We should be able to make it back before nightfall."

"What are you going to do for food and water?" Pearl asked.

"We can fill up by the spring near the cave," Opal said.

"Those small bottles won't be enough for an all-day hike."

"Marconi made it up without water, and he stayed overnight."

"What about the order of visits to the hexagon?" Pearl asked.

"We'll have to go out of order tomorrow," Jeff said. "And Kelly's going to have to accept our decision."

Pearl appeared worried.

"Get over whatever's making you look like that," Opal said. "I need you to cover for me."

"How?"

"If anyone asks why I'm not at the hexagon, tell them I'm suffering from a migraine and that I'm sleeping."

"What if they want to check on you?"

"Tell them I don't want to be disturbed and that I'll report to the hexagon when I feel better." Opal turned to Jeff. "Can anyone cover for you?"

"Already covered. Hiroko's covering for me."

"Are you sure she be trusted?"

"No...but she agreed to help and didn't ask me any difficult questions."

"Well then...we'll find out tomorrow if she's on our side."

Jeff hoped his gut feeling about Hiroko was correct—that she was an honest woman. He wanted to trust her. He wanted to do many things with her, and the visuals he produced in his mind made him smile. I also smiled. Blossoming love gives Me a good buzz.

Only Fiction

Blaze woke from his sleep after he had been violently shaken. Astrid sat in front of him with her legs and arms crossed, rocking back and forth.

"What happened? Did someone hurt you?" Blaze went to hug Astrid, and she pushed him back.

"I should be asking you that question," she said while continuing to rock. "I have been in the pillar many times, but the imprint I connected with today was awful...so vile and unspeakable."

"Imprint? Of what?" The end of the world wasn't nearly as terrifying for Blaze as this moment. "What did you see in there?"

"Did I really have an aneurysm?"

Blaze stopped breathing. All the muscles in his body stiffened and locked.

Astrid slapped him hard across the face. "Answer me!"

Blaze didn't flinch, didn't answer, didn't have anything to say. His brain had momentarily shut down.

"Why didn't you tell me I was raped?"

"You...seemed so sad talking about how much you missed playing your cello. I didn't want you to suffer any more. I thought you were better off not knowing."

"I know now," she said while crying. "That man—I can still see his face. He violated me, and I remember it all."

Astrid's pain brought Blaze back to the night of her murder when he was tied up and forced to watch her assault. Right before she took her last breath, Astrid looked at him long enough to whisper, *"Je t'aime."*

"I love you too," Blaze had responded in a whisper.

The visual memory still haunted him. He never forgot the terror in his wife's eyes when she spoke those words.

"What else do you remember?" Blaze asked, hoping one detail of the night remained forgotten.

"All of it. I remember him laughing at me and tearing off my nightgown." Astrid placed her hand around the front of her neck." He then choked me, and I felt his nails digging into my skin."

Blaze was crying now. "I couldn't stop him. I had to watch him do what he did to you. Every night since then, I went to sleep with your murder playing through my mind in full color and the volume turned up to maximum."

"The illusion of security," Astrid said. "Why did you choose that phrase?"

"I saw through the illusion that night."

"I have a new phrase, as well. The illusion of trust." Astrid pointed to the door. "I want you out of here."

"If I had to do it all again, I still wouldn't tell you." Blaze got up from the bed.

"You would let me continue living a lie?"

"Sometimes a lie is better than the truth."

"It never is. It builds an artificial foundation that eventually crumbles as it did today for us. And now all I see is emptiness where there used to be a deep connection...the deepest one I've ever had with anyone."

"How does it make you feel remembering what happened? Does it make you happy?"

"No. But if you had told me, I would have been prepared to meet my murderer in the pillar."

Blaze crinkled his forehead. "I thought the purpose of the pillar was to make us live our dreams?"

"It does. The Custodians' technology captures imprints of people and events in our lives by tapping into our memories, both pleasant and not so pleasant."

"This is all so unnatural, Astrid." Blaze shook his head. "Did you ever think that the reason you couldn't remember before I came here was because you weren't meant to? You never recover from something like this. Once the veil is lifted, you see that security is an illusion. We'd like to think we're the highest lifeforms on Earth. However, the truth is that from the moment we're born, we're as exposed as the zebras in the Serengeti. Vulnerable to the predators who stalk us, always ready to attack when we least suspect it. That's the way things work, the way they've always worked. There are no guarantees given to us, no contract we sign that grants us a long life, and—" Blaze stopped himself and smiled at a revelation that had just come to him.

"Get off the stage," Astrid said. "This is not one of your poetry slams." She went to the dresser and picked up a crystal sphere. She threw it at Blaze, and he caught it.

"That was supposed to be for Anya. You can stay at her place until she returns."

"I was wrong," Blaze said.

"If that is your way of apologizing, it is very weak."

"*Everything* is an illusion."

"My mother was right about you. You are a very strange man."

"True. But you'll get why I did what I did once you understand."

"Understand what?"

"It's coming to me, but I can't quite get it yet." Blaze snapped his fingers. "Can the pillar help me make sense of what I'm thinking?"

"It can, but—"

"Great." He kissed Astrid's forehead. "I'll see you later, hopefully with a little more clarity."

He walked away, then stopped in front of the doorway. Without looking back he said, "I'm sorry," and then left.

I initially intended trust to connect sentients to their inner Light, which isn't capable of betrayal. Humans turned it into something that resembled a religion. Blaze ascended to godhood at the top level of the Eiffel Tower where Astrid worked as a tour guide during her college years. The foundation of their code of worship began when Blaze told Astrid that the view reminded him of a poem he'd just written. While gazing out at the city below, he recited it to the tour group. The few who understood English applauded, and Astrid fell in love with him. She often joked to friends over how cliché their first meeting was and how their connection had been cinematic. But in the end, Blaze proved to be a mere mortal.

Inside the hexagon, Blaze stared into the lens. The floor vibrated, and his skull felt as though it was about to crack open. He walked toward the center of the room and stood on the large circular panel. The roof opened up, and the vibration got stronger. A light pillar emerged from the floor, extended from around him and burst out of the open ceiling. His jumpsuit clung to him from an outpouring of sweat. He pressed hard against his temples and feared his head would explode from the pressure. As he was about to pass out, the light pillar cleared. Blaze opened his eyes and gasped. He was now standing in his fifth grade classroom.

"Mr. Kenyon, what are you doing away from your desk?" his teacher asked.

"Mrs. Dexter?"

"How peculiar." She tilted her head. "You look as if you don't even remember me."

"I do. But I don't know why I'm back here."

"I'm sure you'll figure it out once you return to your seat." She pointed to it. "Now!"

Blaze inspected himself. He had the limbs of an adult and still had on his jumpsuit. "Strange."

"You're the strange one," Mrs. Dexter said, and the whole class laughed.

One blink from his eyes later, Blaze was walking in the school hall with his friends. They approached a boy who had just pulled a few books out of his locker. Blaze knocked them out of his hand. Everyone cheered as the frightened boy squatted to pick them up.

Blaze kicked the books out of the boy's hands. "Did Charlie Trip have a nice trip?"

Blaze punched the side of Charlie's face as he tried to get up. "That's for murdering my wife, you psychopath!"

One of the teachers came out of the classroom, and Blaze stepped out of the way.

Charlie got up. "You're going to regret this one day!" He ran away.

Blaze chased after him, knocking over the teacher. Once he got outside the school, he stopped and almost fell over. He was now on Rue Marc Sequin, the street where he and Astrid had lived in Paris. He ran to their building and entered. Once inside the apartment, he entered the bedroom. Charlie was inside.

"You're a few years too late," he said. "She's already dead."

Blaze sat on the bed and gazed out the window that had been left wide open. A white linen curtain blew gently in the breeze as it had on the night of Astrid's murder.

"Don't you want to fight anymore?" Charlie asked.

"You already killed her. Along with yourself. Nothing I do here will change that."

"How did you feel when you woke up in the hospital? Were you disappointed that I was dead long before the police got to me?"

"Mostly angry." Blaze rubbed his chin. "But I still don't know why I'm here with you now."

"You don't know? Your wife is dead because of you."

"I know, but I'm missing something," Blaze said to himself.

"Not surprising. You weren't too smart in school. Unlike you, I had aspirations. I loved animals and volunteered my time at the animal shelter. I dreamed of being a vet when I grew up. Then I met you. You devoured my compassion until there was nothing left in me but hatred. Unfortunately for Astrid, there were no space monks around to give me the antidote to treat my infestation." Charlie pointed at his own eyes. "Is this how you envisioned the Bradley Simpson's stare?"

Blaze's heart felt as though it were going to burst out of his ribs.

"You never knew?" Charlie placed his right hand in the middle of his chest. "As the inspiration behind one of your most notorious villains, I'm insulted."

Blaze shot up and pointed his hand at Charlie. "There's no connection!"

"You created Bradley Simpson because you felt guilty over your wife's death...and mine. You're not only intellectually inferior. You're a loser."

Blaze clenched his fists and gritted his teeth. In the midst of his rage and Charlie's smug smile, the clarity he'd sought after arrived. "I'm also an impatient jerk who made a kid cry before the Earth was destroyed, and an author who can't handle criticism all that well." He fell backwards onto the bed and laughed. "And that's just the beginning of my list. I can go on all night with this."

Charlie looked down at him. "You find this funny?"

"Hysterical! I can't stop laughing!"

"You're crazier than I ever was." Charlie stormed off.

Blaze sat up and met a slap across his face. "Welcome home, Son!" Mr. Kenyon flashed a picture of himself with his arm around a woman. "You had no business getting in between me and your mother!" He hoisted Blaze by his shirt and threw him to the floor. "You can forget about my exemption letter. You're going to serve your two years and find your own way to get into college."

"I was going to tell you I was sorry, but I'm not anymore! I'm glad Mom left you!"

Mr. Kenyon spit on his son. "You're no better than a worm crawling into its hole. You should've come to me. A real man doesn't tattle. He confronts his opposition. Maybe a tour in the demilitarized zone will help turn you into a man because you sure as hell aren't one now."

Blaze snarled, leapt to his feet, and threw a punch that landed on the side of a truck. He winced in pain while trying to recognize the city street he now stood on. When Blaze noticed he was holding a gun, he remembered the place.

Charlie approached Blaze. "I don't see what you're all worked up about. Your father hit you only once while I got beaten almost every day at school."

"I lost everything that night."

"If you kept your mouth shut about the affair, you would've gotten into the best university for creative writing and wrote better books. That would've impressed Trevor Forthright."

"I doubt it," Blaze said as his father's young, flaxen-haired girlfriend arrived in front of her apartment with her dog. She leaned down to pet him.

"Go ahead," Charlie said. "Shoot her. I know you want to."

"But you didn't," a female voice replied.

Blaze turned and saw Kay. David was standing next to her.

"You're a nurturer, not a murderer," Kay said, then gestured to David.

"Why did you tell me my mother was never coming back?" he asked.

"What she did was selfish."

"Sounds just like your father," Charlie said to Blaze. "They would've made a lovely couple."

"Why didn't you shoot her?" Kay asked.

"It was the dog," Blaze said. "I didn't want him to be without an owner and possibly euthanized."

"You're joking?" Charlie replied. "You didn't kill that slut because she had a *dog* with her?"

"You wouldn't under—"

Blaze was pushed from behind. He turned with his fist aimed, and he landed it on his father's face.

Mr. Kenyon stepped away from his son.

Blaze grabbed him by his shirt. "And you said I wasn't a man?" He laughed. "I never realized this until now, but you're the worm crawling back into its hole. You were never a man. A man doesn't abandon his loyalty. A man stays true to himself, even when things get difficult. A man honors his responsibilities." Blaze froze for a moment as another realization struck him. "But a woman can do all those things too. Mom did. And we did okay without you."

Blaze pushed his father, who ran away.

"No wonder you turned into a coward," Charlie said. "You're the son of one."

"I don't agree." Kay walked in front of Blaze and held both his hands. "You risked your life to save me."

"I saved no one." Blaze peered at David and then back at Kay.

"You took care of us and made us your family," she reminded him.

"I wish I could've brought both of you here with me."

"How could you save us if you didn't even know you could save yourself?" David asked.

"I don't know. I don't know anything anymore."

"You know one thing." Charlie pointed to Blaze's *illusion of security* tattoo. "You exposed the myth of security, which I never bought into because I never had it. Whenever you and your friends came around to torture me, I was forced to take it. I had no control in my life."

"Seems as though I never did either."

"Welcome to the club. You're not a man, You're a..."

"I know! I heard that enough times. But what does that even mean? To be a man? To be a woman? I just finished telling my father that my mother was more of a man than him." Blaze laughed.

"That's because you're confused along with being a brainless coward. It's a miracle you made it past high school."

"I was all of those. But you still haven't answered my question. And you won't be able to because beyond the obvious physiology, everything else is nothing more than a role. I created my characters the same way. By varying their accents, careers, and idiosyncrasies, they acted according to the characteristics I gave them. How is that different from us?" Blaze pointed at Kay. "You're a WSA agent and wife." He pointed at David. "You're a son and a boy, and I'm a man, son, husband, brother and author." Blaze pointed at Charlie. "What are you?"

"A data entry clerk."

"Other than that being your job, what are you?"

"Bored with this conversation."

"We all exist in our own story, writing our own reality as we move forward," Blaze told them.

Charlie pushed his hand forward. "A weak premise."

"Why is that?"

"If that was true, I would've written myself a happy life and made myself popular. I would've had a girl for every day of the year."

"Who said all writers write their best story?"

Kay pointed to Charlie. "Not him. Even his edits don't improve his story."

"Same here," Blaze said. "But I have no regrets because I found my answer." He smiled, and it felt like the first time he had ever done so. "I'm only fiction."

The whiteness returned with the vibration, but it no longer hurt him. Blaze recognized the tones as a language that told him his presence was no longer required in the pillar. The light pillar switched off, and Blaze took a moment to adjust his eyes to the environment. Removing his sweat drenched jumpsuit, he threw it into the hamper and cleaned himself up. Afterwards, he went to the nourishment panel and received a plate full of cubes. He took a bite, and every flavor imaginable attacked his taste buds. He'd never tasted anything so savory, sweet, bitter or sour. Every culinary experience he ever enjoyed exploded from the once flavorless cubes.

Blaze opened the hexagon door with a wide grin on his face. Hiroko stood at the other side with her mouth wide open. Blaze now noticed he'd forgotten to put on his jumpsuit. Nonetheless, that wasn't what left Hiroko in a state where the slightest breeze would've knocked her over.

"Blaze?" Those were the only words Hiroko could squeeze out.

Blaze looked down at his feet and then at his arms. His tattoos were gone. "Be right back. It appears I'm naked." He closed the door, got a clean jumpsuit and dressed while laughing over how absurd he must've appeared to Hiroko. He felt no embarrassment and would have opted out of the jumpsuit altogether had it not been for the others.

Street Life

Nestor went outside early in the morning and caught a glimpse of Opal jogging towards the western path. He hadn't suspected anything unusual until Jeff came outside of his unit, shortly afterward.

"Good morning, Lieutenant Theobald."

"That it is." Jeff would've told Nestor to drop the title, but he was still suspicious of him. He thought it best to maintain his role as an authoritative figure.

"A great one for a run," Nestor added.

Jeff observed Opal entering the path. "You read my mind."

"I remember those days well, and I don't miss them at all. Takes a special breed to do what you do."

The two exchanged a few more pleasantries, then Jeff headed toward the western path. Rajni stepped outside when Nestor was about to trail after him.

"I want to apologize for my behavior yesterday," she said.

"You don't have to apologize."

Nestor watched Jeff disappear into the western path.

"Can we talk about what happened?" Rajni asked.

Nestor spotted tears in her eyes and forgot all about Jeff.

"I didn't want to hurt you yesterday, but the words came out anyway. I couldn't stop them. It's as if I was momentarily possessed by a *pishacha.*"

Nestor hugged Rajni. "I know that feeling well." He felt unfaithful holding her even though he knew he'd never see Becky again.

"When I thought you died, I wanted to tell you that I didn't blame you for leaving me," Rajni said, "and that I forgave you and loved you."

"Let's start over...me and you." Nestor surveyed the area. "Not that we have a choi—"

Luna screamed from inside the unit, and they ran in to check on her.

"I don't want to go! I don't want to go!" Luna yelled from inside her room.

Nestor and Rajni went in, and Nestor sat beside her.

"It's cold!" she hollered. "It's too cold! Make it stop!" She sat up quickly.

Nestor hugged her, and she grabbed onto him tightly.

"You were dreaming." Nestor gently caressed Luna's back.

"It seemed so real. I couldn't do anything to make it stop."

"Do you want to talk about it?"

Luna pushed Nestor away. "No. I'm okay now."

Rufus, who was standing on the bureau, flew over to Luna and perched on her shoulder.

Luna smiled. "Good morning, Rufus."

"Good morning. Beautiful morning. Beautiful bird," Rufus said, and then went through a circuit of his vocabulary and sound effects.

"Rufus can talk a lot," Nestor said.

"At least he never says anything mean." Luna glared at Rajni, got up, and walked into the living room.

Nestor held Rajni's hand. "Give her some time."

On their way to the hexagon, Nestor and Luna spotted Blaze rubbing his hands against the bark of a tree.

"Who's that?" Luna asked.

Nestor approached Blaze and when he recognized him, he asked, "What happened to your tattoos?"

Blaze turned to Nestor and grinned. "Did you know molecules are tiny building blocks of miracles? They produce an infinite array of creative output." He pulled out a branch. "This tree is one such miracle. It inspired me to write a poem." He glanced at Luna. "Would you like to hear it?"

Luna slowly nodded her head.

Within this dream,
We're what we write.
Fluttering, dancing, being.
All shining within a sphere of light.
Playing music that's freeing.

"That's very...inspirational, Blaze," Nestor said.

"This whole place is a cornucopia of inspiration."

Luna crinkled her forehead at Nestor who winked his eye. They left Blaze to commune with nature and continued towards the hexagon.

"I don't want to go in there," Luna said when Nestor opened the door.

"Blaze already had his turn. He seems okay."

"Okay? All his tattoos disappeared, and did you see how weird he's acting? He never stops smiling."

"He's a happy guy."

"Too happy, and I liked him better with his tattoos."

Luna pointed to Blaze who was handing a bouquet of flowers to Hiroko.

"If I walked around looking like that, my mother would've thought I was on drugs." Luna crossed her arms. "There's no bloody way I'm going inside if that's what's going to happen to me."

"I can go in first if you like."

"You would do that?"

"I could use a little cheering up."

"Don't leave your brain in there like Blaze did."

Nestor stepped on the panel, and the door slid open. "See you when I get out...with my brain neatly packed inside my skull."

Nestor panicked when the light pillar activated. He wasn't comfortable in enclosed spaces. The humming knocked him off his feet. Rolling to his side, he wrapped himself into a fetal position to deal with the pain. After the light pillar had disappeared, he stood up in the middle of a quiet street.

A man wearing an expensive suit walked over. "You seem tired and lost. Do you need any help?"

"Not your kind of help," Nestor said. "I'm not going anywhere with you."

"Where are your parents? Would you like me to call them for you?"

"My parents have been dead for a very long time."

"Sorry to hear that." The man bit his bottom lip. "I can help you if you need a place to stay."

Nestor laughed. "I can't believe I fell for your lies."

"My lies, as you call them, saved your life. You never had to eat another roasted rat again."

A car pulled up, and the front door opened. Nestor's mother stepped out of the vehicle. "Nestor, what are you doing with that strange man? Didn't I always tell you never to talk to strange men?"

"Your mother's not here. She's dead," the man said.

Nestor wept as he looked at his mother. All the feelings he'd suppressed since her death surfaced. "Why did you leave me, Mama?" he whimpered in a child-like voice.

"I can see you're too immature to be left alone." She pointed to the car. "Get in."

Nestor sheepishly walked over to the car and got in the passenger's side. His mother slid into the driver's seat and started driving.

"Do you know why you're here?" Nestor's mother asked.

"To dream."

"Do you know what the purpose of a dream is?"

"To reveal what's hidden in the subconscious mind."

"Stop talking like a textbook, and speak for yourself."

"What do you want me to say?"

"What do you think you're seeing here?"

"I'm not sure. This seems more real than a dream."

"If it's only a dream, why are you so frightened?"

"I don't know." Nestor covered his face. "I don't even know why I'm here."

"Why do you think I did what I did?"

"You were weak. You gave up."

"Who are you to judge her for taking her life?" the man with the expensive suit said from the back seat. "You sold your body every night to men and women for me. Didn't matter what sex, so long as they had the credit. You had no value in your own life. No self-respect. And look at you now. All grown up with a job most people only dream about, and you're still whining about the same things. Blah, blah, blah."

"You can leave," Nestor told the man. "No one asked you to listen." He looked at his mother. "Why did you leave me?"

"It was your father who abandoned us first."

"First, second—the order makes no difference when you lose both your parents."

"I tried to hang on, but we lost everything. I thought you'd be better off without me, that maybe you'd be placed into a better family."

"That didn't happen."

"Because we're alike. We both gave up."

"No...I didn't. I hung on."

"I suppose you blame me for everything that happened," a male voice said.

Nestor turned to face the back seat, where his father was now also seated.

"We were already in trouble before I left," Nestor's father said. "Your mother kept threatening to go back to Greece."

"A whole regiment died because of you, Dad. Mama lost most of her friends, and the kids at school whispered and talked about me. I was the son of a man who betrayed his homeland."

"I make no apologies. I wanted a better life and saw the possibility for one in the Eastern Sector, so I went for it."

"We were the perfect family. All my friends loved coming over to our house because they admired you and Mama more than their own parents. I never knew you were unhappy. I thought we were enough for you."

"Love saves the day. Is that what you believed?" Mr. Zaras laughed. "A syrupy attitude that will get you nowhere in life."

"I'm glad they caught you," Nestor said. "Did your execution hurt?"

"Didn't feel a thing."

"You and Mama both got off easy. I lived in a smelly old dormitory where the caretakers treated us worse than animals."

"You should thank your father," the man with the expensive suit said. "Your career came out of working for me."

Mrs. Zaras stopped the car and looked ahead. "What's that?"

Nestor looked out the front window. There was someone lying in the middle of the road. Nestor got out of the car and went to investigate. On the ground was the same man he tried to save in front of Rajni's apartment building.

"Get out of the way, kid!" a man yelled. "We're in the middle of a shoot!"

Nestor turned around startled and then grinned when he recognized who called him. "Jake!"

"Nestor? You should know better. Why did you screw up my shot?"

"I had no idea you were here. I was with my parents." Nestor gestured to where the car was parked, but it was no longer there. He smiled again at Jake. "It's good to see you."

"How's your career going?"

"Thanks to your mentoring, I got off the streets and became a successful documentarian."

"Wish I were alive to appreciate your accomplishments."

"I'll never forget what you did for me. I dedicated all my documentaries to you."

"That's quite an honor."

Jake morphed back into the man with the fancy suit.

"Why are you back?" Nestor asked.

"To remind you of who you really are."

"I'm not him anymore." Nestor ran off, yelling, "I became more!"

Red fire materialized in front of him. He jumped through it and landed on a seat in the shuttle.

"It's your turn."

Nestor faced Rajni. They were in the middle of a game of Pachisi on one of her custom boards. Each home space displayed the Buddha sitting upon a lotus.

Nestor rolled the dice and smiled. "Double sixes, almost home." Nestor picked up a blue pawn and moved it forward to the home space. He then moved another pawn nine spaces, which brought it to the safety zone. "And now all my pawns are in the safety zone."

Rajni rolled the dice. "This game is about to get boring. At least with Leela I'd have a better chance of catching up."

"I never knew this was an ancient game until you asked me if I wanted to play Pachisi. I thought you said Parcheesi."

"They're technically the same game."

"With a slightly different face"—Nestor waved his finger—"I got it!"

The shuttle disintegrated, and Nestor was now at a playground. Becky was pushing Joey on a swing. Nestor ran over to them and embraced his wife.

"Congratulations," she said, "you got all your pieces home."

"That was the longest game I ever played." Nestor kissed her.

"I'm glad you won, Daddy," Joey said.

"So am I." Nestor halted the swing and picked up Joey. "But just because I'm playing a new game doesn't mean I have to forget you." He leaned over towards Becky. "Or you." He kissed her.

When Nestor exited, Luna sprang up from the ground where she'd been sitting.

"How long was I in there?"

"I have no idea, but it wasn't long." Luna inspected Nestor's face. "You don't look as spacey as Blaze."

"That's a relief."

"What was it like?"

"You'll have to go inside and find out for yourself."

Luna petted Rufus. "I have to go myself."

"I'll watch him." Nestor extended his arm as he'd seen Opal do.

"Go to Nestor," Luna said.

Rufus hopped onto Nestor's arm and climbed to his shoulder. "I'll wait for you right here," Nestor said.

Rufus fluffed his wings. "Me too. Right here."

Luna stood on the panel, and the door opened. She entered, and the door shut behind her.

Flashback

Jeff arrived at the oasis ahead of Opal and headed to the pond. After drinking all his water, he refilled the bottle and surveyed the surrounding mountains. They weren't too high. He surmised it would take them half a day to reach the peak.

"Sorry I'm late."

Jeff swung around and sighed when he saw Opal.

"Good reflexes." She slowly turned as she examined the landscape. "Think we should head farther north. Marconi said there was a path that was easy to climb." She laughed. "Never thought I'd prefer an easier climb, but I'm feeling a little tired today."

"Same here." Jeff chuckled.

Opal kneeled down to fill up her water bottle. She drank it all and refilled. "Let's get going then."

Opal and Jeff proceeded north, never knowing the path they followed was one ring outside the one Anya and Seth had traversed. They discovered the error when they found themselves underneath the stone bridge. Another nearby path that was more challenging also led up the mountain.

"It never gets easier." Opal shook her head and entered the path.

He followed behind her. "Could use the workout."

The path had more steep ascents and got them up quicker, placing them on the northern side of the bridge.

Jeff glanced out at the rows of mountains. "Marconi wasn't kidding. We're in a maze."

"A very large one." Opal glanced up at the spiral peak.

"At least mice get cheese," Jeff said. "We perform for flavorless cubes."

A low hum started to sound, and Opal rubbed her forehead.

Jeff glanced at her. "Everything all right, Commander?"

"The humming is starting to get to me."

"What humming?"

"You don't hear it?"

Jeff shook his head. "We should return to the refuge."

"Never mind me. We have to find Anya." Opal scrutinized the ridge directly across from where they stood. "She couldn't have crossed this."

"Think he killed her?" Jeff asked.

Opal stared over the precipice. "Either that, or she fell, and Marconi went nuts."

"Or both." Jeff stared over the horizon. "I don't see a golden star anywhere."

The humming grew louder. Opal fell to the ground and covered her ears.

"I'm taking you back." Jeff grabbed hold of her arm, and Opal screamed out in terror.

"It's all around us!" she yelled. "We can't escape!"

Jeff scanned the area and couldn't see what Opal was talking about. Everything looked exactly as it had moments before. However, from Opal's perspective, she was surrounded by a landscape of buildings on fire. Smoke saturated the air, blocking out Sun's rays. She was witnessing a city street with people collapsing, dying, lamenting, crying, praying and all the things one would expect to happen after the destruction of a city.

"It's heartbreaking!" Opal cried. "All the people, the children—they're all dying."

Jeff assisted Opal to her feet.

"We can't fight this! The whole perimeter's frying!" She coughed. "Where's my damned gas mask? I can't find it anywhere."

Opal's reaction reminded Jeff of his mother. He decided the safest way to handle the situation was to play along. "We left our supplies at the bottom of the mountain. We should start heading down and find shelter."

"That's a good idea. What rank are you?"

"Lieutenant."

Opal observed a large explosion that formed into a mushroom cloud. "There's no way out from this!"

"We can't give up!" Jeff yelled. "We can't let the enemy break us!"

Opal glared at Jeff. "You dare raise your voice at your superior?"

"I'm sorry, Commander."

Opal smiled. "I like your confidence. We're going to need a lot more of it to make it back alive." Opal marched ahead. "Let's get moving."

Jeff shook his head and followed her down the trail. They had to stop a few times to take cover from the bombs Opal saw exploding all around her.

Cutting the Cord

Luna slowly turned inside the light pillar, unaffected by the humming. Once it deactivated, she found herself flying over the passengers in the shuttle.

"No! I don't want to go! I don't want to go!" Luna yelled as she flew over Jeff and his wife who'd just died. An explosion followed, and she ended up in her room where her friend Jodi was positioning a Space Ex action figure in his spaceship.

"Jodi!" She ran over and kneeled beside her. "You don't know how much I missed you."

Jodi threw the spaceship against the wall. "You're a liar!"

"Really...I did. I never found a friend like you again. There was no one around who liked the same things we liked." Luna picked up the smashed space ship and removed the Space Ex figure.

"Then why don't you want to be my friend anymore?"

"You died"—Luna threw the Space Ex figure—"and I stopped doing all the things that reminded me of you."

"That's not what I mean, and you know it." Jodi sprang to her feet and barreled out of the room.

Luna followed behind her. "I got into a lot of trouble because of you."

"Is that why you don't want to come back?"

"Come back? I'm here."

"You flew away. You didn't care about anyone but yourself." Jodi mimicked Luna's voice. "'I don't want to go. I don't want to go. It's too cold.' You're such a big baby."

"I don't understand."

"You don't care."

"I do!" Luna cried. "When I found out the judge let his old mother drive, I broke all the windows on the first floor of his house. You never would've died if he didn't lie about her vision test."

"And what did that get you?"

"Arrested...when they caught me. But I didn't apologize. He deserved it. Took the police almost a year to find out it was me. The judge dropped the charges because he didn't want the negative publicity." Luna smiled. "But he was fired anyway."

"So?" Jodi walked away. "You still act like a big whiny baby."

"Stop calling me that, or I'll..."

Jodi turned and put her hands on her hips. "Or you'll what? Hit me?"

"No. I'd never hit you. You're my best friend."

"Were. I'm dead." She slapped Luna's face. "Wake up!"

Luna found herself sitting beside the kitchen table at her house. Her brother, Aaron, and some of the neighbor children were busy sketching. Luna's mother came over and gazed over her shoulder.

"Why aren't you drawing anything, Luna? I'm sure there are things you'll miss about Earth."

Luna pushed the paper off the table. "None of this will make a bloody difference."

The other children stopped drawing, and Aaron seemed as though he was about to cry.

"This was a bad idea, Mum," Luna said. "You all died anyway."

She ran upstairs and into her room, inspecting every picture that hung on the wall. One depicted her favorite actor, James McConnor, who portrayed Space Ex in the movies. The picture to the right was of a band she followed, Tearing Nations. On her bureau was her jewelry box filled with jewelry, most of which she never wore. Luna opened one of the drawers, removed a charm bracelet, and cried. One of the charms was of two hands shaking, and Jodi had the same one. They bought them together at the mall.

Luna's mother entered the room. "Did you enjoy spending most of your last night on Earth locked up in your room?"

"I wouldn't have enjoyed living in a fantasy world downstairs with you either."

"What would've been your ideal way to spend your last night?"

Luna sat on her bed and crossed her arms.

"Don't you have an answer?"

"There's no *ideal* way to die," Luna answered. "It sucks, and I can say that because I'm the only one who didn't die. No one here can explain how that happened. I want to know where all of you ended up. No one here can tell me that either."

Luna's mother sat beside her. "Why did you come back?"

"I wanted to see you, but now I wish I didn't because it makes me miss you more." Tears trickled down her cheeks. "I wish you were really here with me."

"What makes you think I'm not here?"

"You're dead."

"We never die."

Luna gazed at her mother until she built up enough emotions to convince herself that their reunion was real. "I'm sorry I got into so much trouble this last year. I was so mad that Jodi had to die because that judge gave a driver's license to an old lady who couldn't see well."

"Did it make you feel better when you broke his windows?"

Luna peered into her mother's eyes. "Would it make me a bad person if I said yes?"

"What do you think?"

"I don't know." Luna lay on her back. "Everything seemed as though it was getting better, until I got caught. Dad canceled our trip to Rome, and Aaron wouldn't speak to me for the longest time. He wanted to see Pompeii ever since he watched that documentary about Mount Vesuvius." Luna began to cry again as she thought about Aaron. "I was mean to him. I always chased him away because he followed me and my friends around, acting stupid and embarrassing me with his lisp." Luna got up and hugged her mother. "I'm sorry I was so mean."

The environment surrounding Luna's bed blended and swirled into a whirlpool of luminous colors. After everything had recombined, Luna stood in front of a broken window. She recalled the house. It belonged to the judge that she blamed for Jodi's death.

The judge came outside, and Luna approached him.

"Not running away anymore?" the judge asked.

"Why did you give your mother a driver's license when you knew she was almost blind?"

The judge pointed to a rock Luna was holding. "What do you plan on doing with that now?"

"You should've been the one who died." Luna hurled the rock at the judge, striking him on the head. He collapsed, and Luna gasped. She ran to him and got onto her knees. Blood trickled down from his forehead. "I didn't mean to. I didn't want to...I couldn't stop myself."

"Time to confess. You wanted to do this."

"I did. But I'm glad I didn't."

"You can't un-break my windows."

"You got new ones to replace them, but I can't ever replace my best friend. She was one of a kind."

The judge nodded. "I lost everything because I didn't want to be bothered with my mother. And then I lost my life because of all the stress from the lawsuits resulting from the accident...and not knowing who kept on breaking my window."

Luna cried. "I don't want to lose anything else." She closed her eyes. "Why can't things stay as they are?"

"Would you really want them to?"

Luna opened her eyes, and she was back in her room, lying on her bed. Her mother sat beside her and handed her a paper and pencil. "Are you ready now?"

Luna took the paper and pencil and went to her desk. She started to sketch. She wasn't sure what to draw, but as the lines connected, she drew quicker and with less effort. After she had finished, she examined the sketch. It was of Jeff and his wife in the same pose as the picture Jeff looked at on the night before Earth was singed.

"What did you draw?" Luna's mother asked.

"One of the lottery winners and some lady I never saw before."

"Are you sure about that?"

Luna looked down at the sketch. "The only thing I'm sure of is that I miss you, Dad, Aaron, and Jodi."

"Do you want things to stay as they are always?"

"I do."

"Think about what you'd miss out on if you got your wish. You'd never grow up, never learn new things. Everything would be the same. *Always.* Would you like that?"

"Sounds boring, but I still miss all of you."

"We're with you whenever you think of us."

"It's not the same."

"We only ever exist in your memories, Luna. What you're missing is them, not us. The only thing that matters is *now*. Make new memories here."

"You're more than a memory."

"Not anymore."

Luna cried, and her mother hugged her.

"You have a full life ahead of you. Don't allow fear to shut you out of the new adventures that await you."

"Like Space Ex?"

"Exactly."

Luna smiled at her mother. "I love you, Mum—"

The sketch of Jeff and his wife caught fire. The orange flames expanded and swallowed everything in the room. Luna gasped and found herself flying over the shuttle, and over Jeff and his wife. To gain confidence, she imagined herself as Space Ex and continued her flight until she flew over Rajni. Right then, as recognition struck her, Luna found herself back in the hexagon. As she went through all the stations, Luna became deeply worried by her revelation.

Nestor went to check on Luna as soon as she exited the Hexagon.

"How did everything go?" he asked.

"Great." Luna fought to contain her tears. "I want to go for a walk."

"Do you want to talk about what you saw?"

"You'd be bored if I told you. Not much happened." Luna glanced at Rufus. "Come on, Rufus."

Rufus flew onto her shoulder.

"Don't stay out too long," Nestor said.

Luna nodded and headed towards the eastern path, passing Kelly and Astrid who were seated at the marble table. She entered the path without saying a word to them and quickened her pace. When she was far enough away, she began to cry. "I don't know what to do, Rufus. Just as I was starting to be happy again, everyone I ever cared about was taken away from me."

"Luna happy, Rufus happy, everyone happy," Rufus said.

"Not everyone."

Rufus continued with his vocalizations throughout their walk. When Luna passed the extended ridge, she looked ahead in dismay. All the sunflowers in the meadow were wilted and lifeless. Luna cried as she approached the dead garden, unable to believe anything so drastic could happen after one day.

"Where am I going to go now, Rufus? This was the only place where I could be alone." She wept. "I don't understand what I'm supposed to do." Glancing at the garden again, the pressure inside her was too intense to contain. She ran, and Rufus flew off her shoulder. She kept running until she arrived at the mountain on the north side. Staring up the steep ascent, she thought about Jodi. They both loved to go camping and went on many hikes together. While most of the other children at summer camp preferred to go swimming, Luna and Jodi made it their mission to climb every tall tree and hike every mountain trail they could find during their trips.

Luna glanced up to admire the mountain peak. Whenever she had problems, they always seemed to leave her on a climb. She spotted a path ahead that she believed she could navigate. Upon reflecting over Astrid's warning and Seth's account of the golden star, she entered the path.

Unified Man

Kelly returned to the marble table after Astrid had called him back from going after Luna.

"She seemed a little off to me," Kelly said. "Maybe her session didn't go well."

"She is missing her parents. I know I miss mine."

"You haven't said that in years." Kelly picked up a water bottle and rubbed his thumbs along the surface. "But I can relate. Ever since the others arrived, I started missing beer again. It's as if they brought all our memories with them."

Astrid didn't hear Kelly's statement. She was thinking about her murder and Blaze's betrayal.

"Have you seen Blaze around?" Kelly asked. "I haven't seen him since he left the pillar."

"I am not his keeper!" Astrid snapped back. Rubbing her forehead she said. "Sorry about that. I am feeling a little tired." She looked at Kelly. "Do you think something happened to him?"

"Maybe. I spoke to Hiroko earlier on. She told me he gave her flowers shortly after she saw him open the door to the hexagon. He was naked. *Completely.* Even his tattoos were gone."

Astrid widened her eyes. "Did he say anything to her?"

"Before handing her the bouquet, he recited a poem about how we should all discard our clothing in reverence of the *Divine's artwork*. Has he always acted that oddly?"

Astrid shook her head. "He claimed he had some new understanding and was eager to go into the pillar to figure it out. But if what you tell me is true, Blaze sounds more confused than enlightened. If anything happens to him, it will be my fault."

Kelly held Astrid's hand. "You can't control what happens to anyone in the pillar. If he doesn't make it through, it will be better if he's removed now rather than risk our progress."

"Towards what? We still don't know why the Custodians brought us here. What if they are lying to me?"

"They never have before."

"But now one of us is missing, and Blaze might very well have lost touch with reality. All the questions I had when I first arrived here are resurfacing."

"Such as?"

"How is it that we ended up here?"

"They captured us before we died. You told us that."

"But what does that mean? Were we cloned? I never got a straight forward answer. And how can I know for certain that I was near death? That any of us were? I stopped asking questions because I was thankful to be alive, thankful to be taken care of and...*kept safe*. That used to be enough for me but not anymore."

"What more do you want to know?"

"What do the Custodians have in store for us next? I think that is a fair question. Don't you?"

"The three of us agreed that since there was no way out of here we'd make the best of it...and we have." He held Astrid's hand. "I loved our time together."

She took her hand away. "I don't want to be a prisoner any longer."

"You never felt that way before."

"I have been here for so long, my experiences before my arrival now seem unreal. I cannot even trust the ones that happened here. How can I be sure of anything?"

"We can't. But the three of us agreed that we had it better here. No violence, no famine, no war."

"But we cannot leave, and we may never be able to," Astrid said. "I was able to put that thought out of my mind for a long time. Now, it is all I think about. I feel trapped."

"What's wrong? You've been upset ever since you left the pillar this morning."

"Blaze and I had a fight before he left."

"I hope it wasn't about me."

"No. He understood complete—" Astrid's eyes opened wide when she spied Blaze walk out of the western path with Jeff and Opal.

Kelly turned to see what Astrid was looking at. "Is that Blaze?"

"And exactly how I remember him." Astrid ran to him.

When he spotted her, he pondered over how to explain his experience.

"What happened to you?" Astrid asked him.

"We'll talk later when the right words come to me. Xavier Starfly was right when he said that our language is very limiting."

Opal stepped in front of Astrid. "There may not be a later if we don't retaliate soon."

Nestor and Pearl joined the gathering.

"Did you find Anya?" Pearl asked.

"What regiment is she in?" Opal asked.

Pearl looked at Jeff. "What happened up there?"

"They blew everything up. All hands are lost," Opal said. "There's nothing left of San Diego. The whole fleet was destroyed as well."

"Let's get her inside the pillar," Kelly advised as he approached the group.

"She can't go in there like this," Jeff said.

"It's the best medicine when you're delusional."

"This happened to you?"

"Why are you all just standing around?" Opal yelled. "We're in the middle of a war-zone!"

"I'm sorry, Commander," Jeff responded. "Let's go inside and come up with a countermeasure."

"Not sure we can come up with one that can counter what just happened, but as long as I can walk and fire my weapon I'll keep fighting till the end."

Jeff was stirred by Opal's bravery. "I'm honored to serve under you, Commander." He saluted her with full conviction.

"Lead the way, Lieutenant." Opal followed Jeff to her unit.

Astrid, Blaze, and Kelly quietly sat around the marble table. Blaze was absorbed by the moment, taking in the sights from all around him. Kelly was absorbed by Blaze's behavior, and Astrid felt awkward being alone with both men.

Blaze loosely crossed his hands on the table and recited a verse that had come to him. "Silence is soothing. A perfect time for a retuning."

Astrid tilted her head, noticing a shift in his expression. It had a calming effect, and her anger toward him dissipated. "What do you mean?"

"Don't censor yourself around me. You and Kelly should celebrate the love and support you shared with each other. Freedom of expression is tantamount to building healthy relationships."

Astrid gawked at Blaze. "Your session went well?"

"It was the most enlightening experience I've ever had." Blaze sighed with a wide grin. "I feel high from the experience and don't want to come back down from it ever."

Kelly eyed Blaze curiously. "What happened to you in the pillar?"

"Nothing. Everything."

Astrid grazed her fingers against Blaze's forearm. "And your tattoos?"

"I'm not entirely sure, but I'm a new man, a unified man, no longer separated by artificial labels and definitions."

"Did you get a message towards the end of your session?" Kelly asked.

"I was told I never have to enter the pillar again."

Astrid faced Kelly. "How is that possible? He only went inside once."

Blaze knocked on the table. "I'm here, Astrid. You can ask me anything you want."

"I'm not sure what to ask."

"No worries." He got up. "When the time is right, we can talk again. I had a long day, and I'd like to rest for a while. You know where to find me." Blaze whistled "Winter Wind" as he walked away.

"Strange man," Kelly commented.

Astrid watched Blaze enter Anya's unit. She wanted to tell him to come back to her and that she didn't mean to throw him out. But the way he looked at her made Astrid feel as if he could read into all her most secret thoughts. Thoughts that she preferred to keep hidden from everyone, including herself.

I could feel Astrid pushing her darkness farther inside her, not wanting to let it out. I shined Light on her to counter it. As she was receptive to My call, I whispered to her, using her own inner voice. "Look inside."

She heard Me, excused herself and ran into her unit. I hoped I didn't come on too strong. Sheim told Me I could be a little too loud at times.

Waving the White Flag

Seth watched Hiroko as she sat in a lotus position beside the sundial. He lingered in front of her until she opened her eyes and stared up at him.

"How long have you been here?" Hiroko asked.

"According to that antiquated timepiece, about ten minutes."

She stood. "Did you want something?"

Seth stared over Hiroko's head to avoid her gaze. "Why didn't you tell me you wanted a divorce?"

"I was afraid of you. Your extreme mistrust scared me. I feared you might hurt me."

"I would've never hurt you, Hiro."

"It didn't take much to get you angry, and towards the end I had to watch everything I said to you."

"The only violence I ever committed was during the 1st sector war." Seth paced nervously as his memories of his tour flooded his consciousness. "So many innocent lives were lost. I could never kill another person after that."

"The Eastern Sector had many casualties as well."

"That's what I meant."

Hiroko was surprised. Seth made it his mission to design aircraft that could wipe out the Eastern Sector.

"Those of us with guns—we weren't the innocent ones. Made no difference whose side we were on." Seth recalled a memory of a family running out of their home. "It was the children that got to me."

"How come you never talked about this with me?"

"Because what I did was reprehensible. The United Republic gave me the permission to kill, and I believed that it absolved me of any wrongdoing. But everything I witnessed out on the battlefield told me I was in the wrong." He peered deeply at Hiroko. "That's why I surrendered to the enemy."

Hiroko widened her eyes. "Why did you do that?"

"After a raid, I saw some children who lost their parents. The youngest—couldn't have been older than four—asked if I could...get his mother a bandage because she was bleeding. I went with him."

Seth's gaze unfocused and surrendered to his brain that retrieved and transmitted his most horrific memory. He experienced all the sensations he did on the day the memory was formed. His legs felt as if they were about to collapse, but the pressure of his heart pounding against the wall of his chest is what made him stagger back a few steps.

"His mother's chest had been blown open," Seth said quietly.

Noticing the terror in his eyes, Hiroko walked closer to him.

"The boy's face haunted me every night before I went to bed," Seth said. "I couldn't take the violence anymore. When my regiment was asleep, I walked over to the other side holding a white flag and gave myself up. I thought they'd appreciate my act of compassion. Instead, I was arrested. The guards honored me with the nickname, Traitor. They called me that until the day of my release."

Hiroko held Seth's hand. "I still can't imagine what you must have gone through during those years."

"As I sat in my cell that first night, I realized I would've lost either way. You're either forced to fight or forced to surrender. I vowed that if I ever made it out alive, I'd become so rich that I'd never have to bow down to those in authority again. When you have enough credits, you own the authority."

"You became the authority," Hiroko said.

"And I got my revenge against my captors when my fleet helped us win the 3rd sector war. The problem is that the power I accumulated never erased what happened to me during my years as a POW. I felt betrayed by both sides. I might as well have been killed in action because my soul died there."

"You can start over here, Seth."

"I don't want to. I'm too tired."

Hiroko hugged him. "I'll help you."

Seth put his arms around his wife, relieved that his secret was finally out and that Jeff had kept quiet about what happened on the shuttle. He planned to tell Hiroko the truth, but revealing one secret exhausted him. He needed some time to rest before the next confession.

Opal paced back and forth while Jeff continued to go along with her delusion. Pearl knew Jeff was handling the situation exactly as she would have, but it didn't ease her trepidation. Her own illness was starting to take its toll on her. As soon as Pearl entered the unit, she collapsed on the couch, exhausted. Without her medication, Pearl didn't know how much longer she'd last. She couldn't bear the idea of dying before Opal was liberated from her past hurts.

The door chime sounded. Pearl, who was too exhausted to get up from the couch, gestured for Jeff to answer. When he opened the door, Rajni and Nestor entered in a panic.

Rufus, who had been perched on Nestor's shoulder, flew off and landed on Opal's shoulder. "Rufus!" She stroked his belly. "You came back!"

"What happened?" Jeff asked.

"Luna is missing," Nestor said. "Rufus came back without her."

"Rescue Luna. Rescue Luna," Rufus repeated.

"Could he know where she is?" Rajni asked.

Opal nodded her head once. "He knows."

Jeff and Pearl smiled at each other and then at Opal.

Opal glared at them. "Why are you two oafs standing there? The furniture in this room is demonstrating more purpose."

"Yes, Commander." Jeff smiled and saluted.

Opal glanced at her sister. "What about you? Clear the fog from your brain. We have a child to find."

"I can't walk far. I won't be of any help."

"You can inform the others that we went out to search for Luna."

"Yes, Ma'am." Pearl smiled.

Opal opened the door. "Find Luna, Rufus."

"Rufus rescue Luna." Rufus flew outside.

"What an amazing bird," Rajni said.

"Let's get going," Opal said.

Jeff headed out with her.

Nestor glanced at Rajni.

"I'm okay." She sat on the couch. "I have Pearl to keep me company."

"See you later then." Nestor forced a smile, then left.

"The strong go off while the weak ones stay behind," Pearl said. "That puts me next in line to go into the hexagon." She smiled at Rajni. "Unless you'd like to go ahead of me?"

"No thanks. I'll wait for my turn."

"I don't blame you."

"What I would like to do is help find Luna," Rajni said.

"I'm sure she'll understand why you can't."

"She hates me. I don't know why. Every time I try to reach out, she lashes out at me."

"She lost her family. Give her time."

"I said something similar to Nestor, but Luna gets along fine with him. He's always been good with kids. I never wanted them, and here one is forced on me." Rajni glanced at Pearl and then quickly looked away. "I must sound like an awful person to you."

"No." Pearl held Rajni's hand. "You sound honest."

The door chime rang. Rajni struggled to get up.

"I'll get it." Pearl answered the door, and Kelly stepped inside.

"I can't find Jeff or Opal, so you'll have to go to the hexagon next," Kelly told Pearl.

"Luna is missing," she said. "The others are searching for her."

"That leaves you and Rajni available to continue with the schedule."

"How can you be so cold?" Pearl asked. "She's only a child."

"The Custodians won't let anything bad happen to her."

"How can you be so sure?"

"They find Luna too important to lose."

"Why is she even here? She wasn't on the shuttle with us."

"I can't answer you because I don't know. Now please, Pearl. You need to go to the hexagon for your session."

"What happens if we refuse to participate?" Rajni asked. "Your cryptic responses won't work with me anymore. I need a better reason to go along with your schedule."

Kelly sighed. "Do you ladies want to eat?"

"So Seth was right? We are no better than lab animals," Pearl said.

"If that's how you choose to view yourself, you'll never adjust to this place. Eating and drinking is our way to survive...to continue. You did the same before you arrived at the refuge. At least here, there's no risk of getting blown up by a bomb or shot in the street by a violent gang."

"Surviving isn't enough for me," Rajni said.

"Then you'll die."

"If I must, so be it." She turned around and went back to the couch.

"That would be suicide."

"Let me talk to her," Pearl said.

"Take your turn at the pillar. I'll handle this," Kelly replied.

"She needs compassion, not a lecture."

"One on one, I'm not so bad."

Pearl looked at Rajni and then back at Kelly. She raised her index finger, and Kelly cupped her hand gently.

"I promise," he said, "I won't do anything to upset her." He released her hand.

"You better not, or I'll do something to upset you. I've just about had it with you bossing everyone around." She smiled at Rajni. "Stay as long as you like, dear." Pearl left the unit.

Kelly glanced at Rajni, hoping she'd go easier on him.

"I'd rather be alone," she said.

Kelly sat next to her. "I won't say a word. It'll be as if you're alone."

Without replying, Rajni got up, limped to the door, and left.

Blaze stood outside admiring the tall floral bushes that encircled the refuge. A poem came to his mind and without anything to write with, he committed each line to memory. Glancing up at the clear blue sky, he spotted Rufus fly by. He then looked ahead at Opal, Nestor, and Jeff who were walking toward him.

Opal and Jeff gawked at his appearance.

Nestor whispered to Jeff, "That's nothing. Wait till you hear him speak."

"I would like to share my experience in the pillar with you," Blaze said, "along with an inspirational poem that just came to me, but I can see you're all in a hurry."

"How observant of you," Jeff said.

Opal pointed at Blaze. "What happened to your tattoos?"

"The story is too involved to get into now. What's going on?"

"Luna is missing," Nestor said. "We're on our way to find her."

"I'd like to help."

"The more of us, the better," Opal said.

"And on the way, I'll tell you what I learned in the pillar."

"I take it you enjoyed your experience in that technological masterpiece?" Opal asked as they continued to the eastern path.

"It went beyond enjoyment, beyond anything I've ever experienced in my entire life. The pillar—whatever technology the machine uses—gets you to probe into your mind where you can discover your deeply guarded secrets."

"What kind of secrets?" Opal asked.

"The kind we keep from ourselves. Once I took a peek, I discovered what I hid inside wasn't so bad. Wish I knew this before. My life would've been a lot easier."

"I don't know if I'd like a machine roaming inside my head and changing me," Jeff said. "It's our personal struggles that shape us into what we are."

Opal patted Jeff's arm. "That was very philosophical, Lieutenant."

"The problem is that some of us can't tell between a self-induced struggle and one that's real," Nestor said. "I don't see anything wrong with having technology that helps us improve ourselves."

Jeff shook his head. "I'll stick to improving myself the old fashioned way, through hard work."

"I agree...with both you and Nestor," Blaze said.

"But they contradicted each other," Opal replied.

"One of the interesting side effects from the illusions we create." Blaze smiled.

"If that pillar transformed all the world leaders like it did you, there would never have been any sector wars," Nestor said.

"I'm glad the Aristocrats never had their hands on that kind of technology," Jeff added. "They would've found a way to use it against us."

"Who's to say they're not using it right now?" Nestor asked.

"We lack the scientific know-how to invent anything like the pillar," Opal said. "The material it's constructed from is way beyond our technology."

"Could be a black ops program," Nestor said.

"Hah! Stop getting your news from conspiracy theory pubpages," Opal said. "It would take us the next ten centuries to match what they have here."

"And that will never happen because Earth has been destroyed," Blaze added.

"Has it really?" Nestor asked. "Isn't it possible that all of this is part of some Aristocrat plot to see how we react in stressful situations?"

Opal looked at Blaze, who smiled at her. "It can't be," she said and raced ahead of everyone.

I could hear Opal's inner voice screaming loudly, *I must overcome this. Give me the strength.* I sprinkled some Light into her being, and Sheim questioned Me about My recent meddling. My response: "They call out into My silence, and I answer."

Rajni opened the door to her unit and was annoyed to discover Kelly standing outside.

"You don't have to check on me." She went back in and limped to the couch. "You can go now. I'll be all right."

"You announced you were going to starve yourself to death. You're far from all right."

"It's none of your concern."

"Why are you doing this?"

"Why do you care?"

Kelly sat down on the edge of the couch. He didn't want to say the wrong words that would make Rajni think killing herself seemed the better option. Words were never his strength, and he wished Hiroko was here with him. She always knew the right thing to say.

"I don't know why I'm here anymore than you do," Kelly said. "I was never good at leading, yet here I am...leading."

"Why are you going along with this?"

"The reason we're all here is because of my poor judgment. I won't let anything bad happen under my watch again. As the captain, it's my duty to ensure you all survive."

"Let yourself off the hook. Your job ended ten years ago."

"So I thought." He peered at Rajni. "Until you told me you were willing to die."

Rajni turned away from him. "My wanting to die has nothing to do with this place. I wanted to die long before I even won the lottery."

"Why do you want to die?"

Rajni put her hands on her thighs and massaged them. "I can barely feel my legs, and I have no cane to get around. Every time I stand, I get dizzy and have to concentrate on my balance to keep from falling. I do the same whenever I walk. Each step I take is planned. I had an easier time with ballet." Rajni pressed her fingers against her temples. "Without my medication, I'm in pain all the time, except when I'm asleep." She dropped her arms to the side. "Surviving only to eat isn't enough for me."

"How about for your family?"

"Nestor and I are no longer family."

"There must be a reason they placed you here together."

"Why would they, whoever they are, want Luna to stay with us? I never wanted children. That was Nestor's dream, not mine."

"I can't answer your question, but you can't either. Maybe you should postpone your suicide until you get your answer."

Rajni recalled all the discussions she had with her grandmother about Hindu mythology, along with her own fascination about alien life. Her curiosity to discover where she was returned and eclipsed her pain. "I'll go along...until I get the answers I want."

Nightmare

Astrid sat on the couch in her unit, quivering. She played back the sequence of key events in her life, attempting to construct meaning. When she first arrived at the refuge, her sessions in the pillar had been frightening. They dealt with her precognitive work with the police. After a few visits, Astrid only had pleasant visions that were whimsical and relaxing. The imprints she captured during her sessions yielded the most creative and exhilarating encounters. She traveled the globe, played cello in the most famous concert halls, and even performed in a trio with Mozart and Chopin. On several occasions, Astrid relived her experiences with Blaze, but she eventually stopped because they only made her miss him more.

Astrid's latest session in the pillar began with a visit to her grandmother who made her apple strudel with a dollop of vanilla ice cream. While Astrid sat and enjoyed her treat, her grandmother stared at her.

"Do you have anything to tell me?" she asked.

Astrid put down her spoon. "I love you."

"Is that all?"

"Thanks for the dessert." Astrid resumed eating.

Astrid's grandmother shook her head. "You like keeping secrets."

Astrid dropped the spoon. "We already went through this. I did not warn you because I believed my visions were nothing more than nightmares."

Astrid's grandmother wept. "It hurt so much. When the car ran over me, I could feel each wheel rolling over my body."

"What do you want from me?" Astrid leaned back against her chair and crossed her arms.

"To admit the truth."

"I have been completely honest with you."

Astrid's grandmother leaned forward and glared at her. "You have done nothing but lie to yourself since you got here. And I know what you're lying about."

Astrid pushed the plate off the table.

"You must end this now," her grandmother told her. "We don't have an eternity to sort through these matters."

"Why won't you just tell me what you want?"

"I cannot see your truth. Only you can." She picked up a mirror from the counter and placed it in front of Astrid's face.

Astrid materialized on a bed, lying on her back with her wrists tied to the posts.

Charlie Trip sat over her. He leaned down and stared at Astrid with a crazed expression. "Allow me to introduce myself before I take my vengeance on your husband for beating me up almost every day in school."

Astrid turned to face Blaze who was tied to a chair.

Charlie grabbed Astrid's face and turned it to face him. "I'm Charlie Trip, and I'm going to make you suffer as much as your husband made me suffer. By the time this night is over, you're going to die hating him."

"Leave her alone, Charlie!" Blaze said. "It's me you have a problem with!"

Charlie jumped out of the bed and squatted in front of Blaze. "A problem? Is that what you call what happened to me? A problem? You made my life a living hell. School was a prison to me. I thought I'd be free once I got out, but my memories never left. They haunted me, followed me around wherever I went. I was programmed by you to be like this. You made me into what you see before you now."

"We were just kids!" Blaze thrust himself forward and stomped his foot on the ground. "All kids rip on each other!"

Charlie slapped Blaze across the face. "I'm not going to let you avoid your responsibility anymore. Tonight, I'm going to give back what you gave me. That's why you won't die tonight. If you die, you won't suffer. To suffer, you have to be alive as I was when I was forced to deal with your brutality."

Charlie went back to Astrid and climbed on top of her. "Before your wife dies, I want you to admit that you're going to be responsible for her death." He turned to face Blaze. "Say it."

Tears trailed down Blaze's cheeks. "I'm sorry, Astrid. I'm so sorry I killed you."

Astrid cried as the memories of that horrific night flooded her mind. "Commence emergency shutdown! I have seen enough!"

"I don't think you have." Charlie tore off her nightgown. "You've been living in denial ever since you got here. I won't let you deny me any longer."

Astrid remembered her last words to Blaze. *Je t'aime.* She squeezed her eyes shut and yelled, "Make it stop now!"

Strange blips, buzzes, and clicks sounded. She opened her eyes and gasped as an alien being, whom she recognized as a Custodian, stared down at her. Its oblong visage was composed of a constantly shifting and blending array of colors. Astrid understood this movement to be language.

"We fix, so you continue," the Custodian said.

Astrid turned to the side where Rajni lay on a table. Between them was a light green beam of light. A fetus floated from within, and its arms and legs slowly moved about.

The scenery around Astrid rearranged, and she stood in front of the hexagon. Hiroko stood in front of her with her arms crossed.

"Have the last ten years happened?" Astrid cried. "I cannot tell what is real anymore."

"You are real," Hiroko said.

"How can I be sure?" She clutched Hiroko's arm. "Are you one of them?"

"One of who?"

"The Custodians. They took us on board their ship."

"I'm not a Custodian," Hiroko said.

Kelly appeared next to Astrid. "We're all Custodians." He laughed, and his face morphed into one of the Custodians.

Astrid awoke from her nightmare, screaming. She was now convinced the last ten years never happened.

Flying Toward Home

Hiroko strolled back to the refuge with Seth. Hearing his confession made her question every assumption she'd made about him. Nevertheless, she had no interest in resuming their relationship. Too much had happened since the day of the crash. Hiroko never believed in looking back. At present, she felt a strong connection to Jeff. She remembered how he had saved her life, and him being the first person she saw when her eyes opened. His concerned expression seemed more sincere to her than Seth's.

"Thanks for listening to me," Seth said.

"I'm glad I could help, but a long time has passed."

Seth stopped and took Hiroko's hand. "I don't expect you to come back to me, Hiro. But we're going to be seeing each other every day. It'll make things easier if we could forget the past and start over as friends."

"I'd like that very much, Seth." She glanced towards the path entrance from where Opal, Jeff, Nestor, and Blaze had just entered through.

"Luna is missing," Jeff said.

Blaze extended his hand towards Seth. "Let's put our anger aside and work together."

Seth shook Blaze's hand while creasing his forehead. "Blaze?"

Blaze smiled and bowed his head.

"Do you have any idea where to start looking?" Hiroko asked.

"We're following Rufus." Blaze pointed to the sky.

"Can you also get him to search for Anya?" Seth asked.

"He's looking for Luna now," Opal said, "but if he finds Anya, he'll let us know. Rufus was trained to locate people in trouble."

Seth looked up at Rufus. "What an amazing bird."

"He truly is." Opal marched ahead. "Come on everyone! Let's put on some speed!"

The lottery winners trekked northward, keeping their eyes on Rufus. When they arrived at the base of the mountain, Rufus changed his direction and headed west. Jeff pointed at the natural land bridge, and Opal acknowledged him with a nod.

"I remember now," she said. "We're completely surrounded."

"By what?" Nestor asked while instinctively reaching for his camcorder, then remembering he didn't have it.

"We're in a maze." Jeff and Seth noted at the same time.

"Over there!" Opal pointed towards a path that Rufus was circling over.

The lottery winners followed Rufus, with Opal and Jeff in the lead.

Nestor caught up with them. "I'm impressed by your physical strength," he said to Opal.

"Why? Because I'm a woman or that I'm old."

"Both." Nestor grinned.

"You'd be impressed over some of the other things I'm still capable of doing." She winked one of her eyes at Nestor and then raced farther ahead.

Opal's comment reminded Nestor of Becky. "Stick around after dinner, and I may impress you with my other talents," she'd told him after he had complimented her on her culinary skills. Nestor pictured Becky's face so clearly, he was ready to reach out and pull her to him. The confusion over his senses intensified his suspicion that they were part of an Aristocrat experiment and that Becky and Joey were at home waiting for him. Turning to Jeff, he said, "I think we're still on Earth."

"What makes you say that?" Seth asked.

"The star system in the sky is the same as our own," Blaze added.

"I didn't know you were an astronomer," Seth said.

"Had a character who was. I did a lot of research about the Solar System and what lurked beyond. The stars in the sky are the same stars we've always seen."

"He's right," Jeff confirmed. "I noticed the same thing, but I'm not so sure we're still on Earth."

"Where do you think we are?" Blaze asked.

Nestor looked up at the sky. "Plugged into some virtual freak show conjured up by the Aristocrats."

Opal pushed her hand toward Nestor. "Get out of that path and find a new one. The Aristocrats could never come up with anything as sophisticated as this place." Opal turned to Jeff. "What do you think, Lieutenant?"

"I don't know what to believe anymore."

"Why believe in anything?" Blaze asked. "Does it matter where we are as long as we can experience all that we are experiencing?"

"It does to me." Jeff glanced at Hiroko. "Where do you think we are?"

"I want to say another world, but I don't think that's the correct answer either. When Kelly and I first awoke here, we were all alone. We believed we were still on Earth, yet nothing in the refuge was like anything we had seen before."

"Did you start following their rules right away?" Opal asked.

"An electronic tablet was left for us in the hexagon. It only worked for me. On the screen were instructions on how the pillar operated and how we could get our food. Kelly and I didn't follow the instructions, at first."

"What made you change your mind?" Seth asked.

"I was dying from starvation, and Kelly entered the pillar to get food for us. After we saw everything was all right, we started to go along. We even started to prefer it here over Earth."

"Do you still have the tablet?" Opal asked.

"In my unit, but it's useless now. Once Astrid arrived, the Custodians only communicated with her."

"Maybe she's one of them," Seth said.

"She isn't," Blaze replied.

"How can you know that?" Jeff asked. "You haven't seen her in years."

"Astrid is a medium. Before her death, she worked, unofficially, for various law enforcement agencies and helped capture several criminals."

Hiroko appeared confused. "She never mentioned any of that to us."

"Doesn't surprise me. Astrid hated having precognition. She witnessed many horrific crimes, some of which gave her sleepless nights."

Hiroko nodded her head. "I can see how that would be disturbing."

"I used to agree with you, but now I know she has a gift," Blaze said. "It's something to be appreciated and not feared." He stretched his hand toward the sky. "Just like this world is a gift to us from the Custodians...a refuge from the destruction we've left behind."

"What type of bliss pills are you on?" Seth asked.

"The same ones all of us have a prescription for."

Blaze's expression reminded Seth of Xavier Starfly.

"You're chasing after an illusion," Seth said.

"Everything is an illusion, so why not make the illusion something you like?"

"Already tried that. My colony was the grandest of all illusions, and it now sits unused because I believed in what's producing that ridiculous smile on your face."

"Your smile is radiant," Hiroko said to Blaze. "It shows that you're connected to your inner purpose."

Seth shook his head. "I'm outnumbered by a band of deluded cultists."

"Interesting you'd say that," Nestor interjected, "considering you worshipped a man who claimed to hear the *Divine Voice* and who ordered you around with garbled messages in his notebook."

Jeff and Opal laughed.

"And who also happened to be right about Earth's destruction."

Nestor recalled his interview with Seth. The eeriness of the prediction was hard to ignore. He lulled himself back to the comfort of his opinion. An Aristocrat conspiracy was far easier to deal with than the destruction of a whole planet that took Becky and Joey along with it.

The speculation about their whereabouts continued as the lottery winners approached the mountain path. The discourse grew intense midway through their climb and ended when they heard Luna yelling for them.

Nestor pointed towards an extended ridge halfway up the cliff face from where Luna was waving at them.

"How did she get up there?" Hiroko asked as she scrutinized the treacherous climb.

Nestor yelled out, "Stay calm, Luna! We're coming to get you!"

From on top of the ledge, Luna smiled as she gazed down at the lottery winners. Rufus landed on her shoulder, and she petted his head. "I knew you'd get help for me."

Opal stared up at Luna. "Stay still! I'm coming up for you!"

Jeff approached her. "Commander, let me go instead. You're a better leader than I am. If anything happens to you—"

"Don't underestimate your ability to lead. I'm going up alone. I *insist*."

"Can't argue with you. You outrank me."

"Glad you know your place, Lieutenant." She smiled. "I appreciate the concern, but I've probably climbed more mountains than you."

Seth approached. "I've climbed a few mountains myself. If you need company, I'll join you."

"I don't need a chaperone." Opal stepped back to get a visual map of her climb. Once she found the perfect trajectory, she began her ascent.

Invisible Daughter

Pearl collapsed when the light pillar activated. Too dizzy to stand, she crawled around trying to find a way out. But no matter where she maneuvered herself, she couldn't escape the blinding light. She closed her eyes and screamed for help.

"What are you doing down there?"

Pearl opened her eyes and saw Harry sitting on the couch in her old apartment. He attempted to help her up, and she swatted his arm.

"What's wrong?" he asked.

"This whole situation." Pearl got up and headed for the door.

Harry followed after her. "Why did you call and tell me to come over?"

"I was lonely, but not anymore."

"Just a few minutes ago, we agreed how Bertrand and Opal were selfish to put outside obligations before us."

"And we were selfish to act on our feelings. We disregarded the vows we made to Opal and Bertrand."

"You never would've disregarded yours if they meant anything to you."

"They meant everything!"

"Did they really?"

"Yes! And you can't make me believe otherwise!" Pearl opened the door and was surprised to find Father Stephen standing in front of her.

"But I can." Stephen pulled Pearl into his arms and kissed her.

Excited and frightened by the strength of her passion, Pearl pushed Stephen away. "I always wanted to do this, but it wasn't right. It still doesn't feel right."

"What's not right about it?"

"It's a sin."

"A convenient excuse to hide behind, so you won't have to deal with your true feelings."

"I didn't hide behind anything. I loved Bertrand."

"Then why did you tell me something was missing between the two of you?" Harry said from behind her. Leaning his chin on her shoulder, he whispered, "Remember what you told me after the first time we made love? After we went through a whole bottle of wine together?"

"I never had passionate feelings for Bertrand."

"And when I asked you why you married him, what did you tell me?"

Pearl gazed at Stephen. "The man I truly love I could never have," she said as a rain of tears trailed down her cheeks.

"You could have me right now."

"Is it a sin to sin in your dreams?"

Stephen hugged her. "How can it be a sin to be with the one you love?"

The two kissed again, and Pearl felt a tap on her back. She ignored it, and another tap followed seconds later.

"Even here I'm invisible."

Pearl pushed Stephen away and swung around. "Christina?"

"Oh. You remember my name?" Christina said with her arms crossed.

"Of course I do, sweetheart." Pearl became teary eyed as she hugged Christina, who didn't reciprocate the embrace. "I missed you so much. We spent years looking for you."

"It's too late now. I'm dead. I would've appreciated this while I was living at home. Maybe if you showed me that you cared about me, I wouldn't have cut you out of my life, and you would've had a relationship with your grandchildren."

"I have grandchildren?"

"Three. A boy and two girls."

"I was always there for you."

"Your body was, but you weren't. I was an obligation. A *mistake.*"

"Don't ever say that."

"Whenever you weren't criticizing me for everything you thought I did wrong, you were ignoring me. Opal supported me more than you did, until after the shuttle crash. Why did she stop speaking to me? What did you tell her?"

"Nothing, I..."

Stephen pulled Pearl over to him and kissed her. "If you came to me sooner, you wouldn't have gone to Harry."

"You should have sinned, Mother," Christina said. "Then I wouldn't have been born into a family that didn't want me."

Pearl examined every feature on Christina's face as though seeing it for the first time. "Whenever I looked at you, all I saw was my betrayal." She sobbed.

"Finally, an admission. But what good will it do me now?"

"I always loved you." Pearl cupped her daughter's face. "I never stopped searching for you, but you died before I could find you. Our chance to make peace is over, and I have to keep living each day knowing I hurt you." Pearl dropped her hands to her sides. "I have no choice but to accept that you died hating me."

"I don't hate you. I don't feel anything for you. You've become nothing more than a forgotten memory."

Pearl closed her eyes. "Please take me out of here. Please. This isn't helping. There can be no resolution without Christina being here with me."

A crackling sound made Pearl open her eyes. Behind her daughter, a large orange fire flickered. She stepped back terrified. Believing she was staring into the ingress of hell, she pointed at Christina and shouted, "You're not really my daughter! I don't believe anything you're saying!"

Father Stephen held Pearl, and she pushed him away. "And you're not Stephen! None of this is real. I want to get out now! Let me out!" Pearl felt a sharp pain in her abdomen and fell to her knees. "Please, shut this off! I can't take this anymore! It's too much!"

Pearl opened her eyes. She was lying on her back in the hexagon.

Kelly helped her up. "Give yourself a few minutes. You'll be all right."

"How did you get in here?" Pearl asked. "I thought no one could enter once the pillar is activated."

"The alarm went off, and the hexagon went into automatic shutdown. What happened?"

"I'd rather not talk about this. It's personal."

He nodded. "You can return to your unit. You're finished for today."

Pearl clutched both of Kelly's arms. "No! Not only for today! I don't ever want to come back in here again!"

"Get your nourishment, and I'll be outside waiting for you. We'll talk then. Okay?"

Pearl nodded her head, and Kelly left the hexagon to give Pearl some privacy. She thought about her daughter's words to her and cried more.

When the private investigator that Pearl had hired found Christina, she thought she'd have plenty of time to reconnect with her. Fearing that her daughter would push her away if she attempted any contact, Pearl decided to wait for the right moment that would be revealed by a sign from God. It's not as fantastical as it sounds. I'm filled with right moments, and Pearl was sensitive enough to detect them. Nevertheless, her right moment never materialized as she missed My cues. Her fear that Christina would turn her away continued to block My signals. Having already lost Opal, Pearl didn't want to feel the sting of rejection again. She would have risked it now, but it was too late. Christina was gone forever. There would be no reconciliation. "Hindsight can be both the cruelest enemy and the wisest teacher," Sheim had once told me. Sheim wasn't kidding.

Pearl opted out of the water and nutrition cubes and exited the hexagon wondering how long it would take for her to starve to death. Kelly and Rajni approached her.

"Don't go in there," Pearl warned Rajni. "It's not what they told us it would be. They should call this thing the nightmare machine."

Rajni eyed Kelly with concern.

"You'll be okay," he told her.

Pearl pointed at Kelly. "Why don't *you* have to go in the pillar? What makes you so special?"

"Don't worry about me, Pearl," Rajni told her. "Nestor went in, and he's okay."

"And Luna disappeared."

Rajni held Pearl's hand. "I'll be all right and so will Luna. Opal and the others will find her." Rajni went inside, and the door shut.

Kelly helped Pearl to the marble table so she could rest. He handed her a bottle of water, and she drank half the contents in one gulp.

"I don't need to go into the pillar anymore because I have nothing more to offer," Kelly explained.

Pearl put down the bottle. "I don't want to offer anything more."

"It would trouble the Custodians if you gave up."

"I'm old. My loss won't make any difference."

"It will to me," Kelly said. "All of you are here because of actions I took, and it's up to me to make sure you are comfortable and secure."

"What actions?"

"I was the pilot. Your lives were in my hands from the moment you climbed aboard the shuttle."

"We survived then, but I'm not so sure we will here. I don't even know where we are, and I want to know. I have to know."

"Why is that so important to you?"

"My whole life, I prayed, went to church each week and tried my hardest to keep the commandments. Was everything I did all for nothing?"

"Aren't you reason enough?"

"After my experience in that pillar, I've learned I'm not." Pearl closed her eyes and tried to envision her grandchildren that she wasn't even sure she had. She wept when no image came to her mind. "I'm not putting myself through this again. I'm still shaking." She opened her teary eyes and peered at Kelly. "There's nothing you can say to make me change my mind."

"How about Opal?"

"She'll be all right."

"How do you think she'll feel about you giving up?"

"She'll think I got what I deserve."

"Do you honestly believe that?"

"I do. It's the truth." Pearl stood. "Now if you don't mind, I would rather be alone." She walked away not knowing what to believe in anymore. It was as if the ground was pulled from beneath her, and she had nowhere to land. That was how Opal preferred to live. Pearl, on the other hand, never fathomed the allure of uncertainty until she acknowledged her feelings for Father Stephen. However, that same uncertainty also terrified Pearl because letting go meant letting go of her faith in a religion that told her falling in love with a priest was a sin. But that same faith failed to stop her from sinning when she slept with her sister's husband and gave birth to a daughter whom she neglected.

When Pearl returned to her unit, she knelt on the ground, did the sign of the cross and recited the *Our Father*. She repeated it because the words comforted her. Pearl cycled through the prayer several times until she disappeared into the verse and connected to the Light within her. A dose of My energy flooded her from inside, and she smiled. "Thank you, God. Thank you for not abandoning me."

I was tempted to respond, and Sheim scolded Me. "You are not a god."

"Are there any gods?" I asked.

Sheim answered Me as Sheim always does...with silence. It's maddening.

Unexpected Path

Opal grasped a jagged rock and pulled herself onto a narrow ledge. She glanced overhead at the ledge from where Luna was looking down at her.

"Are you all right, Commander?" Jeff yelled from down below.

"Just taking a rest," Opal yelled back and continued her climb. About six feet away from her destination, one of the rocks she'd latched onto dislodged, and she slipped. She grabbed another rock on the way down. Both her feet dangled in mid-air.

"Do you need assistance?" Jeff hollered from below.

"Stay where you are! I'm all right!"

"I'm sorry," Luna cried from above, worried that Opal would end up getting killed.

"Hang on. I'll be up there shortly." Opal swung her legs forward, planted her feet against the cliff face, and thanked herself for keeping up with her pull-ups.

"Are you okay?" Nestor shouted.

"I will be when you stop distracting me with all the questions!" Opal yelled.

From down below, Seth and Hiroko approached Jeff and Nestor.

"We should go help," Seth said.

"If she needs us, she'll let us know."

"You have a lot of confidence in her."

"She's been through far worse than this."

"I can relate," Seth said.

Hiroko clutched Seth's hand and gave it a gentle reassuring squeeze.

Jeff misunderstood the gesture and walked over to Nestor. "Where's Blaze?" he asked.

Nestor shrugged his shoulders then widened his eyes, pointing off to the side where Blaze had begun to climb the mountain.

"Blaze, get your ass back down here before you get yourself killed!" Jeff yelled.

Blaze ignored the command and continued his ascent.

"Impressive," Seth said. "Never thought he had it in him."

Nestor looked up at Luna, cupped his hands around his mouth, and yelled, "They're coming for you! Don't be scared."

"I'm not!" Luna stroked Rufus's wing and said to him, "I'll never forgive myself if anything happens to Opal."

"Almost there!" Opal shouted from beneath her. She clasped the brink of the ledge, jammed one of her feet against the jagged rock, and hoisted herself to safety. Glancing over the precipice, she saluted the lottery winners down below, then fell onto her back.

Luna knelt beside her. "Are you okay, Opal?"

"Oh, yes." Opal outstretched her arms and smiled. "That was one of the most invigorating climbs I've had in a while."

Back at ground level, Jeff yelled up to Blaze. "You can come back down! She made it up!"

Blaze continued to climb, surprised by his own heroic display. He hadn't felt this good in years, and his actions reminded him of Drake Kent, who would've climbed any mountain to save a life. The feeling of satisfaction Drake had after every rescue was something Blaze wanted to experience for himself. He was tired of basing his life on his literary success and wanted to be more than an author.

Meanwhile, up on the ledge, Luna was hugging Opal. "I'm so sorry I put you in danger."

"This is nothing. I've been in worse situations," Opal said as some rocks fell from overhead.

"Uh-oh. Trouble," Rufus said.

"And we'll be gone before it arrives," Opal said as she directed Luna toward the rim of the ledge. "I'll head down first. Follow my lead."

Luna petted Rufus. "I can't. It's too high."

"I don't have rescue gear. The only way down is the same way you came up."

Luna stared at the ground. "I'm scared."

"Stay behind me, and you'll be all right."

Some more rocks fell, and Luna backed up until she bumped into the mountain wall.

Opal got on her knees and held both of Luna's hands. "You're going to have to put your fear aside if you want to live."

"Like Space Ex," Luna said as she reflected over the conversation with her mother in the pillar. *You have a full life ahead of you. Don't allow fear to shut you out of the new adventures that await you.*

"Great example," Opal said. "Can you be brave like Space Ex?"

"I'll try."

"Luna is brave," Rufus said.

"That she is." Opal stroked his belly. "See you on the ground."

Rufus flew away.

"Let's get moving." Opal maneuvered herself off the ledge and slowly began her descent.

Luna trailed behind her and froze when she looked down.

"Keep moving," Opal said.

Luna closed her eyes. *Space Ex would never stop. He'd die before giving up.* With renewed vigor, she lowered her foot onto a protruding rock.

"You're doing great—" Opal stepped on a rock that dislodged.

Blaze, who was beneath her, stretched up his hand and caught her foot. "Glad I decided to come up after you," he said.

"That was a crazy stunt." Opal smiled. "Thanks."

"Any time."

The three reached the ground safely, and the lottery winners cheered.

Opal surveyed the ledge overhead. "Where's Rufus?"

"Over there!" Luna pointed to a smaller ledge where Rufus was perched. Some rocks were rolling down in his direction.

All the lottery winners yelled and made flapping gestures for Rufus to fly away. The rocks struck the ledge, and he disappeared from view.

"Rufus!" Opal and Luna yelled out.

Nestor kept his eye on the ledge. Seconds later, Rufus flew into the sky.

"He's okay!" Nestor yelled. "Yeah! He's okay!"

The lottery winners applauded.

Rufus came down and landed on Opal's shoulder.

"You truly are an amazing bird, Rufus," she said. "You never fall."

Jeff saluted Opal with a smile. "Just like you, Commander."

Universe of the Shades

The light pillar turned off, and Rajni stood on stage as Nikiya from *La Bayadère*. It also happened to be the same ballet where she connected to Me. During our union, all traces of what had defined her disappeared. She became Nikiya. This is what you humans refer to as *being in the zone*.

She took it a step further...

At the grande finale, her whole body charged up with My creative energy, so much so that she couldn't come back down after the curtain had dropped.

If you can imagine My explanation, then you'll be able to grasp why Sun became overactive. It's really not all that different from what happened to Rajni. When she connected to the main link I use to communicate with all sentients, she witnessed a spark of Light she erroneously believed was a camera flash. Once My current entered her, a strong surge of euphoria flooded her whole body, making her feel as though she were flying. The sensation lasted several days.

My energy surged unrestrained through Rajni's nervous system, pushing her deepest fears to the surface. She tried to force them back into her subconscious netherworld, but once she'd connected to Me, there was no going back. I cleansed her with Light to assuage her, but she refused to accept Me. Her resistance brought upon terrifying visions. The most frightening of them all was of Kali.

The Hindu goddess with black onyx skin and fiery red eyes stood at the foot of Rajni's bed. Around her neck was a skull lei. From out of her wide open mouth, her tongue protruded and stretched down past her chin. Her four arms extended out to the side holding a sword, trident, bowl filled with blood, and Rajni's severed head.

"I'm here to stay," Kali said. "I'm not leaving until you die." She swung the sword forward, jolting Rajni out of the vision.

Less intense visions followed, but Rajni couldn't blot out Kali's phrase or image from her mind. She found it difficult to concentrate on anything, including her dancing. After a month of sleepless nights, she started seeing a psychiatrist. He prescribed medication that stopped her visions but also blocked My energy that had the potential to heal her. She soon experienced her first symptom of multiple sclerosis when both her legs went completely numb during a rehearsal. Rajni never danced again after that day.

Most humans would've gone mad with the amount of My energy Rajni had absorbed. But she endured. Her will was strong.

Sheim told Me I was similar to her in My youth, always drifting off into the void, insisting that I could exist on my own. It made me think about Sun and how he took after Me. I could no longer be mad at him as I would then have to be angry at Myself. Anger stunts My evolutionary growth, so I forgave him and looked forward to hearing about his future orbits around the galactic center.

In Rajni's pillar fantasy, "No. 27 Allegro" from *La Bayadère* echoed throughout the theater. When the music softened and the harp sounded, Rajni's legs moved as though they had been beckoned by the strings. The symptoms from her multiple sclerosis were gone, and she threw herself into her performance as Nikiya. Her legs were now as graceful and flexible as when she danced as a professional ballerina for the United Republic Ballet Company. Refusing to be tied down by the choreography, Rajni improvised her own version of the *Snake Dance*. Her aplomb was steady; her arabesque, flawless; her pirouettes as perfectly executed as during her last performance. Each cabriole, ballonné, grand jeté, and fouetté en tournant, seemed effortless. She went through all the dances without forgetting a single step, leap, or turn.

Nestor's wife, Becky, danced toward her, dressed like her rival Gamzatti. She handed Rajni a basket of flowers. If this were the same *La Bayadère* that was performed by the United Republic Ballet Company, Nikiya would've gotten bitten by a snake that had been surreptitiously placed inside the basket by Gamzatti. But Rajni was too involved with her dancing to analyze why Becky, someone she'd only seen in a picture, would be part of her pillar fantasy.

Rajni strode across the stage, joyfully pulling petals from out of the basket and tossing them onto the floor. She pressed the opening of the basket against her chest and her legs went numb. She pulled the basket away and removed a syringe that stuck out of her chest. Collapsing onto her back she smiled, surmising that the pillar was granting her wish to die, but not before giving her the chance to dance one last time. As she was about to surrender to death, lively orchestral music that strayed away from the score began to play. A healthy version of Rajni danced over, holding another syringe. She knelt beside Rajni and injected her in the center of her chest. "You were born to dance. Being a part of the audience will never satisfy you."

Rajni got onto her knees. Sitting across from her on a throne was Nestor, dressed like Solor, Nikiya's lover. He was smoking out of a hookah, hoping the opium would get his mind off of Nikiya's death.

Oh God, please don't tell me he's going to dance, she thought to herself.

The stage lights dimmed, and the Shades, thirty-two ballerinas dressed in white tutus, glided onto the stage in single file and began to dance all around Rajni. She crawled past them, stopping in front of Nestor. He took a drag from the hookah mouth tip and blew out an impressive smoke cloud that masked his face.

Rajni got onto her knees, inhaled the smoke, and felt a wave of euphoria enter her. Explosive orchestral music interspersed with tabla drums and a sitar sounded, completely detaching the score from *La Bayadère*. Nestor tossed the hose on the floor, sprang up, and began to dance all around Rajni. She giggled as her normally rigid ex-husband expertly cycled through eighteen fouetté turns. He then stopped and pointed to stage right.

A giant statue of the Buddha, with a stairwell that lead to a platform, rolled onto the stage. The Shades all stopped dancing and bowed as Becky danced over still dressed as Gamzatti. She was waiting for Solor, who she was to marry on that day.

One of the Shades got up. In her hand was a large dagger. She danced over to Rajni and handed it to her. Rajni stared at the blade and then looked up at Becky and Nestor, who now danced together. The music became more dramatic, and all the stringed instruments in the orchestra sped up.

The feeling returned to Rajni's legs. She leapt up to her feet and ran towards Nestor. She stabbed him in his chest and then turned to Becky who dropped to her knees and cried. Clasping her hands together, she desperately pled for her life.

Rajni raised the knife. As she readied herself to stab Becky, the music crescendoed. Rajni stared at her hand holding the knife. Horrified by the violence she never thought she was capable of, she dropped the knife, ran up the stairs of the Buddha statue, and was struck down by a giant lightning bolt.

A white mist formed all around her. She stood, and it slowly cleared away. Beneath her feet, a carpet of clouds swirled and sparkled under a bright blue sky. The sun gleamed brightly, and a large green blaze emerged from out of the cover of the clouds. Rajni sidled towards it. Nestor tapped the back of her shoulder, startling her. He extended his hand, offering to dance. Rajni shoved him, and he grabbed her arms.

Kali materialized off to the side, holding a sword and Rajni's head in two of her hands. "I'm here to stay, and I'm not leaving until you die!" Her tongued rolled out like a snake and headed toward Rajni.

Rajni pushed Nestor out of the way, jumped into the green flames, and landed on a seat in the shuttle that had crashed ten years before. Sitting next to her was Nestor. He handed her an airsick bag. "Looks like you'll be needing this."

"That was the strangest production of *La Bayadère* I ever danced in." Rajni touched her neck to ensure that her head was still attached to her body. "Can't figure out what I was supposed to get out of it other than I have a grotesque imagination."

"Don't ask me. I see too many possibilities to give you one absolute answer."

Rajni smacked Nestor's arm with the airsick bag. "That was the one thing that annoyed me most about you."

Nestor smiled and winked. "We can't all be perfect."

Rajni leaned in close to him. "What would you have said if I told you I was on my way to Compassionate Endings to kill myself?"

"Are you always this honest on a first date?"

"It's your fault I didn't find my peace. The only thing these last ten years added to my life was more pain."

"How did I manage to do all that if I only just met you?"

Rajni leaned back in her seat and stared ahead at the exit sign. "My vision after the crash was nothing but a hallucination. I was never fixed. I based the last ten years of my life believing in a delusion."

Nestor covered Rajni's eyes with a sleep mask. "You're not seeing everything."

A baby cried, and Rajni took off her mask. She now lay on a bed in the hotel room she had stayed in after the shuttle crash. Lying beside her was a baby girl, wrapped in a white blanket.

"Why am I here?" Rajni awkwardly picked up the baby. "And why would I dream about you?" Rajni carried her into the bathroom, laid her on the counter, and undressed her. Four beauty marks encircled her belly button in almost the exact position of twelve, three, six, and nine o'clock. After cleaning and wrapping the baby in a towel, Rajni held her and felt a warmth and contentment she'd never experienced.

"Be careful you don't drop her on her head."

Rajni turned and saw Luna. "I won't."

"The way you were so quick to get rid of her, I don't believe you."

"She wasn't mine to keep."

Luna sat on the bed. "You could've at least changed her diapers."

Rajni caressed the baby's face.

"She was upset, but you didn't want to smell her stinky-poo and damage your precious little nose." Luna held up a translinker. "Do you want me to call security so you can get rid of her again?"

"Why do you hate me so much? I never did anything to you."

"You're so bloody stupid." Luna shook her head. "I get why Nestor left you for Becky. She was smarter. And prettier."

"I thought the same thing." Rajni hugged the baby as though gaining strength from her. The baby then went limp in her arms.

"You sucked all the life out of her," Luna said. "You're a vampire."

Rajni held the baby in front of her and screamed. The room darkened, and "No. 14 Molto Moderato" from *La Bayadére* played. A green flame presented itself, flickering and crackling to the beat. The center of Rajni's chest vibrated, producing a low hum. She reached out her arms and when her fingertips touched the flame, she found herself lying on a cold, hard surface. The fire faded, and bright light seeped in through Rajni's now closed eyelids. Blips, buzzes, and clicks sounded rhythmically. She opened her eyes and screamed in terror when she saw a Custodian flashing its colorful facial lights at her.

Lost Within the Shades

Nestor and Luna looked down at Rajni, who was lying on her bed. Nestor lifted her limp arm and kissed the back of her hand.

"Aren't you guys divorced?" Luna asked.

"Yes."

"Why did the Custodians put you in here together?"

Nestor shook his head. "I'm not even sure why they placed you in here with us."

"I hope she's going to be okay."

"Me too." Nestor gazed at Rajni. The idea of losing her after already losing his family was too much for him to deal with. Patting Luna's back, he said, "We should let her rest."

They walked out into the living room where Kelly, Blaze, Seth, and Hiroko had been gathered.

"How is she?" Hiroko asked.

"She hasn't said a word." Nestor glared at Kelly. "I thought you said the pillar was safe."

"As safe as the user's subconscious is."

"What's that supposed to mean?" Seth asked.

"Astrid once had a difficult time in there," Hiroko said. "She was in a similar state to Rajni."

"How long did it last for?" Nestor asked.

"We counted seventeen days."

"Seventeen days? How is she supposed to eat and drink?"

"When she wakes up, Astrid will give her food until she's ready to continue with her sessions," Kelly said.

"What if she doesn't wake up?" Nestor asked.

"She will...once she assimilates her experiences from her session."

"You should call that thing what it is, a mind reprogramming device," Seth said. "Scientists in the United Republic have been running similar experiments to break down a criminal and then rebuild him or her to be a *productive citizen*."

"I shot a documentary about the Cognitive Liberation Movement trying to expose those experiments," Nestor said. "I was skeptical at the start of the project, but when every corporate scientist I spoke with told me, 'we are not permitted to disclose that information as it is a threat to patent security,' I was convinced. Unfortunately, not enough people cared. The documentary cost more to produce than it made in sales."

"And the Aristocrats chose to get even with you by placing us all in here as part of one of their trials," Seth said half-jokingly.

Luna petted Rufus. "My father said when people do something the government doesn't like, they *disappear*."

"The Aristocrats have nothing to do with what's happening to us," Blaze said. "They made it their mission in life to make us miserable, but I feel more inspired than ever before." He smiled at Luna. "I even feel like writing a new *Drake Kent* book."

"Happy slaves are obedient slaves," Seth said.

"I've had enough of your paranoia, Seth!" Kelly yelled. "None of you are being reprogrammed, and I'm exactly the same as I was when I first arrived here." He rubbed his beard. "Exactly. I never even had to shave. The Fountain of Youth isn't a myth. We're living in it."

"I never knew you to follow anyone blindly," Seth said. "You were always questioning everything the government did."

"I questioned everyone, Seth. Even you. Remember?"

"Remember what?"

Luna crept towards the door and opened it. Blaze spotted her as she slipped out. He signaled to Nestor that he was going after her and left.

"I'm with Seth on this one," Nestor said. "We should have Astrid tell the Custodians, or whoever the hell they are, that we won't perform for them until they tell us what they want from us." He looked at Seth for support. "Do you agree with me?"

"Whole heartedly. Where's Astrid?"

"She's having a difficult time right now," Kelly said. "I'd rather not bother her."

"What's wrong with her?" Nestor asked.

"I don't discuss anyone's private business." He leered at Seth. "I'm sure you can agree with me on that one."

Seth was bothered by Kelly's comment but was unsure why. "I have no problem waiting."

"But I do," Nestor said. "Rajni better wake up because if she doesn't, I'll show the Custodians that not all of us are willing to sit around and blindly follow their orders."

Opal, Pearl, and Jeff stood in front of the hexagon. Jeff was scheduled to go next, but he refused. Opal would've been in agreement with him had it not been for her conversation with Blaze. After hanging off the edge of a mountain, taking a peek inside her mind seemed easy by comparison.

"I don't think it's a good idea, Commander" Jeff said.

"Nestor is okay, and Blaze left his session happier than he's ever been."

"Rajni was carried out of there practically catatonic," Pearl said.

"Kelly said that Rajni will be okay after some rest."

"I never knew you to trust anyone so easily."

Opal held Pearl's forearm gently. "I need to do this."

"You can deal with whatever issues you have out here. You don't need that nightmare machine to do it."

"Agreed," Jeff said. "I'm not taking any chances with my brain. It's the only one I have."

"At least one of you is using it wisely," Pearl said.

Opal stepped onto the panel, and the door opened. "I appreciate both your concerns, but I've been through far worse than anything I could ever dream up in there."

Jeff clenched his fists and tightened all the muscles in his arms to keep himself from questioning his commander's decision.

Opal glanced at Jeff's hands and then peered directly into his eyes. "When I'm finished, you'll see that I'm okay and then you can go in next." She entered the hexagon, and turned to face him.

"I would rather wait until the Custodians tell us what they want."

"That could be a long time from now, and you won't get any food." Opal waved her hand in front of Jeff. "You could also use a shower after that long hike. You stink."

"I don't mean any disrespect, Commander, but how can we just sit here and allow ourselves to be trained by unseen controllers?"

"We were trained in the joined forces by unseen controllers. The generals were nothing but lackeys."

"That was different."

"Was it really, Lieutenant?" Opal smiled, and the door shut in front of her.

"She never listens," Pearl said. "She always has to learn things the hard way. I lost track of all her broken bones, scratches, and bloody noses."

"I won't let anything bad happen to her," Jeff said.

"I know you won't. You're a man of honor. I can tell by the way my sister talks to you. She doesn't have respect for many people."

Jeff sat and leaned his back against the wall. Before Earth was extinguished, there were few people he respected. One of them was his mother. He thought about her and Darla. Memories of them cycled in his mind, and he turned his focus to Hiroko to keep himself from crying. When he pictured her face, he closed his eyes and smiled.

Rajni lay unconscious on her bed as her mind cycled through the simulation from the light pillar.

A Custodian stared down at her, and the colors of her visage flashed, shifted, and blended together to appear like Rajni's face. "We fix, so you continue."

Rajni smiled and closed her eyes. When she reopened them, she turned her head to the side and saw Astrid standing next to the table she was lying on.

Rajni sat up. "Where are we?" The setting was familiar to her, but she had no conscious recollection of what she was seeing.

Next to her table was the baby floating in the green beam of light.

"I am not sure, but I think we are aboard some type of spacecraft."

Rajni approached a table that Nestor was lying on. *Why is this so familiar?*

Astrid pointed at Blaze who was also on a table. "That is my husband."

"Where are we?"

"I am not sure, but one of the aliens told me we would not be harmed."

"You were able to understand it?" Rajni asked, fascinated. "How?"

"The varying color patterns on his face allowed him to communicate telepathically with me. They were transmitted as tones, but I understood them as words in my native language, French."

Rajni sidled towards the door. "How could you tell it was a male?"

"I sensed it." Astrid followed Rajni. "Where are you going?"

"I want to see where we are." Rajni opened the door and peeked her head out, looking from left to right along a narrow corridor. The floors and walls were both pale white, backlit by a soft violet light. "There's no one around."

She exited the room, and Astrid followed her. A faint low mechanical sound pulsed and grew louder as they continued ahead. At the end of the corridor was a large door. Rajni touched the surface, and it vibrated, matching the beat of the pulsing sound. She pushed open the door.

Astrid grabbed her arm. "Maybe we shouldn't."

"You said they didn't want to harm us." Rajni entered and gasped.

The room was the size of two football fields, lined with tables that filled the entirety of the space. Atop them lay a multi-planetary population of unconscious beings.

Astrid came in from behind Rajni and stepped back when she spotted an alien with scaly gray skin. "We should leave now."

"In a minute." Rajni walked ahead and peered down at a being who had blue translucent skin with similar colored hair.

"Is it dead?" Astrid asked.

Rajni stared at the being's chest that contracted and expanded. "He...or she is alive. Can you tell its sex?"

Astrid shook her head.

Rajni touched the alien's skin, which was smooth and warm. "Amazing. Feels just like us." She proceeded to examine the other beings.

"What do you think is being done to them?" Astrid asked.

"Some kind of medical procedure. Think this is their version of a hospital."

Rajni continued to walk around the room, and Astrid kept turning her head towards the door they had come in from. When they reached the center of the room, an alarm sounded. They ran towards the door. Rajni opened it and came face to face with a Custodian. He extended his hand forward. The lights on his face flashed, transmitting a frequency that knocked Rajni and Astrid out.

Nestor sat by Rajni's bedside, holding her hand. He gazed at her, but he thought about Becky and Joey and how much he missed them.

"Rajni, I'm here, and I'm going to talk to you in case you're listening to me." He massaged the back of her hand. "I'd talk to you even if you didn't know I was here." He laughed to himself. "I had a revealing game of Pachisi with you in the pillar. 'Same face, different name,' you told me. Everything made so much sense when I was in there. My experiences don't define me. If I strip them all away, what remains is this constant sense of pure being. I'm trying to understand the implications of what that means out here, and it's not as easy."

Nestor caressed Rajni's cheek. "You haven't changed since I last saw you. When I came over to your apartment and you opened the door, I wanted to take you in my arms and kiss you, as I had all the other times when I came home after a shoot. It was as if the four years that separated us never happened, but I still love my wife. Is it possible to love both of you?"

Rajni opened her eyes, startled.

"Rajni? Are you all—"

"I have to see Astrid!" Rajni leapt off the bed and ran out of the room.

Nestor chased after her. "Wait a minute! You were just unconscious a few seconds ago." He followed her to the door. "Slow down and give yourself a chance to take a breath."

Rajni stopped and faced Nestor. "I'm not dizzy anymore!" She ran her hands up and down her thighs. "And I can feel my legs!"

"You're cured? How?"

"I'll explain later." Rajni kissed Nestor's cheek. "Sorry for killing you."

"Killing me?"

"I'll make it up to you when I get back." She smiled and left.

Raining Roses

Luna strode past the sundial, with Rufus perched on her shoulder. Blaze walked alongside them.

"I want to be left alone," Luna said.

"I won't say a word."

"Whatever."

They continued walking, and Luna kept staring at Blaze.

"What's on your mind?" he asked.

"I liked you better with your tattoos. They were cool."

"So cool," Rufus added.

"I appreciate the both of you for saying that, but I got them for the wrong reason."

"Why did you get them?"

"Thought they would make me as strong as Drake Kent."

"No offense, but if Drake ever got into a fight with Space Ex, he'd lose."

"I'm not so sure of that. Ex is all about muscle while Drake uses his brain."

"Space Ex is also better written. There's too much meandering going on with Drake. Who does all that talking when someone's about to shoot them?"

Blaze raised a brow. "Did you ever think of becoming a literary critic?"

"I read all of Trevor Forthright's reviews...and your responses. They were more interesting than your books."

"If you're trying to get a reaction out of me, it's not working. I'm more than the sum of my books, I'll never confuse them as the core of my existence again."

Luna stopped walking. "What did you see inside the pillar?"

"Can't really find the words to explain my experience, but it helped me see things as they truly are."

"I saw things in a different way, and my life is now more complicated."

"How so?"

"None of your business." She stormed off.

Blaze continued following her. "I'm not leaving you alone until you tell me what's bothering you."

"Fine. Just don't talk to me."

"I can do that."

Luna led Blaze to the sunflowers and was shocked to discover they were all in bloom. "They were all dead before."

"Not anymore."

"But that's impossible. Dead things can't come back to life," Luna said more to herself. She then stared up at Blaze, wondering if he had something to do with the miracle. "Can they?"

Blaze widened his eyes and then leaned down to kiss Luna's cheek. "Thanks! I think you may have helped me figure this out."

"Figure what out?"

"Go back to the refuge. Tell Seth to bring everyone to the spot where Anya was last seen."

"Do you know what happened to her?"

"I'm going to check out my theory now."

"Kelly will never go along with this."

"The others will listen to you."

"Why now? They haven't since I showed up here."

Blaze put his hands on Luna shoulders. "I know you can do this."

Luna shook her head.

Blaze cut off one of the sunflowers and handed it to her. "Show them this, and tell them what you told me."

"They won't believe me."

"They will. I know you can do it."

"What if I can't?"

Pointing to the sunflower, he said, "Believe in the blossoming flower that you are, and you'll do fine." He smiled and ran off.

Luna petted Rufus. "There's no way I'm leaving him alone. He's acting crazy." She tossed the sunflower and slowly trailed behind Blaze. Once they got on the path, Rufus sang the first line to "Goodnight Sweetheart." Luna hid behind a boulder. "You have to stay quiet, Rufus," she whispered.

"Anya, is that you?" Blaze yelled out towards the peak and ran ahead.

Luna breathed a sigh of relief. "That was a close call."

Rufus flapped his wings. "Let's get moving."

"You can't make any more noise. If Blaze sees us, we'll get in trouble."

"Uh-oh. Trouble," Rufus said.

"Exactly. So get everything out now. We'll leave when you're finished."

Rufus went through several of his sound effects, including a door slamming, rattling keys, and a referee whistle. After he had completed his performance, Luna continued on with her surveillance.

Luna tracked Blaze to the stone bridge and crossed over when he was out of view. A flash of light made her look toward the horizon where the golden star sparkled brightly. Pointing to it, she said, "I saw that star right before I came here, Rufus!"

"Star light, star bright," he replied. "Lights up the darkest night."

Luna spotted Blaze on the precipice and gasped when he stepped off and walked across the air. "That's so cool! Space Ex did the same thing, but he was wearing his gravity boots." She stroked the top of Rufus's head, and he went through a few of his favorite sound effects.

Luna continued to watch Blaze until he disappeared from her line of sight. "Where do you think he went?"

Rufus flew off her shoulder and headed toward the spiral peak.

"Good idea! We'll definitely be able to find Blaze from up there!"

She ran towards the peak and started to climb the spiraling path. An hour later, she reached the crest. From where Luna stood, she had a clear view of everything around her. The mountain rings seemed to stretch out infinitely.

Rufus returned and perched on Luna's shoulder.

"Wow! Mr. Marconi was right! We're in a maze! A giant maze!"

A gentle wind blew, carrying a floral scent with it. Red and white roses started to rain down from the heavens. "This is incredible!" Luna smiled and slowly turned with her arms stretched out to the side. Her expression changed when she looked at the ground. The petals were all wilted. Luna knelt, and scooped the dead flowers into her hands. She slowly stood as roses continued to pour down on her. "Why does Blaze want the others to come here?"

Luna peered at the golden star and a sense of recognition came to her. "I remember." The dry petals in her hands reanimated. "Dead things come back to life here, Rufus!" She examined the petals. "But how do I remember that? I was never here before."

Landing on the Ladder

As the light pillar dissipated, Opal clutched her scalp and squeezed it as hard as she could. The pain from the pillar was unbearable.

"Move it, Halifax! We haven't got all day!"

The light pillar switched off, and Opal smiled when she recognized who was talking to her. "You haven't aged a bit, Gary." She examined the clearing they were in, which was in the middle of a rainforest. "We crashed nearby."

"No kidding. Did you hit your head on the way down, soldier?"

Opal laughed. "Feels that way."

"We need to keep moving. They're probably tracking us." Gary pointed his finger at Opal and smirked. "But when we get home, I'm checking you in for a psych evaluation."

"And I'll make sure you have the bed next to mine." Opal winked.

Gunfire reverberated from all around, and the two ran until they distanced themselves from the line of fire. They stopped to rest at a small clearing surrounded by large pine trees.

"We should be safe here for a while." Gary got out his transponder and checked for a signal.

"You're not going to pick anything up with that," Opal said.

"Don't be so negative."

Opal sat on a large tree stump. "I'm not negative. I'm a psychic."

"You can be real cute sometimes."

After several failed attempts for a rescue call, Gary sat beside Opal. "You really must be psychic."

"Told you so."

Gary looked up at the sky. "It'll be getting dark soon. Wish we could light a fire."

Opal stared at him affectionately. "It's a clear night. The moonlight will be enough."

"Not enough to keep us warm." Gary gazed at Opal in a way that made every hair on her body stand at attention. "How about we start off with a romantic dinner?" He pulled out a field ration from his pack and read the label on the container. "Tuna." He winced. "What do you have?"

Opal removed her meal pack. "Lasagna. And no, I don't want to trade."

"You're starting to scare me." Gary smiled.

At this moment in Opal's history, she had teased Gary by telling him that he better not kiss her after he eats his smelly tuna. But in her pillar fantasy, Opal hurled the lasagna into a tuft of bushes.

"Why did you do that?" Gary asked. "I would've—"

Opal pulled Gary by the front of his shirt and kissed him. They ended up on the ground with him on top of her. Opal allowed herself to get swept away by the passion, but when Gary went to unbutton her shirt she pushed him away.

"Why did you stop?" Gary asked.

"Because it was wrong then, and it's wrong now." She got up and paced back and forth. "I turned you down because I wanted to remain faithful to Harry. When I found out about him and my sister, I regretted my loyalty. I used to believe I was being faithful to him. But after I kissed you, I found out that wasn't true." Opal kneeled in front of Gary and cupped his face with her hands. "I remained faithful to my principles." She smiled. "I have no more regrets."

Gunshots fired in the near distance. Gary got up, and Opal watched as he grabbed his gear.

"Why are you just sitting there?" he asked.

"There's nowhere to run."

At the time of the actual incident, Opal and Gary fled as enemy fire continued to echo throughout the forest. Gary got shot in the back during the pursuit. Opal had to keep running when Eastern Sector soldiers came out of hiding from behind a thick cluster of bushes. Leaving Gary in the hands of the enemy was the hardest thing she ever had to do during all her years in the military.

Opal evaded Eastern Sector forces by traveling at night and sleeping during the day. By the time she'd crossed the border and found a village, Opal was almost completely dehydrated. The friendly residents clothed Opal and gave her shelter, but safety gave her discomfort. Gary was still missing, and his fate was unknown.

After the war had ended, Opal scanned through the list of released prisoners, and Gary's name wasn't included. She next read all the names of the deceased soldiers and was relieved that he wasn't listed there either. Still it offered her only limited comfort. Being listed as missing in action meant his fate would remain unknown.

Gary was never heard from again. Opal surmised he must've died, but he was in fact rescued by some hunters from a nearby village. They found him shot and almost dead. After he had been nursed back to health, Gary fell in love with one of the women who cared for him. The two ended up getting married and had three children. You could say they lived happily ever after.

Opal's vision in the light pillar next placed her in the shuttle, minutes before the crash. There was no sound at all, aside from Pearl who grabbed her hand and said, "I have something to tell you."

"I know," Opal replied. "And I'd rather not hear about your betrayal again."

"How did you find out?"

"I'm psychic." She grinned.

Pearl crinkled her forehead. "Then you know about..."

"Christina? Yes."

"How can you be so calm?"

"About your deception or the crash?"

"Both."

"I had ten years to get over it." Opal inspected the cabin, attempting to figure out why she was brought here. Noticing a red glow emitting through the cracks of the cockpit door, she got up from her seat and stepped into the aisle. "Be right back."

"We're crashing!" Pearl yelled. "Where are you going?"

Opal ignored Pearl and hurried toward the cockpit door. She opened it and entered a cavern where a red fire softly crackled. She slowly approached and positioned her palms inches in front of the flames. She felt a warm tingly sensation in her belly. The flames changed to green and crackled at a higher pitch, and Opal felt an intense euphoria. The buzzing in her abdomen moved upward, resting in the center of her chest.

"I'll understand."

Opal turned around and faced Blaze.

He stretched his hand out to her. "Don't be afraid of the truth."

Opal reached for him, and the flames cleared. She was now back in the hexagon. The amount of energy in her had increased. She dropped down to the floor and did fifty push-ups without breaking a sweat and then cycled through the stations. When she ate her nutrition cubes, she reveled in the ecstasy of flavors and thought that this place was the closest to the ideal of heaven. She hadn't been this happy in years.

Opal's energy expanded, pierced through the Earth's atmosphere, and resonated with all that's inside Me. These are the moments I appreciate most. When sentients reach out of their limited space filled with love and desire, it gets redistributed throughout Me. Love truly never dies.

Opal found Pearl waiting with Jeff. "What a wild ride! Can't wait to do it again tomorrow!"

Jeff and Pearl stared at one another and then at Opal.

"You two have to stop doing that. I haven't felt this great in years."

"Glad to hear it, Commander," Jeff said, even though his own doubts hadn't dissipated.

Opal placed her hand on Jeff's shoulder. "It's safe, Lieutenant. You may proceed inside."

"Is that an order?"

"It is. No soldier starves under my command."

He nodded and stood on the panel.

"May you find your green flame."

The door opened, and Jeff entered the hexagon. He turned and saluted Opal, and the door shut.

Opal turned to gaze at her sister, who eyed her curiously.

"Give me your hands," Opal demanded.

"Why?" Pearl cautiously did as asked.

"So I can break them."

Pearl pulled her hands back, and Opal chuckled. "Only kidding. I couldn't resist."

Opal gently took hold of Pearl's hands. "I release you of your guilt. I was selfish for the past ten years. I wanted you to suffer for betraying me because I thought I sacrificed my own chance at happiness."

"What happened to you in there?"

"During my last tour, I was attracted to another man. I ran into him in the pillar, and ooh, ooh wee! It was as steamy as ever between us two."

"You...were unfaithful?"

"No, but I regretted I wasn't, until today. I did the right thing, and if I had a chance to go back and do things differently, I wouldn't. Except for Christina. I should never have cut her out of my life."

Pearl was about to cry but stopped when she felt Opal's hands heat up. The heat traveled through the whole of her body, causing her to perspire. Relief soon followed in the form of a cool, refreshing breeze that caressed her skin.

"What just happened?" Pearl asked. "I feel different. Almost exactly how I felt before I got sick."

Opal released Pearl's hands. "Maybe we're both healed now."

Nestor ran towards Opal and Pearl, who were still in front of the hexagon.

"Have any of you seen Luna?" he asked.

"She's missing?" Opal replied. "Again?"

"I saw her sneak out while Kelly and I were arguing over Rajni's condition, but I wasn't worried because Blaze went after her. Now I can't find either of them anywhere."

Opal shook her head. "That girl must enjoy getting lost." She threw her hand in the air. "At least Rufus is with her."

"What are the chances that he'll come back and lead you to Luna again?" Pearl asked.

Opal looked toward the sky and was concerned as it was late in the afternoon. "I can't wait for him...or for the lieutenant to finish with his session. I'll have to search for her now."

"I'm coming with you," Nestor said.

Pearl pointed toward the center of the refuge where Rajni was dancing. "She's healed!"

"I guess Astrid wasn't home," Nestor said softly as he watched Rajni's performance. He had never seen her that happy during the time they were together.

"How did it happen?" Pearl asked Nestor.

"Think it has something to do with the pillar."

"I would love to be able to do a cartwheel again," Pearl said to Opal. "Maybe I should give the pillar another try."

"I insist that you do," Opal responded. "And if you don't, I'll drag you in there myself."

"Give me time," Pearl said, still troubled by her encounter with Christina. "Everything is moving too fast for me here."

"That's a normal day in my life."

"But not mine." Pearl watched Rajni dance. "I don't want to be afraid anymore. I want to be free."

"You can be."

"Eventually. But there's a lot I have to throw away first, and I was always a hoarder." Pearl forced out a smile.

"Letting go was never easy...for either of us."

"Be patient, and maybe it will happen for us both."

"I'll be patient...for us. But never when it comes to finding a lost child. I want Luna back here, right now." Opal glanced at the western path, but her instincts told her to head east. She came to trust them even more than her own judgement as they saved her on the battlefield and while she was on the run from the enemy.

"I'll head west," Nestor said. "We'll cover more ground that way."

Opal shook her head. "This is my second rescue mission of the day. I don't want a third. You're coming with me."

Rajni danced the death scene of Nikiya around the table, and Pearl watched enthusiastically. After she had finished her performance, Pearl applauded.

"Bravo! Bravo!"

More clapping came from Kelly, who approached the ladies. "Impressive."

"I'm healed!" Rajni stood on the marble table and performed a flawless pirouette. "It's as if I never missed a day of practice."

"I'm glad you're feeling better." Kelly went to leave.

Rajni leapt off the table. "Have you seen Astrid anywhere?"

"She should be in her unit."

"I rang for her, but she never answered."

"She had a rough session in the pillar."

Rajni stared back at the dormitory.

"What do you need?" Kelly asked. "Maybe I can be of help."

"Nothing. Just wanted some company. Now that Pearl's here, I'm okay."

He nodded. "If you need anything, I'll be back in two hours."

"Where are you going?" Pearl asked.

"For my daily walk."

"Mind if I join you?" Rajni asked. "I feel like climbing the highest peak today."

"Please don't take this personally, but I prefer to walk alone. It gives me time to think."

"I understand."

Kelly walked off, and Rajni sat next to Pearl who began to cry.

Rajni put her arm around her. "Want to talk about it?"

"I think my cancer is gone," she said.

"That's terrific, Pearl! Now we're both healed."

"I want to be happy, but I don't know how to resolve my faith with everything that's happening here. Nothing conforms to what I believe in, and that terrifies me."

"What are you scared of?"

"I spent all my life serving God and the church. Everything I counted on, relied on, depended on, may all be wrong. Where does that leave me?"

"My grandmother once told me that each phase of our lives is like the beginning of a new game. Our only job is to keep moving forward."

"Forward to where? Heaven or hell? I have to know."

"Neither. We're not dead."

"Are you sure?"

Rajni smiled. "Even more so now."

Quickening

Jeff found himself in a convenience store after the light pillar had deactivated. With him was the gang that he had wanted to join. Approaching sirens blared, and the leader of the gang slapped Jeff's arm. "Come on! Let's get out of here!"

The gang ran out, and Jeff walked behind the counter. He looked down at Mr. Riker, the store owner who lay dead on the floor. He also happened to be the landlord of the building Jeff's family lived in.

Mr. Riker's eyes popped open. "Why? Why did you bring them here?"

"You were going to evict us," Jeff said.

"It was your father's fault. If he spent his time working rather than shooting up, I wouldn't have thrown your family out, and I'd still be alive." Pointing to Jeff, he said, "You killed me."

A flat line alarm sounded in what was now a hospital room. Jeff stood by the door while a medical staff tried to save Mr. Riker's life.

One of the tending nurses went to work on him with defibrillator paddles. After three jolts, she gave up. "He's gone." She barreled over to Jeff, rammed the paddles against his chest, and gave him a shock that knocked him halfway across the room.

"Satisfied?" the nurse sneered.

"I never was." Jeff rubbed his chest.

"Think you need another," a male voice said from behind him.

Jeff swung around and saw Jericho holding defibrillator paddles.

"I don't hear a heart beating in there, Tin Man." He lifted up the paddles. "Let me see if I can help reanimate you."

Jeff inched back until he ran into the wall.

"*Da dum, da dum, da dum.*" Jericho shocked Jeff with the paddles.

A cacophony of screams and explosions reverberated from all around as the environment rearranged into a setting that Jeff remembered well.

It was a village in the East Sector. Jeff's regiment was in the middle of clearing the perimeter when one of the soldiers came out of a cottage. Something didn't appear right about him. His clothes were torn, and there was a scratch on his face.

"What happened in there, Paulson?" Jeff yelled at the time of the incident. He didn't have to ask that question now. He knew what awaited inside: a naked girl whom Paulson had raped. Jeff found her with a shot to the forehead and with the most frightful expression he'd seen during his whole time in active combat. Jeff went to therapy to try to get over the image burned into his mind, but he never fully recovered. PTSD, they told him. Whenever he closed his eyes, the girl was present, like an eternal snapshot that never faded with the passing of time.

Back when the incident happened, Jeff ordered Paulson to stay behind with him. After the regiment had departed, Jeff grabbed him and dragged him over to the girl's grieving parents.

"If you want justice, I'll serve it for you," Jeff said in their language.

Paulson cried, "Please, Sir. I'm sorry, I'm sorry—"

"Shut your mouth, Paulson!" Jeff rammed the barrel of the gun against the terrified soldier's head and waited for a response.

The father solemnly shook his head and sighed. "All life is sacred. I cannot be a part of its destruction." He turned and left.

Jeff peered at the mother. "What was her name?"

"Kara." She spat in the rapist's face and peered at Jeff. "The only justice would be with his death."

Jeff nodded, took Paulson out beyond the border of the village, and shot him, leaving his body right where it fell.

Paulson shouldn't have been in combat. He had trouble dealing with conflict and was constantly getting into fights with the other men in his regiment. Jeff told his commander numerous times that Paulson needed a psychiatric evaluation, but his warnings had been ignored.

When he was in the joined forces Jeff believed he killed in the name of justice, yet had no recollection of who he killed. He had no more emotional attachment to them than all the ants he'd stepped on during his lifetime. His indifference disturbed him. He wept, now understanding the reason Kara's father wanted no action taken against Paulson. Even with all the blood and violence that he had to endure daily, he clung to his faith in Humanity. Jeff's own faith had been stripped away layer by layer, each time he pulled the trigger of his gun.

Within the pillar, Jeff's rage towards Paulson was as intense as it had been on the day he was reliving.

"Why? Why did you do this?" Jeff asked Paulson. "We were supposed to be the righteous ones."

"Were you righteous when you had that gang rip off your landlord's store?"

"I didn't want them to kill him."

Jeff and Paulson now found themselves in the store staring down at Mr. Riker's body.

"You did right," Paulson said. "You were exacting justice because he was in the wrong. He wanted to throw you and your family out into the street."

Jeff pressed his hands against his face. "I was wrong. My father was a drug addict. He cared more about his next fix than he did for us." Jeff wept when he thought about how hard his mother had worked to feed him and his sister. While his father sunk further into his drug habit, Mrs. Theobald managed to get an education by taking some publink classes in the evening. She got her family out of the dungeon blocks before Jeff's sixteenth birthday. Being a compassionate woman, Mrs. Theobald stayed with her husband and tried to help him get off drugs. But all he wanted was her steady paycheck. He sponged off her earnings until her accident, and he did the same to the nurse with whom he had the affair.

The previous thought transported Jeff to the front lawn of the White House, before its destruction. Blossom and Jericho stood next to him.

"Why are you so sad, Jeff?" Blossom asked.

"Too many reasons why."

Jeff ruminated over the old symbol of freedom. It was a concept humans had long forgotten, including all the lottery winners who had been conditioned to accept their downgraded lifestyles and constant monitoring by watchful eye cameras.

"You did as much as you could," Blossom said.

"I couldn't save you or your baby. I couldn't save anyone."

"You can fight an invading army, but you can't fight the sun," Jericho commented.

"I suppose you're right."

"Of course he's right!" shouted a voice Jeff needed to hear.

He turned around. "Mom!" He hugged her. "I'm so glad to see you!"

"I never realized how many issues you were dealing with," she said.

"I missed our conversations. They always helped."

"The bomb that blew up the Pentagon brought an end to that for us when it brought an end to my mind." Mrs. Theobald laughed, but Jeff didn't get the humor.

"Don't mourn me or regret your survival," she said. "The craziness of all that's happened can drive you insane if you let it. I don't want you to go insane. Do you want to go insane?"

Jeff smiled recalling how much he missed his mother's unique way of delivering advice, and how she continued to do so on their last night together.

"You weren't all gone," he said. "The most important part of you, the part that made you see brightness even in the darkest of circumstances, it was always there."

A strong explosion shook the ground, almost shattering Jeff's eardrums. The White House burst into green flames that silently sparkled and swayed. Under the hypnotic spell of their rhythm, he advanced toward them until a baby started to cry. Jeff swung around and gasped when he saw his mother holding Darla in her arms. She handed Darla to him, and he hugged her tightly.

Jeff walked towards the inferno with Blossom, Jericho, and his mother following alongside him. They arrived at the door, and the flames cleared away. Jeff slowly reached his hand towards the knob. He opened the door, went inside, and turned to face his mother.

"Open your heart," she said, "and find the beauty in life again. You deserve to be happy."

The door shut, and the flames overtook him as he hugged Darla. "You gave me my heart back." He kissed Darla's cheek and surrendered to the warmth that made his whole body tingle and vibrate. He yelled out in pure joy and when the flames cleared, he was back in the hexagon. After he had gone through all the stations, he opened the door and saw Hiroko. They gazed at one another, threw themselves into a passionate embrace, and kissed.

Luna hurried along the path with Rufus flying overhead. Twilight had arrived, and she wanted to make it back before dark. Halfway through her journey, she found a large rock and climbed onto it to rest. Rufus landed on her shoulder. "I'm so tired. Wish I had wings like you to fly."

Rufus sang through a line of "Goodnight Sweetheart."

Luna laughed. "I can't be sad when I'm around you." She caressed his belly. "But I still think about my family...a lot. I miss them so much."

"We go home. Home sweet home," Rufus said.

"I can't ever go home. None of us can."

"Go home," he insisted.

"We'll go back to the refuge soon. But I found something out in the pillar that I'm still trying to figure out."

As Luna analyzed her visions, she became unsettled when she recalled flying over Jeff and his wife. Remembering the happiness she'd felt in the sunflower garden, she began to sing "Sh'ma Yisrael."

Opal and Nestor, who were headed in Luna's direction, heard her singing. They ran towards Luna, who now stood upon the rock with her head tilted towards the sky. Nestor and Opal stood back a few feet and listened quietly.

"I have the shivers hearing her," Opal whispered as she rubbed her forearms.

"Me too, and I feel something else."

"So do I...a rush of excitement sweeping throughout me. It's the same feeling I used to get when I jumped out of a flyer. There's no feeling in the world like that. Never thought someone singing could have the same kind of effect on me."

"She could have a great career as a vocalist," Nestor said.

Luna opened her eyes. Spotting her audience, she jumped off the rock.

"Yikes!" Rufus said as he flew off her shoulder.

"How long were you standing there?" Luna asked Nestor.

"Long enough," he said. "That was beautiful."

"I thought you didn't like anything religious."

"Had no idea it was religious, but it makes no difference. I appreciate people who are loyal to their personal faith."

"Where's Blaze?" Opal asked as Rufus flew onto her shoulder.

Luna went over the events, ending with the rain of flowers from the top of the spiral peak. She showed Nestor and Opal some flower petals she'd brought back with her.

"You should have come back to ask us for help," Opal said.

"I would have, but after I asked Blaze if dead things come back to life here, he got all weird and told me to come get you. I was too worried to leave him all alone. I wanted to make sure he was all right."

Nestor stared up at the sky, spooked by its appearance. "We better get back to the refuge."

"We have to find Blaze first," Luna insisted.

"It's too late to trek up the mountain now, and it's going to take us a couple of hours to get back to the refuge from where we are now."

"Didn't you hear what I told you?" Luna asked. "Dead things really do come back to life here! I saw it with my own eyes. I think that's why Blaze wants us to meet him up there. We have to get Mr. Marconi to show us the way—"

"We'll search for him tomorrow." Opal curiously examined the sky. "It should be getting dark soon."

"It should be dark now," Luna said.

"So it's not just me?" Opal scratched her head.

"I knew something was off about it," Nestor added.

"The sky is actually getting lighter," Luna said. "When I first started singing, it was darker."

Nestor and Opal both craned their heads skyward.

"Still think the Aristocrats aren't behind this?" Nestor asked.

"Too elaborate."

"Then how do you explain this?"

"Some things can never be explained, Nestor." Opal thought about Gary and how she'd never know his fate. "The best we can do is march on. And that's what we should do now. Pearl and Rajni will want to know that Luna is safe."

"What about Blaze?" Luna asked.

Opal put her hand on Luna's shoulder. "I promise you that I'll search for him first thing in the morning."

Jeff and Hiroko walked together in the Oasis, holding hands. "I have a confession to make," Jeff said. "I wanted to do this since I carried you out of the shuttle." He took a moment to choose his words. "My wife and I talked about separating. We grew apart after I returned from my tour because of everything I had gone through. When we won the lottery, we decided to try and reconnect with each other during the trip. "

"I too felt a connection to you that day."

"My feelings toward you were confusing. I loved my wife, despite all our problems."

"I can understand that. My relationship with Seth was also complicated."

"Thought you two were on your way to getting back together."

"Seth is part of my past only. I let go of him long before the shuttle crash."

Jeff smiled. "Might I suggest a dark, out-of-work soldier for your future?"

Hiroko draped her arms around him. "I'd rather be with him right now."

The couple kissed and then continued their stroll, stopping by the waterfall.

"I love it here," Hiroko said. "I could stay here for hours and never get bored."

Jeff examined her face and marveled how at peace she appeared.

"You've been here for a while," he said. "Doesn't it bother you that you don't know where you are?"

"Not really. I find this place peaceful. I've experienced a happiness here I haven't known in my previous life."

"Previous life? So you think we're dead?"

"I view the life I led before the shuttle crash as a past life. I have no attachment to it anymore. The Custodians brought me here so that I can start over again and be happy. And I have been."

"I wish I could be as confident as you. In my world, when you take prisoners in a war, you either want something from them or want to hurt them for killing people on your side."

"We don't fall under either circumstance."

"I'm not sure about that. The Custodians obviously want something from us, or they wouldn't have brought us here."

"I would've thought the same way if they didn't give us the pillar. Each time I enter, it seems to take some of my darkness away, and I feel lighter inside. It works a lot faster than meditation."

"My session was explosive. Are they all that intense?"

"Not all, but my last one was. I relived my darkest moments with Seth. Astrid also had a difficult time."

"Why do you think that is?"

"I sense a quickening. It's as though the three of us were waiting to be rejoined with all of you."

"For what?"

"I view this place as a ladder to a new level of reality. I can't imagine what it will be like, but I don't think it's going to be somewhere we won't want to be."

Jeff hugged Hiroko. "I don't share your confidence, but having you with me makes my suspicions easier to deal with."

Comparing Nightmares

Astrid opened the door and smiled when she saw that it was Rajni. "I was coming to look for you. Did you just connect to me?"

"Yes. That's why I'm here." Rajni entered the unit. "Why wouldn't you answer the door?"

"I was unsure of how to process what I saw."

"How much do you remember?" Rajni asked.

Astrid sat on the couch. "We were in the large room filled with unconscious alien beings. They were all different in their appearance."

Rajni sat next to Astrid. "The alarm sounded..."

"And we ran for the door where a male Custodian was waiting for us. I remember it surprising me that I knew his gender."

"He stretched his hand towards us, and I think we passed out."

"The light patterns on his face...I remember them. He wanted us to forget what we saw." Astrid shook her head. "What if the last ten years never happened? The Custodians could easily have confused our understanding of time."

"I don't believe that. A lot has happened in my life since then."

"Are you certain of that?"

"All of us who were on Earth before the last sunrise witnessed a gold star."

"I saw it as well." Astrid closed her eyes. "I do not want to remember what lead up to it."

Rajni saw tears streaming out from underneath Astrid's closed lids. "They saved you. They saved all of us."

Astrid opened her eyes wide. "We fix..."

"So you continue," Rajni replied concurrently with Astrid.

"At first, I thought I was seeing myself," Rajni said. "The Custodians can make themselves appear like anything they want to us."

"And make us forget about our experience with them."

"But we remember now, and I want to know why."

"Did you understand their language?" Astrid asked.

"Only that one phrase. We have to tell the others."

"Tell them what? We still do not know why the Custodians brought us here, or if their intentions are harmless."

"You heard them. They want to fix us."

"I want to believe that, but"—Astrid hugged herself and rubbed her arms—"all those bodies lying inanimate in that room...I cannot erase that image from my mind. Did the Custodians do the same thing to us before letting us go?"

"I don't think they want to harm us. They healed my MS and Pearl's cancer."

"But where does that leave us? Still contained inside this environment, unable to leave."

"Did you talk to Kelly about any of this?"

"I would rather keep this between you and me until we figure out what's going on."

"You don't trust him?" Rajni asked.

"Right now, you are the only one I trust and not because of our shared experience."

"What about Blaze?"

"Although I do not agree with his reason for lying to me, he wanted to protect me...as I wanted to protect you."

"From what?"

"On the day of the shuttle crash, I ran into you at the departure waiting room. I had a vision that confused me. It showed me a newborn baby, which made me believe you were pregnant. But then this dark emptiness followed. Whenever I had this feeling, it usually meant someone was going to die." Astrid wiped some tears from her eyes as she thought about her grandmother.

"You got the last part right," Rajni said. "I made an appointment with Compassionate Endings, but I was never pregnant."

"I distinctly picked up a baby in your future. Did you become pregnant when you returned home?"

"I was never pregnant."

"This is very peculiar. My vision was very detailed. It stayed with me throughout the flight. I would purposely excuse myself to use the bathroom so that I could pass you by and hopefully trigger another vision." Astrid laughed. "I got up so many times, Blaze suggested I visit a urologist when we returned home."

"You never told him you were clairvoyant?"

"He knew, but I never discussed my visions until I made sense of them first. After a few more trips down the aisle, he grew worried, and I told him about you. He wanted me not to get involved any further because he saw how upset the vision was making me. But I could not leave you alone."

"Why?"

"When I was a little girl, and my psychic awareness was first awakening, I had visions of my grandmother dying. They were so real in that I experienced all my senses while they came to me. I told my mother and she said, 'Do not worry, Astrid. You are only dreaming.' But one day, when my grandmother crossed the road on her way back from her daily walk, a drunk driver ran her over, and he did not stop to assist her. I gave the police the license plate number from my vision, and they apprehended the owner of the car soon after that."

Rajni pointed her finger towards Astrid. "I remember you now. You tripped over a passenger whose foot was sticking out in the aisle. You smiled at me and said—"

"Timber," Rajni and Astrid said together.

"Did you have any other visions about me?" Rajni asked.

"After the crash, when I saw you again, the darkness lifted. But I still saw the baby. I have no other explanation other than maybe I was wrong. I have been wrong before. Readings are never completely accurate."

The door chime rang.

"Remember. Not a word about this to anyone." Astrid answered the door.

Nestor and Luna entered.

Luna smiled when she spotted Rajni. "I'm glad you're okay."

There would be no time for a reunion. Astrid received a telepathic message from the Custodians, who told her Blaze was unharmed. They also instructed her to take Luna to the fire cave.

Astrid and Luna silently walked along the western path. The sky was bright, and Astrid wondered why Sun hadn't begun to set.

"Are you worried about Blaze?" Luna asked.

"The Custodians ensured me he would be all right."

"You believe them?"

"They've never lied to me before." Astrid didn't say this with full conviction. Since her last session in the pillar, she felt as vulnerable as the ones who had recently arrived.

"When you entered my unit, I received a message from the Custodians."

"What was it about?"

"You."

Luna stopped. "What did they tell you?"

"I am not sure yet. Perhaps if you tell me what you saw during your session—"

"I have to talk to Jeff first."

"Was he...in one of your visions?"

Luna nodded. "I'm not sure what I'm going to tell him. It's kind of a weird situation."

"How weird?"

"Weirder than the usual weird that goes on around here."

"That's pretty weird." Astrid smiled.

"Tell me about it. I'm not even sure I understand what I saw. It seems too impossible to believe."

Astrid lifted her brows. "I go to a special place where I can think clearly. Would you like me to take you?"

"As long as I don't see any more dead flowers."

Prism

Astrid and Luna hiked to the oasis, where Hiroko and Jeff were kissing in front of the waterfall. Hiroko quickly pulled back when they approached.

"Sorry for the intrusion," Astrid said. "I am taking Luna to see the fire cave."

"You'll love the cave. It's very *weird* inside," Jeff said with a grin.

"This whole place is weird." Luna pointed toward Sun. "Did any of you notice that the sky is getting brighter?"

Jeff looked toward the sky, surprised he hadn't noticed. He'd never let his guard down for a woman before. He played back the sequence of events before Earth's destruction: his argument with Lynn, holding Darla for one last time, picking up his mother at the hospital, running into Sirene at the convenience store, interrupting Jericho and Blossom's party in the Old White House, Mrs. Bellamy, her cat Spunky, all of them aboard Kara, the fire in the sky, and then the golden star. After that, he was in the pillar with the other lottery winners. "This feels too much like a PSYOP."

"We are nowhere near the Eastern Sector," Astrid countered. "It's the Custodians who are pulling the switches here."

"Whoever they are, I've had enough of begging for my meals." Jeff glanced at Hiroko. "Are you ready to take off your leash?"

Hiroko disagreed with Jeff's mistrust, but she was concerned that Sun was up in the sky, when it should've been Moon. "Why don't you go on to the fire cave?" she said to her. "We'll have plenty of time to discuss all of this later." She forced a smile. "More sun means more time for fun."

Luna wanted to roll her eyes but held herself back because she respected Hiroko. She left with Astrid.

Jeff couldn't shake the bad feeling he got when he looked at the brightening sky. "We can't do anything to free ourselves." He looked at Hiroko. "Can we?"

"There's nothing we can do."

"I don't believe that. There's a countermeasure for everything. We have to get the others together and figure one out."

"And what if we can't?"

"I won't even think of an answer unless that happens. Until then, we fight back. There'll be no more performing tricks for our food."

Luna and Astrid approached the cave. "Do you see the glow coming from inside?" Astrid asked.

Luna approached the ingress. "A white glow."

"White?" Astrid's eyes widened.

"Yes. What's wrong? You seem surprised."

"You see beyond the colors."

"What color do you see?"

"Purple. Since my arrival."

"Why do we see different colors?"

"Some religions on Earth view the body as having seven main chakras. Purple is the seventh chakra and located in the crown."

"My mom always read books about that kind of stuff. My father called it nonsense." Luna entered the cave. "What is the white chakra?"

"I do not think there is a white chakra. But if I were to take a guess, all the colors are passing freely through you which means you are open."

"To what?"

"Other than what I have mentioned, I know very little about chakras. I spent most of my time playing my cello before I arrived here."

They entered the chamber and witnessed the blaze in their own respective colors. Luna walked around the fire, and she noticed a small opening where the tunnel continued. Along the cavern walls, glowing rocks lined up on either side as though leading somewhere. She wandered towards the passageway and admired the ambience. "Have you ever gone farther in?"

"It's too dark."

"Even with all those lights?"

"You see lights?"

"Yes. Don't you?"

Astrid shook her head and gestured toward the opening. "Lead the way."

425

Luna entered and when Astrid attempted to follow her in, she was struck by a fierce headache.

"Why did you stop?" Luna asked.

Astrid massaged her temples. "I think the Custodians want you to go alone. I'll wait for you here."

"Don't leave me!" Luna grabbed Astrid's hand.

"You will be okay if they are showing you the way."

Luna looked back at the lights.

"Don't be afraid. The Custodians are allowing you to see more than any of us have ever seen. I think that is why they asked me to bring you here."

"Did they tell you why?"

"No, but if they want you here, it must be for an important reason."

"Do you think it may have to do with my family?"

"The only way you will find your answer is by going inside."

The possibility of discovering her family's fate beclouded Luna's fear. She crept farther into the tunnel. The side walls sparkled, and the rocks glowed in various colors, flashing off and on.

This is amazing! she thought. *Jodi would love this place!* All the painful emotions Luna usually experienced whenever she thought of Jodi were gone. Her tears had been spent on everyone she left behind, and that made her feel guilty. Nevertheless, she kept going until she reached a dead-end. The whole face of the rock wall glowed bright, and the environment around her changed to the interior of the shuttle.

Luna flew over a row of seats. When she passed over Jeff and his wife, she yelled, "I don't want to go! I don't want to go!"

Luna flew over Rajni, and a loud explosion rang in her ears followed by a bright flash.

A name came to her: *Teryl.*

Now back in the cave, Luna covered her mouth and gasped. She now comprehended the meaning of her vision in the pillar.

Luna and Astrid returned to the pond and found Hiroko and Jeff kissing again.

"Don't they ever stop for air?" Luna asked.

Jeff and Hiroko turned to face Luna.

Astrid clasped Luna's hand. "Don't be nervous to speak the truth. You will be okay."

Luna approached Jeff. "I have something to tell you."

Jeff looked down and smiled at her. The familiarity of the expression made Luna more uncomfortable.

"I..." She glanced up at Astrid. "I can't do this."

"I don't bite," Jeff reassured her.

Luna looked at him. "This is going to sound weird."

"If it wasn't, I'd think there was something wrong." He smiled at Luna again. "Weird is the new normal around here."

"I...I"—Luna shut her eyes—"used to be your wife."

Jeff laughed. "My what?"

Luna opened her eyes and glared at him. "Your wife, you mute jackass!"

Jeff staggered back. Whenever he'd gotten angry with Teryl during their many arguments, he refrained from speaking to keep from losing his temper.

Astrid held Luna's hand that was shaking. She had trouble discerning that her rage came from her experiences as Teryl.

"Give him a moment," Astrid said.

"What did she see in there?" Hiroko asked.

"White flames."

Hiroko turned to Jeff. "Luna speaks the truth."

"How can white flames make her think she's my wife?"

"*Was* your wife," Luna said. "I'm just a kid now. And a different person."

"Kelly has also seen the white flames," Hiroko said. "Did you travel deeper into the cave?"

"The walls glowed, and these colorful rocks lit up and made a path."

"This has to connect to the quickening I mentioned before. I've had this sense that things were moving faster since your arrival," Hiroko said.

"I sensed something similar," Astrid added. "The Custodians' messages to me changed. They never gave me direct orders, but today, they insisted I take Luna to the fire cave."

Hiroko pointed to the sky. "It should be dark by now, but the Custodians are keeping the light turned on for us."

Luna looked toward the mountain she'd climbed. "It's as if they're showing us the way to somewhere."

"I still don't trust this situation," Jeff said, "and neither should any of you."

Hiroko held Jeff's hand. "After what Luna just told us, I'm more sure than I ever was before that the Custodians don't intend us any harm."

Jeff looked at Luna. "What do you remember about Teryl?"

"Ever since I arrived here, I had a dream of flying over you and Teryl. I then flew over Rajni. After that, everything around me got dark and cold. I'm still not sure what that means."

Astrid gasped. "I do!"

Interrogations and Revelations

Seth Marconi squeezed his scalp with both his hands when the light pillar activated. Refusing to demonstrate his weakness, he laughed at his pain until he could no longer feel it. With fists raised in the air, he yelled, "I can take a lot more than you can ever give me! That's why I came in here! To show you that you can't break Seth Marconi! Nobody can!"

The light pillar dimmed in response to Seth's challenge. He now sat tied to a chair. A woman wearing an Eastern Sector uniform slapped him across the face and said something to him in a language he'd learned during the war.

Refusing to be the victim in his pillar fantasy, Seth took over the direction of his dream and broke out of his binds using superhuman dream strength. Wrapping his hands around the interrogator's neck, he choked her until she died. He violently threw her body against the wall and shouted, "Aristocrats! Custodians! Whoever you are makes no difference to me! I'll die before I let you control me!" Pointing to the interrogator who lay on the floor, he said, "If you come anywhere near me, I'll do to you what I did to her!"

Seizing a gun from the table, he snuck out of the room and shot the two guards outside the door. He ran to the men's room, looked at the bathroom mirror, and laughed when he scrutinized his perfect, unmarred face. Grazing his fingers against his cheek, he thought about Anya, and how she would've been attracted to without his scar.

"Is that all you wanted?" Hiroko said from behind him.

Seth glanced at her reflection in the mirror.

"To be attractive to the opposite sex? After your struggle to survive in the prison camp and your accomplishments with your company, I thought you had more depth than that."

Seth turned and faced Hiroko. "If this is one of those *It's a Wonderful Life* moments, that won't work on me. The old Seth is dead, and I don't ever want him back. "

Hiroko crossed her arms. "You wish your life was wonderful."

"Exactly. I wish, and it's now my reality. You can't control me anymore."

"I never controlled you, Seth. It was you that tried to control me, and everyone else around you."

"I don't have to listen to you either. Goodbye, Hiro. You can have your officer. I don't care about you anymore."

Seth looked at his reflection in the mirror which morphed into clouds. He was now in the shuttle, piloting the craft. He turned to face Kelly. "Why am I at the controls?"

"Because you're Seth Marconi, ruler of the world."

"I told you Maxwell was testing his prototype."

"And it was almost an exact copy of this model."

"I insisted you fly over Maxwell's building so that I could prove that my shuttle was part of the best fleet on Earth. But you refused and..." Seth gasped. "I flew the shuttle!"

"Pow! Straight into the Custodian's craft."

Seth looked at the sky in front of him. "How did I forget all this?"

"I can see how being responsible for the death of half the passengers, including your wife, would be something you'd want to forget."

"Everything would've worked out okay if the Custodian's ship didn't get in our way." Seth pointed at Kelly. "Are you one of them? Did you make us crash and then erase our memories?"

"You're talking to yourself, Seth. The only one in here is you." Kelly punched Seth's cheek. "Wake up!"

Seth coughed and was now seated in the smoke-filled cabin of the shuttle. Beside him was Hiroko, who was unconscious.

Her eyes sprung open. "You left me here to die on purpose."

"No," Seth said as tears fell down his face, "I was coming back for you."

"I see through your tears. You're crying because you know I speak the truth."

Seth let out a long wail and materialized on a hospital bed where a nurse was in the middle of removing a bandage from his face. He glided his hand against the side of his cheek, which was still smooth. "Why am I here? My scar is gone."

"Is it?" The nurse's appearance changed to that of the interrogator. "I own you, Traitor."

"And I killed you!"

"You can kill me a million times, but I'll never die."

A burst of purple fire shot up from around Seth and spread throughout the room. The interrogator entered through the flames and struck Seth with a whip. "I'm inside your mind when you wake up in the morning."

Seth lifted his arms in a defensive posture.

"I show up after you fall asleep at night and haunt you in your dreams." The interrogator whipped Seth again. "I come out of you in your present relationships, whenever you think someone is controlling you. It's by my hand that you attack them." The interrogator thrashed Seth again. "I pull your strings and control your mind. You don't have any power. You never had power."

Seth lunged at the interrogator and seized the whip. "It was you! All these years. Whenever I lost control of myself, I felt as helpless as when you were interrogating me. I hated that. Couldn't understand why you were still with me after I was freed. They said it was PTSD. I didn't care what it was. I just wanted you to stay away, but you kept returning. No matter what I did, you followed me like a shadow, forcing me to do things that made me hate myself more than I hated you."

The interrogator laughed. "I'm not a shadow. I am you, Traitor. Every decision you make is mine. Every action you take is mine. Every thought you make is because of me."

"I get it!" Seth whipped her. "And as of now, you're dead to me."

The interrogator disappeared. Seth laughed as the purple flames engulfed him.

Seth exited the hexagon, disappointed to find the scar on his face, but angry enough not to care. He pondered how he could've forgotten he'd flown the shuttle and headed towards Kelly's unit to find out how much he knew. Playing back the sequence of events, Seth now remembered everything. *Clearly.* He stood on the panel in front of Kelly's unit and yelled for him to come out.

Jeff and Hiroko, who'd just returned to the refuge, heard him and came to see what was wrong.

"Why are you shouting, Seth?" Hiroko asked.

Seth turned around and smiled, but his eyes appeared manic. "Have any of you seen Kelly? I have a question to ask him."

"He's in the middle of his daily hike," Hiroko said. "He goes every day."

Seth gazed up at the sky. "How lucky for him the sun decided to stick around longer today."

"You look pale," Hiroko noted. "Are you feeling sick?"

"How has your memory been since you arrived here?" Seth asked Jeff.

"Got no complaints. And yours?"

"Funny you should ask. I forgot a very important detail about the shuttle crash, and I'm trying to figure out how something so glaringly obvious could've escaped my mind." Seth shook his head and thought aloud. "We all experienced missing time between the crash and when the rescue team arrived. The Custodians must've brought me aboard their ship and erased my memory before returning me to Earth."

"What are you talking about Seth?" Hiroko asked. "You sound confused."

"Very good, Hiro!" Seth clapped his hands. "You should've been a psychiatrist. You could've then told me I've been delusional since my arrival and given me some drugs to convince me everything around here is normal. That's the only way I'll believe this place"—Seth pointed towards the hexagon with his thumb —"is normal."

"Stay cool, Marconi," Jeff advised.

"Oh, I am. I am...cool. Which is strange, considering I was surrounded by a purple fire." Seth smiled. "It was the most beautiful fire I've ever seen." He snapped out of his reverie and narrowed his eyes at Hiroko. "I'm on to you and your two accomplices."

Seth marched off, and Jeff watched him suspiciously. "He's up to something."

"Seth is always up to something."

"I'm going after him."

Seth spied Kelly walking toward the oasis and shadowed him all the way to the fire cave. He hid behind a rock near the entranceway of the cavern. The flames, that Seth saw as purple, illuminated the cavern enough for him to see Kelly remove a wand-shaped device from his pocket. He aimed it towards the cavern wall, and a large beam shot out, expanding into a swirling gold vortex. A pink beam directed back towards Kelly, and his body changed into that of a Custodian. Recognition hit Seth who now recalled his time aboard their vessel after the shuttle had crashed.

The Custodian basked in the swirling vortex, gaining energy from it. When he had his fill, the vortex shifted to blue and emitted a green beam that transformed him back into Kelly's form.

Seth snuck up to Kelly and shoved him against the cavern wall.

"Give me the device you were using!"

"What device?"

"Don't you even think of playing me. We humans are dangerous when we have nothing left to lose." Seth forced one of Kelly's arms behind his back.

"Have you completely lost your mind?" Kelly asked.

"I saw you change into a Custodian! You took me aboard your ship! I remember!"

"You're hallucinating."

"We'll see about that!" Seth forced Kelly's other arm behind his back and seized the wand. "If I'm hallucinating, then what's this?"

Kelly remained unresponsive.

"What are you?"

"Kelly, the pilot who used to work for you."

Seth flipped Kelly around and slammed his back against the wall.

"I'm impressed, Seth. Did you continue with your martial arts training?"

"I switched over to boxing. I never had the patience to memorize all those forms. And I have even less patience for your stalling. Now tell me who you are."

"Right after you let go of me."

Seth shook his head. "I'm the one waving the magic wand here." Seth thrust the device in front of Kelly. "What would your friends say if I activate this thing now?"

"No. You can't do that! They'll find out, and you'll ruin everything!"

"Things can't get any worse around here. We're all your prisoners."

"You're not. You'd all be dead if it wasn't for the Custodians."

"And you'll soon be dead if you don't get me out of—" Seth heard footsteps and swung around.

Reuniting

Luna entered her unit with Astrid and was stunned by the sight of Rajni dancing.

Nestor walked over to them. "She hasn't stopped since she got the use of her legs back." He smiled. "She's not even breaking a sweat."

"She's amazing," Luna said.

Rajni stopped dancing, extended her hands to the side and bowed. "Thank you. I can teach you if you'd like."

"I took ballet every Thursday for two years."

Astrid coaxed Luna towards Rajni.

"But I can always use some more lessons."

"Well, there's no time like right now." Rajni grabbed Luna's hand. "Let's go outside where there's more room."

"I have something to tell you first." Luna nervously looked at Astrid. "This is harder than what I had to tell Jeff."

"Never fear the truth. It may hurt you, but it will never betray you."

Nestor put his hand on Luna's shoulder. "You're free to say whatever you want here. This is a free-speech zone. No suppressed opinions are allowed."

Luna peered at Rajni. "You're my...my..." Her stomach churned as she forced the remaining words out of her mouth. "You're my mother."

Rajni's eyes widened. She searched for a response but none came.

"Were you pregnant on the flight?" Nestor asked.

"I wasn't."

Luna turned to Astrid. "Told you she wouldn't believe me."

"Remember the green beam of light?" Astrid asked Rajni.

"There was a baby floating inside it," Rajni said.

"What beam of light?" Nestor asked.

"Astrid and I remember being taken by the Custodians after the shuttle crash," Rajni said.

"My vision of you was accurate," Astrid said. "You were pregnant at the time of the flight, and the fetus must've been injured. The Custodians saved her life."

Rajni rubbed her forehead. "That baby was almost full-term."

"Considering all the technology they have here, speeding up the gestation cycle doesn't seem beyond their ability," Nestor said.

"No." Rajni shook her head. "This is impossible. I never wanted kids. I would've gotten rid of..." Rajni cut herself off, but it was too late. Luna knew what she inferred and started to cry.

Astrid put her arm around Luna. "I asked the Custodians, and they confirmed my suspicions. You are her mother."

"Why didn't they tell you this sooner?" Nestor asked Astrid.

"I am not sure of the reason, but I believe that they wanted our memories to return on their own. But now, they want us to move along faster."

"Sounds like they're losing patience with us," Nestor said.

"Or they don't think we're smart enough to figure things out for ourselves," Luna added.

"If they read any of our history books, I wouldn't blame them for believing that," Nestor said.

Rajni snapped her fingers. "The baby in my hotel room!"

"What about her?" Nestor asked.

"You knew she was female?" Rajni asked.

"The officer who changed her at the station told me."

"You gave me away?" Luna asked.

"There's no way for us to know if you were the baby that was left in my room," Rajni said. "And even if we could verify it, I wasn't pregnant."

"We thought one of the maids abandoned her," Nestor said. "It's not uncommon for poor mothers to leave their babies to people they think will give them a better life, although they typically don't leave an infant with a single woman. They scope out young married couples that appear as though they have a lot of credit."

"Nestor did a documentary about mothers who have gotten more desperate since the water and food shortages during the last sector war," Rajni said. "More babies are abandoned now than in the past few hundred years combined."

"All of that is irrelevant now," Astrid said. "Luna is your daughter. There would be no other reason for her to be here with us."

Rajni peered at Luna and noticed something she hadn't before. "You have my mother's eyes." She remembered another detail from the pillar. "Do you have four beauty marks?"

"Around my belly button."

Rajni placed her trembling hands over her mouth.

"Who was my father?" Luna asked, hoping it was Nestor.

Rajni thought about that time period in her life. She had been very promiscuous. Sex kept her mind off her disease, and at times she had more than two liaisons a week.

"I don't know."

"What do you mean, you don't know?" Luna asked. "Were you a prostitute?"

Tears brimmed in Rajni's eyes.

"I'm sorry," Luna said. "I didn't mean that."

"I felt like one at times. But now that I'm looking at you, I don't feel as bad about it anymore." Rajni extended her hand to Luna, who took a step back.

"I don't expect you to call me Mom. I don't feel like one anyway. How about we get to know each other and see what happens?"

Luna crossed her arms.

"It's okay," Rajni said. "Whenever you're ready."

"What if I never am?"

"I won't like it, but I'll understand. I wouldn't want me as a mother either." Rajni closed her eyes and envisioned her mother's face. "When I think of my own mother and how she raised me, I know I would've been a disappointment to her." Rajni peered at Luna. "When she died, she took a part of me away with her."

Luna wept. "My mother took a part of me with her too."

"A mother can never be replaced."

Luna nodded her head. "Never."

"But the parts of us that remain here have to go on," Rajni said. "We can create a new life, make new memories, and still have enough time to honor the older ones. That's what I plan on doing."

Luna peered at her. "Italian food is my favorite. Do you think it's because I'm part Italian?"

"Could be. I like it too."

Nestor smiled at Rajni. "I miss your eggplant Parmesan."

Unmasked

Jeff stormed into the cavern and pointed at Seth. "What the hell is going on in here?"

Seth gestured to Kelly. "Ask him. He's one of the Custodians. I think they wiped out our memories."

"There's nothing wrong with my memory," Jeff said.

"We were taken aboard their ship after the shuttle crash."

"Do you know how crazy that sounds?" Jeff said.

Seth waved the wand. "I found him using this."

"What is it?" Jeff asked.

"My insurance on getting some answers around here." He aimed the wand at Kelly. "I'm sure you don't want me to shoot you with this."

Kelly took a step back.

"It wasn't wise for you to think I'd voluntarily play the role of a rat in your maze," Seth said.

"I'm not here to fight you, Seth."

"We'll see about that after you contact your friends."

"I'm not your enemy. You're confused."

"What is this then?" Seth waved the wand.

"The Custodians gave it to me to communicate with them."

"Why didn't you tell us?" Jeff asked.

"They instructed me not to say anything."

"Why not?"

"They knew you'd react exactly as you're reacting now."

"Did they predict I'd do this?" Jeff grabbed Kelly by the shirt and pushed him toward the cave's exit.

"They did."

Jeff eyed the wand in Seth's hands.

"Don't even think of asking for it," Seth said. "This stays with me."

Jeff shook his head and followed Kelly. "Why did you pretend to be one of us?"

"Isn't it obvious?" Seth said. "They're spying on us."

"You're both making a big mistake, and you're going to mess this up for everyone."

"Turn off the phony team leader pitch," Jeff said. "I'm not buying it." He shoved Kelly. "Keep moving."

Jeff stepped on the panel in front of Opal and Pearl's unit. Hiroko, who had been nervously waiting, ran over.

"What's going on?" she asked.

"He's one of the Custodians." Seth showed her the wand. "I found him using this to communicate with them. It also made his whole body change. He looked like one of them."

"It's not true, Hiro," Kelly said.

"If you're telling the truth, you'll have no problem telling the commander everything," Jeff said.

As if on cue, Opal opened the door. Crossing her arms, she said, "Did someone else get lost?"

"It's a little more complicated," Jeff said.

Opal motioned for everyone to enter, and Pearl got up from the couch.

"I'm almost afraid to ask what's wrong," Pearl said.

"We found a spy." Jeff pushed Kelly towards Opal.

"Are you sure?" She glared at Kelly. "He doesn't seem devious enough to be a spy."

"That's because I'm not a spy," Kelly said.

Seth flashed the wand in front of Opal. "I found him using this. It shoots out a beam that creates some type of vortex."

"Let me see that."

"Sorry, but this stays in my possession."

"What do you intend to do with it?" Opal asked.

"Use it as a bargaining tool. His life for our freedom."

"And where will we go?" Pearl asked. "The Earth has been destroyed."

"That's debatable after the deception I witnessed here today."

Everyone stared at Seth.

"Don't you get it? Our memories were erased. For all we know, the last ten years never happened."

"You're reckless Seth," Kelly said. "Just as reckless as the day of the crash."

"What does he mean by that?" Jeff asked Seth.

"I'm a pilot. I wanted to fly, so I flew."

"His need to show off his shuttle is why we crashed," Kelly said.

"It was business, Kelly. Business. Something you couldn't comprehend. And everything would've gone fine if your people or whatever you call yourselves didn't knock us out of the sky."

"I told you to engage the thrusters and leave! You're the one who wanted to stick around!"

Seth shrugged his shoulders. "I misread the situation. I see that now and plan on correcting it."

"Tell them about the cute little light exhibition you performed for the visitors."

Everyone stared at Seth.

"Start talking now, Marconi," Jeff said.

"Our flight was ahead of schedule, and I asked Kelly if we could fly over New York City to demonstrate the new shuttle during Stone Maxwell's pitch to the joined forces. I used to work for Maxwell Aeronautics before I opened my company. My new fleet of shuttles was supposed to be the final nail on his proverbial coffin. Kelly argued with my decision to take over the flight, and he told me to document his disapproval. After I gave my authorization, I took over the controls and navigated to where we could be seen. I flashed on the lights a few times hoping to get the attention of the media, but I attracted someone else's attention. An alien vessel appeared from out of nowhere. It was massive, at least ten times our size. Our radar failed to detect it."

Seth glared at Kelly. "And I did engage the thrusters, but the aliens must've overrode them somehow because I lost control of the shuttle. We were suspended in mid-air. Kelly was terrified, but I wasn't. I believed the ship was a sign that what Xavier had said about the sun was true. He told me the day would be marked by the arrival of advanced beings who would teach us the knowledge that was washed away by the great flood. I flashed the lights to attract the vessel's attention, and they flashed their lights back at me. That's when Kelly ordered me out of the cockpit with the barrel of his gun aimed at my face."

"I would've done the same thing," Jeff said.

"You were out of your mind then, and you still are," Kelly said.

"I hoped and prayed the aliens would take me with them," Seth said. "I thought they listened. After the crash, I woke up, lying on a bed. Two beings were staring down at me. Their faces flashed in various colors, and one of them said, 'We fix, so you continue.' I thought that meant I'd be staying with them, but I ended up back on Earth, living amongst a horde of useless empty shells lumped under the label of Humanity."

"I never passed judgement on anyone," Pearl said, "but never before in all my years as a counselor have I come across a patient as egotistical as you. You try so hard to disassociate yourself from what you are, and you can't even recognize that what you're describing is yourself. You're the empty shell."

"We all are! Compared to the Custodians"—Seth tapped his head—"nothing of value exists in here. Who can blame them for treating us like their inferiors?"

"Speak for yourself," Pearl said.

"See what I mean?" Kelly said. "He's crazy." He faced Hiroko. "Tell them I'm okay, Hiro. I've never done anything but help you and Astrid."

Hiroko turned to Jeff. "It's true, Jeff. Kelly has never hurt either Astrid or me."

Jeff eyed the wand in Seth's hand. "He'd have more credibility if he wasn't found with a weapon."

"It's not a weapon." Kelly turned to Seth. "Please stop this now before you ruin it for everybody."

"Did you know about any of this?" Opal asked Hiroko.

Hiroko looked at Kelly and then back at Opal. "I'm as surprised as you are."

"And isn't it convenient how he's the only one who doesn't have to go into the pillar," Seth said.

"You're forgetting Blaze," Kelly said.

"I haven't forgotten."

The door chime rang.

Opal opened the door. Nestor entered with Astrid, who rushed over to Kelly.

"The Custodians contacted me and told me you are in trouble."

"Marconi thinks I'm a Custodian."

"I don't think you're a Custodian," Seth said. "I know you're a Custodian, and you're going to tell me how to contact your friends."

"I can't do that."

Astrid stared at Kelly, surprised.

Seth aimed the wand at Astrid. "You know how to contact them. Do it now."

"What would you like me to tell them?" Astrid asked.

"I want out of here."

Astrid quickly eyed Kelly, who nodded his head. She then turned to Seth. "Okay. I will contact them now." Astrid shut her eyes, pretending to enter a deep trance, but the message she received was anything but pretend. She screamed, "No! Please! Give us one more chance!"

Hiroko grabbed hold of her. "What did they tell you?"

"They are going to let us all die." Astrid hugged Hiroko. "They said there is nothing they can do to save us."

Kelly leered at Seth. "You did this! Now they're all going to die because of you!"

"They're? Did you all hear that? He just admitted he's one of them."

"Give me the device back now, before you destroy everything!" Kelly said.

"You're no longer in control here!" Seth gawked at Kelly, who from his perspective took on the appearance of his interrogator. "You won't break me. I'll die before I let you take me alive!"

Kelly barreled towards Seth who fired the wand. The beam struck Kelly, and he disintegrated. Everyone in the room was shocked into silence.

Seth, believing he murdered Kelly, dropped the wand and ran out of the unit.

Opal picked it up. "Thank God the Eastern Sector never had anything like this."

"God rest his soul." Pearl did the sign of the cross.

Nestor stepped back and examined the floor and surrounding area. He was spooked when there was no trace left of Kelly and spooked that Seth was more than likely right. He glanced at Astrid and blurted out the first thing that popped into his mind. "Think I'll go home and play Pachisi."

4th Cycle

"It is the next step forward on the path to sunrise, and the sun is rising over a new heaven and new earth."
Martha Carey Thomas

What's Inside a Song

Seth stared across the horizon where he'd last seen Anya. A thunderous hum reverberated from all around. He collapsed to his knees and pressed his temples with his hands trying to numb the pain. "I didn't mean to kill him! I only wanted to expose you to the others! Show me who you are! I demand you show me who you are! Or are you cowards, afraid to show your true faces?"

A blast of pain knocked him to the ground. He gripped both sides of his head. "It hurts too much! Make it stop! I don't care if you erase my mind! Erase it! It didn't do me any good anyway!"

The pain increased, and Seth lay on his back and wailed. "Give me eyes to see the Light. I want to see the Light."

When Seth thought he couldn't endure anymore, the pain stopped. He sat up, and in the distance was the golden star. He sprung to his feet with his mouth wide open. Seth slowly walked towards the precipice.

A light path of round disks illuminated in mid-air. Seth stepped onto the first disk and glimpsed down at his feet floating over the light. He laughed and hopped all the way across the light path, touching ground on a floating, circular platform. The floor was translucent and glowed violet. Seth looked up at the golden star that shone on him. His head ached again, and he screamed out in agony. Falling to his knees, he said, "I can't do this."

"You finally have eyes to see the Light."

Seth looked up. "Anya! Thank God you're all right! Can you make them stop? I'll do anything they want."

"The answer is quite obvious. You must find your inner conscience."

"How?"

"Listen to the music, not your voice."

"I can't hear a thing." The pain strengthened. Seth screamed and fell onto his back.

Blaze walked over and smiled. "So the master freak arrives first."

"Told you he would," Anya said. "The higher they fly, the harder they crash."

Blaze put his hands on his hips. "And the faster they run to get away from the flames of a crashed shuttle."

Astrid, Rajni and Luna watched Nestor as he paced in front of them.

"He's been like this since he got back," Rajni said. "What happened at Opal's?"

Nestor stopped and looked at Rajni, Luna and then at Astrid. "What happened? Now that's a question that's usually not impossible to answer."

"The Custodians told me Kelly is all right," Astrid said. It made no difference to her that he wasn't human. She sensed no malice in him. "So are Blaze and Anya."

"How can we know that for sure?" Nestor asked.

"We cannot."

"Of course not." Nestor threw his hands in the air. "After we ended up here, I'll admit things were *unusual*, but they were at least explainable...somewhat. I was leaning toward us being in some Aristocrat mind experiment. But after what happened to Kelly with that device, and after what Marconi found out about him, nothing's adding up anymore."

"Neither are you," Rajni told him. "I don't have any of my Pachisi boards here."

"I know that, Raj! What I meant was I want something familiar, something that connects us to our previous lives. A fork, a hair brush, a board game, any of those would be acceptable."

"Why don't you tell me what's bothering you?"

"Wake up and take a look around you! We're prisoners, and there's no escaping!" Nestor started to pace again. "I can't take not knowing where we are, what we're doing here, or who's doing this to us. I'd rather be dead than live like this!" He pictured Becky and Joey. "Why couldn't they just let us die with everyone else?"

Rajni cried as she understood the desire for death, and Luna cried because she was frightened. They both hugged each other, and Nestor was gratified that his anguish had yielded positive results. It was bringing Luna and Rajni closer together.

"Death will not solve anything," Astrid stated. "It will never tell you why you're here."

"What if we never find out?" Nestor asked.

"Did you answer that question before we left Earth?" Rajni asked. "Why were we there?"

"Nice attempt at an analogy, but it's not the same."

"We were in a contained environment, unsure of how we got there or who put us there. How is this any different?"

Nestor was at a loss for an answer. He sat next to Rajni. "What are we doing here?"

"I don't know any more than you do."

"I don't mean that. I mean us here. Together."

"Maybe to support one another." Rajni held his hand. "When my MS symptoms returned, I pulled away from you. I won't do that again."

"You were there for me in the end." He hugged Rajni. "Is that what's going on here? Are we ended? Are we dead?"

Luna reached into her pocket and pulled out one of the petals that had fallen from the heavens. She placed it in the palm of her hand and showed it to Nestor. "Dead things come to life here. Remember?"

Nestor shook his head, still not believing Luna's story about the reanimated flowers.

"This was dead, and it came back to life," she said. "I saw it happen."

Astrid and Rajni looked at each other and said together, "We fix, so you continue."

Rajni grabbed hold of Nestor's hand. "We have to get everyone together and go to where Anya and Seth saw the gold star."

"And do what?" Nestor laughed. "Walk across the air?"

"There is something special about Luna," Astrid said. "I took her to the fire cave, and she witnessed the flames as pure white. Initially, I believed it was because she allowed the pillar to take away all her darkness, as it did for Kelly. But Luna is beyond that. The Custodians saved her with their technology. There must be a bit of them inside Luna, which makes her sensitive to this environment."

"Did any of you take time to consider all of this could be a trick?" Nestor asked. "Kelly was here spying on us during this whole time, observing how we were acting and reacting." He shook his head. "Go if you want. I'm staying right here—"

The ground trembled.

"Okay, okay, I'll go along!" Nestor said. "I'll eat the piece of cheese like a good little mouse."

"I don't think they heard you," Luna said as the shaking continued.

Astrid stumbled towards the door, opened it, and ran out.

Opal, Rufus, Pearl, Hiroko and Jeff were already outside.

"Do you know why this is happening?" Opal asked Astrid who shook her head.

A hum reverberated, and the light column shot out of the Hexagon startling Rufus, who flew off Opal's shoulder.

"It shouldn't be doing that," Hiroko said. "No one is inside the pillar."

The column swelled and then swirled around the Hexagon. The structure de-solidified and merged with the light. The speed of the gyration increased and emitted an explosive hum. The ground shook violently, and the lottery winners fell to the ground.

"What the hell is going on here?" Opal yelled as she inched closer to Jeff, but she couldn't even hear the sound of her own voice.

The column shot into the sky, pierced through the clouds, and disappeared.

The lottery winners all got up.

"We have no choice now," Astrid said. "We must go find Anya and Blaze."

Rufus flew down and landed on Opal's shoulder. "Luna is brave. Opal is brave. The regiment is brave," he said.

"You got that right, Rufus." Opal charged ahead.

The lottery winners followed her, aside from Nestor.

Rajni turned back to see what was keeping him. "Are you waiting for a personal invitation?"

Tossing his hands in the air, he said, "I don't know how to process all of this, Raj."

"Stop processing. It's not all that complicated. All you have to do is climb the mountain with us."

"But I can't help but ask 'what is the mountain made of? Is it even real?'" Nestor shook his head. "I can't find an answer, and I'm close to losing my mind."

"You've already lost it."

The two stared at each other and then burst out laughing.

Nestor stopped when he thought about Becky and Joey. "There's no going back...ever."

Rajni smiled. "You always told Papà that same exact phrase whenever he insisted the Aristocrats would eventually lose power and that the United Republic would rise again."

"What do you find so amusing? I would've rather lost that bet."

"You did. Your conclusion was wrong. Miracles are real, Nestor. My MS is gone, and all that's happened here changed me, made me see things in a new way. I wouldn't want to go back."

Clasping his hands beneath his chin, Nestor said, "From the ashes something new is always built."

Rajni tilted her head to the side.

"Said that to your father...the night before we ended up here."

"You actually said that? Out loud?"

Nestor pointed at Rajni. "Randy and your father had that same look on their faces. And I had no idea why I said it...until just now. I only wish I could pay your father the one-thousand credits I owe him."

"What did Papà say to you?"

Nestor took a moment to come up with a modified version of the truth. "'You? Optimistic? That scares me more than Rajni's temper.'"

"Sounds like something he'd say." Rajni cried but maintained her smile. "He'd be happy to know that Kali killed me."

"Kali? The Hindu goddess?" Nestor chuckled. "She must've been mad at you for not featuring her on one of your gameboards."

"I had a vision of her shortly before I got MS. She said, 'I'm here to stay, and I'm not leaving until you die!' It scared me."

"You believe Kali actually visited you?"

"I'm not sure. But what I am sure of now is that she appeared to me so I could gain a new understanding about myself. I thought I wanted to die, but what I really wanted dead was my ego, just like Father Thomas told me during my confession."

"I would've loved to be a watchful eye camera for that discussion."

"You can ask me anything about it. I won't be hiding in my room with my 'ings anymore."

Rajni's smile radiated, washing away Nestor's previous assumptions about her. For the first time since his arrival at the refuge, he didn't think his survival was undeserved. Between Rajni's cure and the other miracles he'd witnessed here, he had a feeling something existed in this experience that would make all the subjects of his documentaries pale in comparison, and he wanted to be around to witness it. Upon that realization, Nestor grinned.

Rajni slapped the side of his arm. "Stop smirking. I kept my cool here."

"You did lose it once."

"But I apologized the next day." She hugged Nestor tightly. "I won't do that again. I won't wait for next days."

"Neither will I." He kissed her cheek and then whispered in her ear, "What did you mean when you told me you were sorry for killing me?"

459

Rajni stepped back and patted Nestor on his chest. "I apologized for that too." She winked and walked ahead.

Nestor chased after her, still grinning. "An apology is pointless if you already killed me, Raj!"

"Not to me."

Growing Flowers

The lottery winners arrived at the point of the ridge where Anya had disappeared. They all observed the golden star, but only Luna, Opal and Nestor saw the illuminated pathway that led across.

Luna walked to the edge, and Rajni pulled her back by the arm.

"Watch your step," Rajni said.

"If we stay on the path, we'll be all right."

"What path?"

"Don't you see the lights?" Nestor asked.

"I see them," Opal said. "They lead all the way across...but to where, I don't know."

Pearl stared over the precipice. "I don't see anything but rocks and forest."

Jeff, Hiroko, Astrid and Rajni responded similarly.

"Why is it that only the three of us can see the lights?" Nestor asked.

Opal narrowed her eyes. "The three of us were alone earlier, but I don't recall anything peculiar happening."

Nestor clapped his hands together. "Her singing! We both had a strong reaction to Luna's voice."

Opal widened her eyes. "That rush of excitement I felt—you may be on to something."

Nestor faced Luna. "Start singing."

"Why?" Luna stepped back when she noticed everyone staring at her.

"The song you sang—think it was the way you sang it; it did something to us."

"I don't feel comfortable singing in front of people."

"You did for us," Opal said.

"I didn't know you were watching me."

Rajni held Luna's hand. "Astrid is right about you. Whatever the Custodians did to you makes you stronger than us."

Luna stared at all the lottery winners, petrified.

Rufus flew off Opal's shoulder and onto Luna's.

"Keep your eyes on Rufus," Opal said. "You trusted him before, and he won't let you down now."

Luna gazed at Rufus until the urge to free the music stored within her since birth awoke. She closed her eyes and began to sing her sacred song. Each note rang in the pitch center, one flowing effortlessly into the next. As she continued to sing, the vibrational frequencies of her body were detected and absorbed by the lottery winners.

Rajni held Luna's hand and stared ahead. She could now see the light path as did all the lottery winners.

Nestor put his arm around Rajni. "Isn't it beautiful."

"Still think we're inside a computer simulation?" Rajni asked him.

"Don't care if we are anymore."

Luna finished her song and opened her eyes. "Did it work?"

"You did great," Opal said as Rufus returned to perch on her shoulder. "And so did you." She petted him.

The lottery winners edged towards the precipice.

"You should take the first step," Nestor told Luna.

She hopped onto the first disk, and the others followed behind her.

The lottery winners stepped on the platform where Anya and Blaze had been waiting.

Astrid ran over to Blaze and hugged him. "I should have never let you go."

"And I should've been honest with you." He kissed her.

Nestor pointed to Seth who was still lying on the ground, writhing in pain. "What's wrong with him?"

Hiroko walked over to Seth, and he looked up at her. "Hiro?"

"I'm here for you."

"I'm sorry I left you."

"You didn't leave me. I was going to leave you."

"No." Seth got up and grabbed Hiroko's hand. "I left you on the shuttle to die." Seth looked at Jeff. "He saw me run out without you, but what he didn't know was I did it on purpose."

Hiroko pulled away her hand. "Why?"

"I loved you so much I couldn't think of anything else. Not my work. Not even the prototype. It was too much for me. Everywhere we went, men watched you, admired you, wanted you. It was exhausting, always having to compete against men who weren't deformed like me. When I saw you unconscious after the crash, I thought what a relief it would be not to feel out of control anymore, and I left you to die. But when I looked back and saw the flames, I realized what I'd done. I was about to run back in, but Jeff got to you first. When you died, I knew I murdered you. What I endured after your death was far worse than a loss of control."

Hiroko wept. "You were right to be suspicious. I had an affair with my co-pilot. I was going to leave you to be with him. Your jealousy was suffocating, and I wanted to be free."

"You're free of me, Hiro. I want you to be happy," Seth said with the fullest conviction.

"And how about you?" she asked.

"I'm also free of you, of my scar, and of everything up to my arrival here." He took a deep breath and exhaled slowly, allowing My music to enter into him without any resistance. Raising his hands to the air, he said, "All I want now is to be happy."

All the dark frequencies Seth had carried within him since the 1st sector war detached and disbanded. The star that shone from above released a beam that descended, split in two, and entered the palms of his hands. "I hear what you hear, Anya!" He smiled.

"Why is he getting rewarded for being a psychopath?" Nestor asked.

"Wherever we are, there's no room for the bad," Luna said. "We can only grow flowers here."

Rajni smiled and held Luna's hand.

"You all have to let go as Seth did," Anya told them and smiled at Luna.

"We must grow...like flowers," Luna added.

All the lottery winners stood silent, afraid of the secrets they had kept for so long but wanting to let them go and move forward.

Nestor cleared his throat. "My father snuck military secrets to the Eastern Sector. He got caught and was executed. My mother took her life soon after, and I was thrown from foster home to foster home. None of them ever worked out, and I started living on the streets. It wasn't so bad in the summer, but when winter came, I was thankful when a man took me in and gave me food and shelter. I soon started working for him as an escort, entertaining both men and women. I tried to hide from my past, telling people a socially acceptable version of my childhood. I'm not hiding anymore. My past led me to a successful career as a documentarian." Nestor smiled at Rajni. "Your turn now. I'm sure it can't be as controversial as mine."

Rajni kneeled down in front of Luna and held her hands. "I hope you'll forgive me after what I tell you. I knew I was pregnant."

"Why did you say you weren't?"

"Hearing you were my daughter and seeing your face brought me back to a time I tried hard to forget. I was pregnant with you, but I still wanted to keep my appointment at Compassionate Endings. At the time, I didn't think it would be anything worse than having an abortion; I was only six weeks into my pregnancy. If the Custodians hadn't interfered, you never would've been born." Rajni's eyes filled with tears. "I'll understand if you want nothing to do with me."

"Do you know who my father was?"

Rajni shook her head. "I told you the truth about that."

"It's not important. I had a father who loved me, even when I disappointed him."

"I can't imagine you disappointing anyone."

"My friend Jodi died after an old woman ran her over. The woman shouldn't have been driving because she had poor eyesight, but her son was a judge. He got sick of driving his mother around, so he allowed her to keep driving. I was so mad when I found out. I broke the windows in his house. Each time he'd replace them, I'd break them again. I got caught a year later, and the judge died soon after that. His wife said it was from stress caused by my breaking the windows." Luna cried and peered at Rajni. "Do you think that's true? Did I kill him?"

"It wasn't your fault," Rajni said. "Adults sometimes find it hard to deal with stress. We can sometimes blurt things out without thinking."

"That's what my mother said, but I didn't believe her. I was sad for a long time after that, and when I finally started to feel better, the sun decided to destroy Earth."

"I'm so glad you were given a good home. I never would've done as good a job raising you as your parents."

Luna cried and hugged Rajni. She didn't know how to process everything her birth mother had told her, but she sensed everything would turn out all right. That was enough for her.

Jeff cleared his throat, and all the lottery winners faced him.

"I killed a man in cold blood. During the last sector war, one of the men in my regiment raped a woman. I was so angry, I shot him. I then had to look his parents in the eyes and tell them he died during a raid. I ended up turning him into a celebrated hero in his hometown. He raped a woman and became immortalized as a god. There's no honor in vengeance."

Blaze held Astrid's hand. "There was more to your murder than I told you. When I was in high school, I used to torment this kid every day. He ended up transferring to a different school because of me. I didn't see him again until the night he murdered you to get even with me for ruining his life."

Astrid cried and cupped Blaze's face. "I was hoping you would tell me on your own." Hugging him, she said, "Thank you for being honest."

Pearl turned to Opal. "I suppose it's my turn next."

"Should I brace myself?"

"I already said what I had to say to you. This is about Stephen. I've been in love with him since he gave me the angel charm for my sixteenth birthday."

"He loved you too," Opal said. "He told me on the night I thought you died."

With tears in her eyes, Pearl said, "I'm going to make a promise to you—and to myself—that wherever we end up, I'm going to live my life to the fullest. I'm never going to compromise my life away or give in to my age." Pearl smirked. "You won't be the only one who can still get away with wearing a bikini."

Opal hugged Pearl. "We'll wear matching ones again." She let go of her sister and walked over to Blaze. "There's a reason why I look familiar to you."

"Whatever it is, I can take it." He smiled.

"The night before Earth's destruction, a boy came to me asking for my help. I saw you in the alley fighting that thug...only I thought you were the instigator. I shot you instead." Opal wiped her eyes with the back of her hand. "When the boy told me I shot the wrong man, I ran away."

"I forgive you, Opal." Blaze hugged her. "You're a compassionate woman."

"I'm not." Opal pushed him away. "I asked myself if I would've done the same thing without all the insanity that was going on that night. I couldn't come up with an honest answer. I'd like to think I would've taken the time to assess the situation more accurately, but I'm not sure that I would have. I'm not sure of anything anymore, even my actions during the 1st sector war." Opal looked at Pearl. "You were right about me. Violence was always my way of dealing with things."

Pearl did the sign of the cross. "Forgive me for saying that. I was only upset by what was happening...and of losing Christina. I admire you. I always have...for having the strength to stand up for your convictions. And even after the sector wars that followed, you never abandoned them. You're an inspiration to me."

"And to me," Blaze said. "After what I saw you do for Luna, I want to write a new story with you as the superhero." He outstretched his arms. "Let this go. I have."

"I can't." Opal cried harder. "You were an innocent. I never shot an innocent."

"That wasn't your intention. You were trying to protect David."

"The way he stared at me reminded me of the children during the sector war. They had the same look in their eyes when we raided their villages." More tears spilled from Opal's eyes. "I did that to them. I stole their childhood. I'm not worthy of forgiveness."

Jeff walked over. "I don't know about the others, but I'm not going to give up on you, Commander. You've stayed strong for us since we got here, and now I'm going to be strong for you. Either you go with us, or I'm staying behind with you."

All the lottery winners expressed a similar sentiment, and this is where I gave in and cried after a billion years of abstinence. Sheim kept quiet, somehow sensing I needed to do this.

Luna clasped Opal's hand. "Please, Opal. Don't give up. Rufus would be very sad." She started to sing, "You Are My Sunny Day," and Rufus joined in along with the rest of the lottery winners.

Opal smiled with tears still streaming down her cheeks. She took a step back to appreciate those around her as they sang. When they finished, she applauded. "Thank you. Thanks all of you for showing this old lady a few new lessons. I love each and every one of you."

Imprints

The gold star lowered down and enveloped the lottery winners, immersing them in the whiteness they'd experienced when they first entered this strange and whimsical world. A loud hum sounded, and they all sensed a big change was taking place within themselves. Opal petted Rufus to ensure he was still on her shoulder. Pearl sensed Opal beside her and held her hand.

"How remarkable!" Pearl said. "I know you're standing next to me even though I can't see you!" When no response came, she said, "You probably have that silly smile on your face."

"What silly smile?"

"Whenever you're fascinated by something, the right side of your lip shoots up and slams your right eye shut."

"You know me well, Sis."

Nestor and Rajni stood behind Luna, each with a hand on one of her shoulders. Jeff and Hiroko held hands, as did Seth and Anya.

Astrid squeezed Blaze's hand. *"Je t'aime."*

"Moi aussi," Blaze responded.

Jeff and Hiroko embraced.

"If this is our last moment, I want to tell you I love you," Jeff told Hiroko.

She kissed Jeff. "I love you too."

Nestor squeezed Rajni's hand. "This is very unsettling. Everyone sounds different, and I can't even recognize my own voice."

"It's time for you to let go and embrace the unknown."

"That's what Space Ex would do," Luna said.

"Then so will I. Can't let a fictional character make me look bad."

"I'll hold you to it," Rajni said.

Nestor hugged her. "You won't have to. I'm glad we're finishing this game in a tie."

Seth ambled toward Anya. "Strange how I can find you although I can't see you."

"Not strange. Different," she said.

"Either which way, I don't want to be alone for whatever is coming."

"Got a feeling it won't be that bad."

The light cleared, and the lottery winners were inside a spacious hexagonal room. It made the hexagon they were familiar with seem minuscule by comparison. Encircling them was a group of Custodians.

The lottery winners scrutinized each other's appearance, and Luna was the first to proclaim, "We look just like them!"

"And sound like them as well," Seth chimed. "We're not speaking in words."

"All except for Rufus." Opal petted him. "He's exactly the same."

The lottery winners recognized one another by the unique color patterns flashing on their faces.

One of the Custodians advanced toward them and stopped in front of Rajni. Placing his hand on his chest, he said, "We fix, so we continue."

Rajni smiled, recognizing the being as the one who'd spoken to her during the crash.

Seth walked over to Kelly, who was in his evolved form. "Sorry I shot you. Guess I went a little crazy."

"Working for you for as long as I had, I got used to your eccentricities." Kelly's lights flashed in a way as to suggest laughter. "But, as you can see, no harm was done. I returned to my evolved physical form."

"When did you change over?" Hiroko asked.

"The Custodians needed one of us to act as a liaison between you and them to ensure you were developing properly. They chose me after I witnessed the white fire."

"Where are we?" Nestor asked, hoping he could continue his work as a documentarian.

"On a ship," Kelly said. "The same ship we were on ten years ago."

A large door retracted, revealing an expansive light blue meadow. Kelly and the lottery winners walked outside. Out of everyone, Rajni was the most excited about this alien world. She studied the rainbow colored sky filled with swirling white clouds and then turned back to study the ship.

"It's shaped like a *vimana!*" Rajni said to Nestor with a colorful display of lights that flashed and shifted on her face. "What do you have to say about that?"

"Wish I had my camcorder with me."

Rajni approached Kelly. "What are we?"

"Part of a race of explorers and scientists who travel throughout the Universe studying life. If we feel a species can add to our knowledge, we imprint several of the lifeforms into our integration system. At the moment of death, they're reanimated here. I'm told not all the species make the transition. Letting go of all the definitions you placed on yourself isn't easy, so celebrate your success." He placed his palms together and bowed. "Welcome to your new life."

Rufus kissed Opal on the cheek and then flew onto Luna's shoulder and did the same. He then took flight and soared across the sky of a new sunrise. Everyone craned their heads to watch him as he disappeared into the clouds and back to the place from where he began...My breath. For his loyal service, I honored him by reanimating him as part of a race even more advanced than the Custodians. A fitting gift for one truly amazing bird.

Epilogue

By delivering the lottery winners' energy forms to the Custodians, I saved their lives. The outcome was worth the scolding I received from Sheim. The doubters among you may ask, "Why would I, the Universe, focus on a small insignificant lot when there's so much going on inside Me?" As I am the Universe, I don't have to explain Myself. I do so only to those who listen with their hearts. Inspiration flows freely in Me, waiting to be captured. What you read here is just one story among the many. A book would have to be as large as Me to explain Universal happenings during every given microsecond.

There is no ultimate truth, even from My perspective. This used to drive Me crazy until I accepted Sheim's advice to accept what I cannot know and enjoy existing and experiencing. It sounded simplistic, but when I followed Sheim's advice, it all became clear to Me. *I am experience.* I'm not exact. Within Me exists a potential for anything. Miscalculations and misinterpretations are to be expected. With ignorance, mistakes are sure to follow. Nevertheless, they are necessary as they lead to an infinite stream of possibilities. So if you happen to roll the dice and find yourself sliding down the snake, remember there's always the chance of landing on a ladder that will bring you back up higher than ever before.

My family plays a similar game. The day Sun ventured off without Me, I ruminated over not being strict enough during his upbringing. Fortunately, Sheim predicted My fallibility and created one of My Universal laws that you sentients know well. With each action there is a counteraction, and the same law applies to Me. At Sun's crucial moment of defiance, I fragmented into two Universes. While Humanity's demise couldn't be undone within Me, it continues inside my newly born sister Universe. Nestor was correct; from the ashes something new is always built. I was surprised he heard Me when I whispered it to him.

In reaction to what happened to Humanity, My sister kept Sun on a tight gravitational leash, and he remains in a predictable orbit. I once visited to see how things were going on inside Her. She was happy that I created Her and boasted over how the shuttle never crashed. Nevertheless, this change also meant the Custodians left Earth with an indifference to humans. Earth survived, and Seth Marconi built his ideal society off-world, waiting for a disaster that failed to arrive. He eventually started to view himself as a prophet of God and sent Xavier Starfly back to Earth. Xavier spent the rest of his life in the Himalayas, living alone in a cave, and Anya became a famous slam artist who toured the world. Nestor returned home to his family, and Rajni made another appointment at Compassionate Endings and kept it. Opal attended Pearl's funeral the following year without ever having the chance to forgive her. Blaze continued his sparring with Trevor Forthright, and Astrid gave birth to a lovely baby girl named Daryn. She happened to be the reincarnation of Jeff's wife, Teryl. This was the only change I appreciated. With Rajni never giving birth to Luna, Teryl's essence would at least continue. I disagreed with everything else, but I kept silent. My Sister would have to deal with Her growing pains just as I had to deal with Mine.

I can't help but view this version of Earth as tragic. I've seen a lot of individual growth in the lottery winners. Together, they made a formidable team and once again validated Sheim's assertion that mistakes can lead to positive outcomes.

Before leaving My Sister's tragic Earth, I decided to travel back in time and say hello to Blaze. Enjoying the time I spent sharing Rufus's form, I presented Myself as a sparrow and flew into a small neighborhood park near his home. In this timeline, he was in his sophomore year at high school. I would've introduced Myself as a human, but it would've been too obvious for Blaze who always loved a good metaphor. His own name is also highly symbolic. In Arizona, there exists one small, insignificant spot called Blaze Canyon. It got its name because each summer, Sun's rays would singe everything that grew there. But each spring, life would blossom again, just as it had for My lottery winners and the rest of Humanity that continued through My Sister.

I landed on a park bench where Blaze was writing. He was so absorbed in his storytelling that he never noticed My presence, but he heard Me whispering to him. My transmission was interrupted as he worried over how he would tell his mother about the week's detention he was given for beating up Charlie Trip.

I chirped until Blaze glanced at Me and then cocked My head to the side in the way birds typically do. He reached his hand to Me, and I hopped on. After he had expressed shock over My trust in him, I chirped again and flew away. I felt his eyes on Me as I soared higher.

He heard Me.

Blaze never bothered Charlie Trip again and a year later, I ended up in his debut book, *Beyond Omega's Sunrise*, which was about a group of lottery winners who banded together after Earth had been annihilated by Sun. They ended up on an alien world with a hexagonal building and a white pillar of light that made people's dreams come true.

I chirped, Blaze listened with his heart, and he understood. I also relearned a lesson I'd long forgotten...a Universe can dream too.

About The Author

Eleni Papanou wrote her first poem when she was an outcast at school. Honored with the name, "Greek Freak." She started to feel like one and believed life was plagued with torment and endless suffering. A spontaneous kundalini awakening thrust Eleni on a spiritual path and constantly tested her to the breaking point by challenging her world-view and everything else she held sacred. Through visions and personal insights, Eleni eventually discovered the Universe has a sense of humor. She started laughing more—mostly at herself—whenever she caught herself taking things too seriously. After many years on the path of self-rediscovery, along with a bout with cancer and caring for her two daughters, Eleni had a lot to say. Having already written several screenplays, she started writing novels where she could freely express her spirituality. The book you now hold in your hands is a product of that desire.

Acknowledgements

Beyond Omega's Sunrise is an amalgamation of an old concept about an elitist who makes a bet with a friend that a wedding photographer couldn't convince anyone the world will end the next day. It was the kind of idea that, on the surface, sounded unbelievable. Nevertheless, I liked it enough to write it down in my concept list. I didn't think of it until years later when I happened across an article in the *Daily Mail* that was about a boy who's allergic to the sun. It's here where I give my first thanks to James Creag, who's brave story inspired me. He was the catalyst that led me to begin writing this novel.

My thanks to my daughter, Tiggy, who's line, "Let's just go home and play Parchisi," led to Rajni's career of gameboard design.

Thank you to my daughter, Daphne. You make a beautiful cover model.

Thanks to my beta readers, Margaret Duarte, Russ Muller, Angel Pricer, and Jodine Turner. Your valuable input helped elevate my book.

Thank you Barbra Lieberstein, for assisting me in the research that led me to the beautiful climax of this story.

Thank you to Dr. George and Amy Jirsa-Smith, who proofread my manuscript.

Thanks to Robin Quinn, for the partial edit of my manuscript.

I reserve the last and most heartfelt thanks to the Universe for allowing me to capture this story that both horrified and captivated me from inception to publication. To me, the Universe is not only teeming with life, *Sheim* is alive. I cannot give an exact definition, but I feel Sheim's presence throughout all that I do in my life. Sheim is ever present, unmoving, and always around. From Sheim, inspiration never ceases.

Love and light,
Eleni

Titles from

Philophrosyne Publishing

Between Now and Forever
By Margaret Duarte
A rookie teacher challenges school tradition and authority to help seven troubled students with psychic abilities fight for their spiritual and emotional freedom.

Jessie's Song
Readers' Favorite International Book Award Winner - Bronze Medal (2013)
By Eleni Papanou
A man must make the greatest sacrifice to save his daughter from a kidnapper. It's a story of love, and how far a father would go to save his daughter.

Unison - Book One of the Spheral Series
Honorable Mention - New York Book Festival Awards (2014)
By Eleni Papanou
A man is condemned to relive his life until he uncovers a suppressed memory.